BAD KiTTY

GOES ON VACATION

NICK BRUEL

ROARING BROOK PRESS
NEW YORK

Dedicated to
Pat Robbins, Bob Butman, and Denny O'Neil,
the three finest writing teachers I ever had.

Published by Roaring Brook Press
Roaring Brook Press is a division of Holtzbrinck Publishing Holdings Limited Partnership
120 Broadway, New York, NY 10271 • mackids.com

ISBN 978-1-250-20808-8
Library of Congress Control Number 2020912185

Our books may be purchased in bulk for promotional, educational, or business use.
Please contact your local bookseller or the Macmillan Corporate and Premium Sales
Department at (800) 221-7945 ext. 5442 or by email at
MacmillanSpecialMarkets@macmillan.com.

First edition, 2020
Book design by Cassie Gonzales • Color by Rob Steen
Printed in China by 1010 Printing International Limited, North Point, Hong Kong

1   3   5   7   9   10   8   6   4   2

• CONTENTS •

CHAPTER ONE
AT HOME WITH UNCLE MURRAY 4

CHAPTER TWO
AT HOME WITH KITTY............ 16

CHAPTER THREE
AT THE AIRPORT 38

CHAPTER FOUR
AT THE HOTEL 55

CHAPTER FIVE
FINALLY 77

CHAPTER SIX
INSIDE THE PARK 88

CHAPTER SEVEN
14 RIDES LATER................ 106

CHAPTER EIGHT
LOVE LOVE ANGEL KITTY JAIL 119

CHAPTER NINE
THE TRIAL OF UNCLE MURRAY
(AND KITTY) 124

CHAPTER TEN
HOME AGAIN.................. 146

•CHAPTER ONE•

AT HOME WITH UNCLE MURRAY

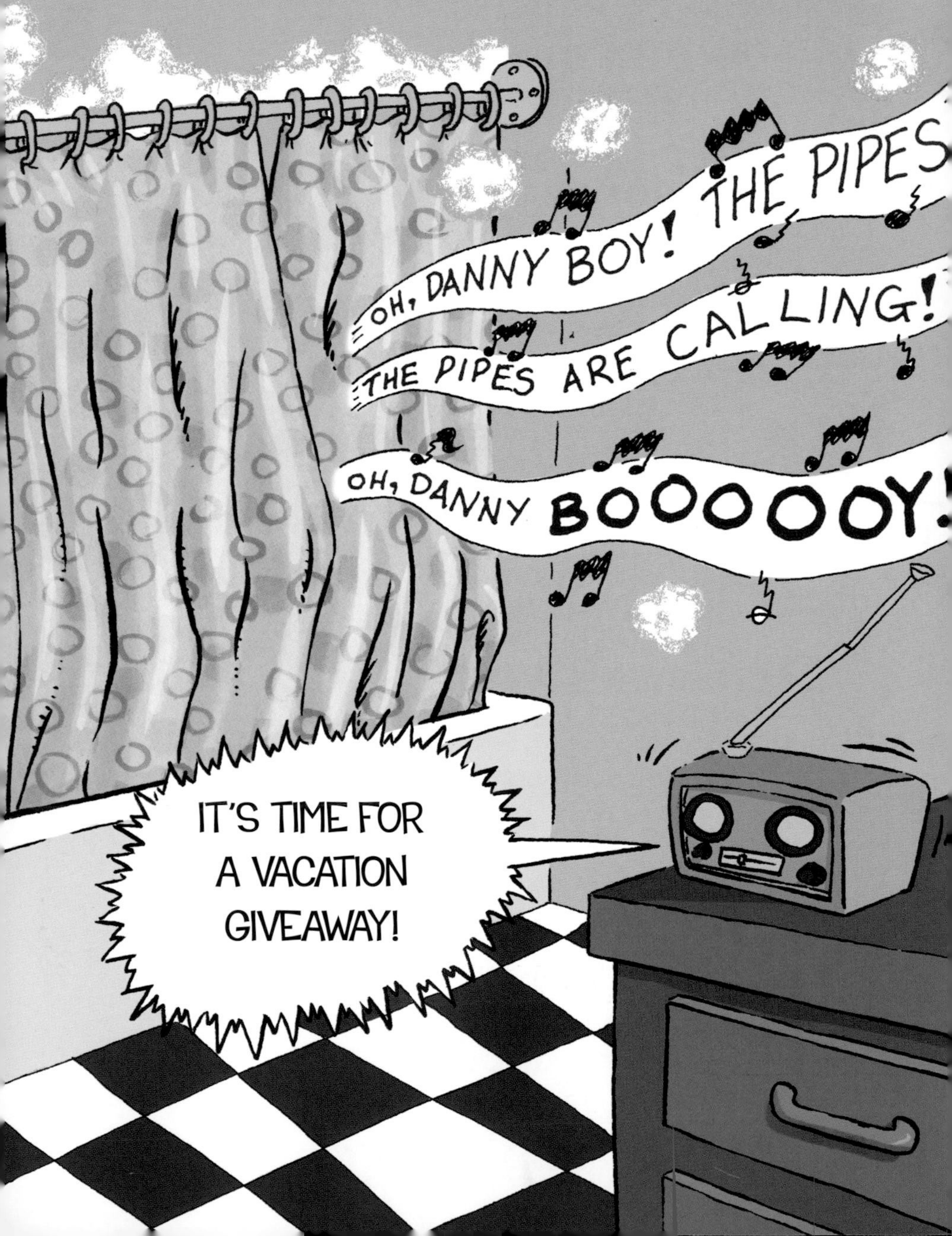
OH, DANNY BOY! THE PIPES
THE PIPES ARE CALLING!
OH, DANNY BOOOOOY!
IT'S TIME FOR A VACATION GIVEAWAY!

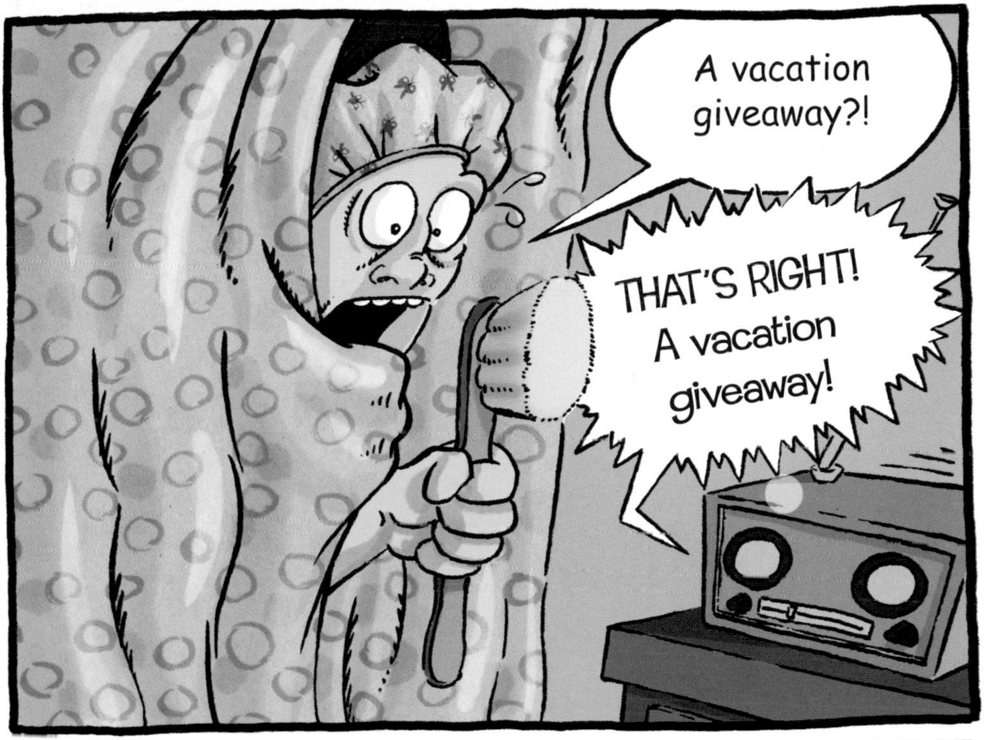
A vacation giveaway?!
THAT'S RIGHT! A vacation giveaway!

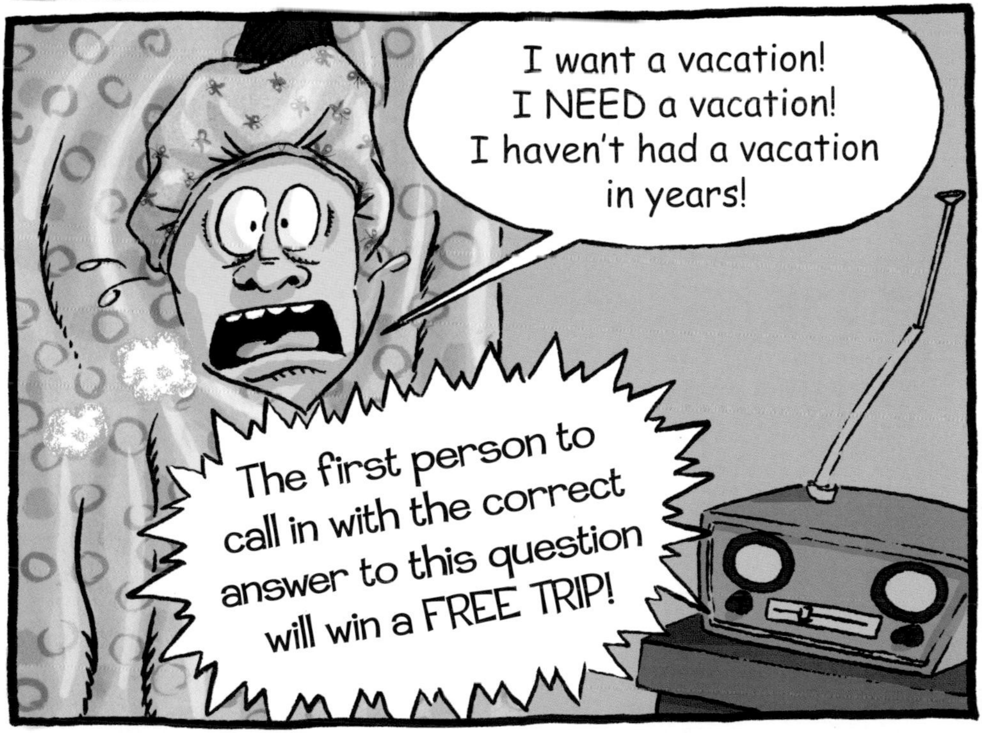
I want a vacation! I NEED a vacation! I haven't had a vacation in years!
The first person to call in with the correct answer to this question will win a FREE TRIP!

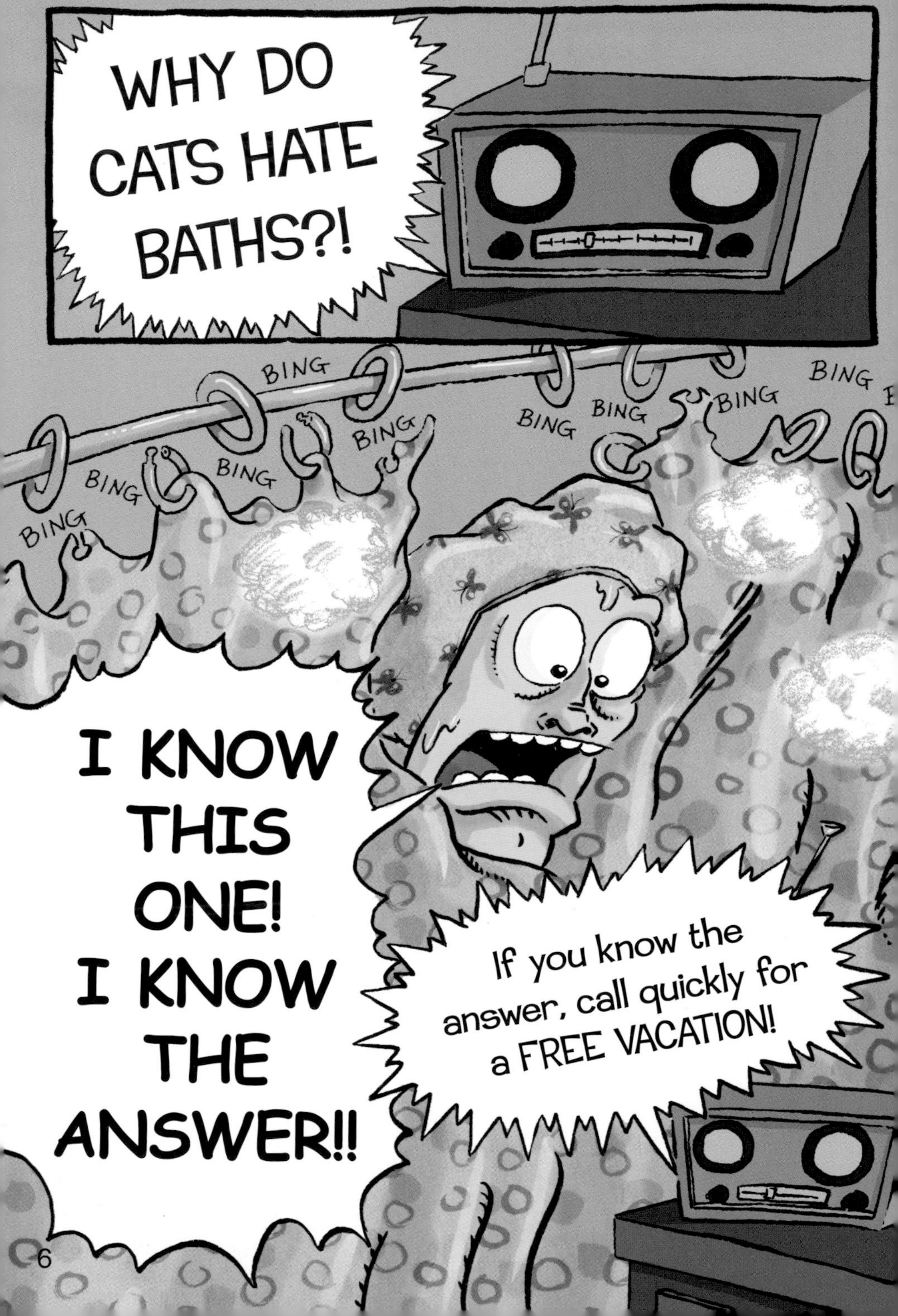
WHY DO CATS HATE BATHS?!
BING
BING
BING
BING
BING
BING
BING
BING
BING
BING
I KNOW THIS ONE! I KNOW THE ANSWER!!
If you know the answer, call quickly for a FREE VACATION!

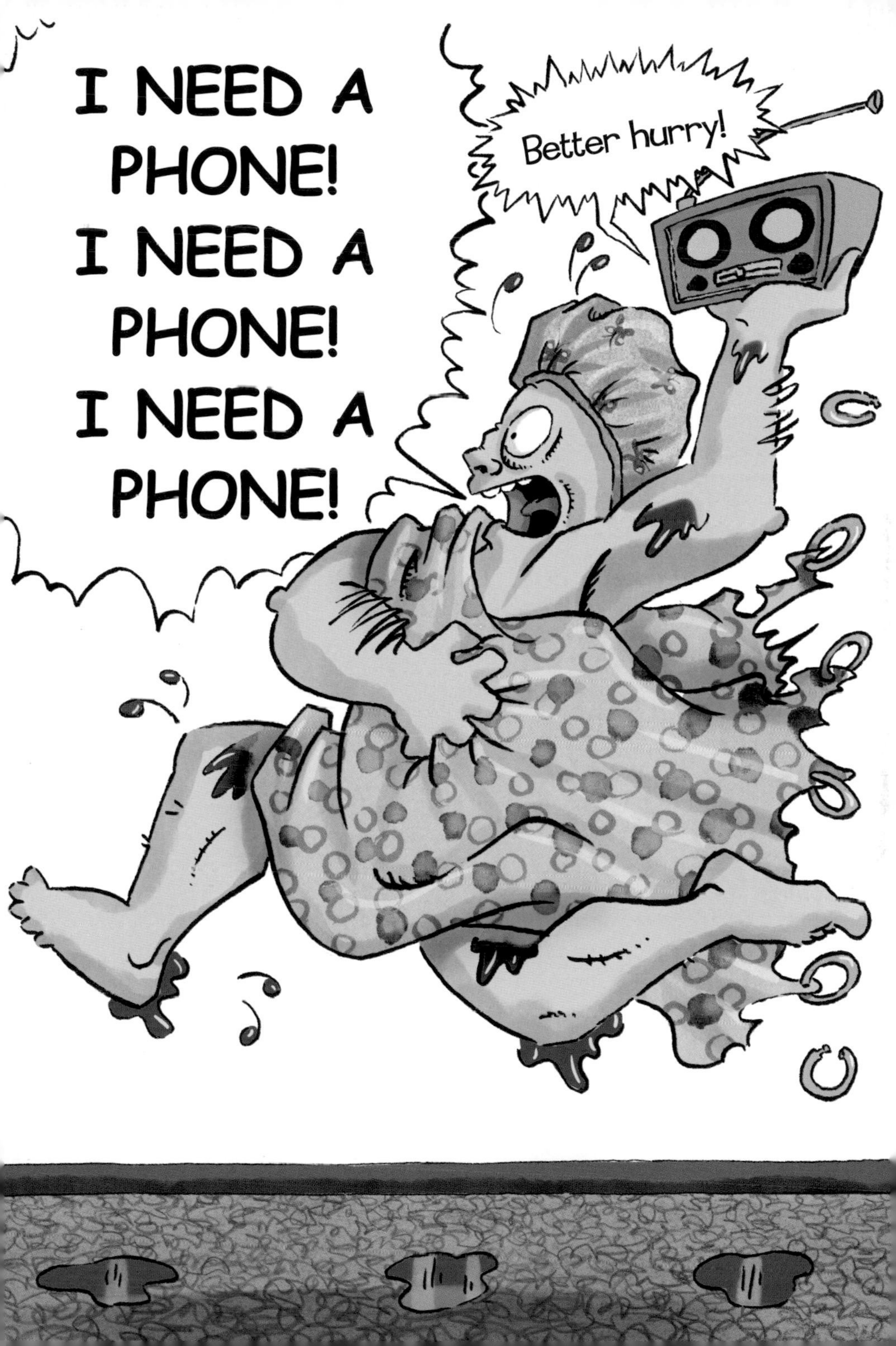
I NEED A PHONE! I NEED A PHONE! I NEED A PHONE!
Better hurry!

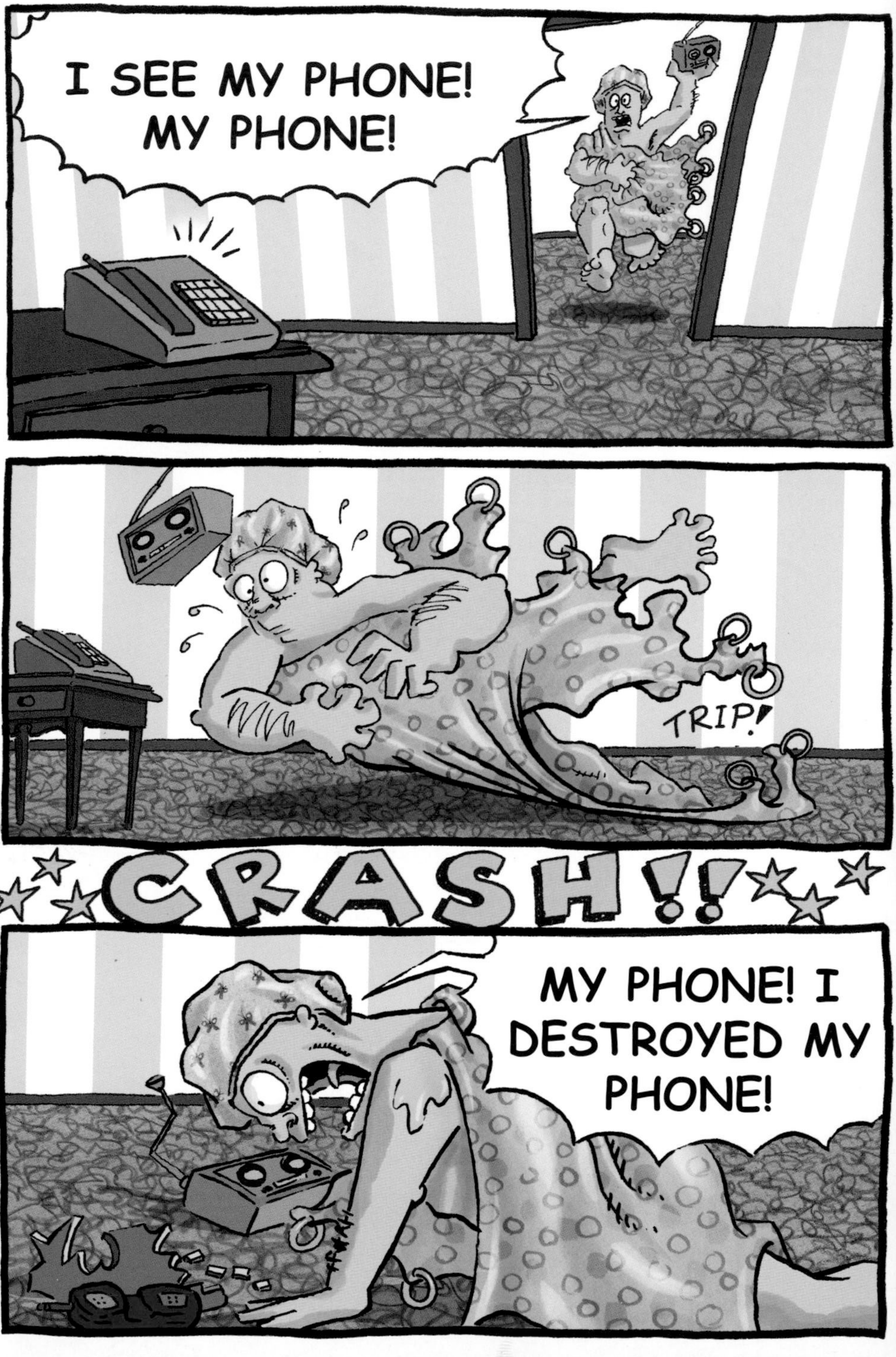
I SEE MY PHONE! MY PHONE!
TRIP!
CRASH!!
MY PHONE! I DESTROYED MY PHONE!

I have Edna Prunelove on the line. Tell me why cats hate baths, and you'll win a free vacation!
Awww.
Is it because they prefer showers?
Sorry, Edna. That answer is incredibly wrong. The lines are still open for anyone who can call in with the right answer!
I've still got a chance! WAIT! I have a cell phone!

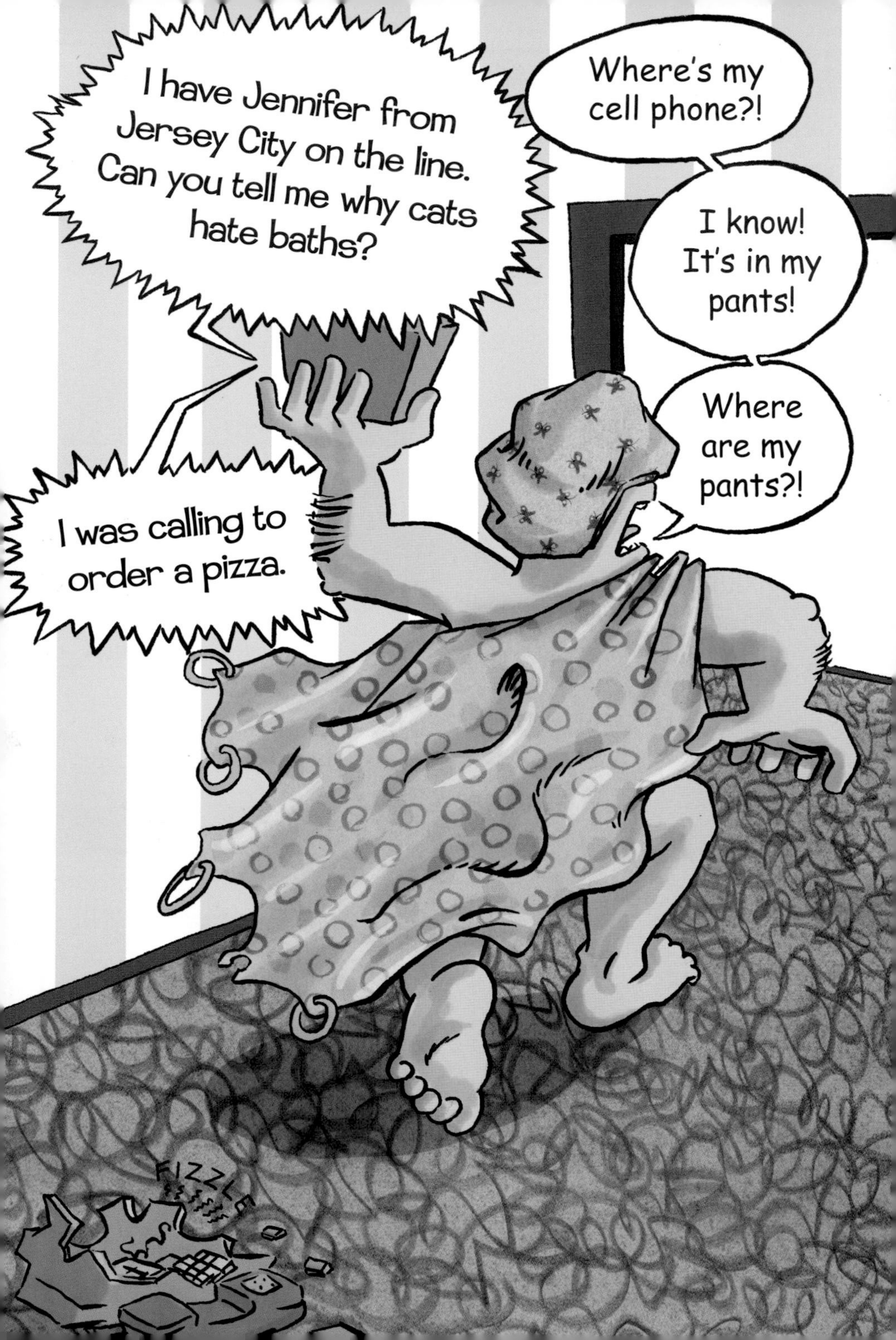
I have Jennifer from Jersey City on the line. Can you tell me why cats hate baths?
I was calling to order a pizza.
Where's my cell phone?!
I know! It's in my pants!
Where are my pants?!
FIZZLE

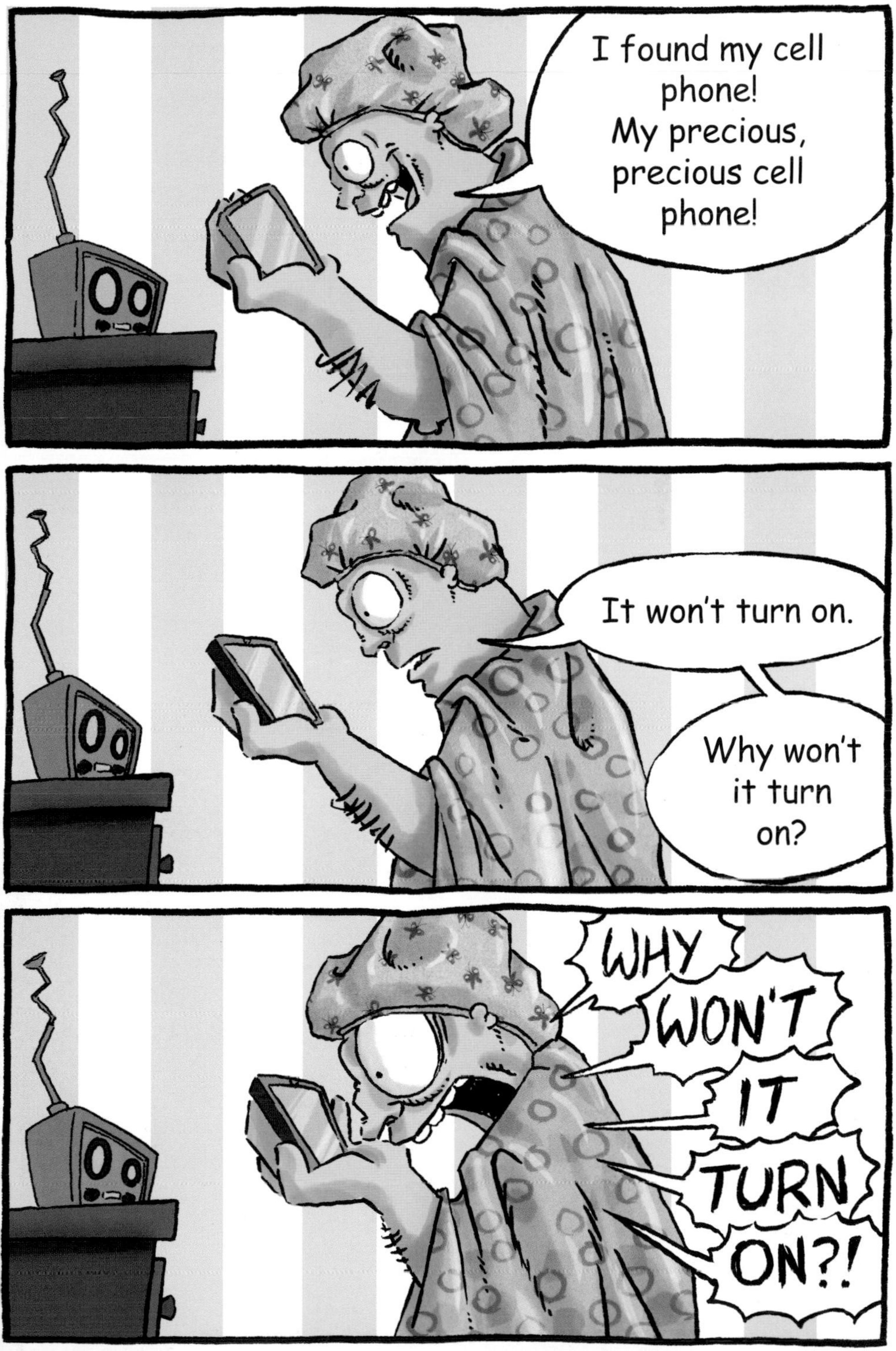
I found my cell phone!
My precious, precious cell phone!
It won't turn on.
Why won't it turn on?
WHY WON'T IT TURN ON?!

THE SEVEN STAGES OF UNCLE MURRAY'S PANIC • PART ONE

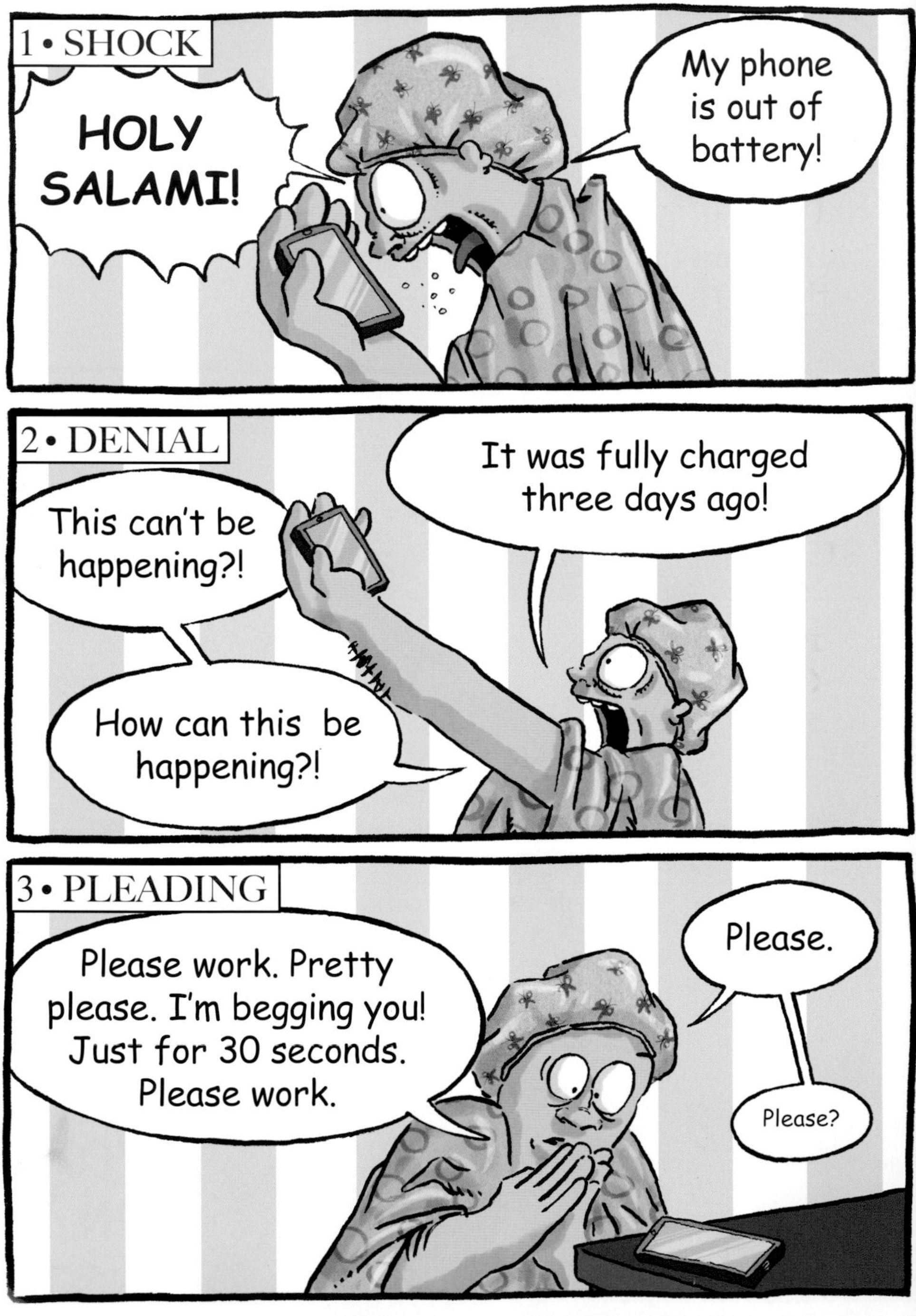
1 • SHOCK
HOLY SALAMI!
My phone is out of battery!
2 • DENIAL
This can't be happening?!
It was fully charged three days ago!
How can this be happening?!
3 • PLEADING
Please work. Pretty please. I'm begging you! Just for 30 seconds. Please work.
Please.
Please?

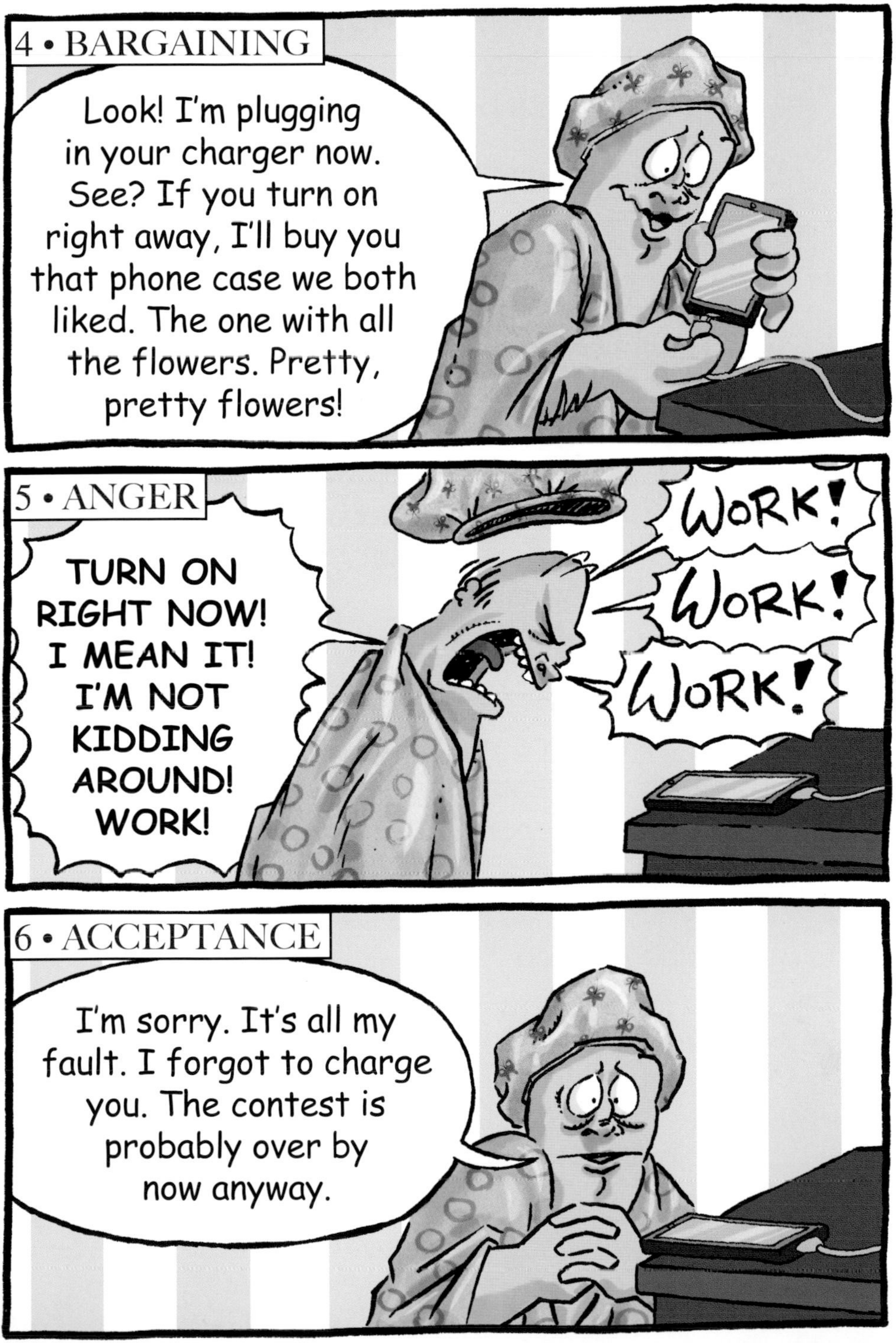
4 • BARGAINING
Look! I'm plugging in your charger now. See? If you turn on right away, I'll buy you that phone case we both liked. The one with all the flowers. Pretty, pretty flowers!
5 • ANGER
TURN ON RIGHT NOW! I MEAN IT! I'M NOT KIDDING AROUND! WORK!
WORK!
WORK!
WORK!
6 • ACCEPTANCE
I'm sorry. It's all my fault. I forgot to charge you. The contest is probably over by now anyway.

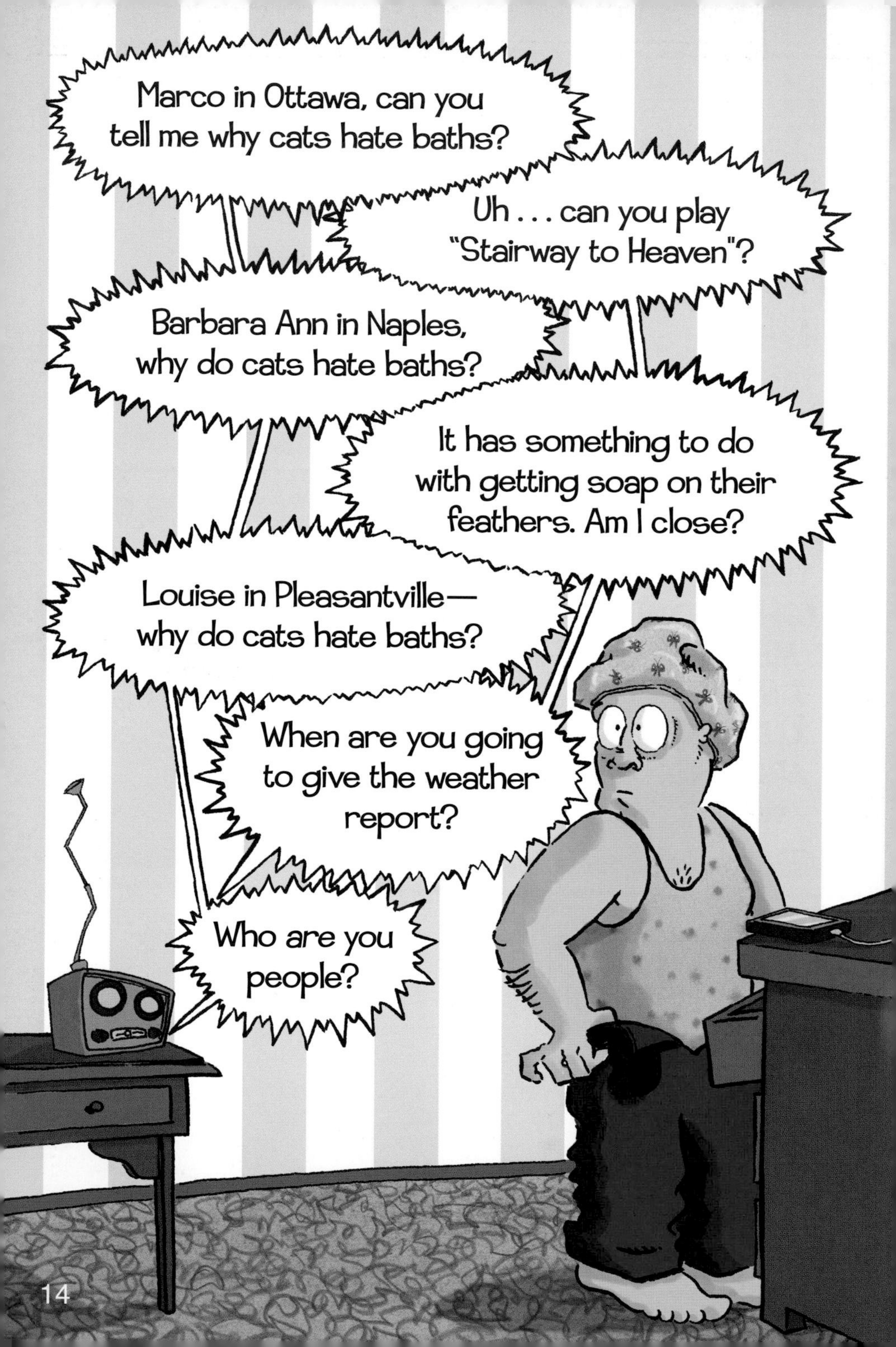
Marco in Ottawa, can you tell me why cats hate baths?
Uh . . . can you play "Stairway to Heaven"?
Barbara Ann in Naples, why do cats hate baths?
It has something to do with getting soap on their feathers. Am I close?
Louise in Pleasantville—why do cats hate baths?
When are you going to give the weather report?
Who are you people?

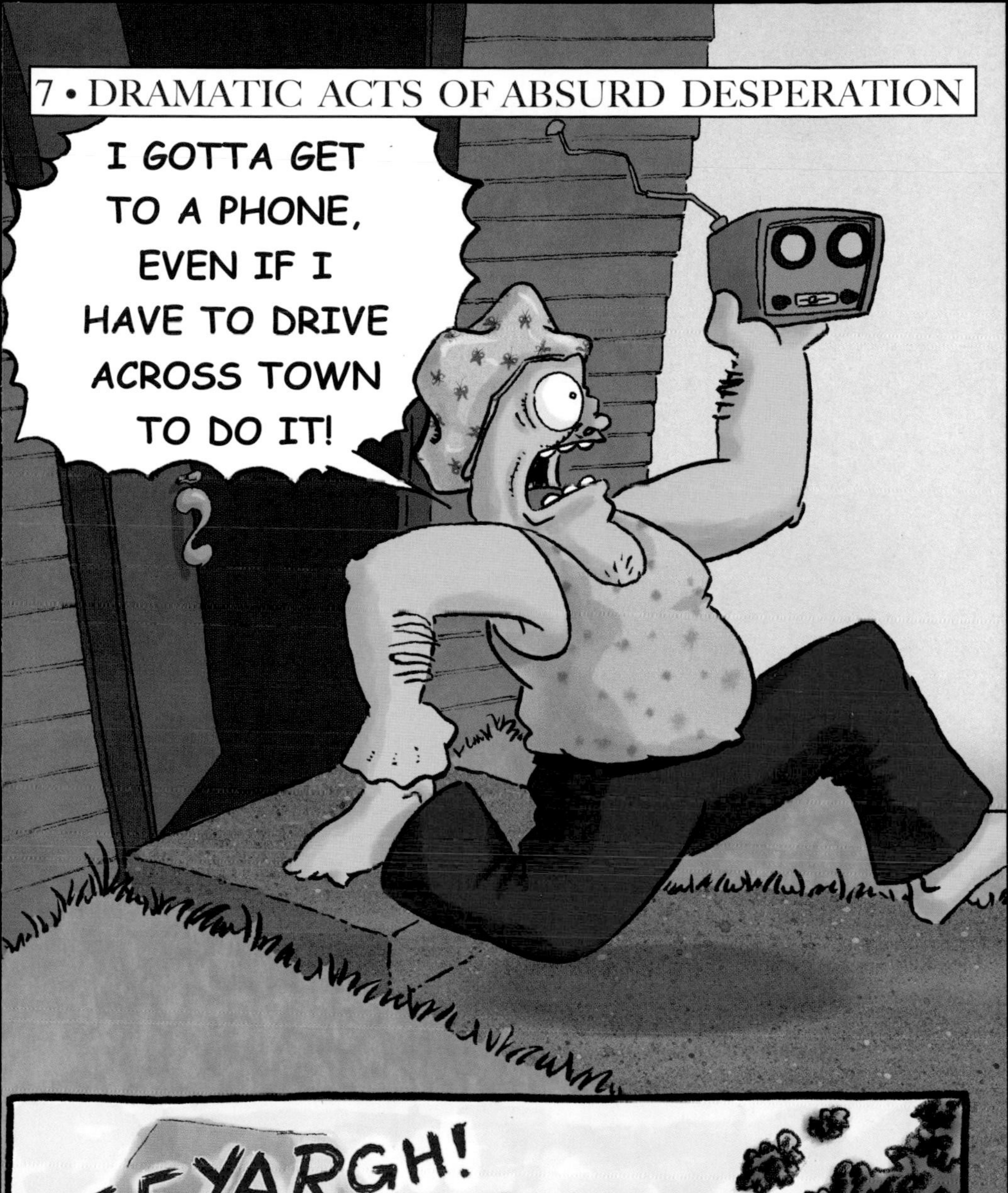
7 • DRAMATIC ACTS OF ABSURD DESPERATION
I GOTTA GET TO A PHONE, EVEN IF I HAVE TO DRIVE ACROSS TOWN TO DO IT!
EEEYARGH!

•CHAPTER TWO•

AT HOME WITH KITTY

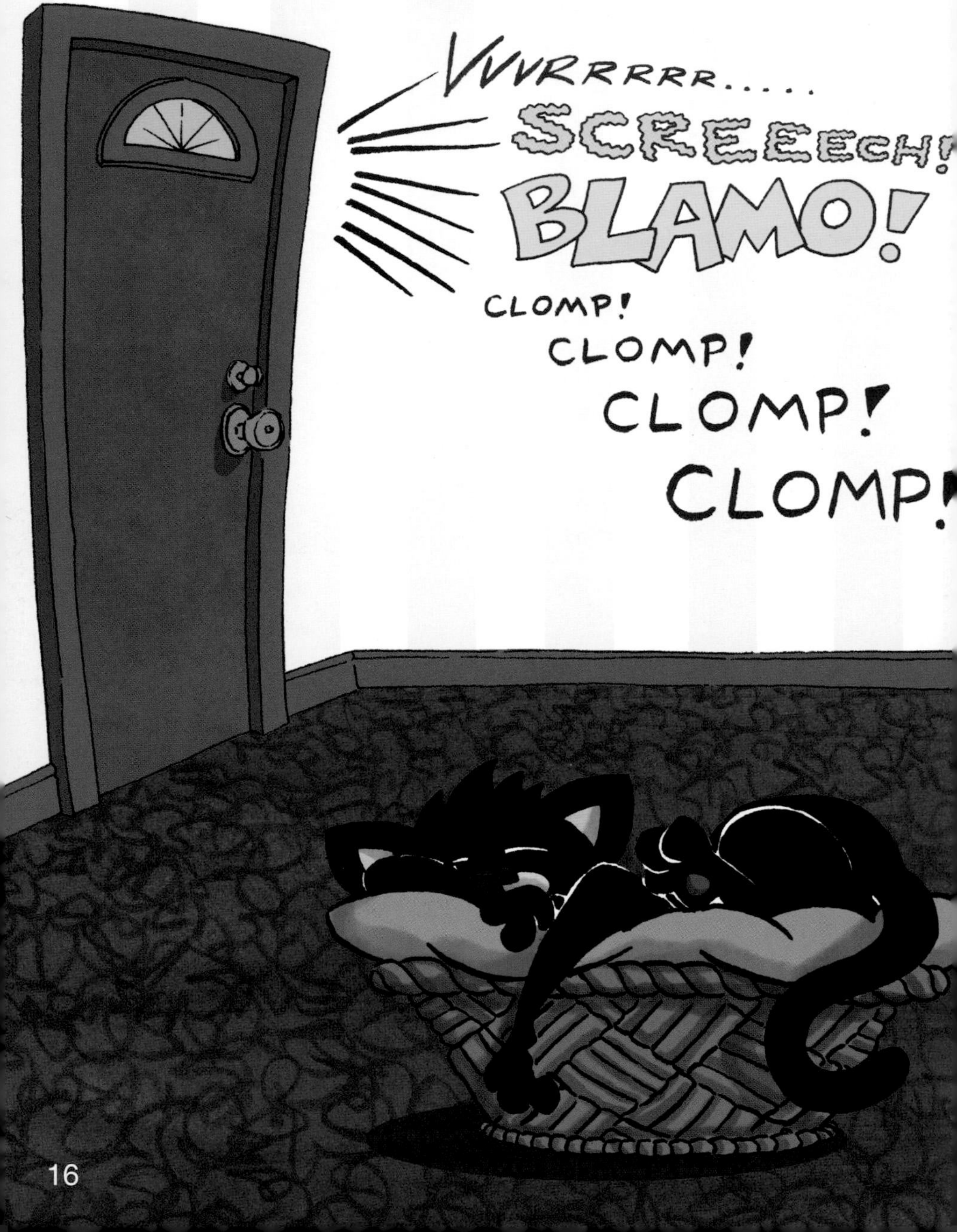
VVVVRRRRRR.....
SCREEECH!
BLAMO!
CLOMP!
CLOMP!
CLOMP!
CLOMP!

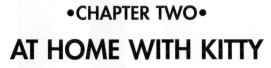

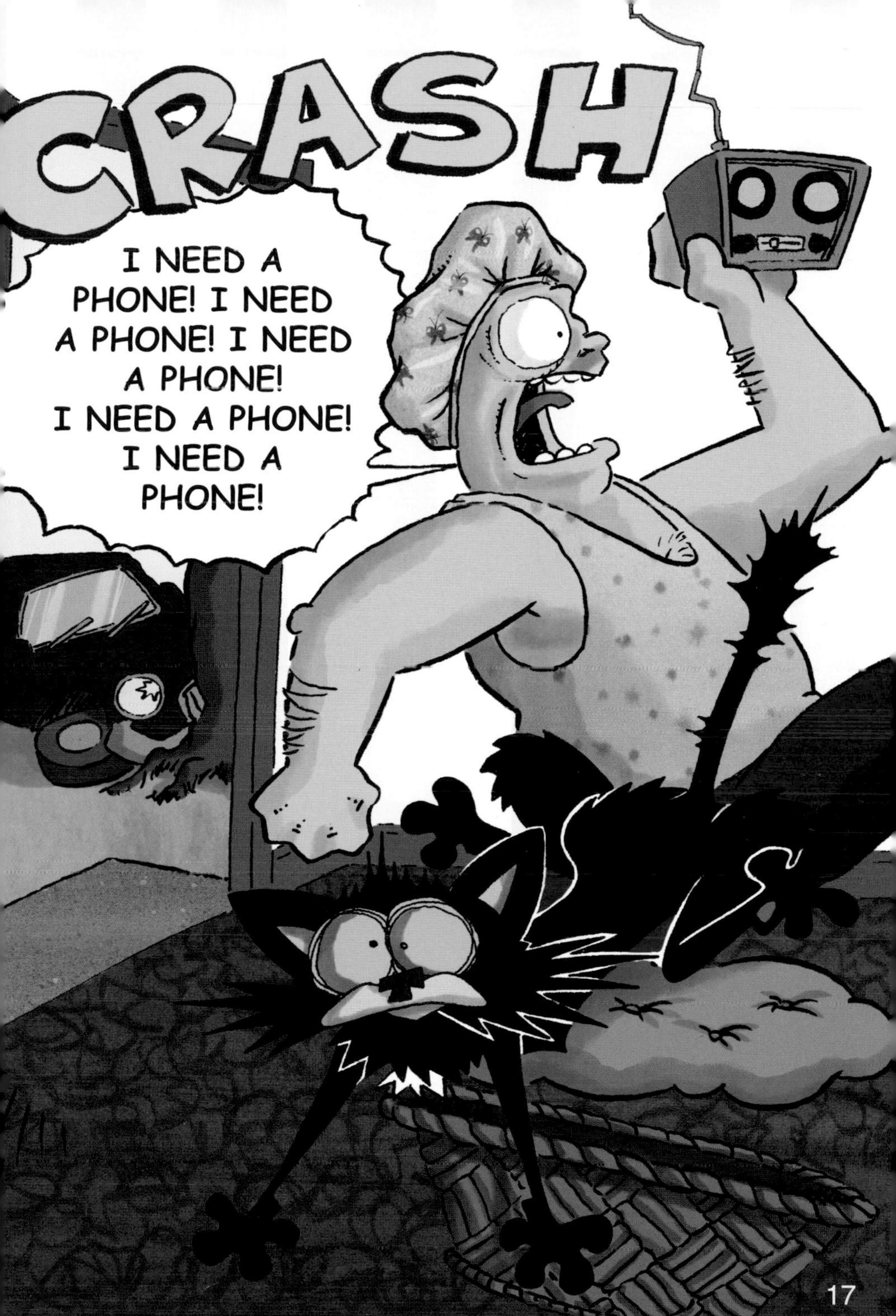
CRASH
I NEED A PHONE! I NEED A PHONE! I NEED A PHONE! I NEED A PHONE! I NEED A PHONE!

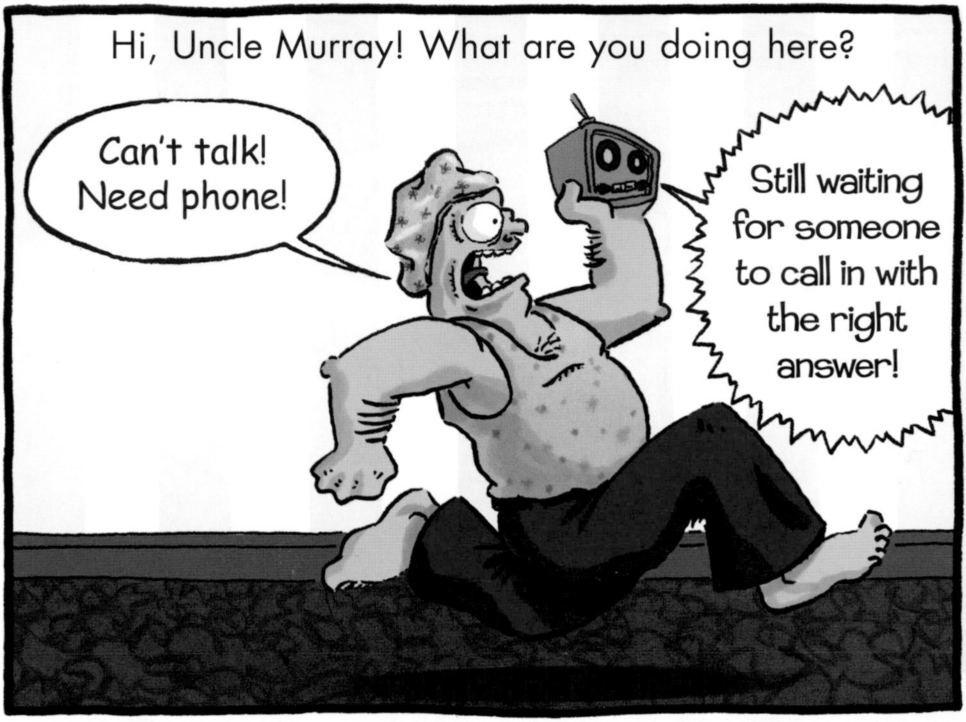
Hi, Uncle Murray! What are you doing here?
Can't talk! Need phone!
Still waiting for someone to call in with the right answer!

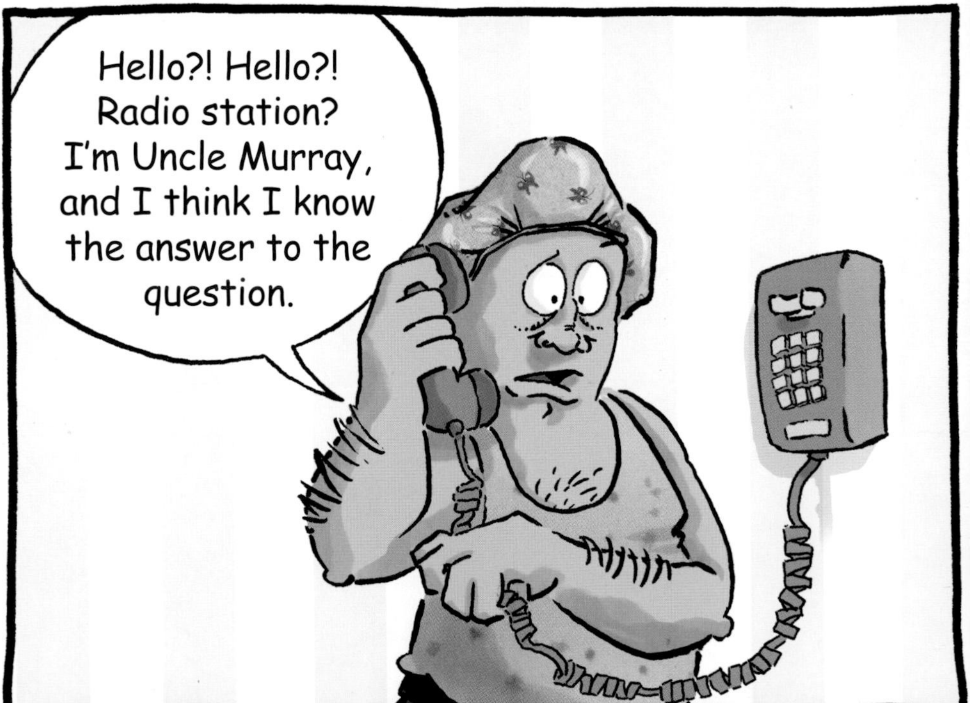
Hello?! Hello?! Radio station? I'm Uncle Murray, and I think I know the answer to the question.

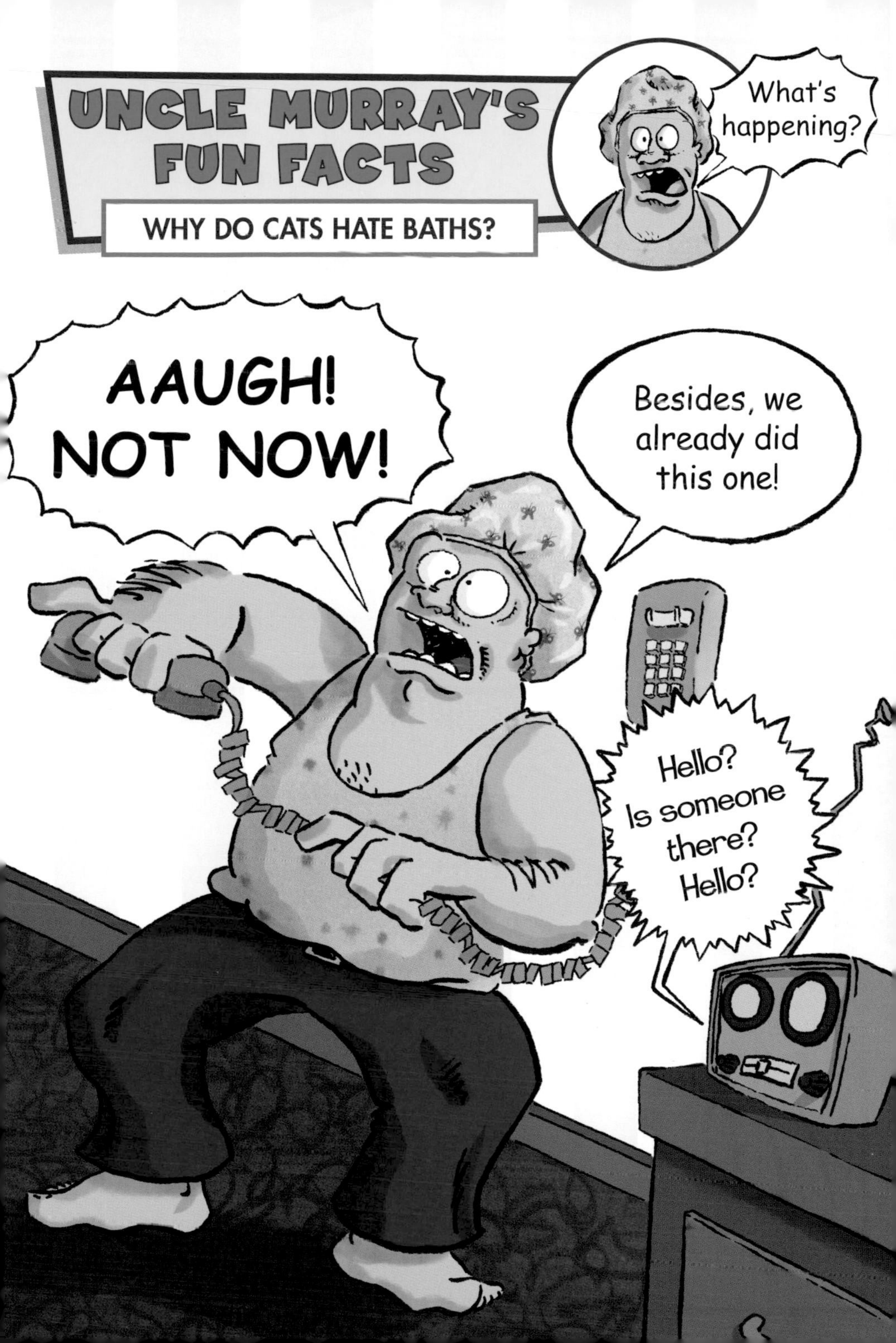
UNCLE MURRAY'S FUN FACTS
WHY DO CATS HATE BATHS?
What's happening?
AAUGH! NOT NOW!
Besides, we already did this one!
Hello? Is someone there? Hello?

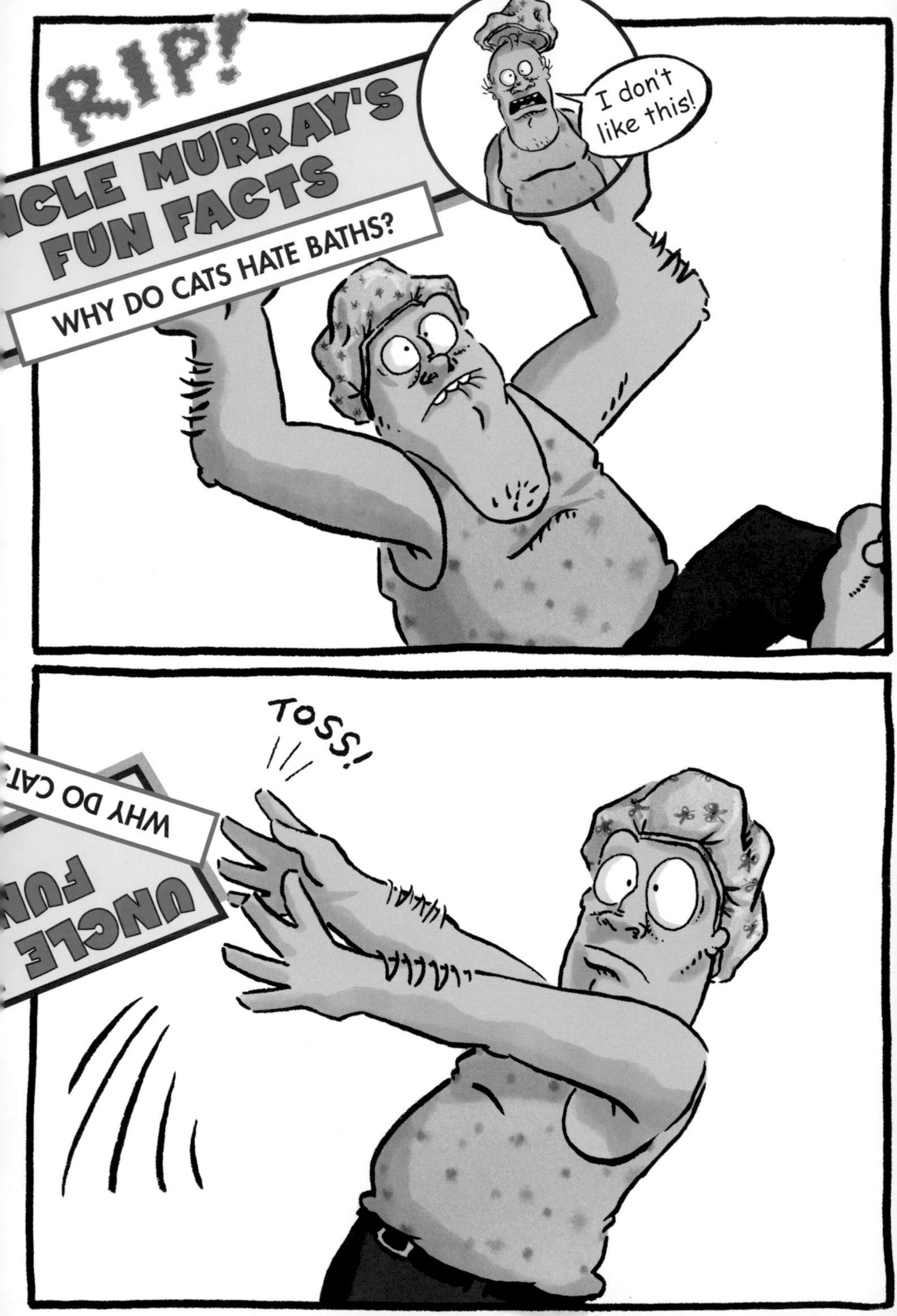
RIP!
CLE MURRAY'S
FUN FACTS
WHY DO CATS HATE BATHS?
I don't like this!
TOSS!
UNCLE

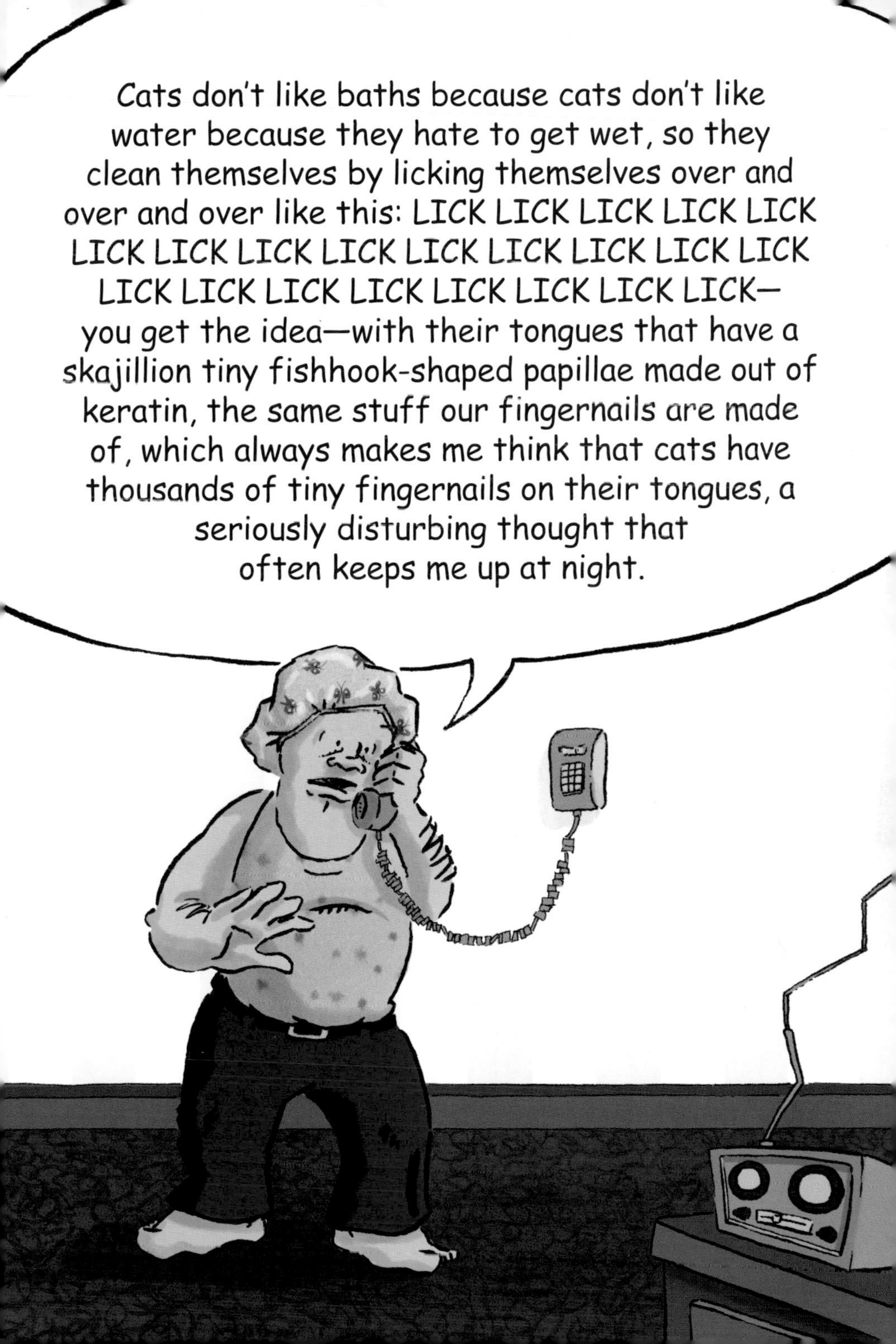
Cats don't like baths because cats don't like water because they hate to get wet, so they clean themselves by licking themselves over and over and over like this: LICK LICK LICK LICK LICK LICK LICK LICK LICK LICK LICK LICK LICK LICK LICK LICK LICK LICK LICK LICK LICK LICK— you get the idea—with their tongues that have a skajillion tiny fishhook-shaped papillae made out of keratin, the same stuff our fingernails are made of, which always makes me think that cats have thousands of tiny fingernails on their tongues, a seriously disturbing thought that often keeps me up at night.

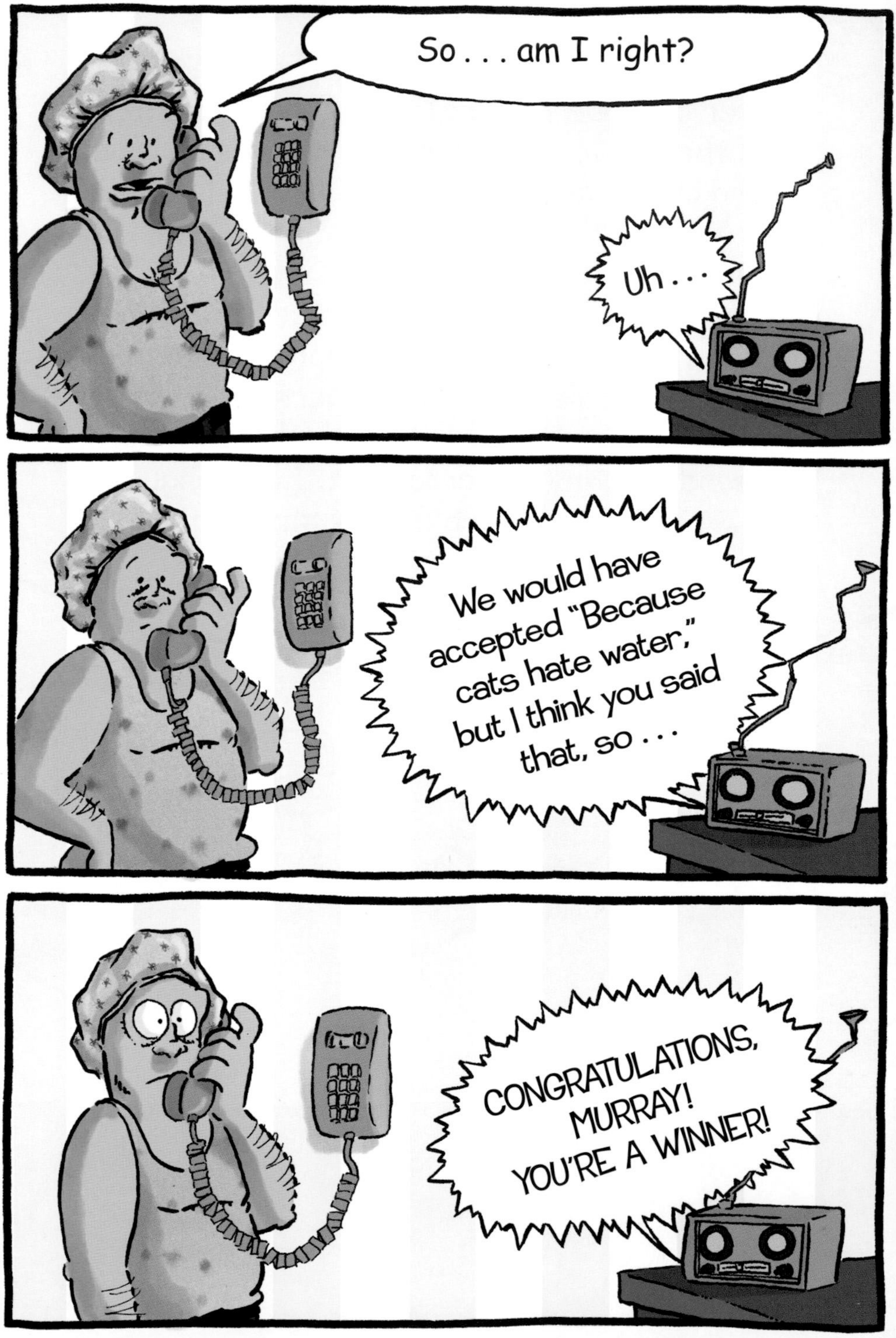
So . . . am I right?
Uh . . .
We would have accepted "Because cats hate water," but I think you said that, so . . .
CONGRATULATIONS, MURRAY! YOU'RE A WINNER!

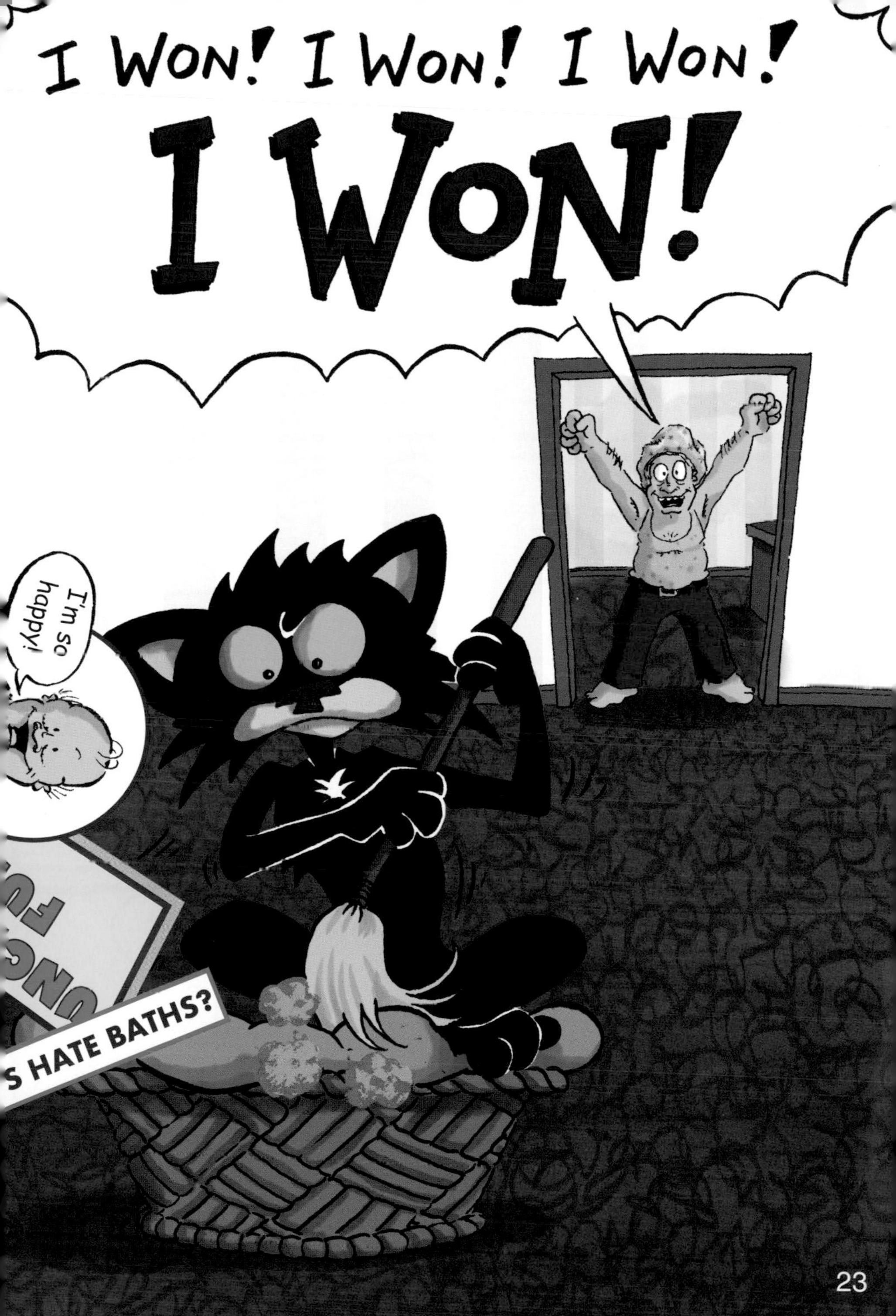

I WON! I WON! I WON!
I WON!
I'm so happy!
S HATE BATHS?

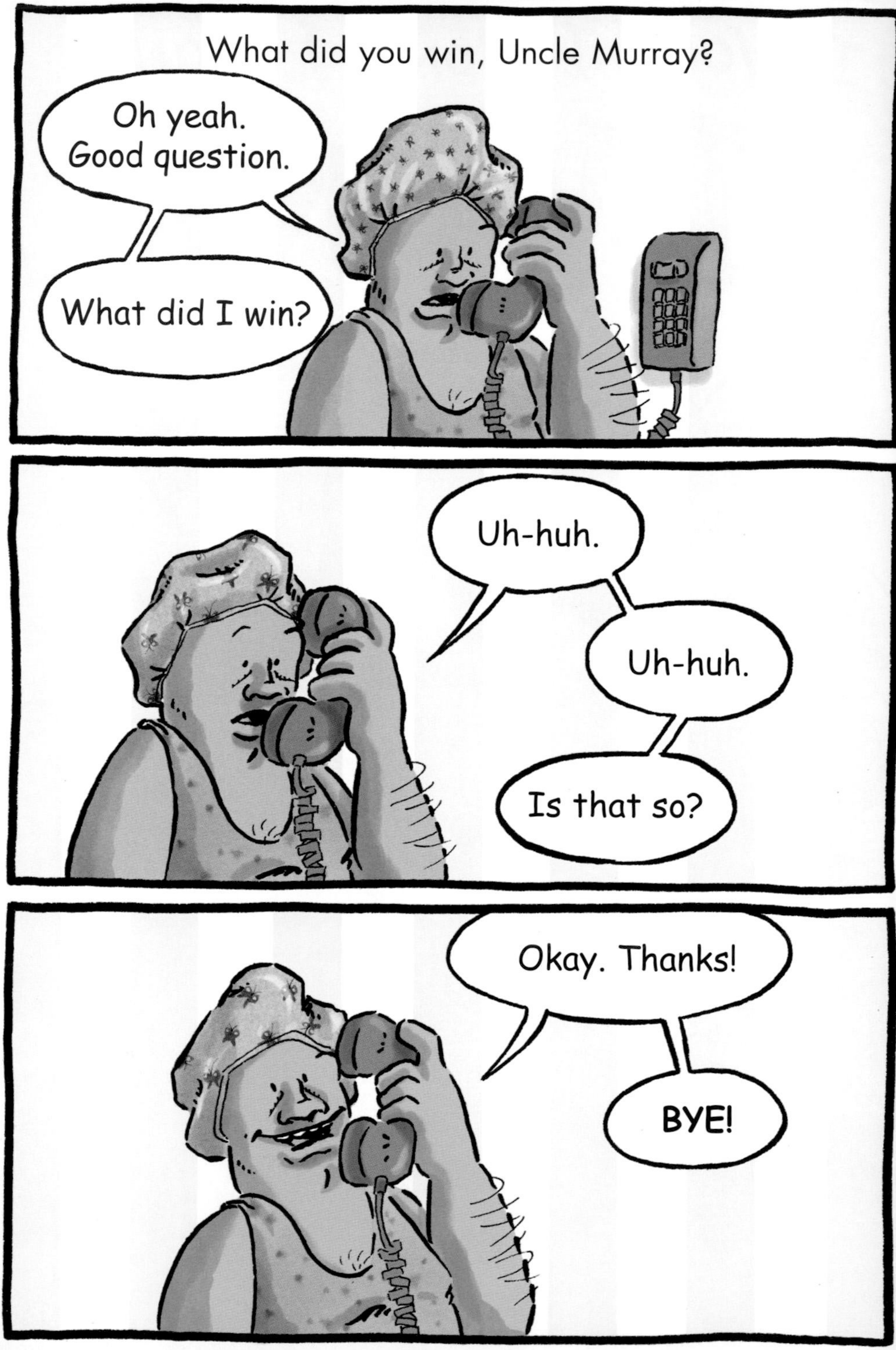
What did you win, Uncle Murray?
Oh yeah. Good question.
What did I win?
Uh-huh.
Uh-huh.
Is that so?
Okay. Thanks!
BYE!

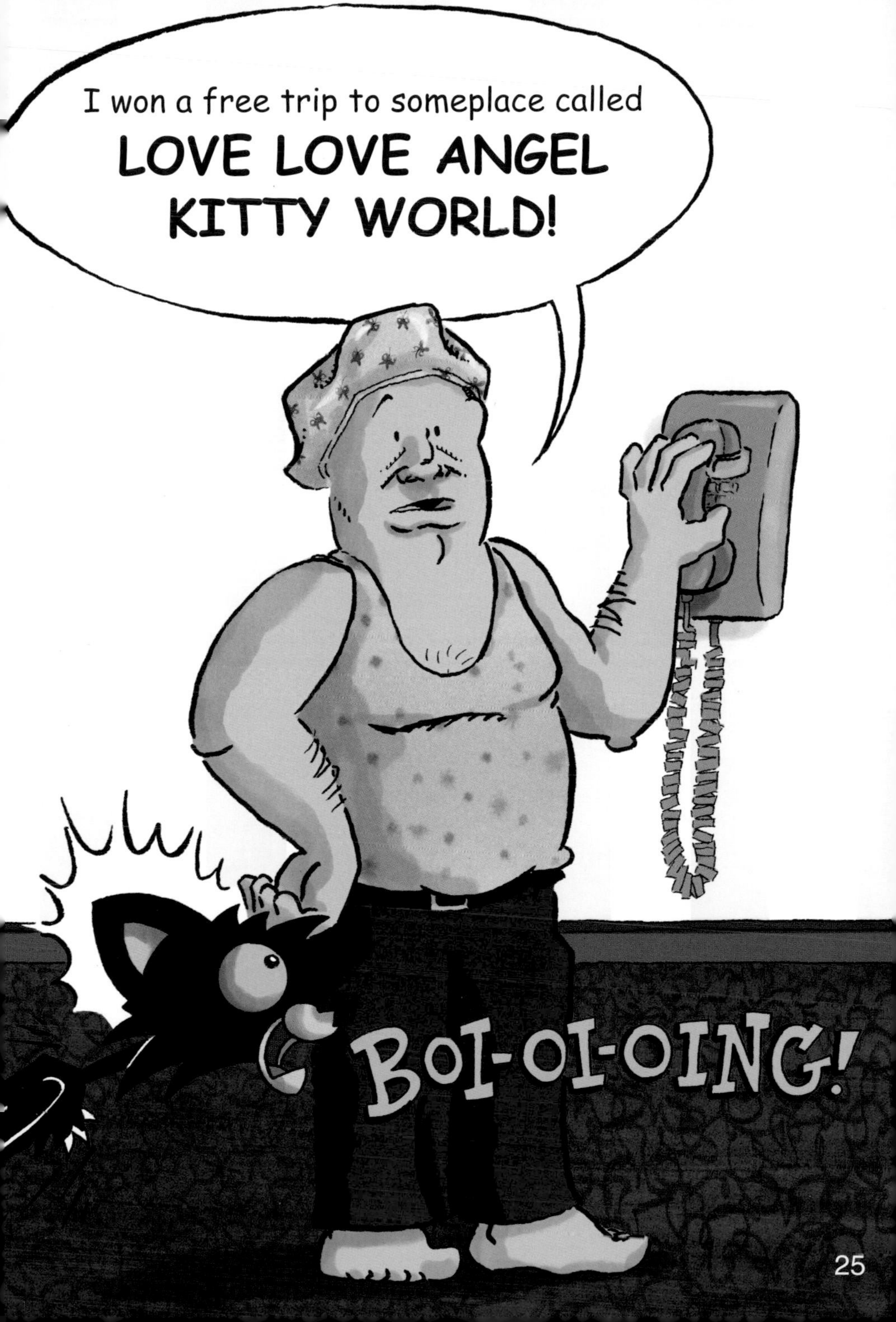
I won a free trip to someplace called LOVE LOVE ANGEL KITTY WORLD!
BOI-OI-OING!

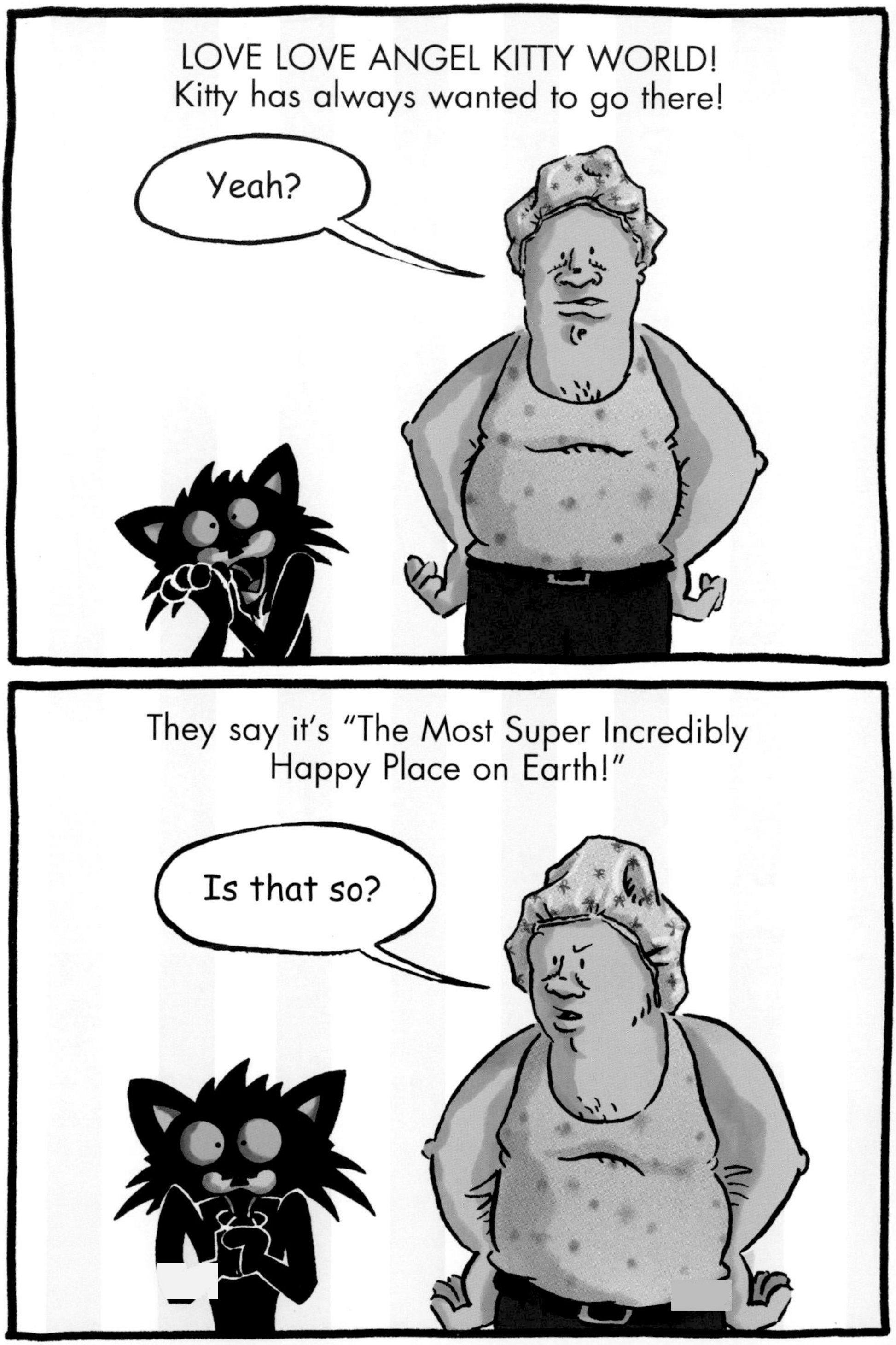
LOVE LOVE ANGEL KITTY WORLD!
Kitty has always wanted to go there!
Yeah?
They say it's "The Most Super Incredibly Happy Place on Earth!"
Is that so?

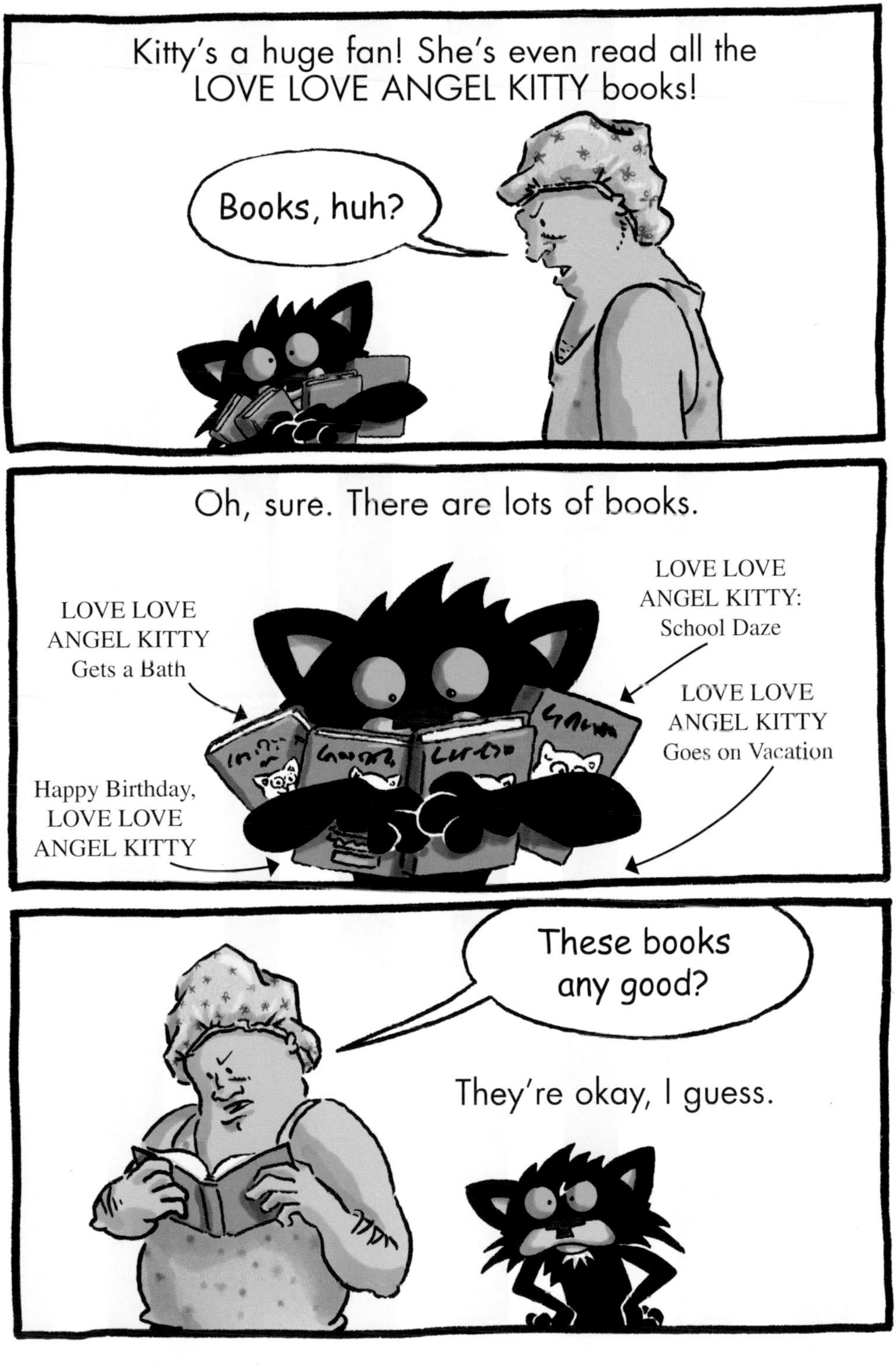
Kitty's a huge fan! She's even read all the LOVE LOVE ANGEL KITTY books!
Books, huh?
Oh, sure. There are lots of books.
LOVE LOVE ANGEL KITTY Gets a Bath
LOVE LOVE ANGEL KITTY: School Daze
LOVE LOVE ANGEL KITTY Goes on Vacation
Happy Birthday, LOVE LOVE ANGEL KITTY
These books any good?
They're okay, I guess.

Show him what else you have, Kitty!

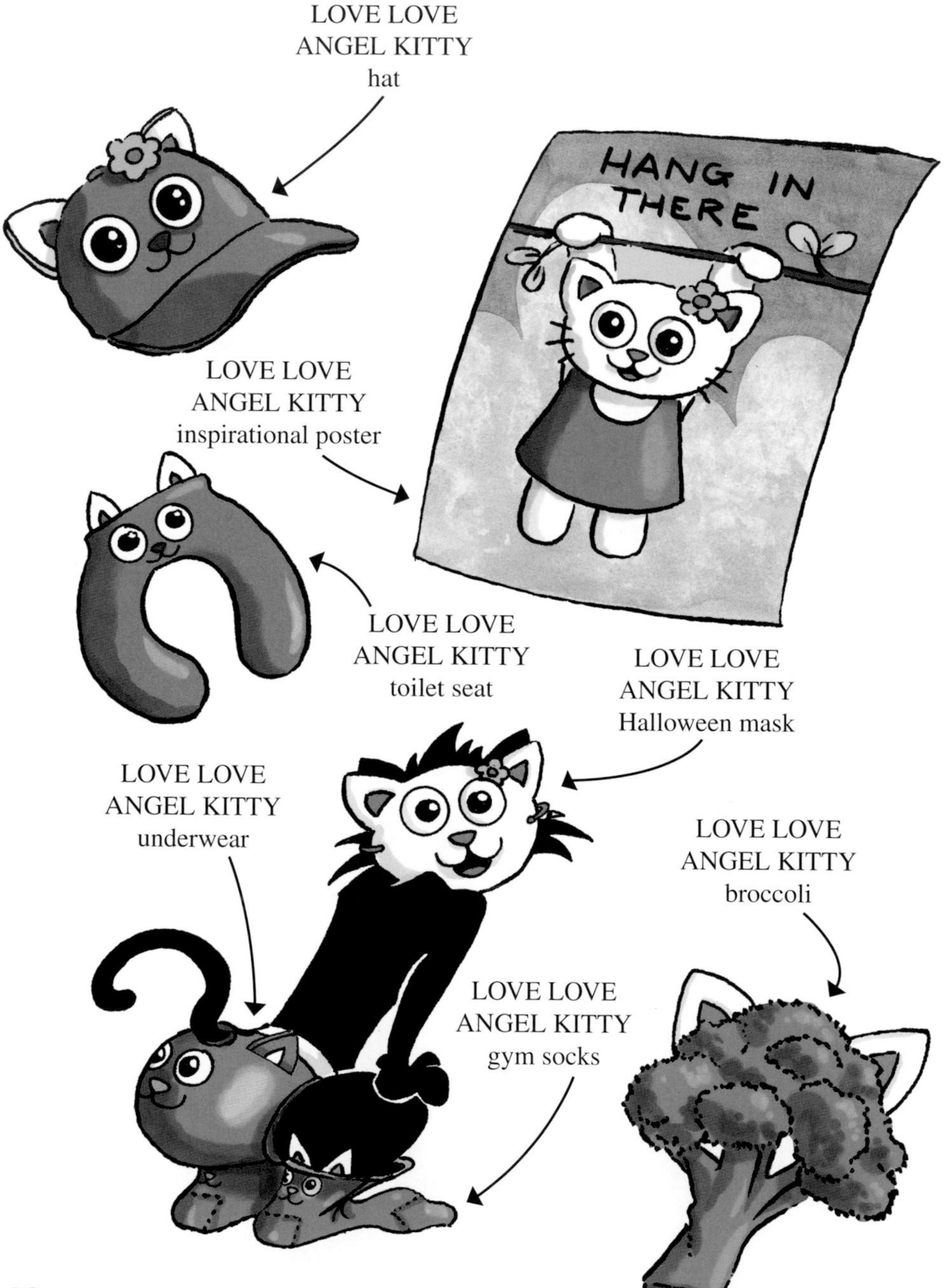
LOVE LOVE ANGEL KITTY hat
HANG IN THERE
LOVE LOVE ANGEL KITTY inspirational poster
LOVE LOVE ANGEL KITTY toilet seat
LOVE LOVE ANGEL KITTY Halloween mask
LOVE LOVE ANGEL KITTY underwear
LOVE LOVE ANGEL KITTY broccoli
LOVE LOVE ANGEL KITTY gym socks

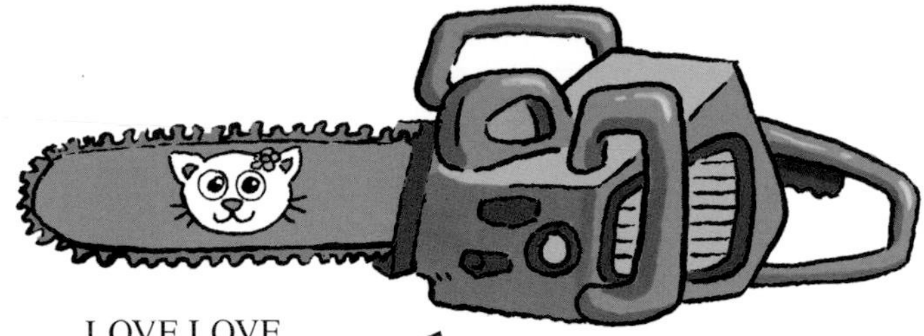

LOVE LOVE
ANGEL KITTY
chainsaw

LOVE LOVE
ANGEL KITTY
table lamp

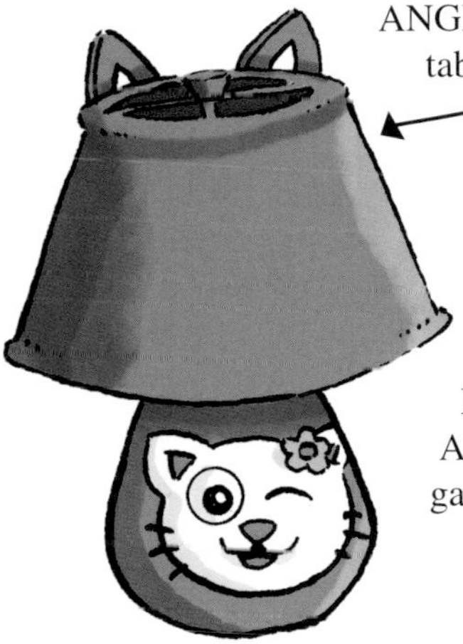

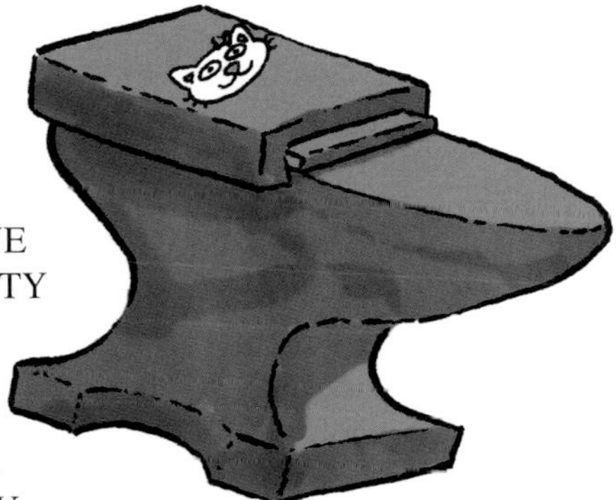

LOVE LOVE
ANGEL KITTY
anvil

LOVE LOVE
ANGEL KITTY
garbage dumpster

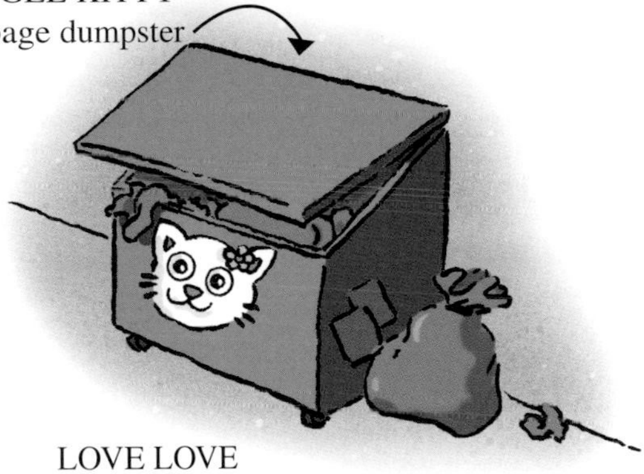

LOVE LOVE
ANGEL KITTY
car battery

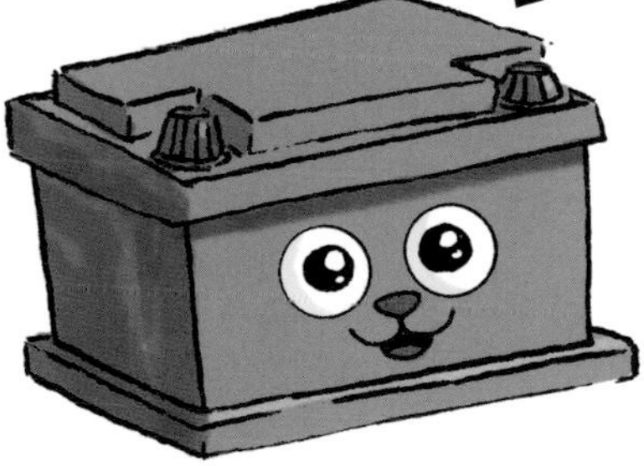

LOVE LOVE
ANGEL KITTY
orbital satellite

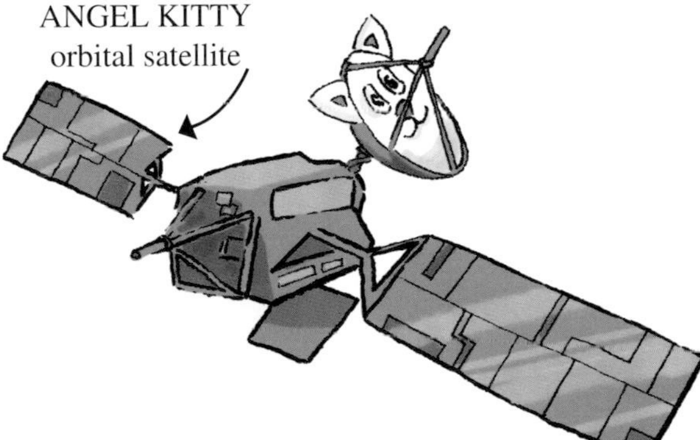

LOVE LOVE
ANGEL KITTY
dryer lint

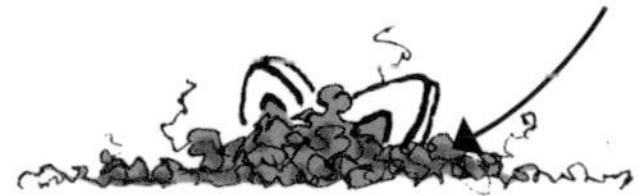

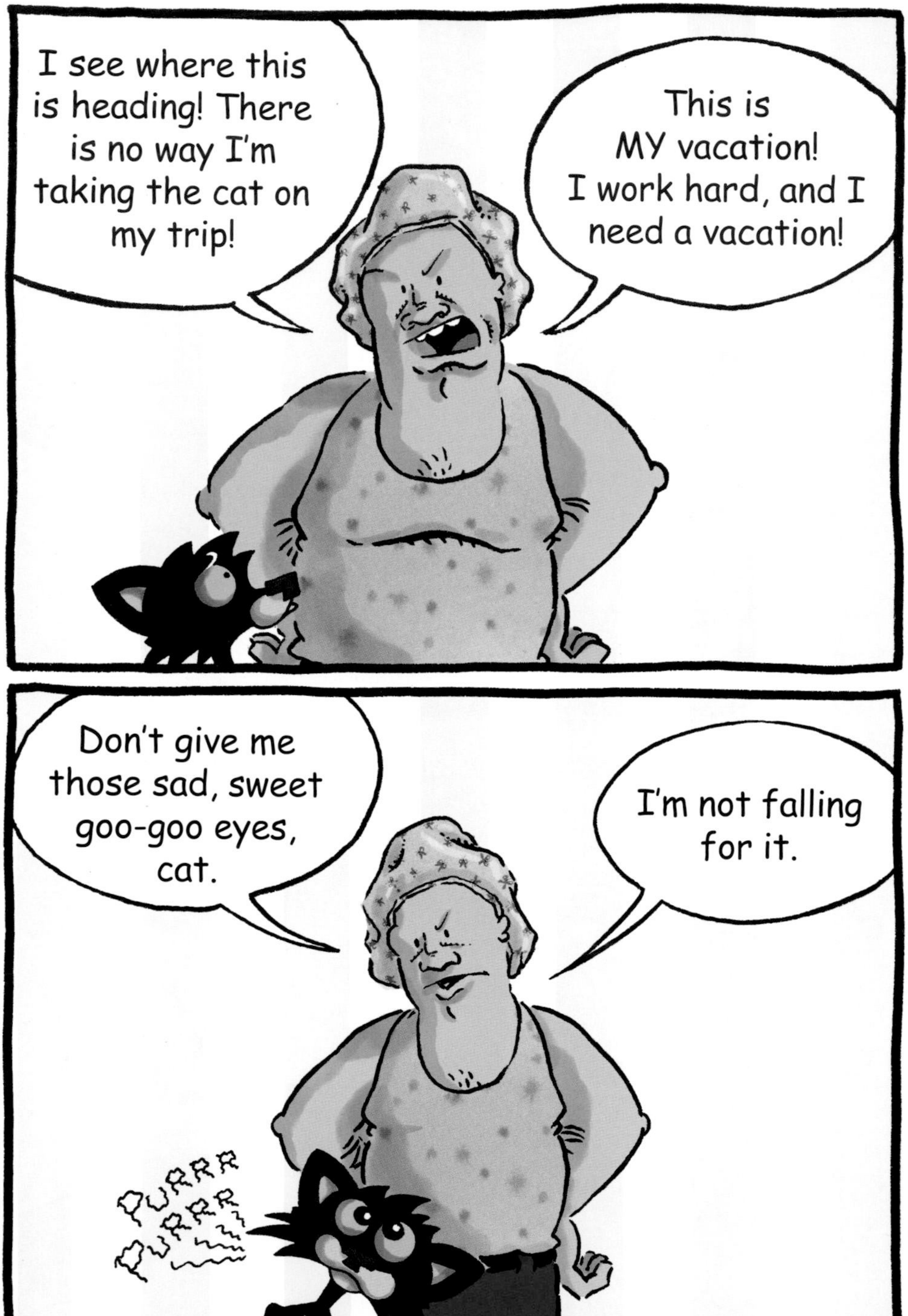
I see where this is heading! There is no way I'm taking the cat on my trip!
This is MY vacation! I work hard, and I need a vacation!
Don't give me those sad, sweet goo-goo eyes, cat.
I'm not falling for it.
PURRR
PURRR

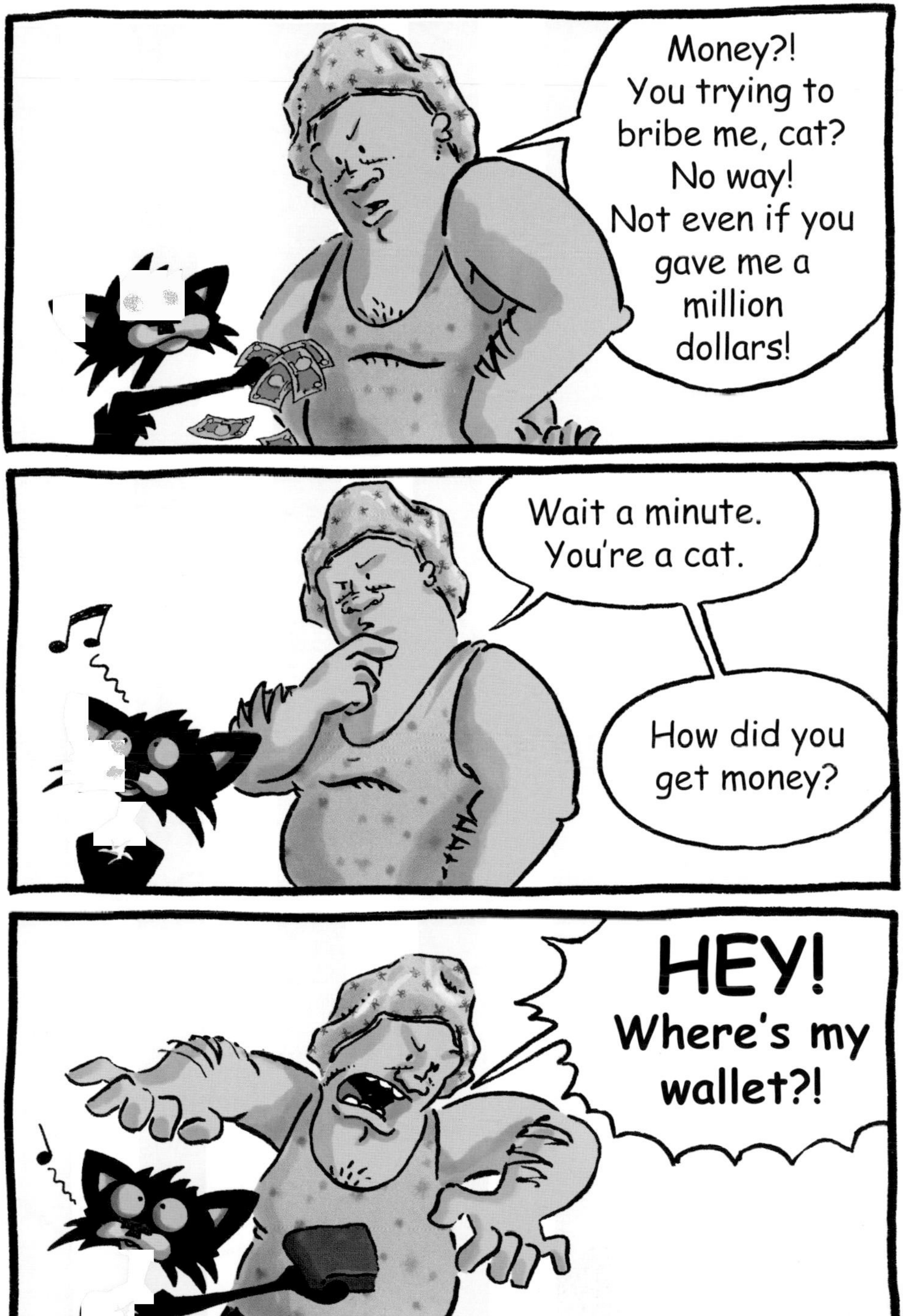
Money?! You trying to bribe me, cat? No way! Not even if you gave me a million dollars!
Wait a minute. You're a cat.
How did you get money?
HEY! Where's my wallet?!

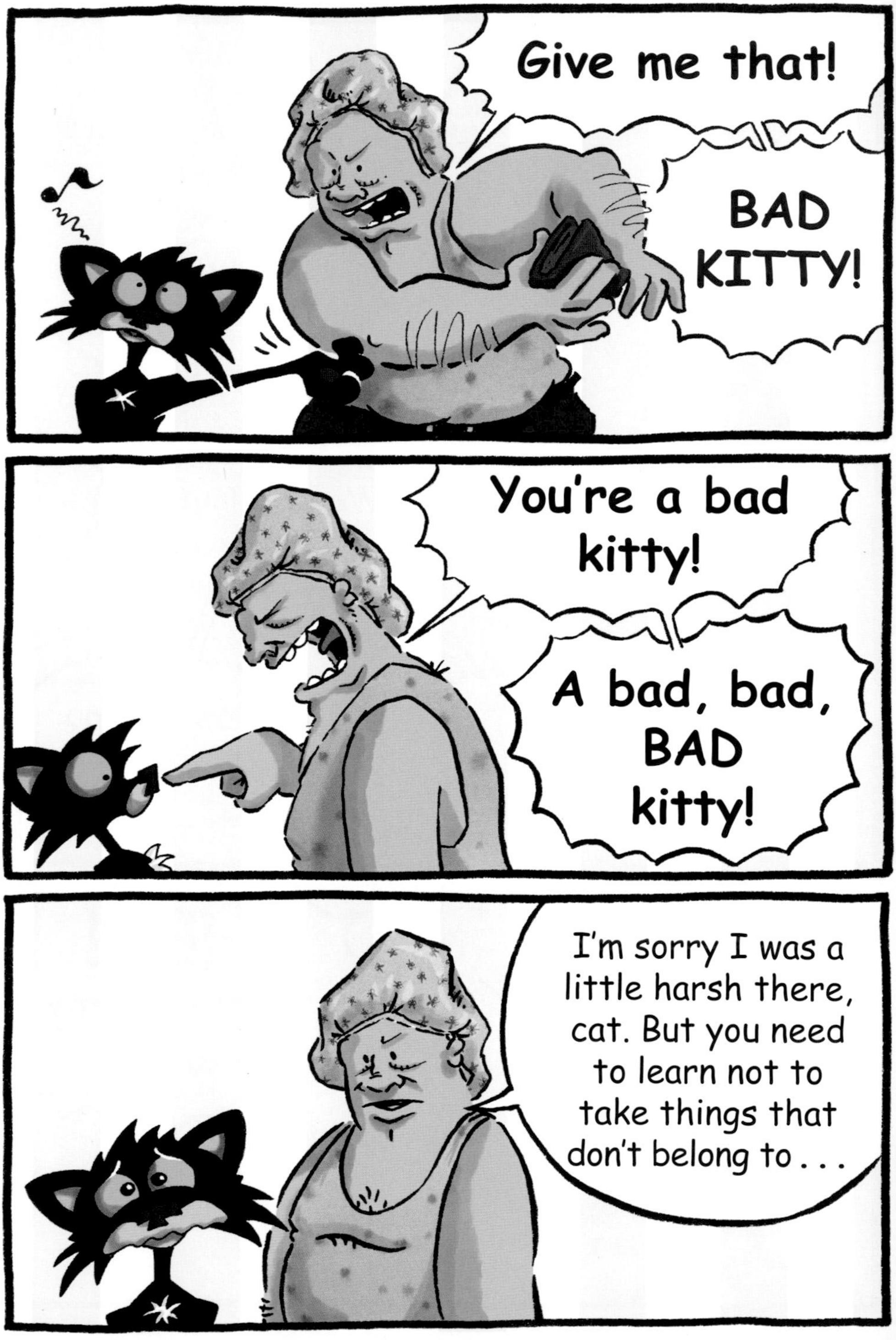
Give me that!
BAD KITTY!
You're a bad kitty!
A bad, bad, BAD kitty!
I'm sorry I was a little harsh there, cat. But you need to learn not to take things that don't belong to . . .

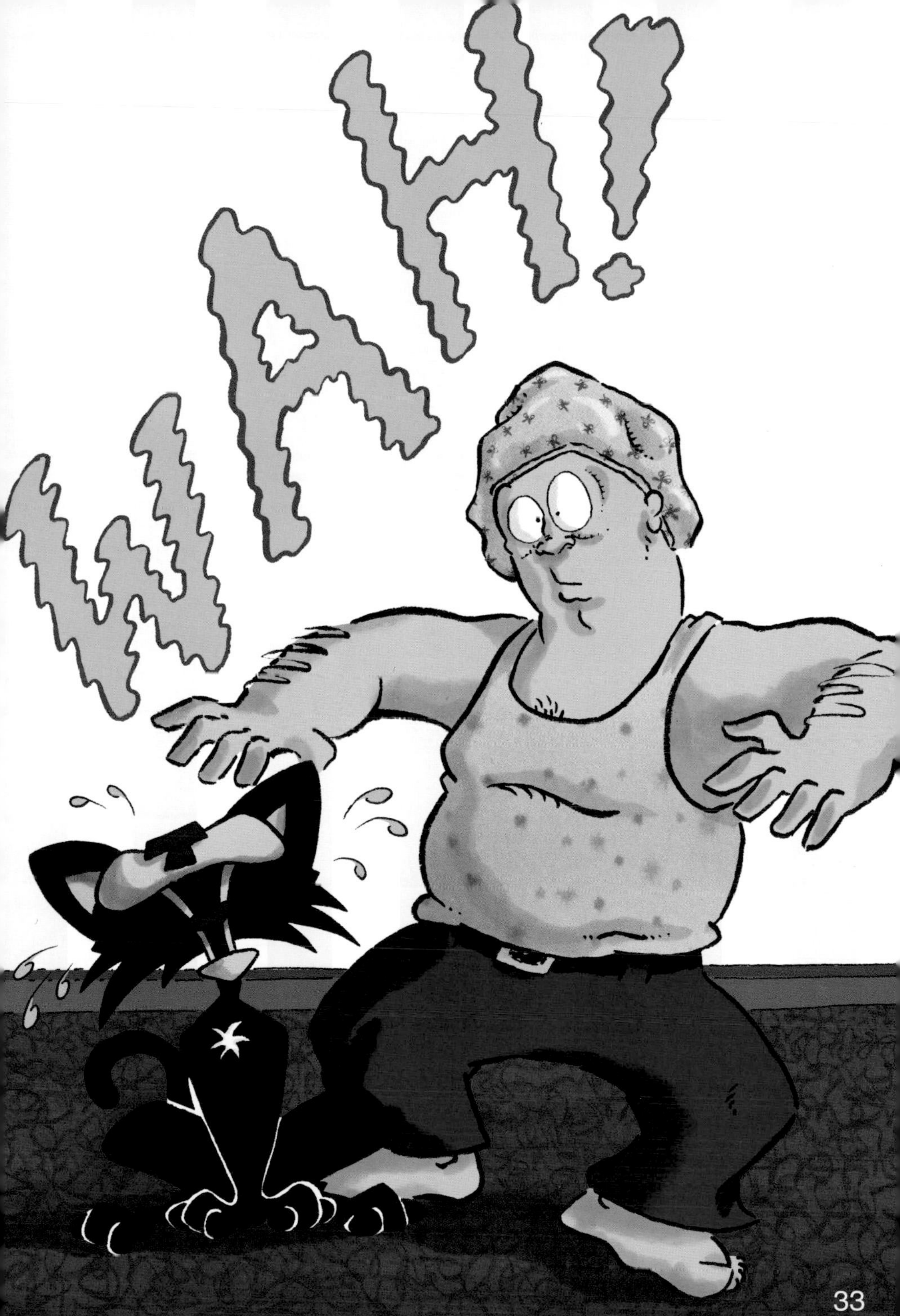
WAH!

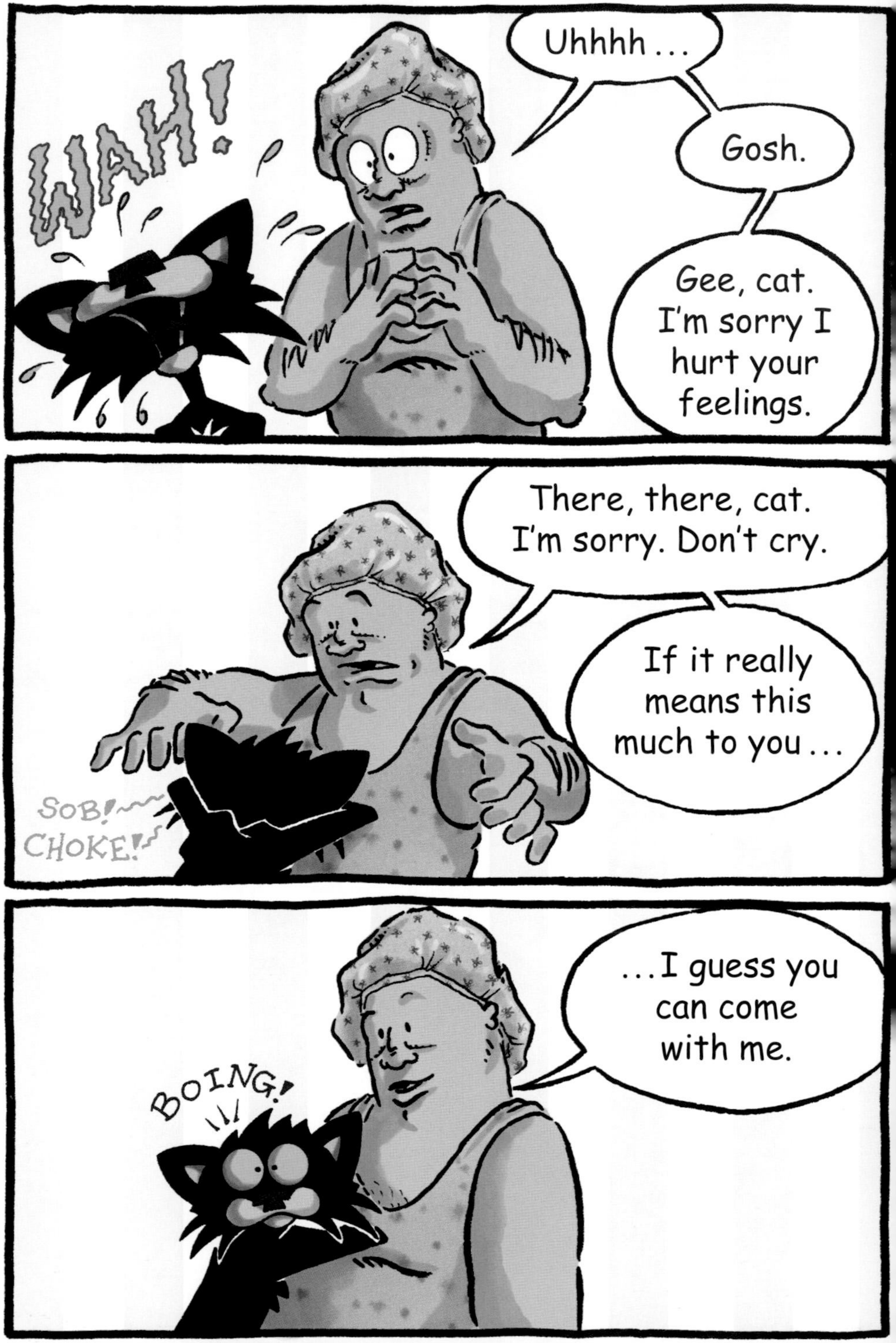
WAH!
Uhhhh . . .
Gosh.
Gee, cat. I'm sorry I hurt your feelings.
There, there, cat. I'm sorry. Don't cry.
If it really means this much to you . . .
SOB!
CHOKE!
. . . I guess you can come with me.
BOING!

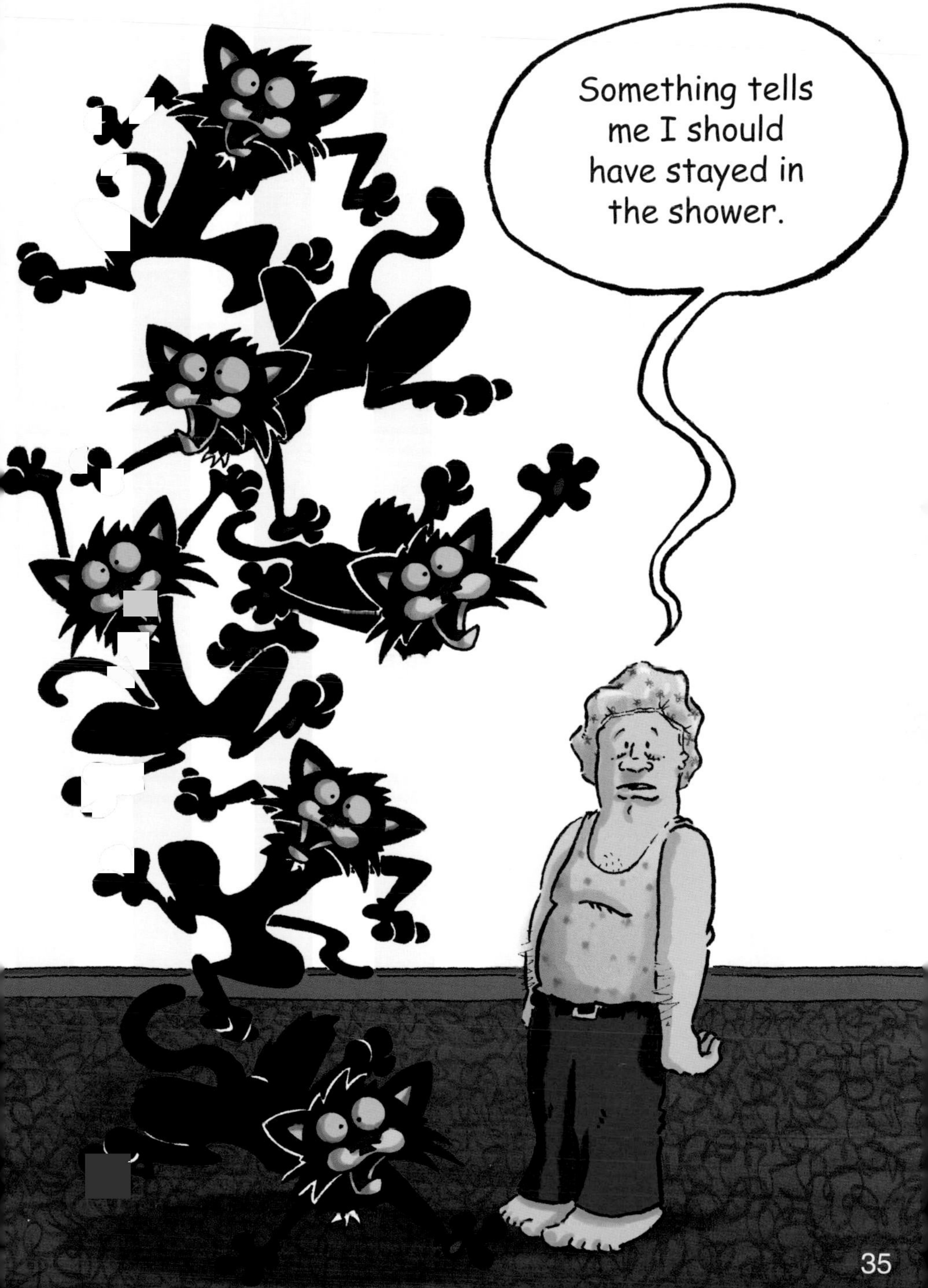
Something tells me I should have stayed in the shower.

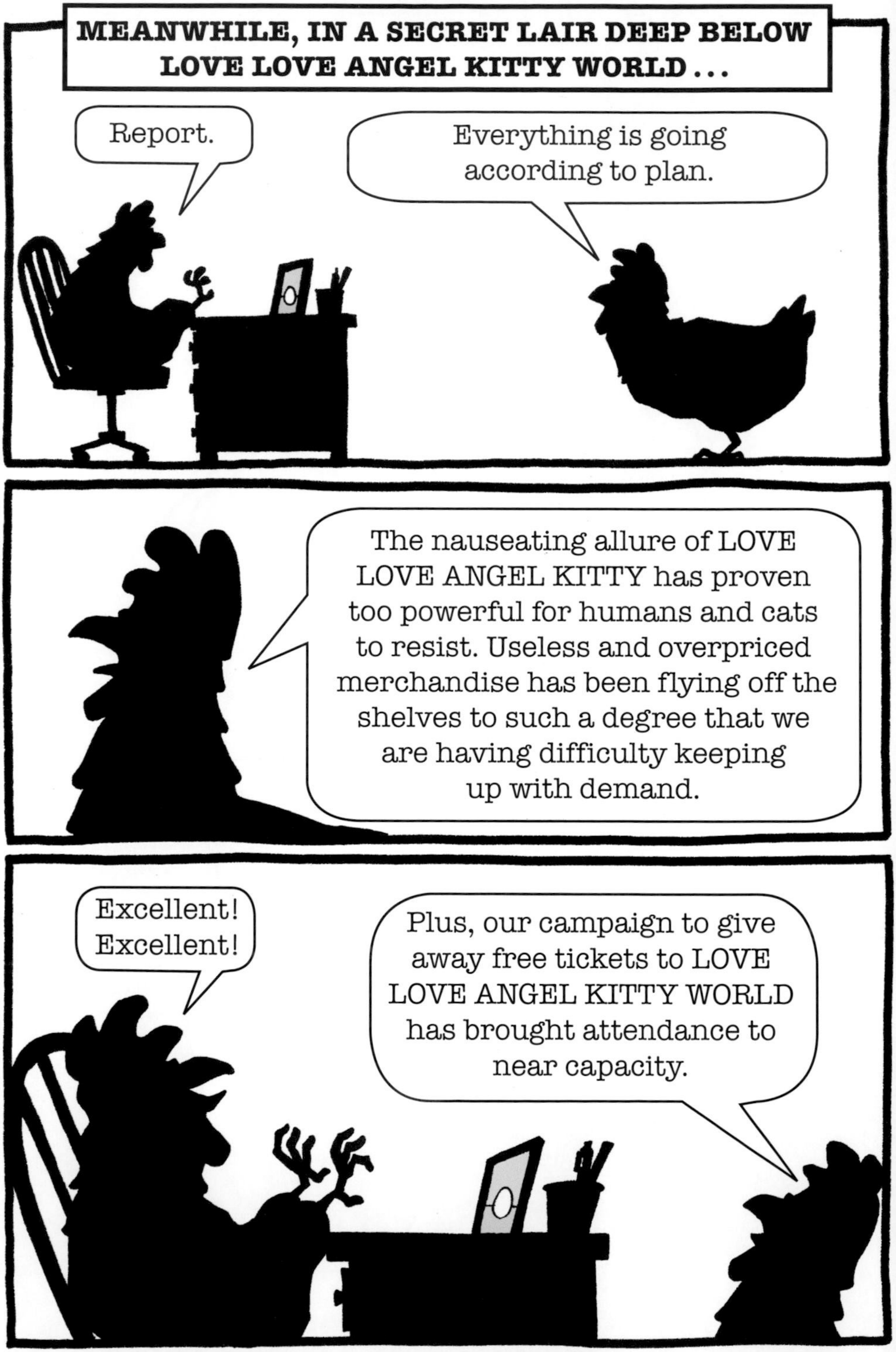
MEANWHILE, IN A SECRET LAIR DEEP BELOW LOVE LOVE ANGEL KITTY WORLD . . .
Report.
Everything is going according to plan.
The nauseating allure of LOVE LOVE ANGEL KITTY has proven too powerful for humans and cats to resist. Useless and overpriced merchandise has been flying off the shelves to such a degree that we are having difficulty keeping up with demand.
Excellent! Excellent!
Plus, our campaign to give away free tickets to LOVE LOVE ANGEL KITTY WORLD has brought attendance to near capacity.

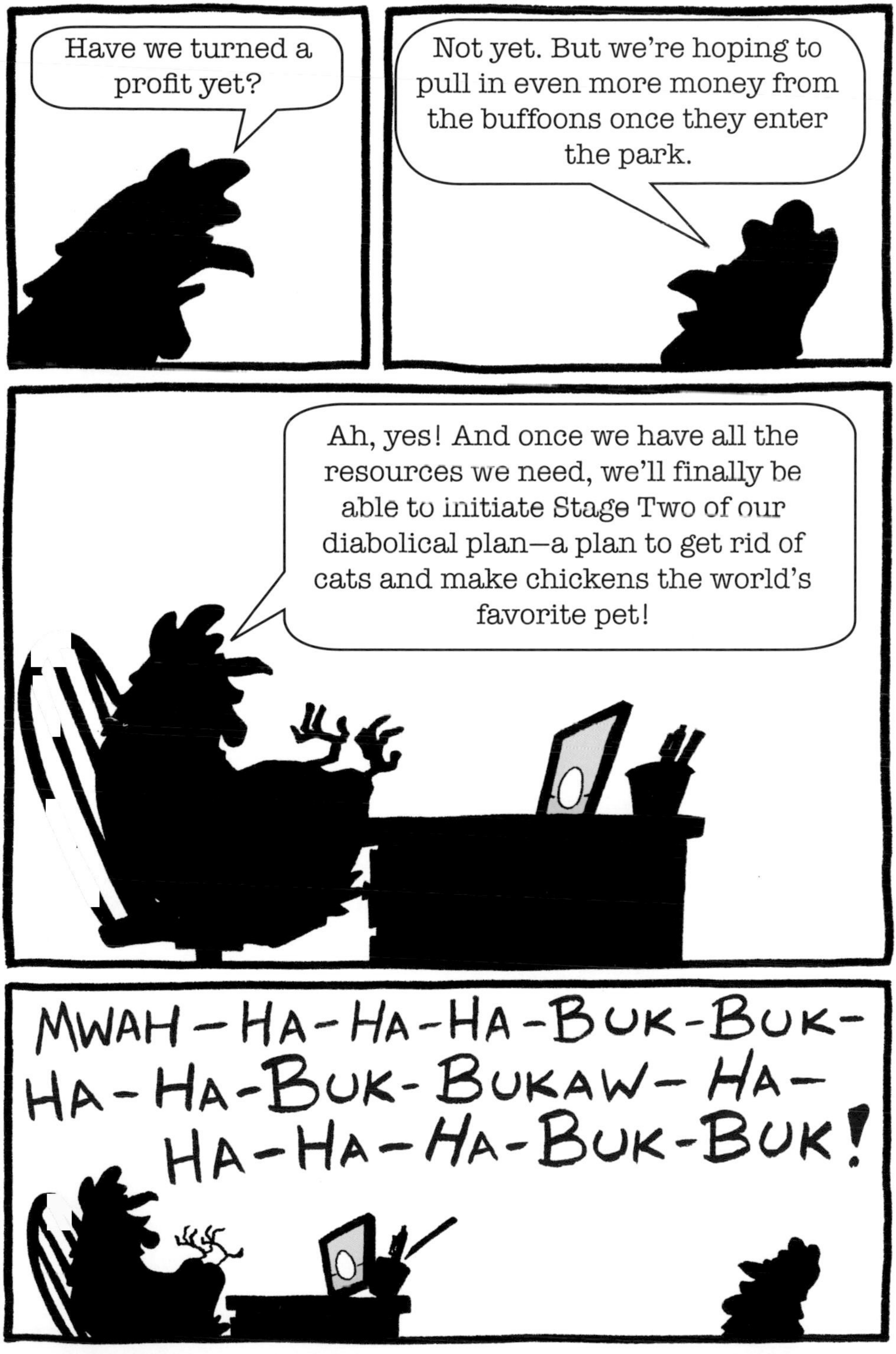
Have we turned a profit yet?
Not yet. But we're hoping to pull in even more money from the buffoons once they enter the park.
Ah, yes! And once we have all the resources we need, we'll finally be able to initiate Stage Two of our diabolical plan—a plan to get rid of cats and make chickens the world's favorite pet!
MWAH-HA-HA-HA-BUK-BUK-HA-HA-BUK-BUKAW-HA-HA-HA-HA-BUK-BUK!

• CHAPTER THREE •

AT THE AIRPORT

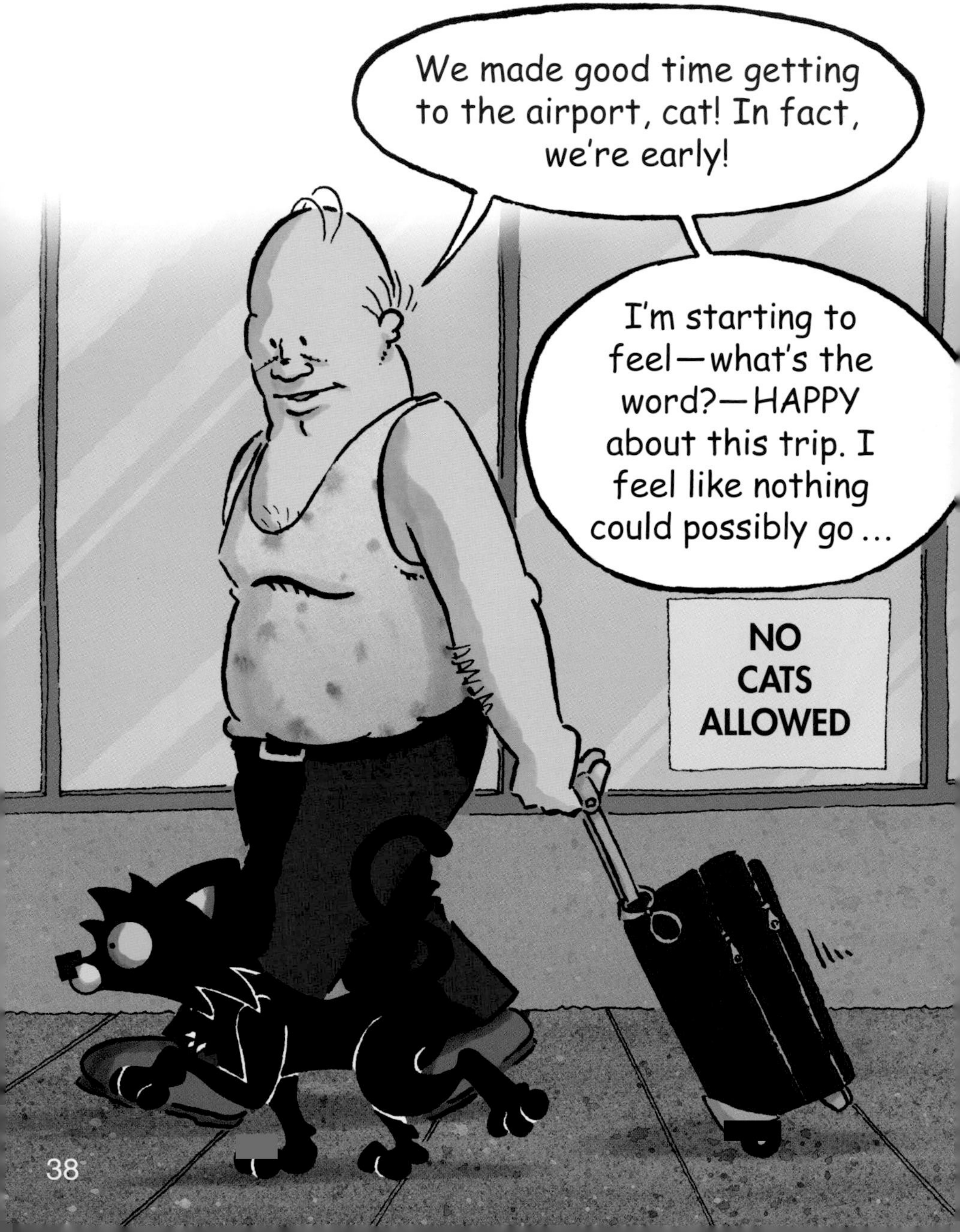
We made good time getting to the airport, cat! In fact, we're early!
I'm starting to feel—what's the word?—HAPPY about this trip. I feel like nothing could possibly go ...
NO CATS ALLOWED

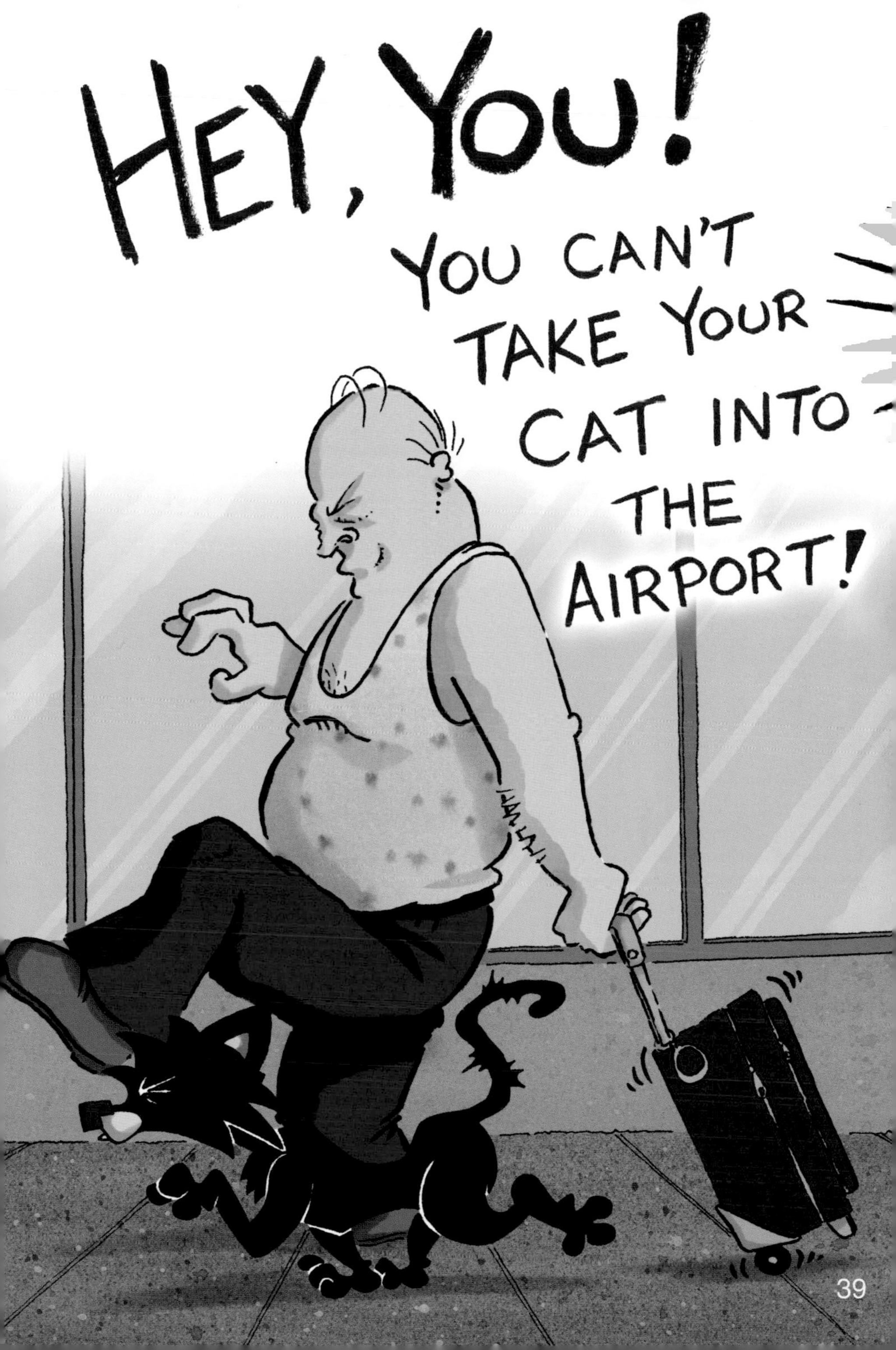
HEY, YOU!
YOU CAN'T TAKE YOUR CAT INTO THE AIRPORT!

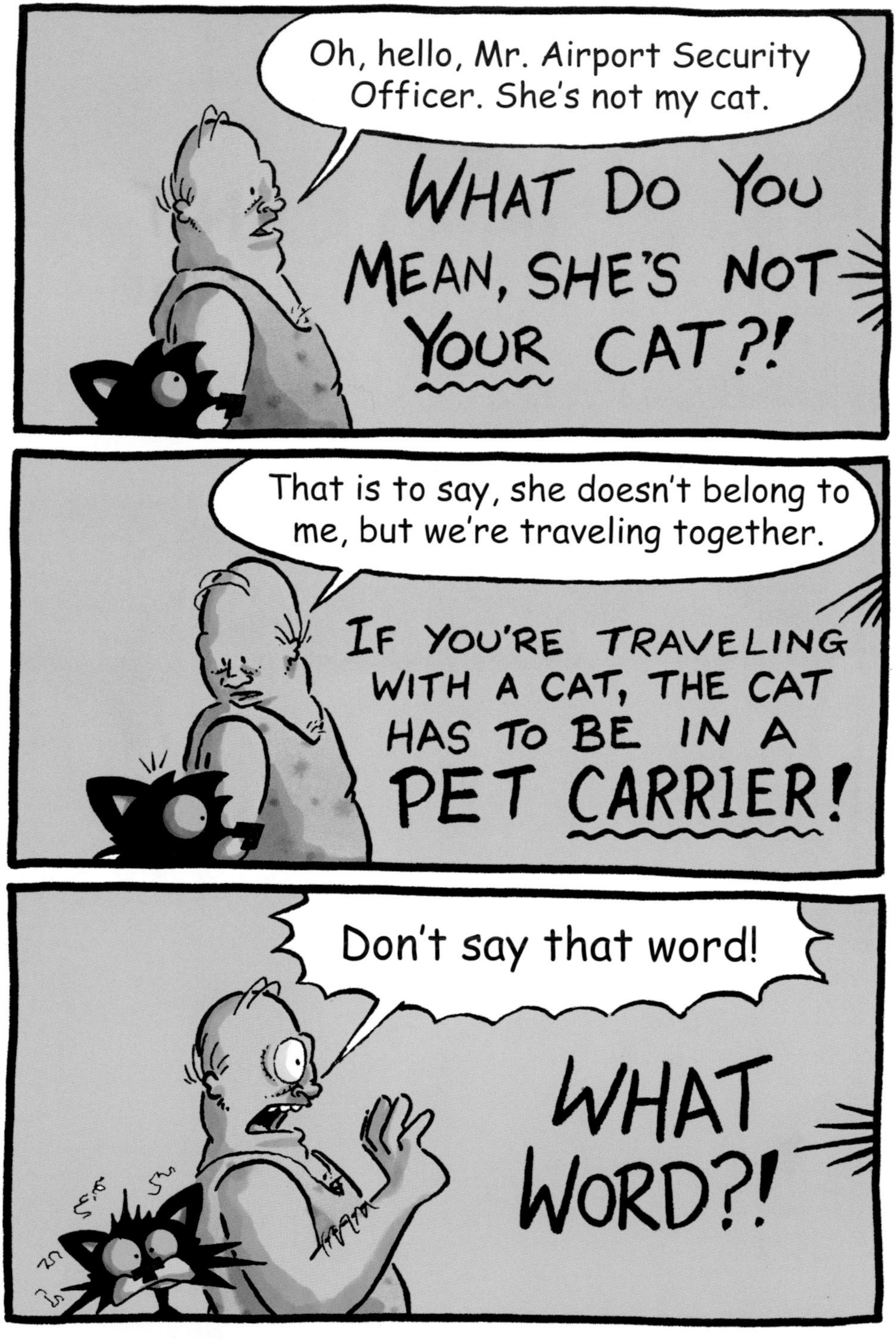
Oh, hello, Mr. Airport Security Officer. She's not my cat.
WHAT DO YOU MEAN, SHE'S NOT YOUR CAT?!
That is to say, she doesn't belong to me, but we're traveling together.
IF YOU'RE TRAVELING WITH A CAT, THE CAT HAS TO BE IN A PET CARRIER!
Don't say that word!
WHAT WORD?!

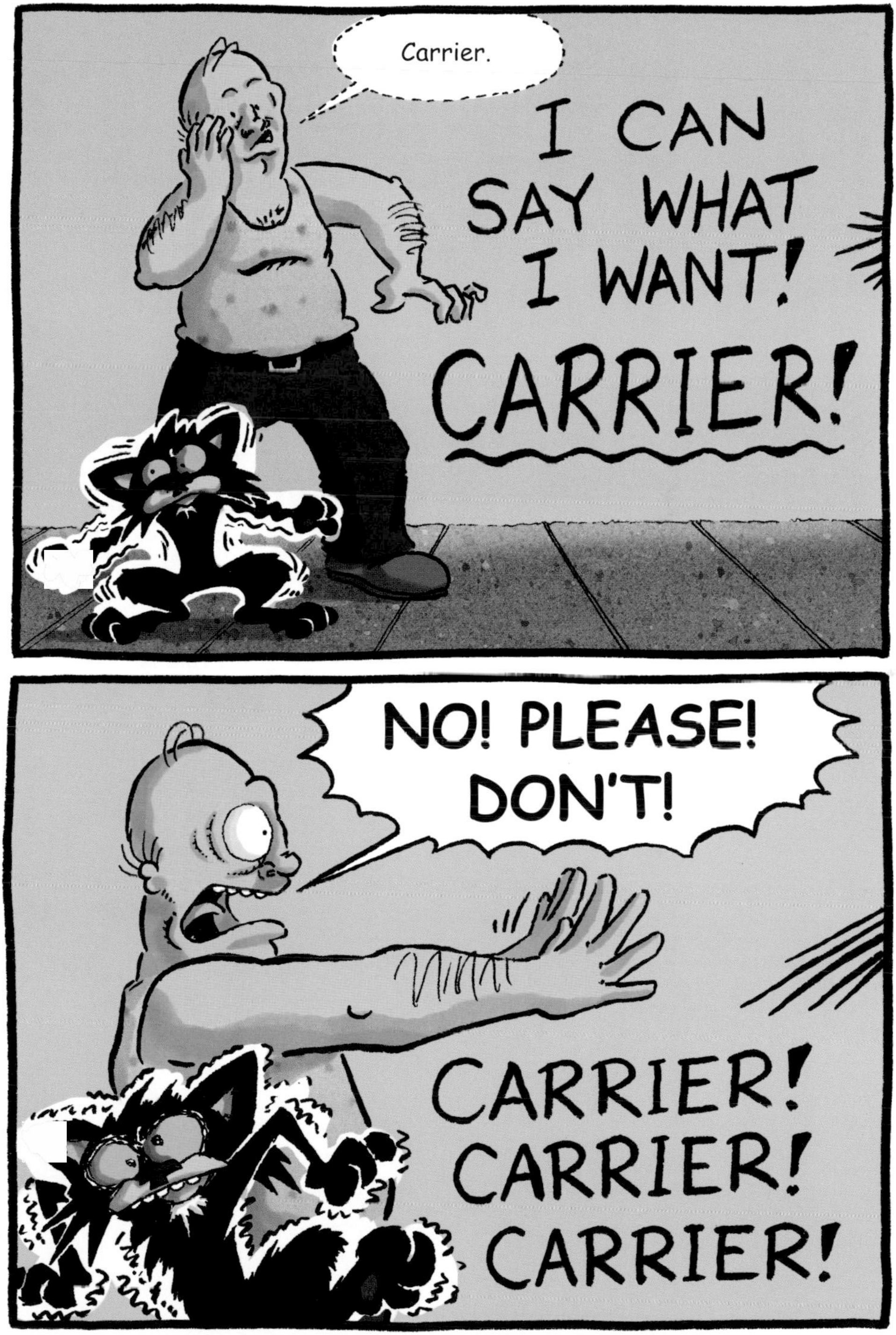
Carrier.
I CAN SAY WHAT I WANT! CARRIER!
NO! PLEASE! DON'T!
CARRIER! CARRIER! CARRIER!

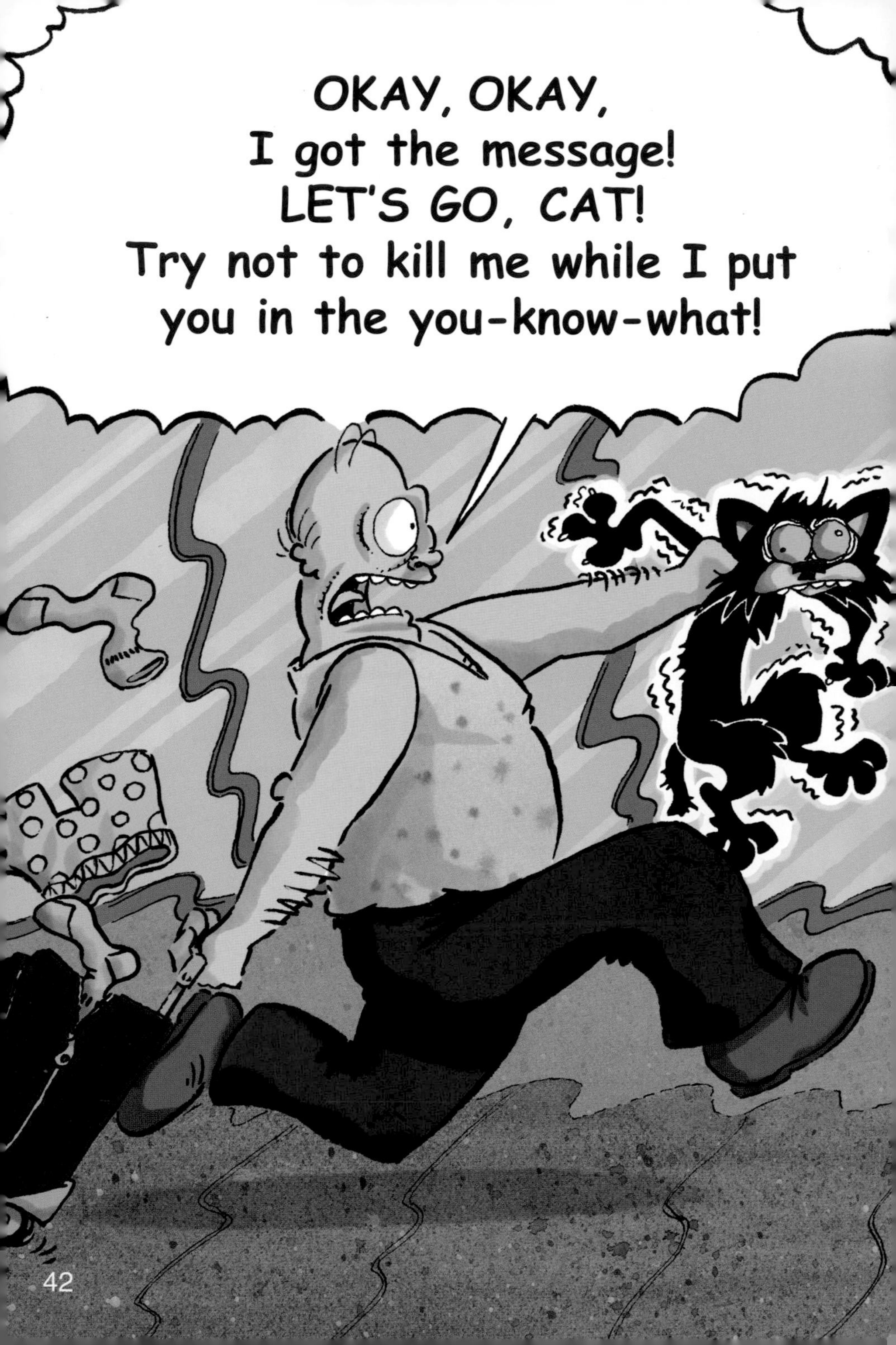
OKAY, OKAY, I got the message! LET'S GO, CAT! Try not to kill me while I put you in the you-know-what!

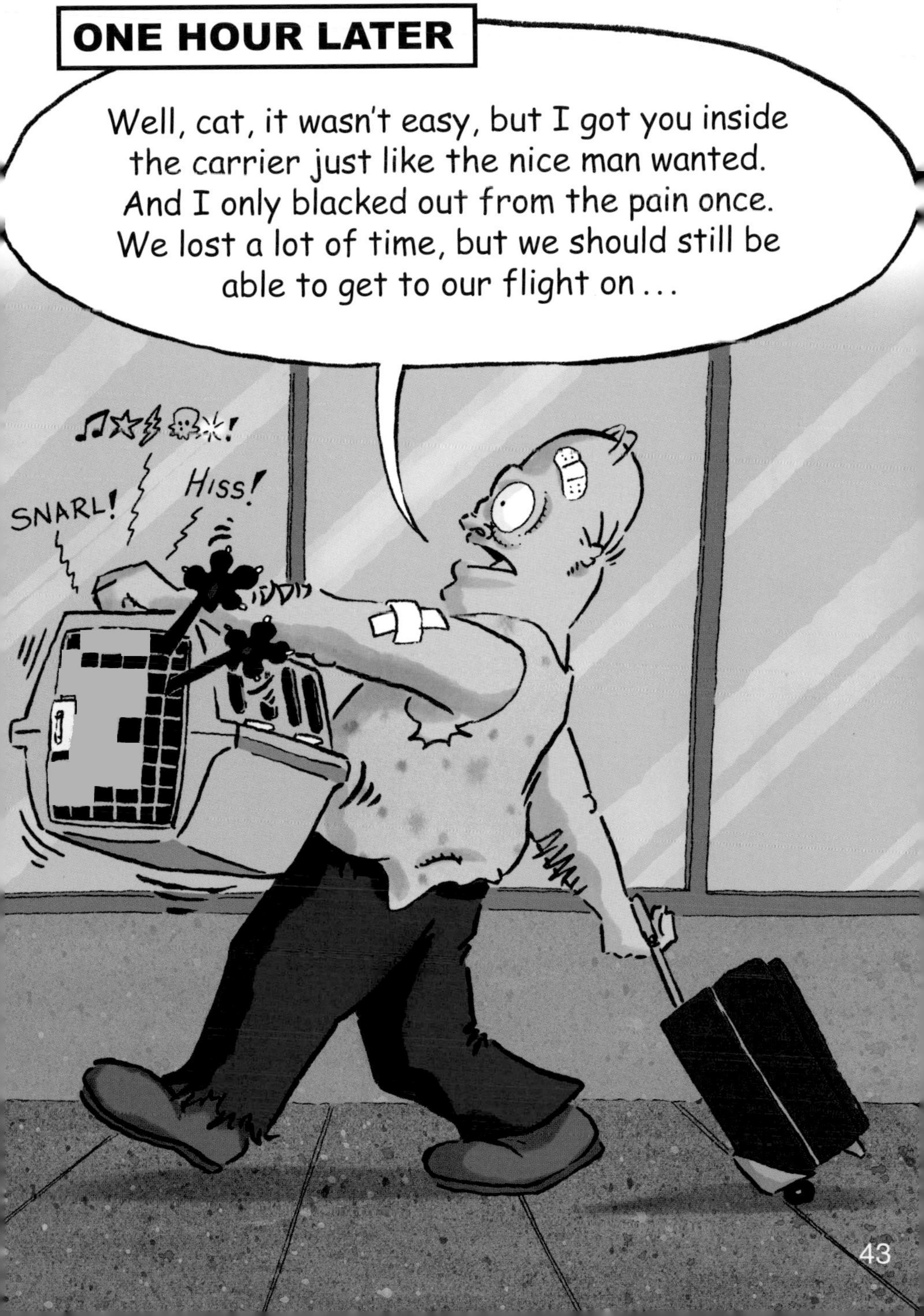
ONE HOUR LATER
Well, cat, it wasn't easy, but I got you inside the carrier just like the nice man wanted. And I only blacked out from the pain once. We lost a lot of time, but we should still be able to get to our flight on . . .
SNARL!
HISS!

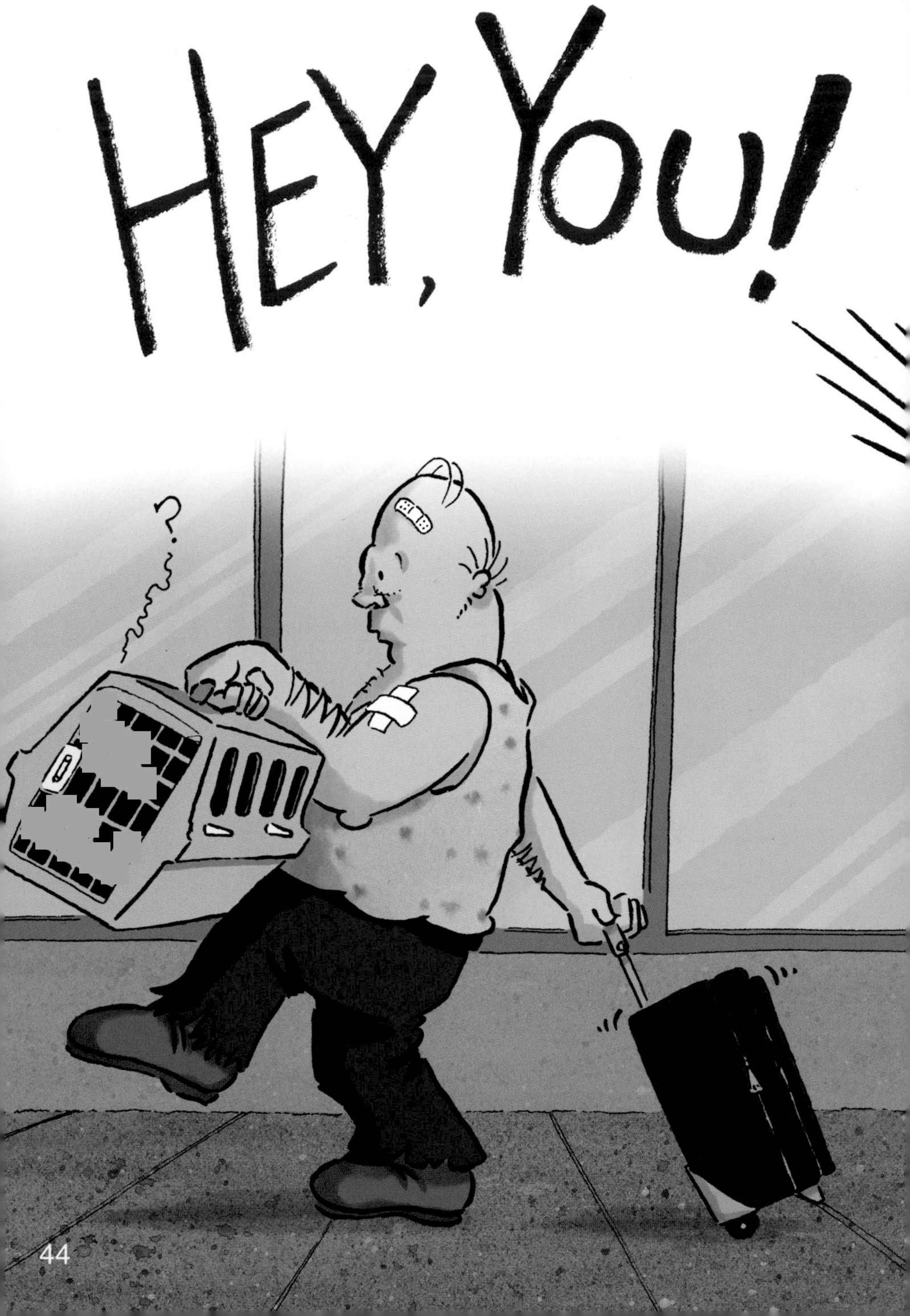
HEY, YOU!
?

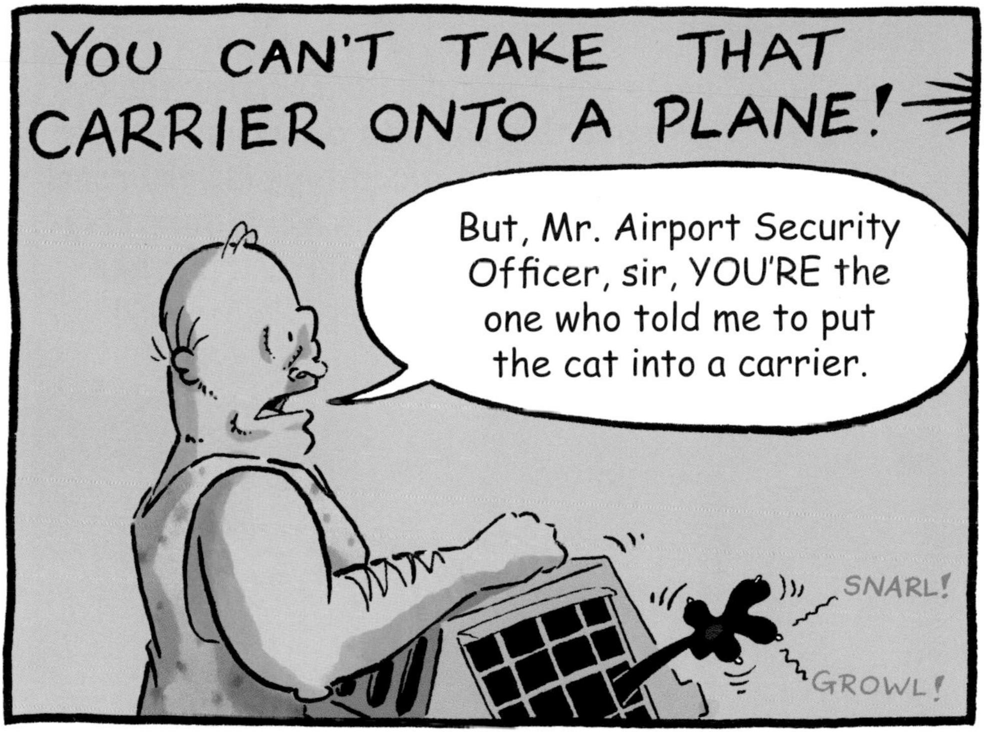
YOU CAN'T TAKE THAT CARRIER ONTO A PLANE!
But, Mr. Airport Security Officer, sir, YOU'RE the one who told me to put the cat into a carrier.
SNARL!
GROWL!

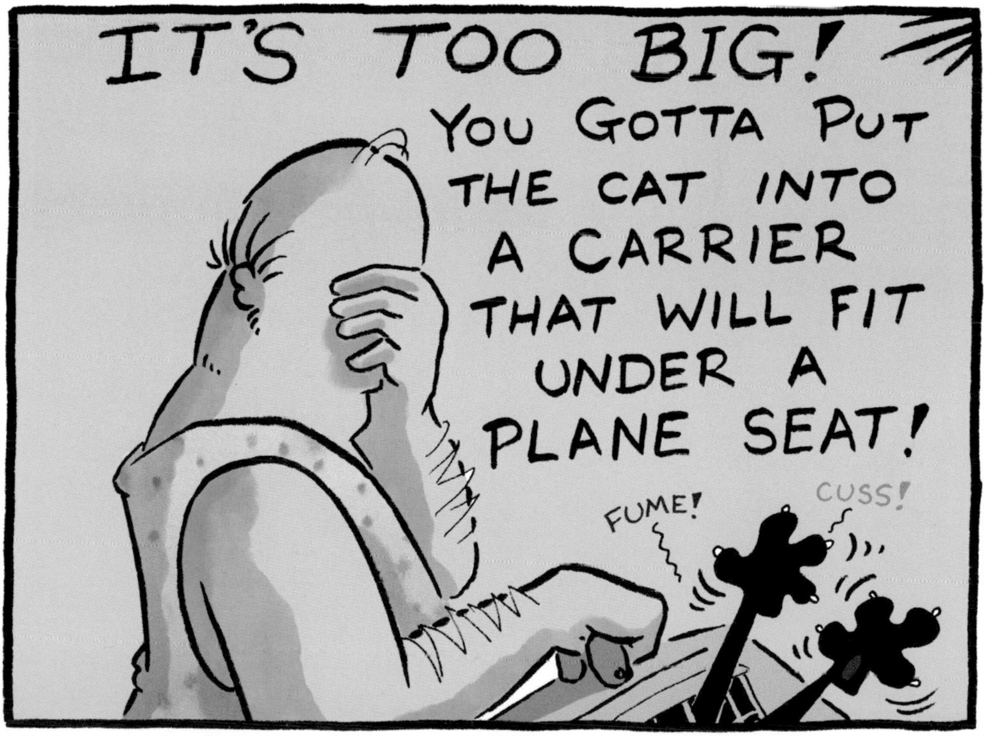
IT'S TOO BIG!
YOU GOTTA PUT THE CAT INTO A CARRIER THAT WILL FIT UNDER A PLANE SEAT!
FUME!
CUSS!

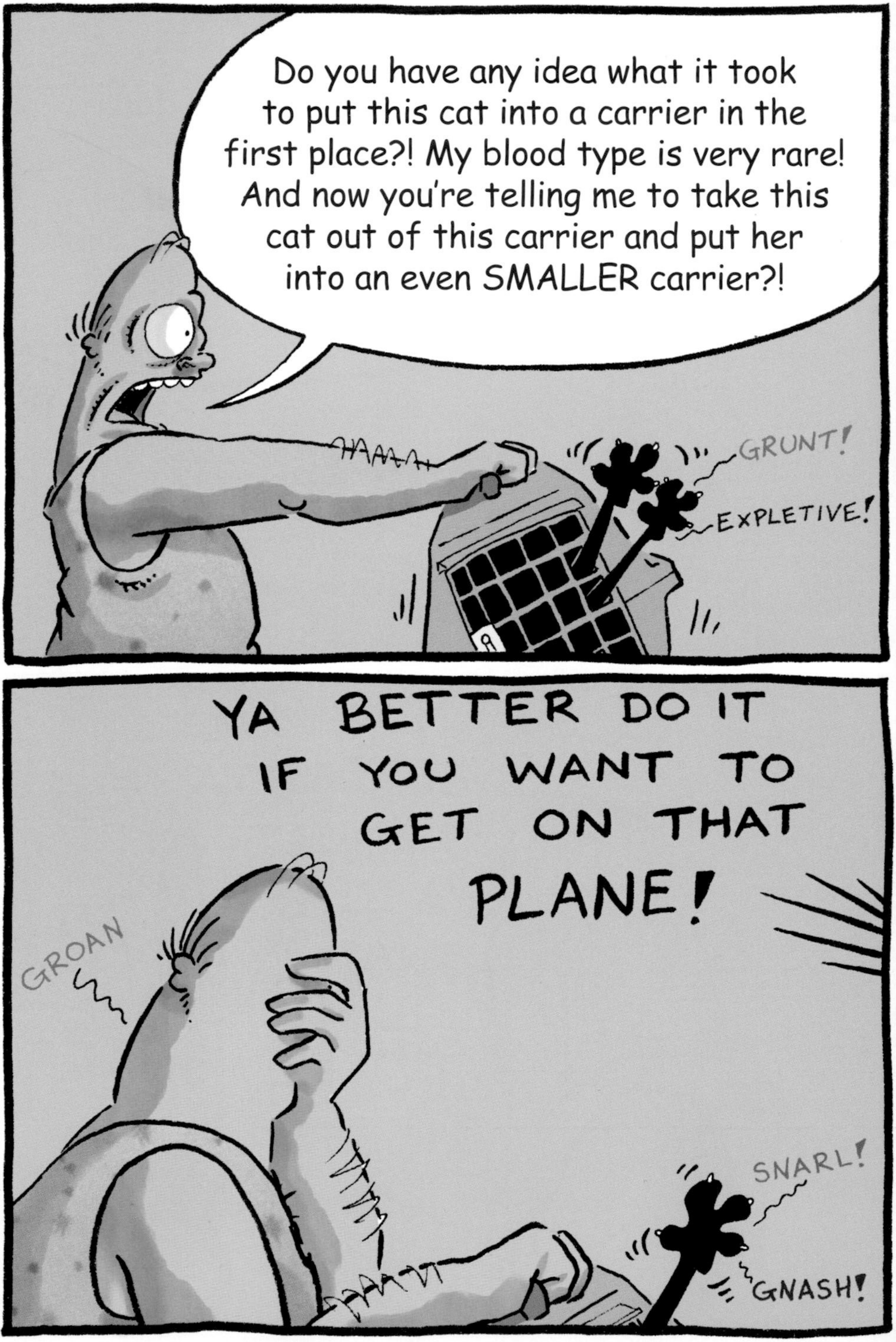

Do you have any idea what it took to put this cat into a carrier in the first place?! My blood type is very rare! And now you're telling me to take this cat out of this carrier and put her into an even SMALLER carrier?!
GRUNT!
EXPLETIVE!
YA BETTER DO IT IF YOU WANT TO GET ON THAT PLANE!
GROAN
SNARL!
GNASH!

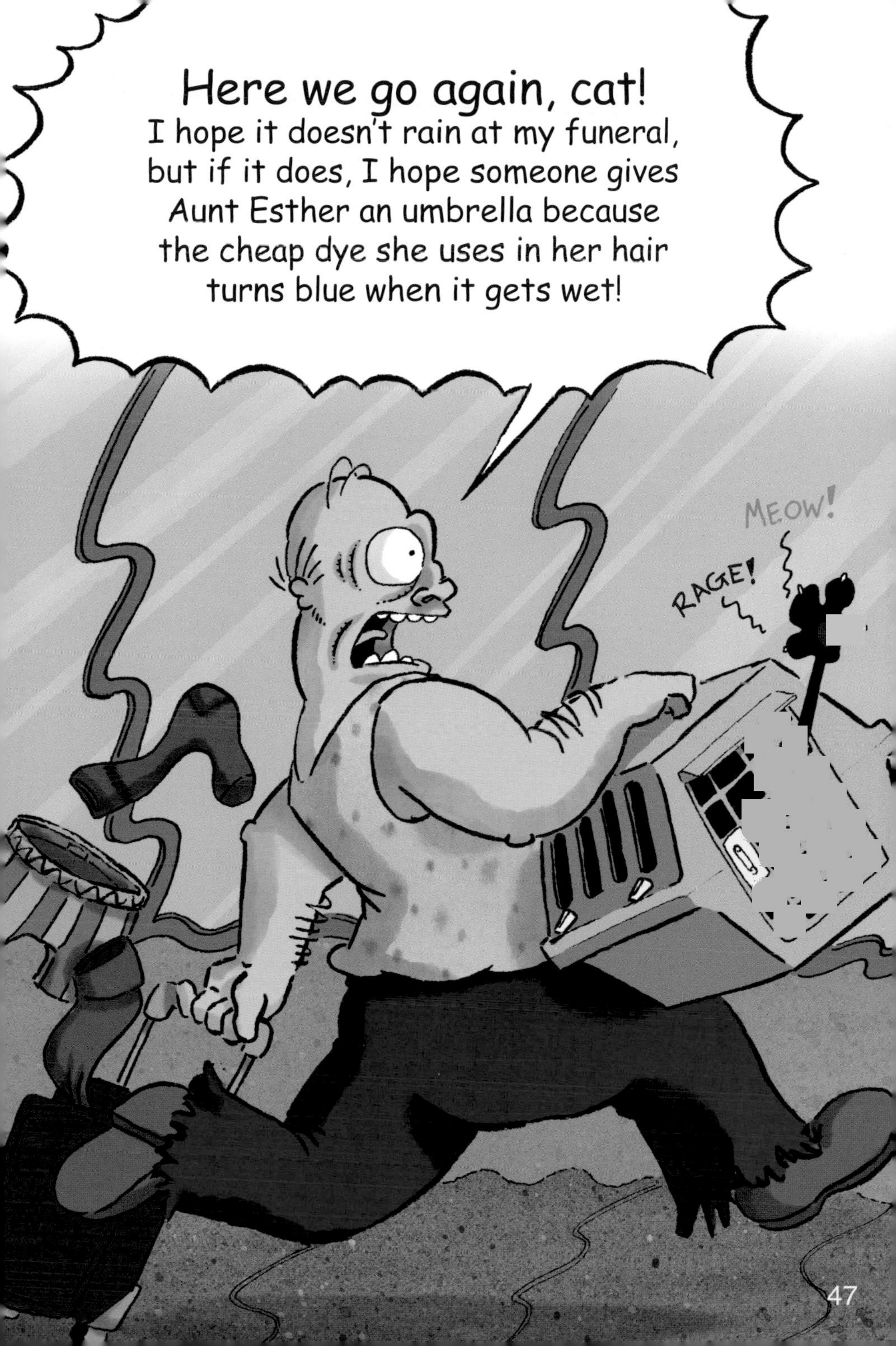
Here we go again, cat!
I hope it doesn't rain at my funeral, but if it does, I hope someone gives Aunt Esther an umbrella because the cheap dye she uses in her hair turns blue when it gets wet!
MEOW!
RAGE!

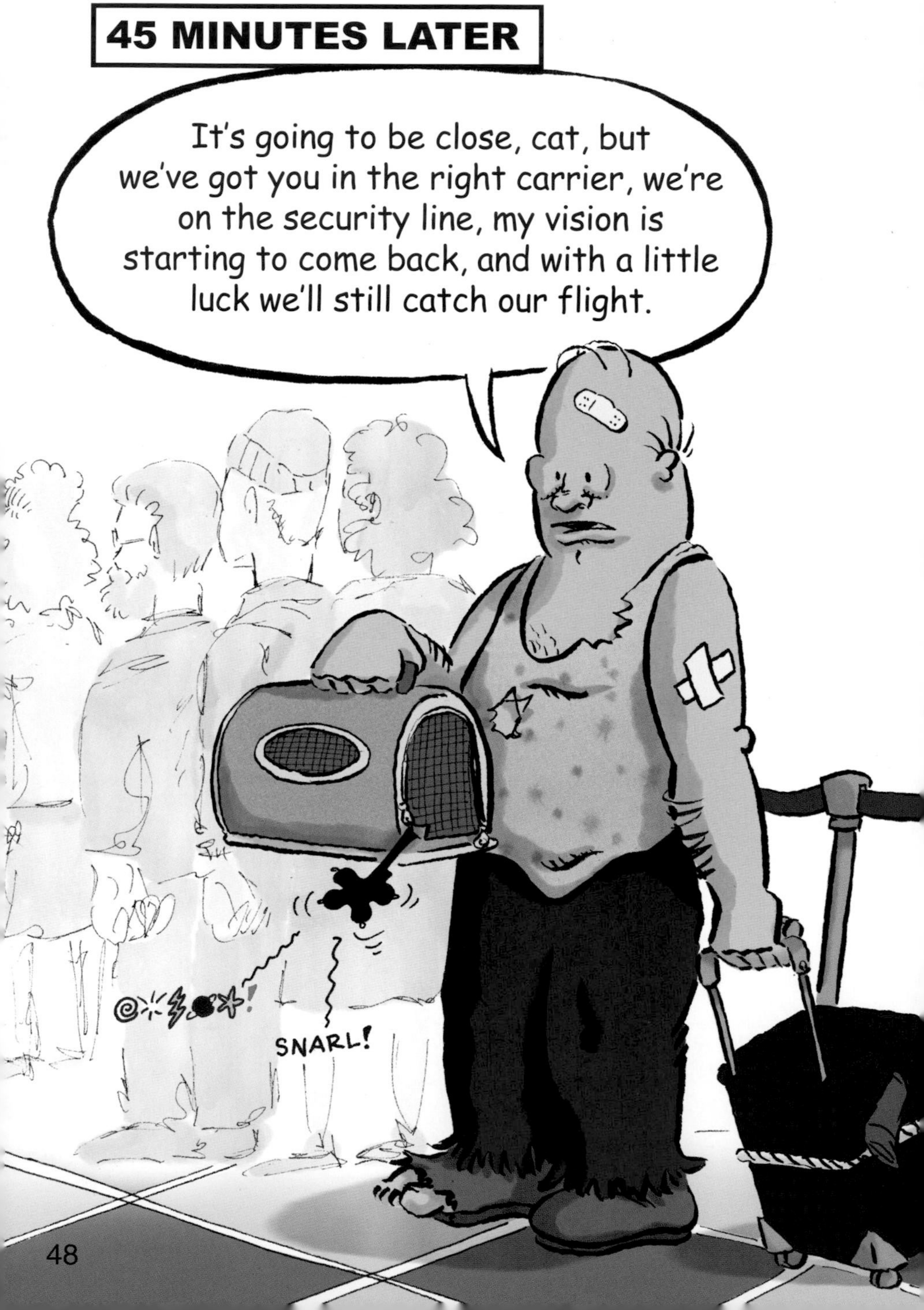
45 MINUTES LATER
It's going to be close, cat, but we've got you in the right carrier, we're on the security line, my vision is starting to come back, and with a little luck we'll still catch our flight.
SNARL!

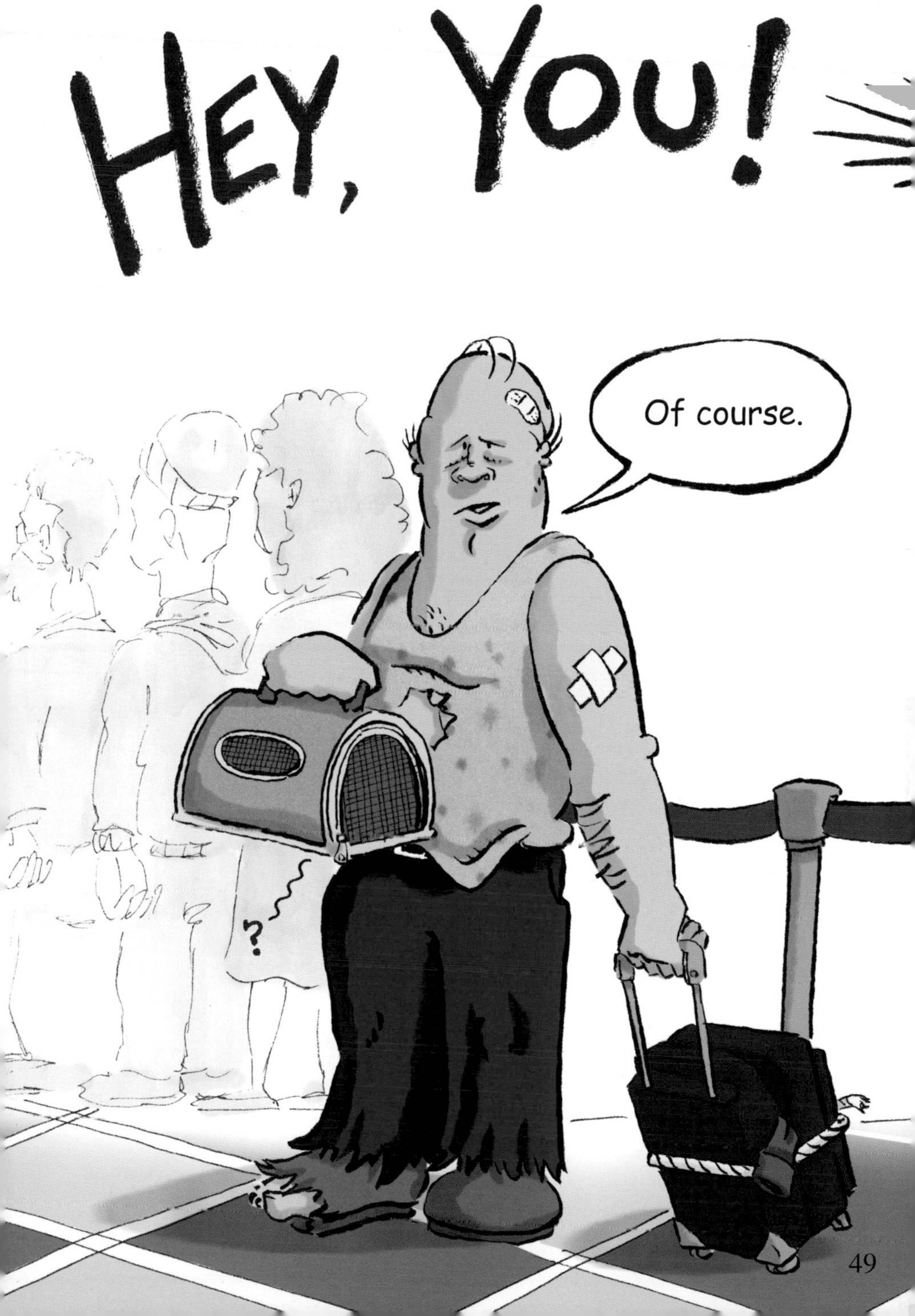
HEY, YOU!
Of course.
?

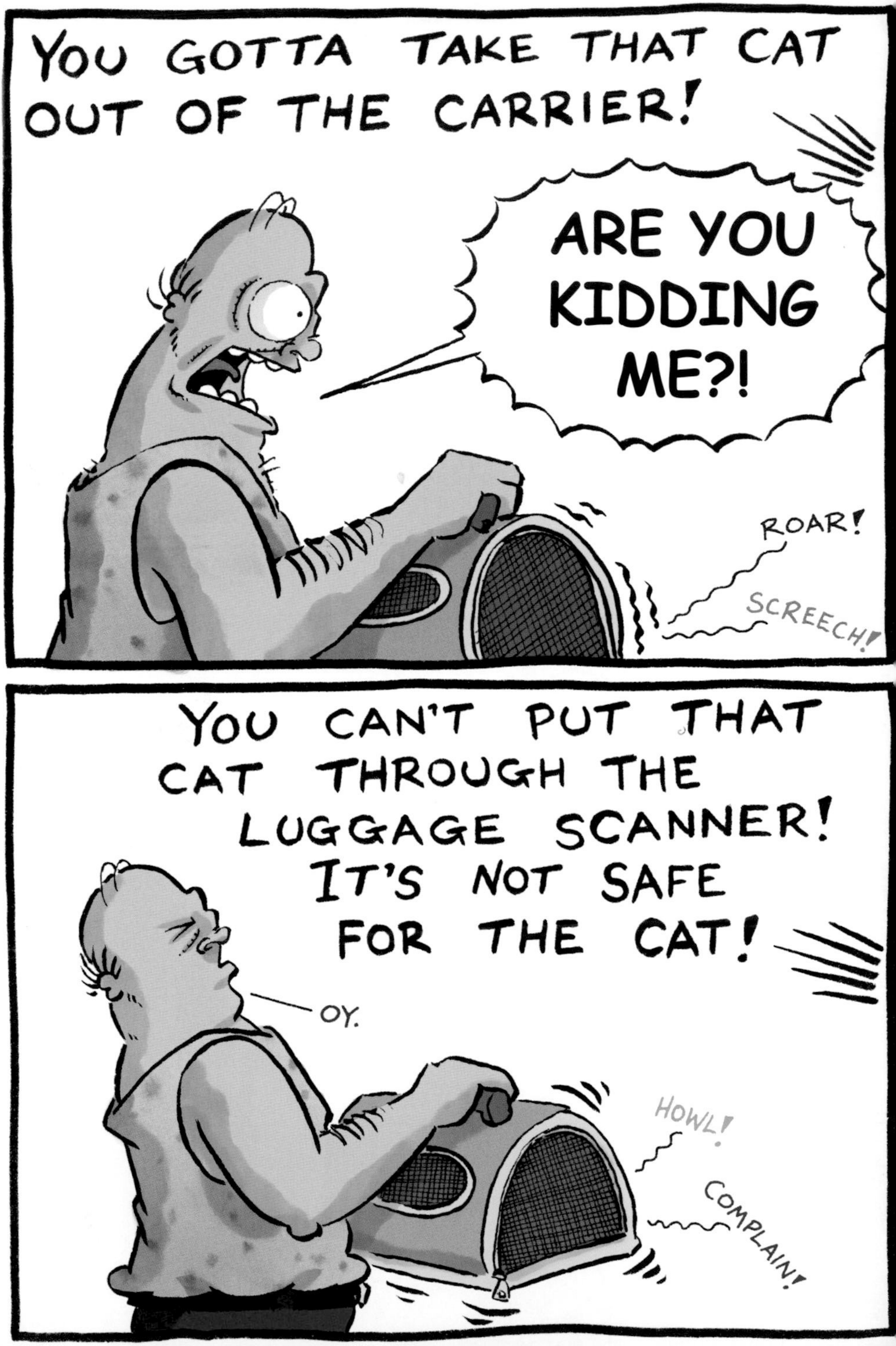
YOU GOTTA TAKE THAT CAT OUT OF THE CARRIER!
ARE YOU KIDDING ME?!
ROAR!
SCREECH!
YOU CAN'T PUT THAT CAT THROUGH THE LUGGAGE SCANNER! IT'S NOT SAFE FOR THE CAT!
OY.
HOWL!
COMPLAIN!

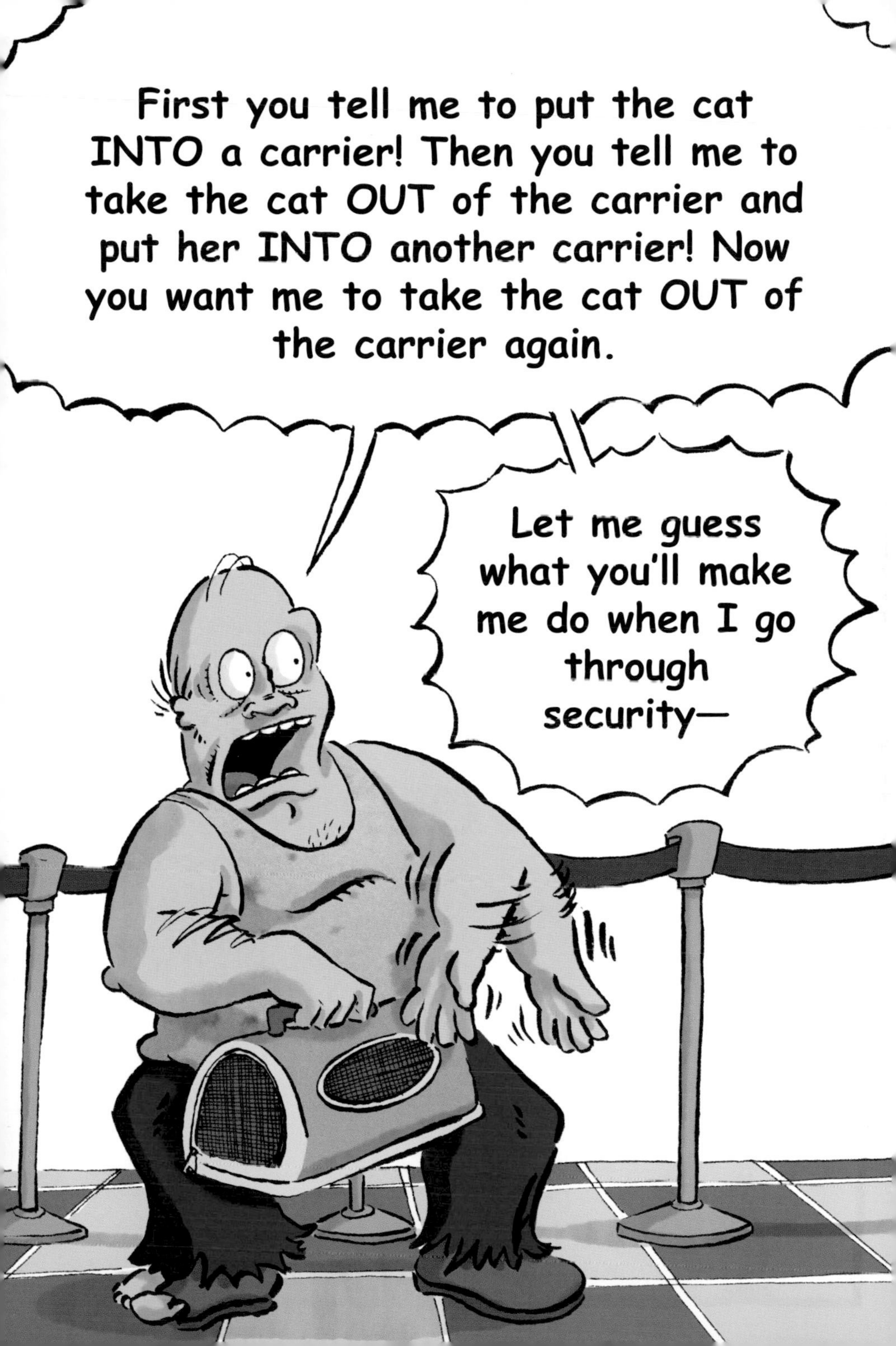
First you tell me to put the cat INTO a carrier! Then you tell me to take the cat OUT of the carrier and put her INTO another carrier! Now you want me to take the cat OUT of the carrier again.
Let me guess what you'll make me do when I go through security—

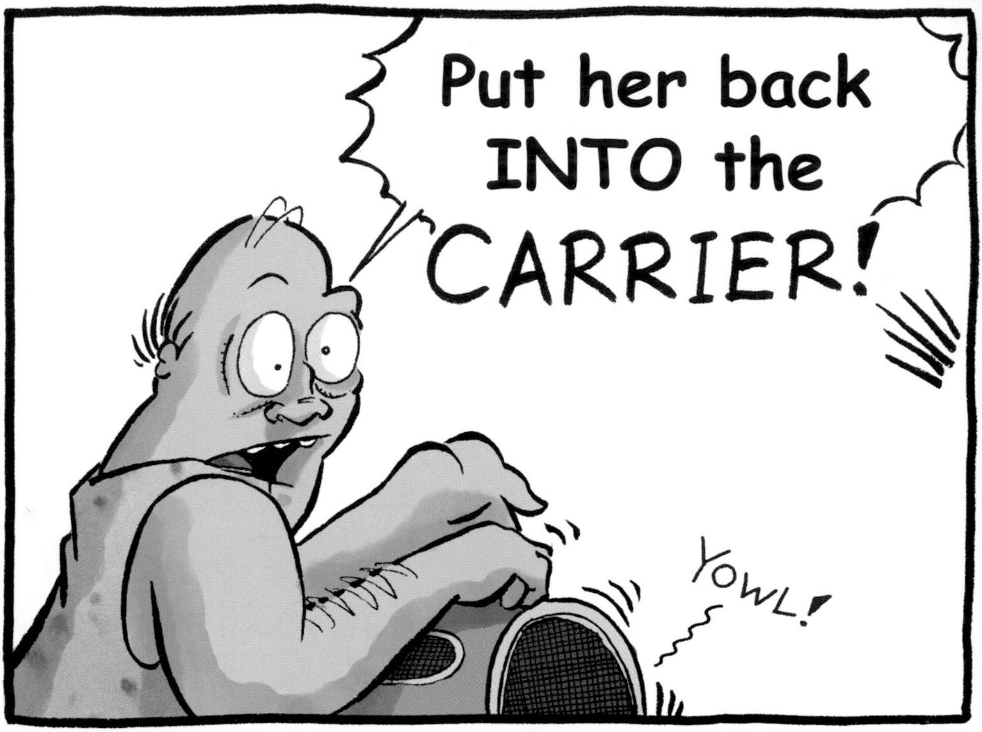
Put her back INTO the CARRIER!
YOWL!

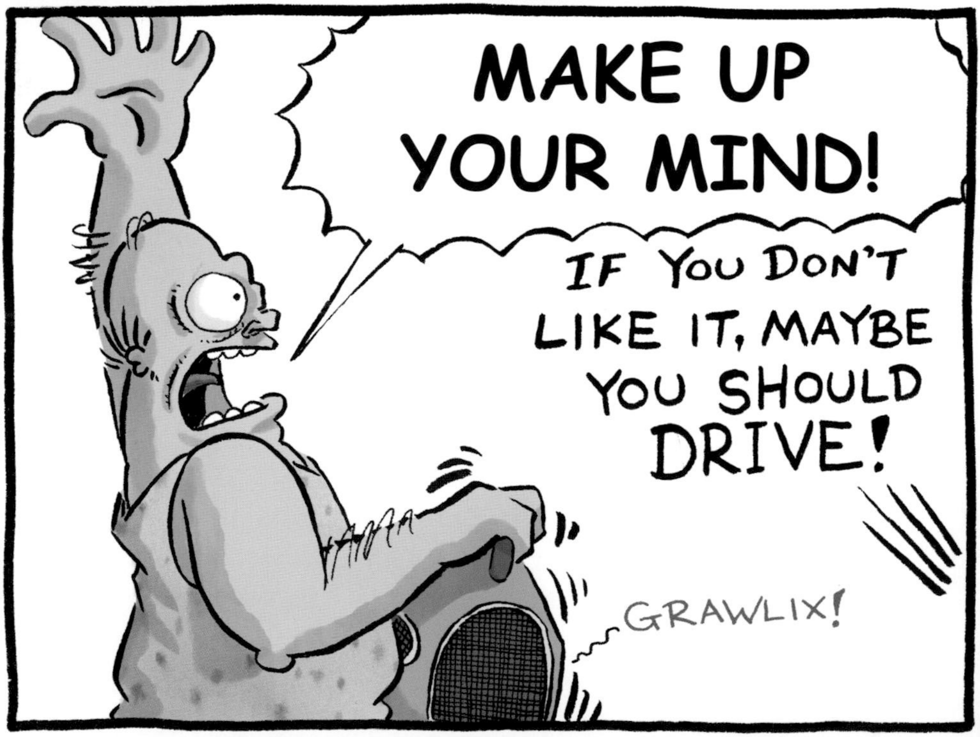
MAKE UP YOUR MIND!
IF YOU DON'T LIKE IT, MAYBE YOU SHOULD DRIVE!
GRAWLIX!

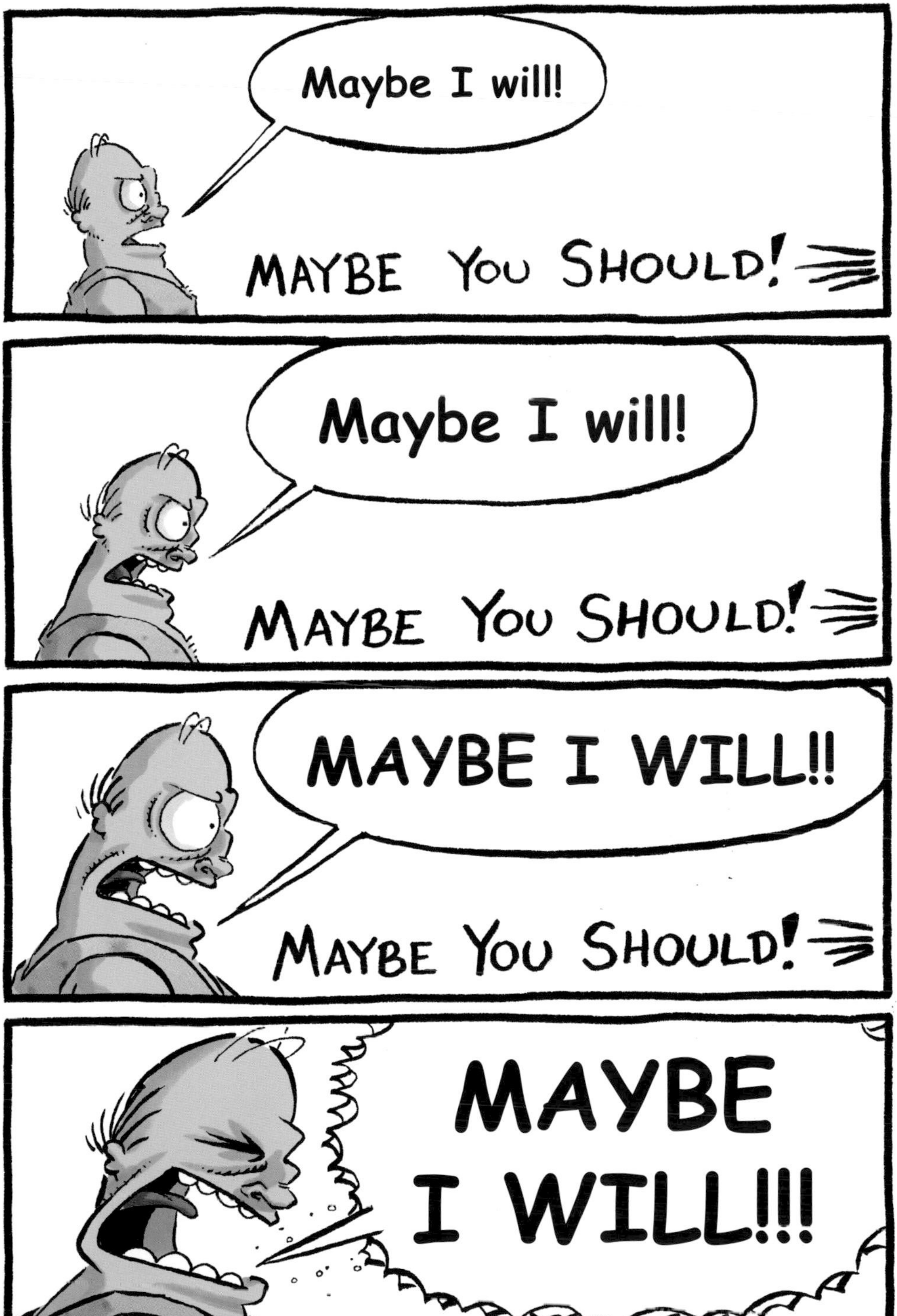
Maybe I will!
MAYBE YOU SHOULD!
Maybe I will!
MAYBE YOU SHOULD!
MAYBE I WILL!!
MAYBE YOU SHOULD!
MAYBE I WILL!!!

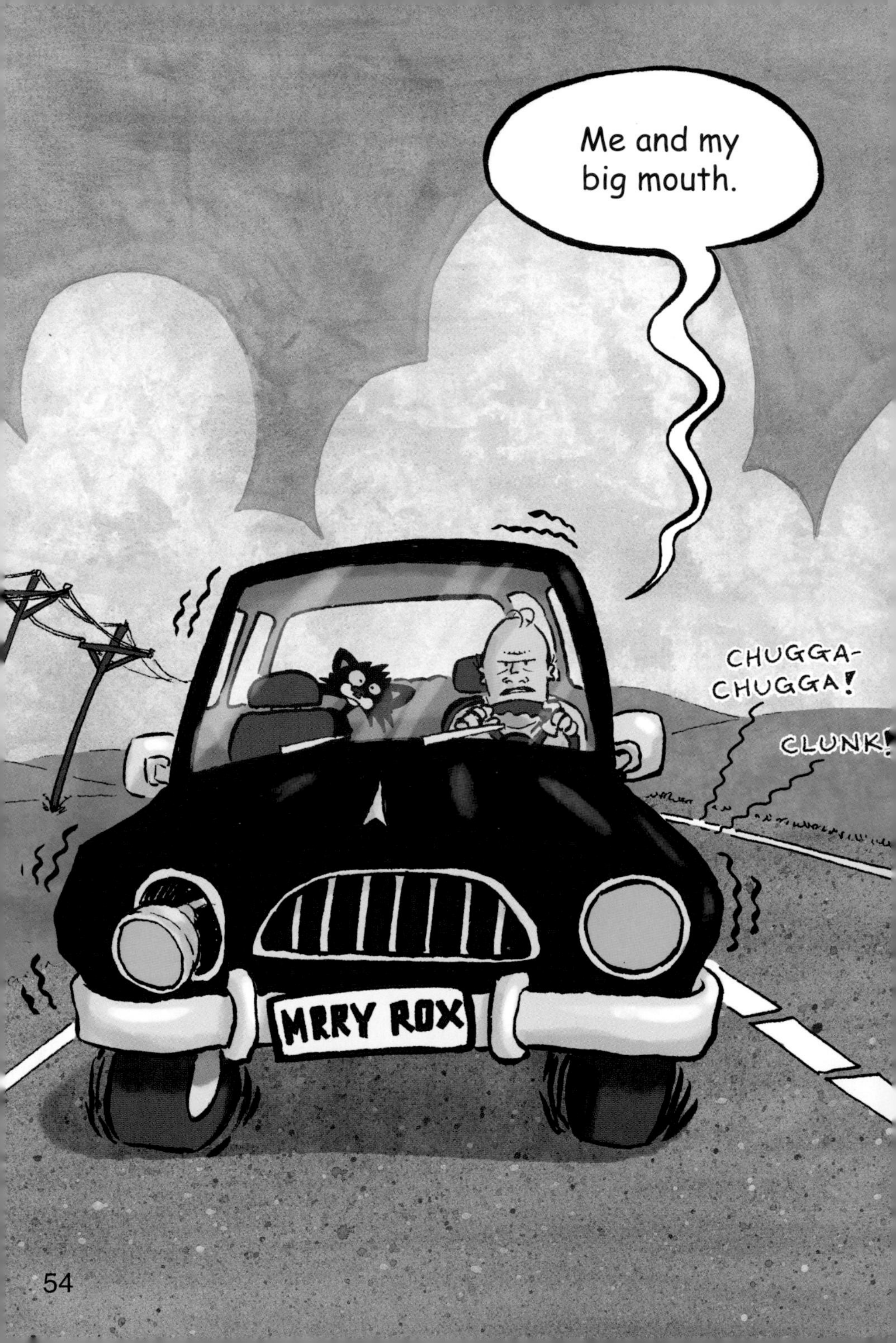
Me and my big mouth.
CHUGGA-CHUGGA!
CLUNK!
MRRY ROX

• CHAPTER FOUR •

AT THE HOTEL

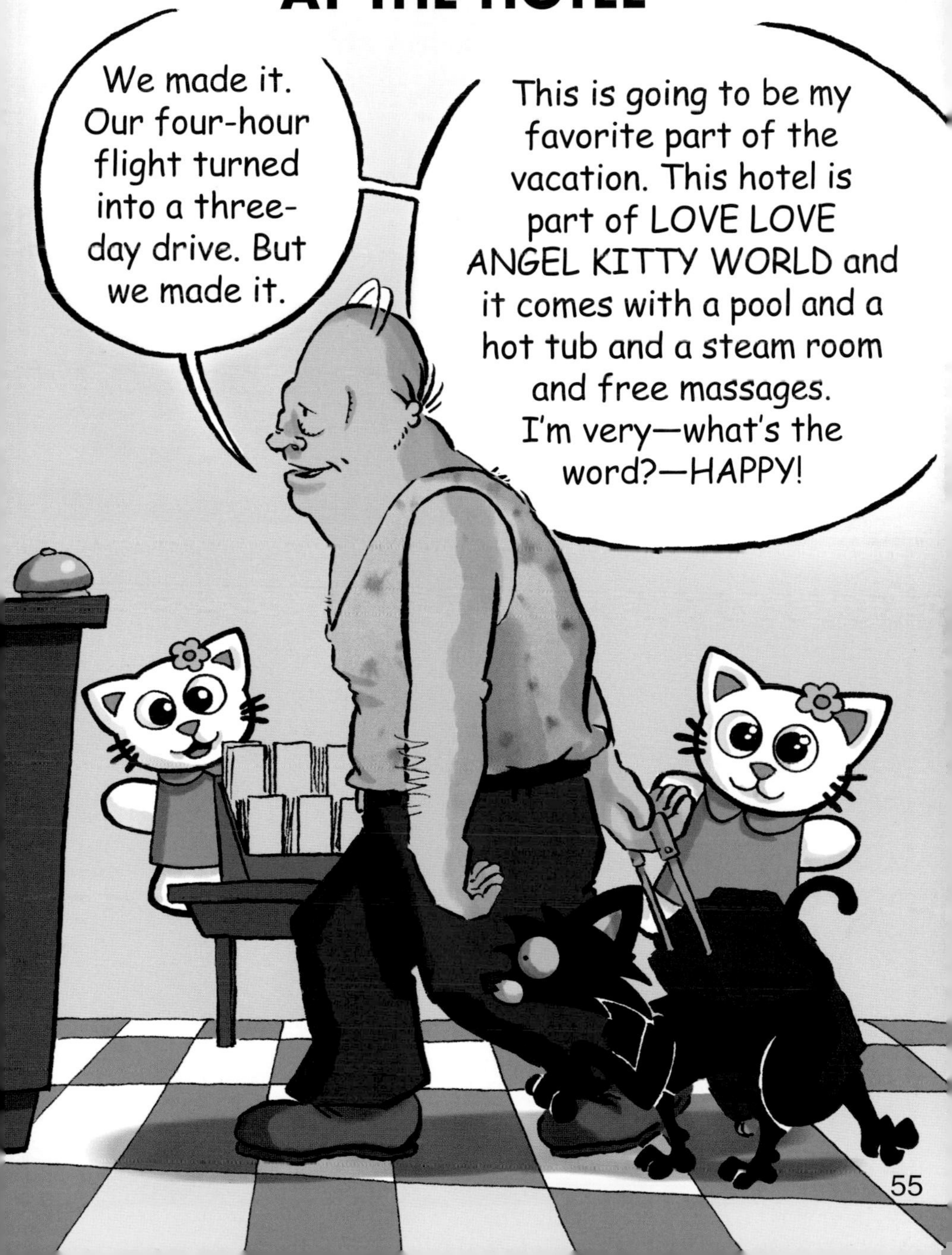

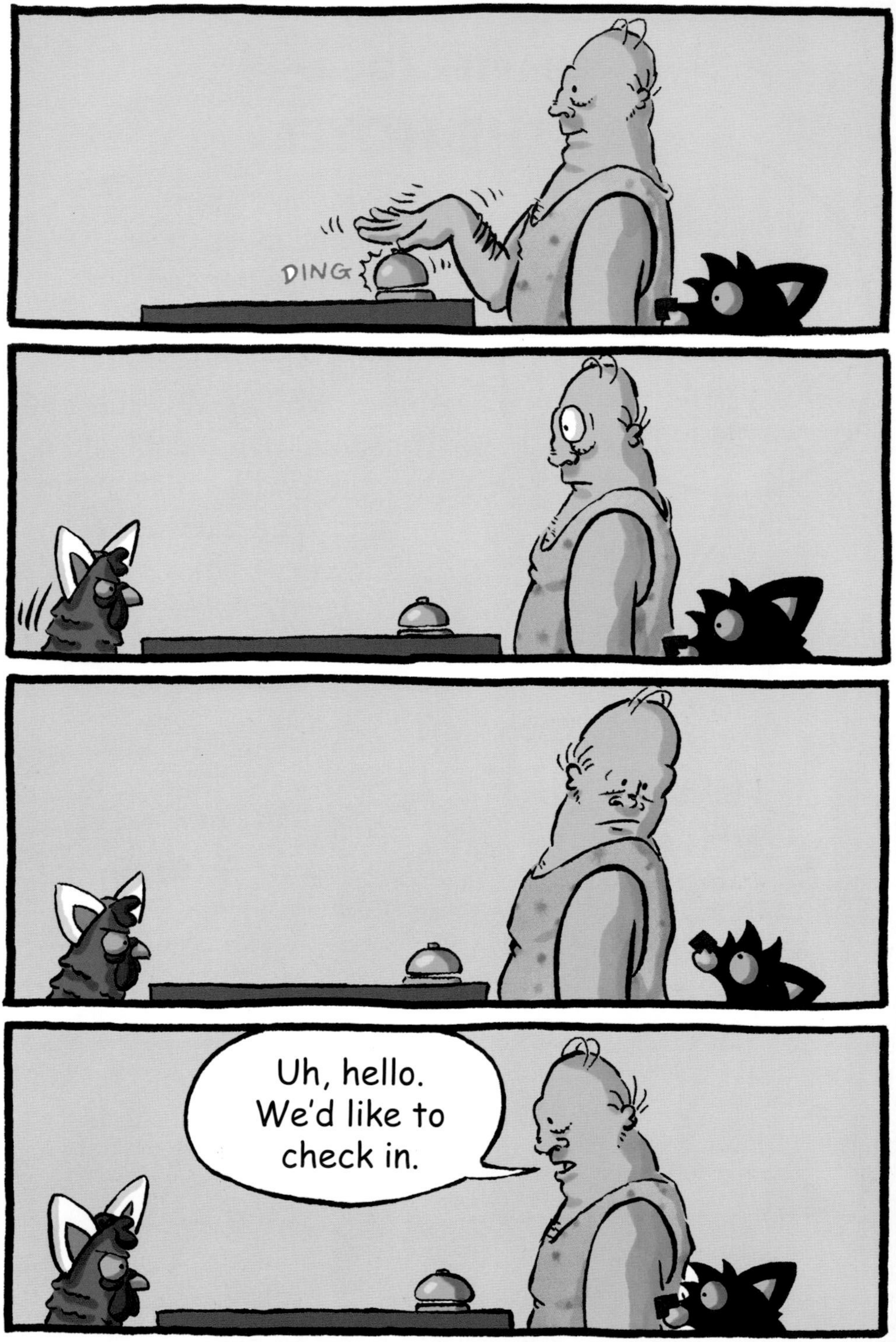
DING
Uh, hello. We'd like to check in.

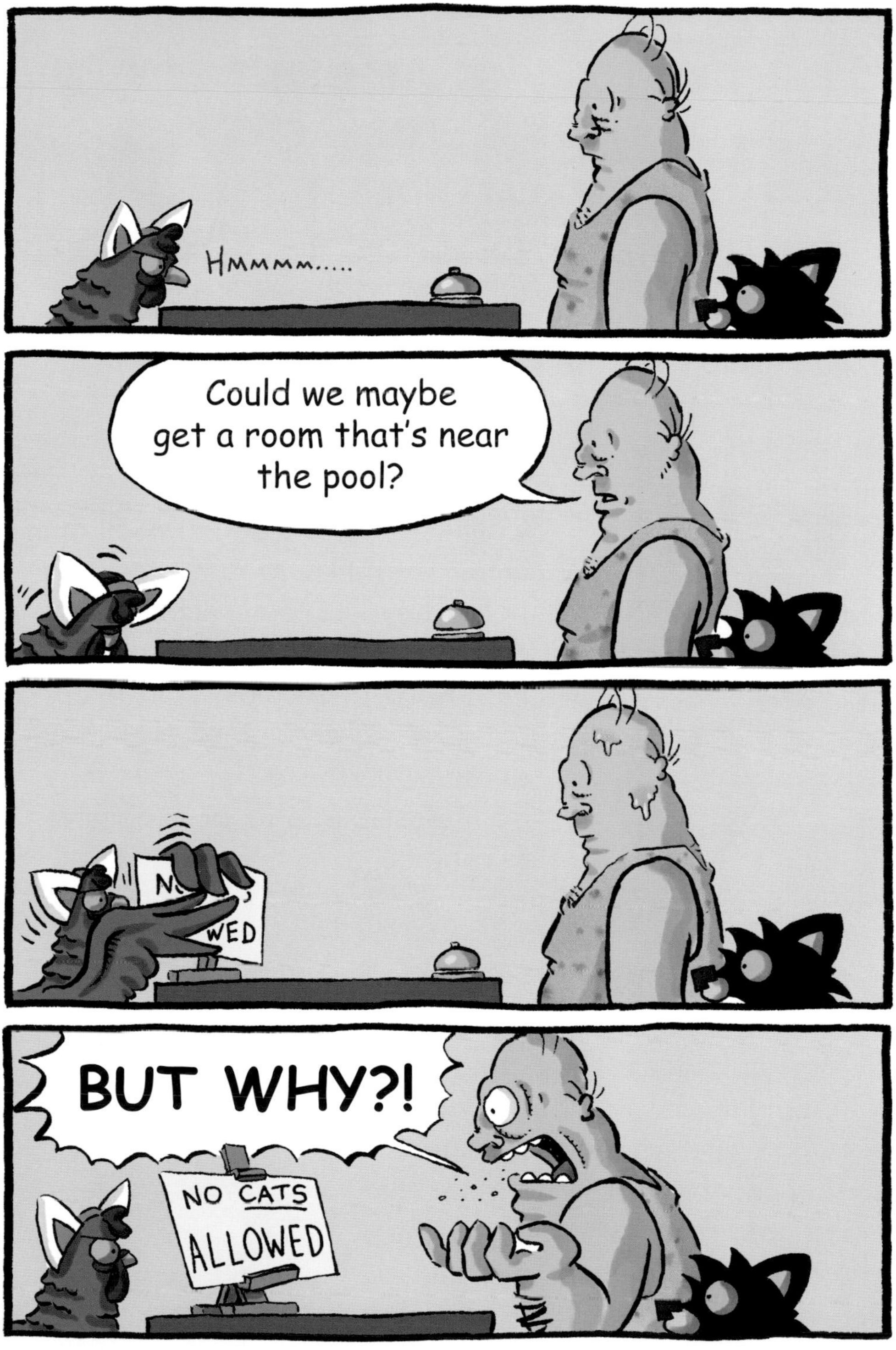
HMMMM.....
Could we maybe get a room that's near the pool?
NO CATS ALLOWED
BUT WHY?!

THE LOVE LOVE ANGEL KITTY CORPORATION'S FUN FACTS

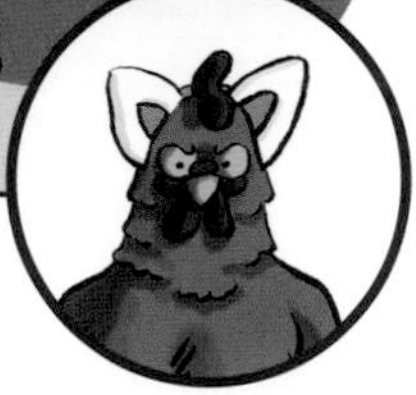

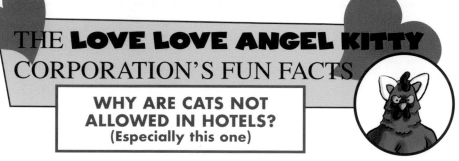

WHY ARE CATS NOT ALLOWED IN HOTELS?
(Especially this one)

Even some hotels that allow dogs to stay won't allow cats. Here's why…

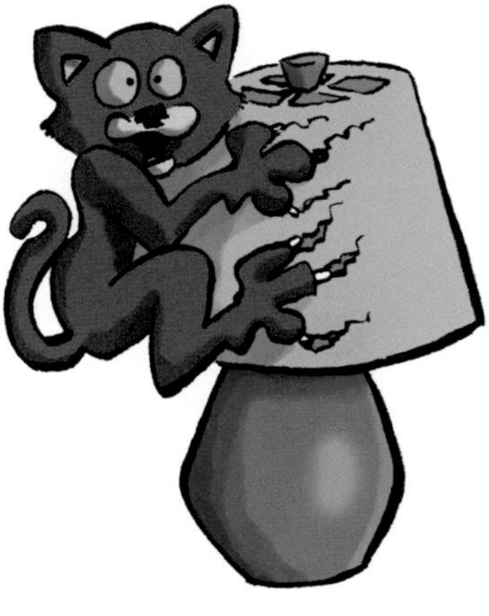

Cats Cause Damage

Cats like to claw at things all the time. They like to claw the carpets. They like to claw the sheets and blankets. They like to claw the chairs and sofas. And every time they claw something, they damage it. These damages may be impossible to fix or expensive to replace.

Cats Have Fur

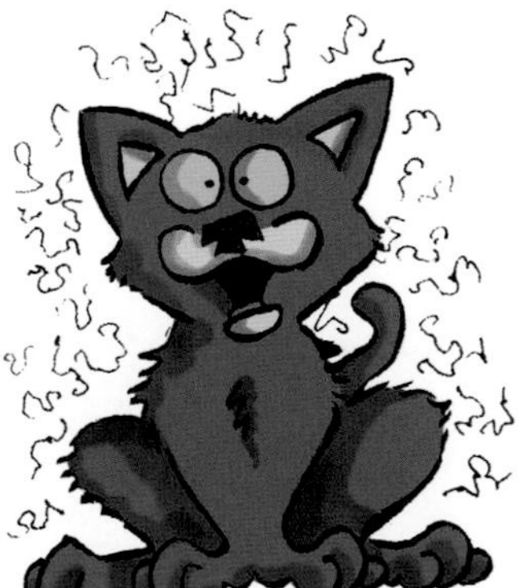

Most cats shed. They can't help it. But their fur can be very hard to pick up, even with a vacuum. This can be a real problem for the *next* guest who stays in that room and might be allergic to cats. An allergic reaction can mean coughing, sneezing, itchy eyes, and maybe even an asthma attack.

Cats Are Noisy

Hotels are quiet places. Guests like to sleep soundly in them. But some cats who don't like being in an unfamiliar place may meow loudly or howl or even screech. This can be a real problem for the people in nearby rooms.

Cats Are Messy

Cat pee smells bad. Really bad. Much, much worse than dog pee. So if a cat has an accident in the room, not only is it very difficult to clean the stain, but it's nearly impossible to get rid of the odor completely. This is why hotels will often charge a cat's owner a LOT of money, maybe even hundreds of dollars, if they have to clean up after a cat.

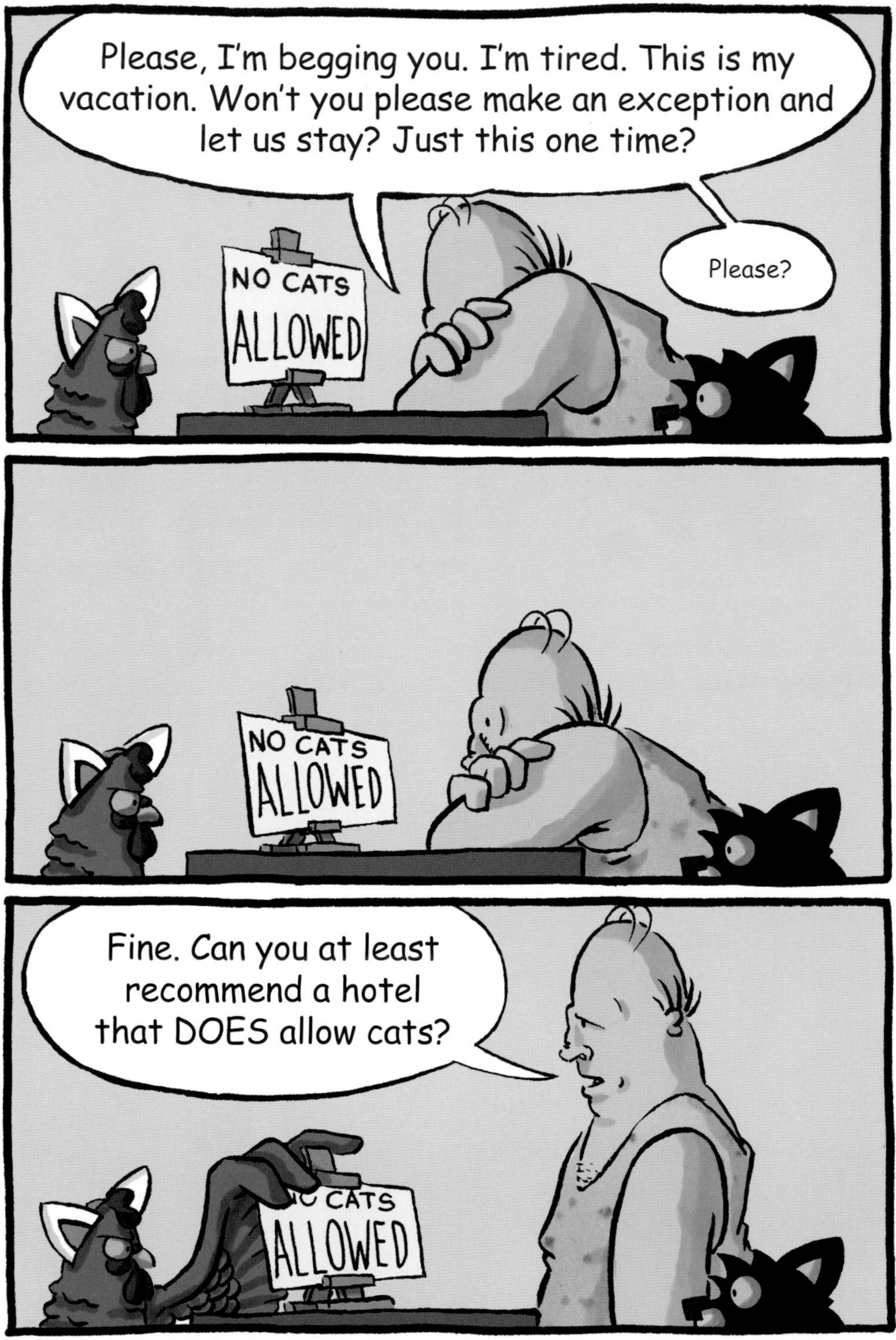
Please, I'm begging you. I'm tired. This is my vacation. Won't you please make an exception and let us stay? Just this one time?
Please?
NO CATS ALLOWED
NO CATS ALLOWED
Fine. Can you at least recommend a hotel that DOES allow cats?
CATS ALLOWED

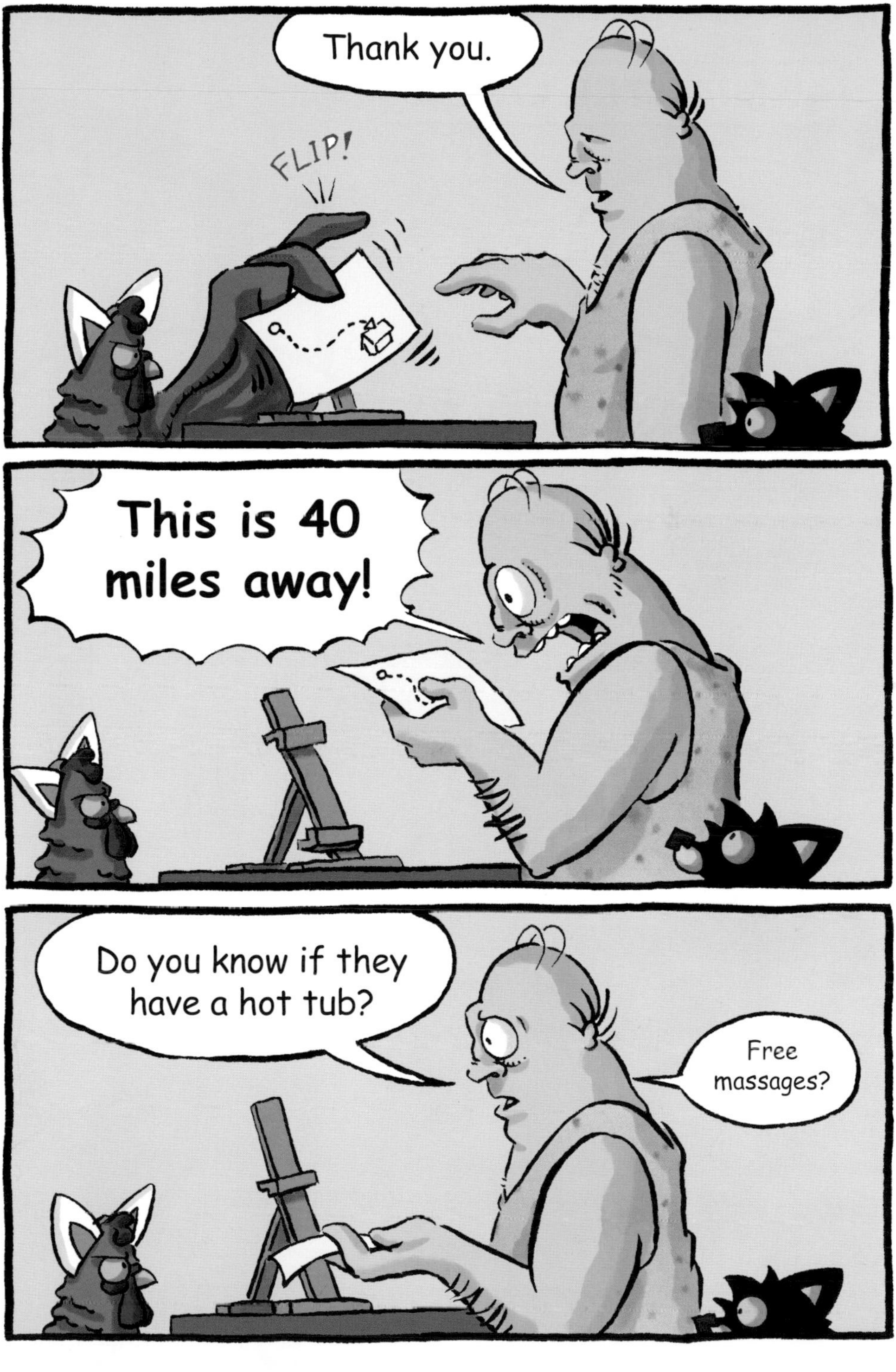
Thank you.
FLIP!
This is 40 miles away!
Do you know if they have a hot tub?
Free massages?

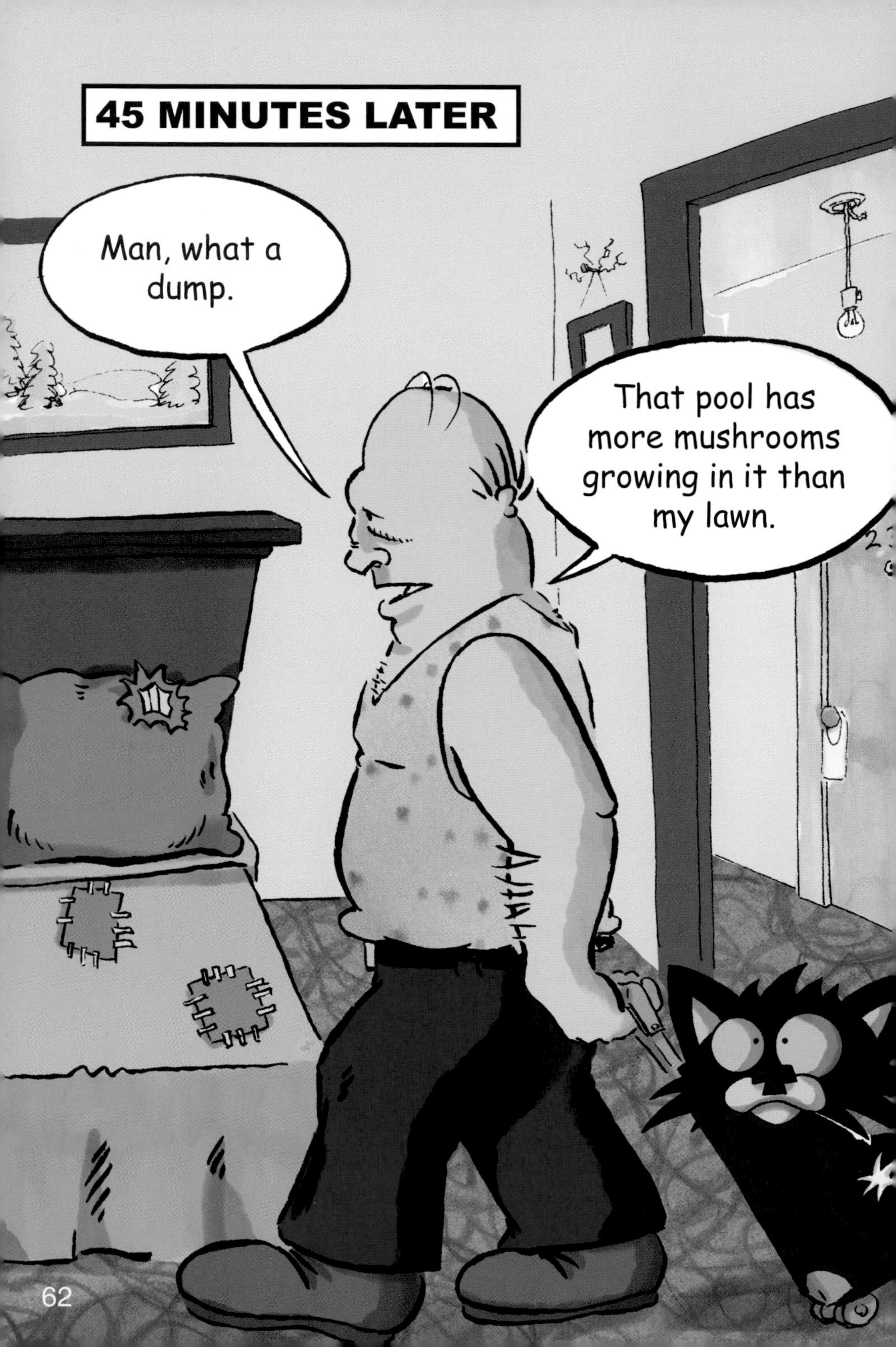
45 MINUTES LATER
Man, what a dump.
That pool has more mushrooms growing in it than my lawn.

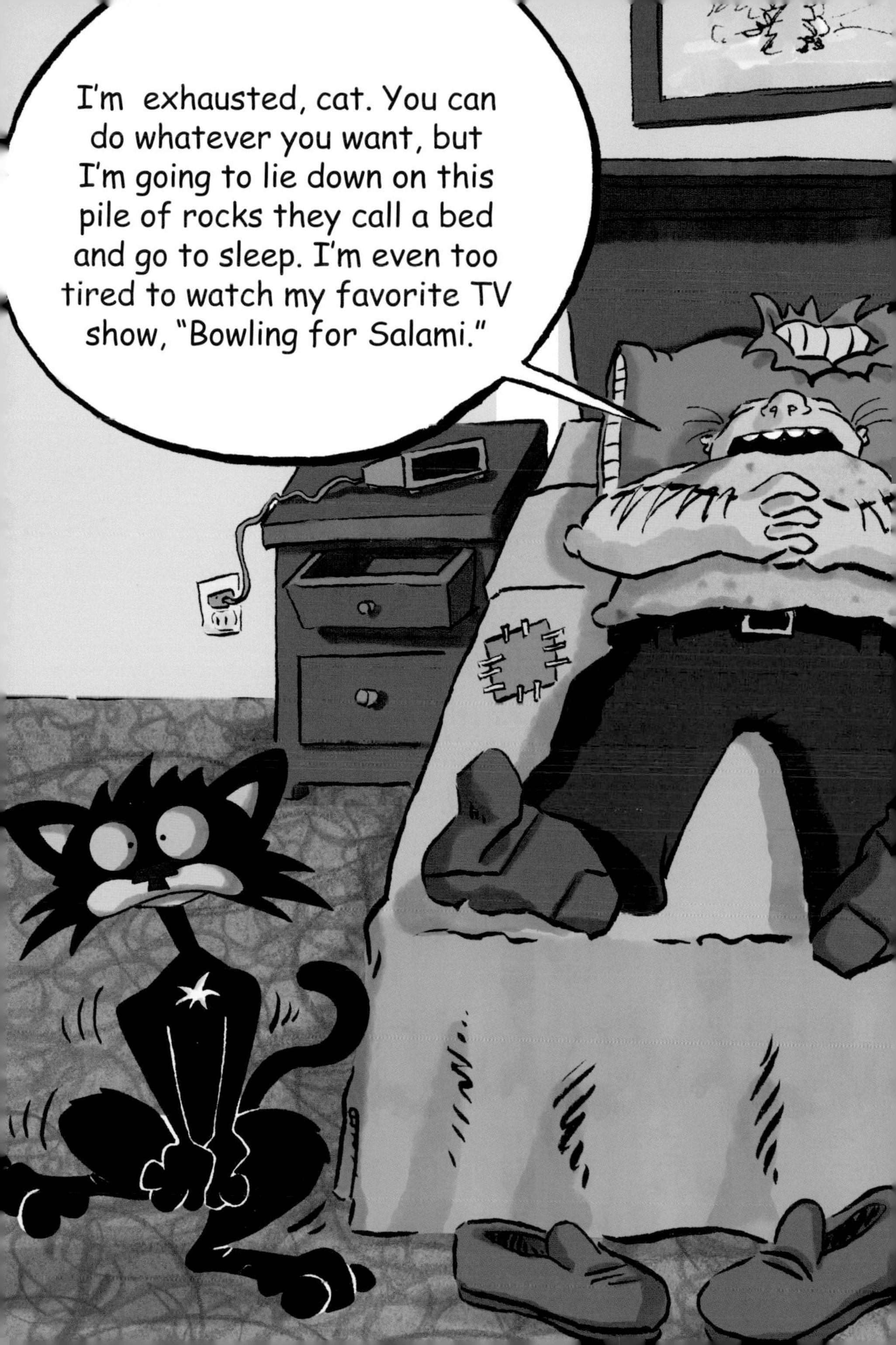
I'm exhausted, cat. You can do whatever you want, but I'm going to lie down on this pile of rocks they call a bed and go to sleep. I'm even too tired to watch my favorite TV show, "Bowling for Salami."

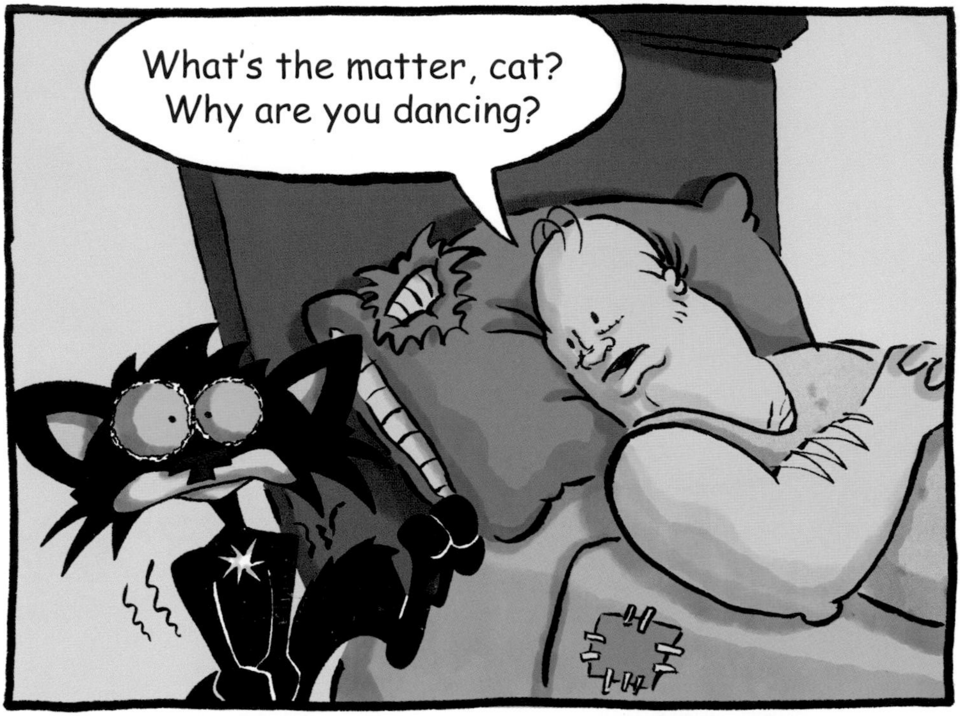
What's the matter, cat? Why are you dancing?

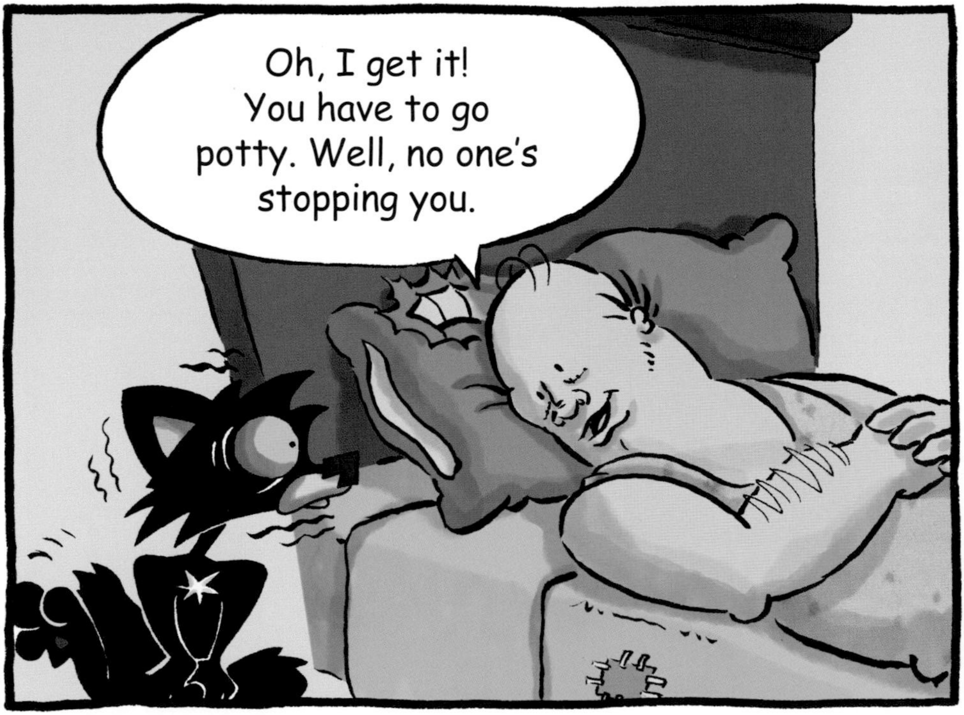
Oh, I get it! You have to go potty. Well, no one's stopping you.

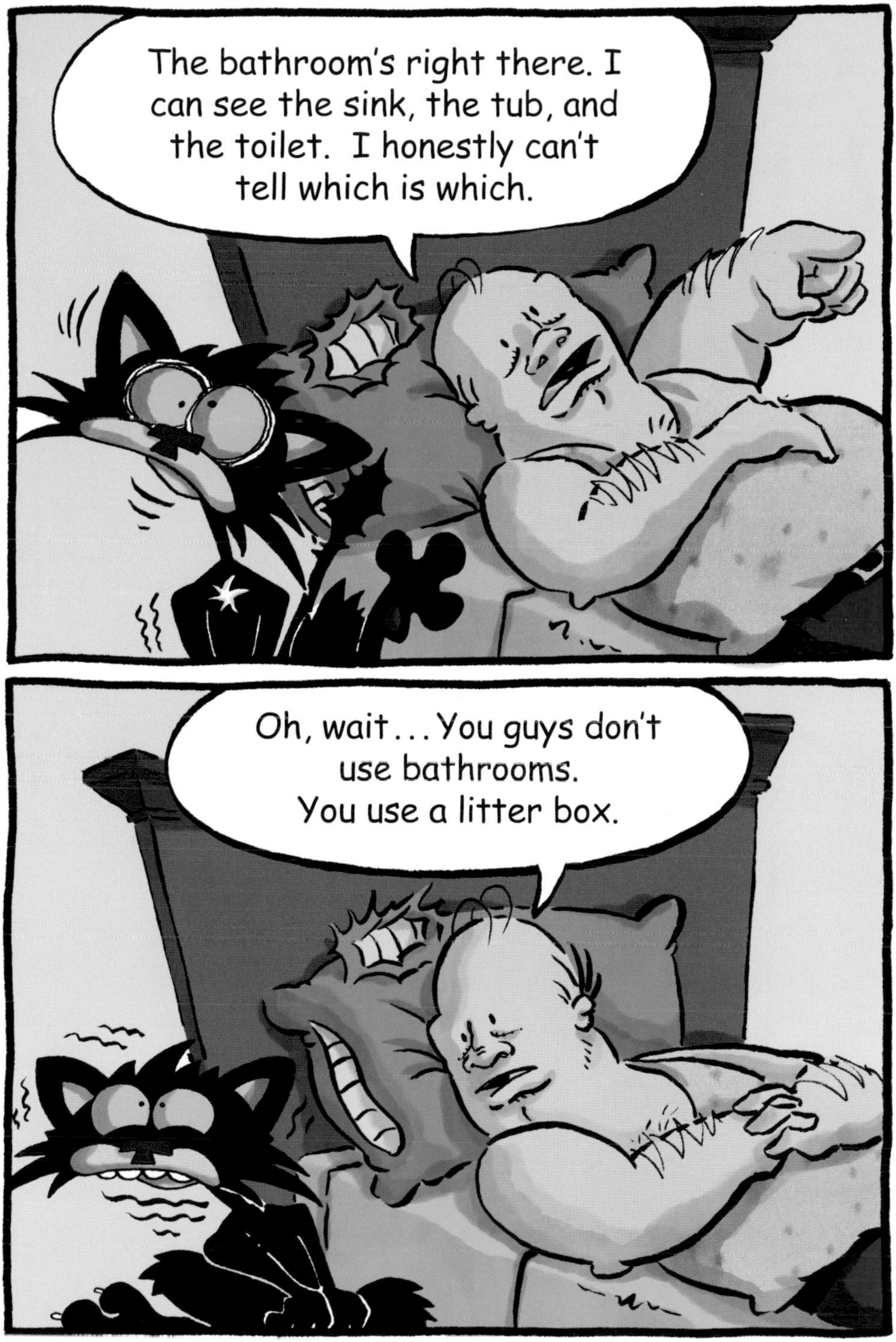
The bathroom's right there. I can see the sink, the tub, and the toilet. I honestly can't tell which is which.
Oh, wait... You guys don't use bathrooms. You use a litter box.

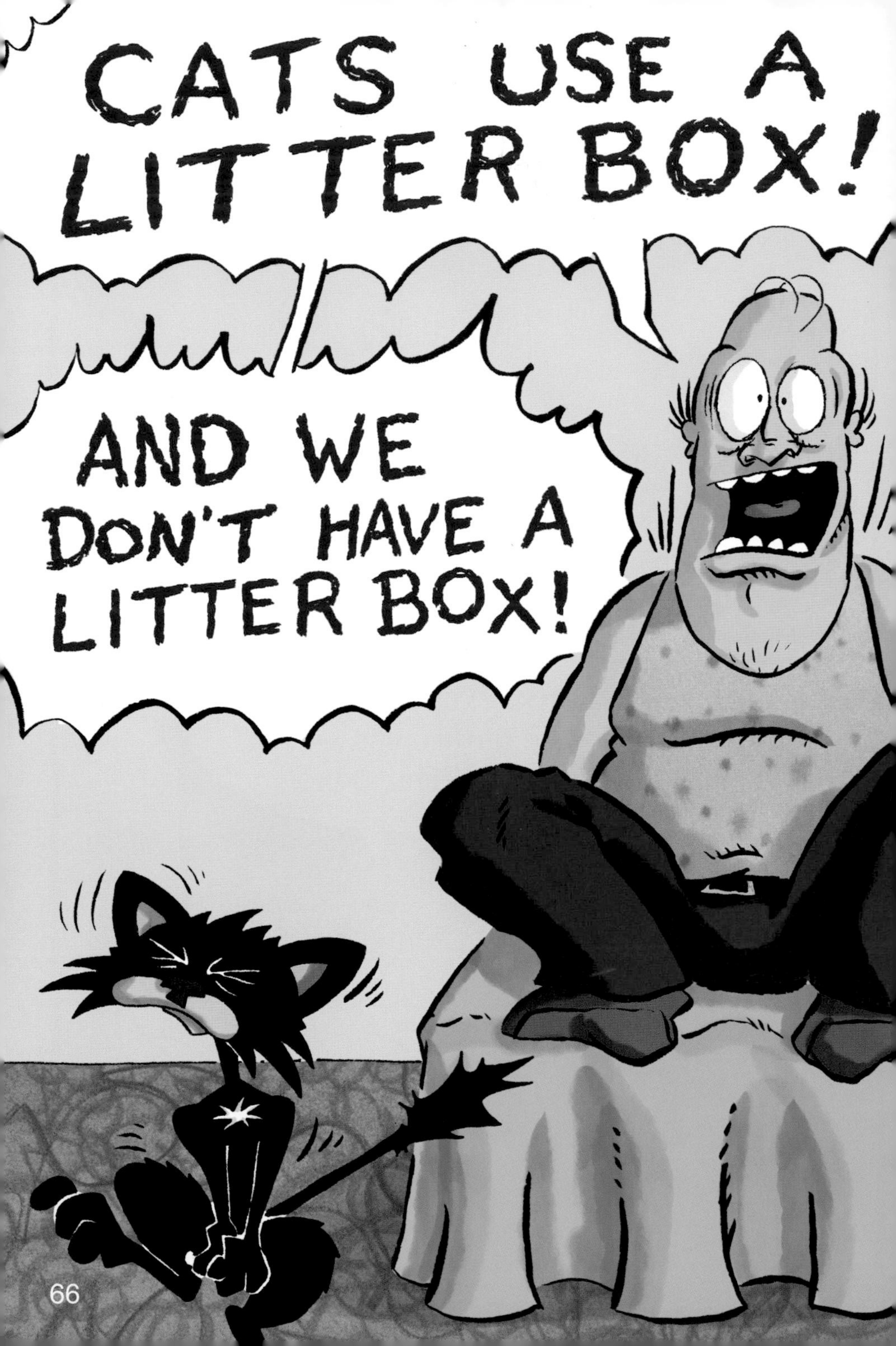
CATS USE A LITTER BOX!
AND WE DON'T HAVE A LITTER BOX!

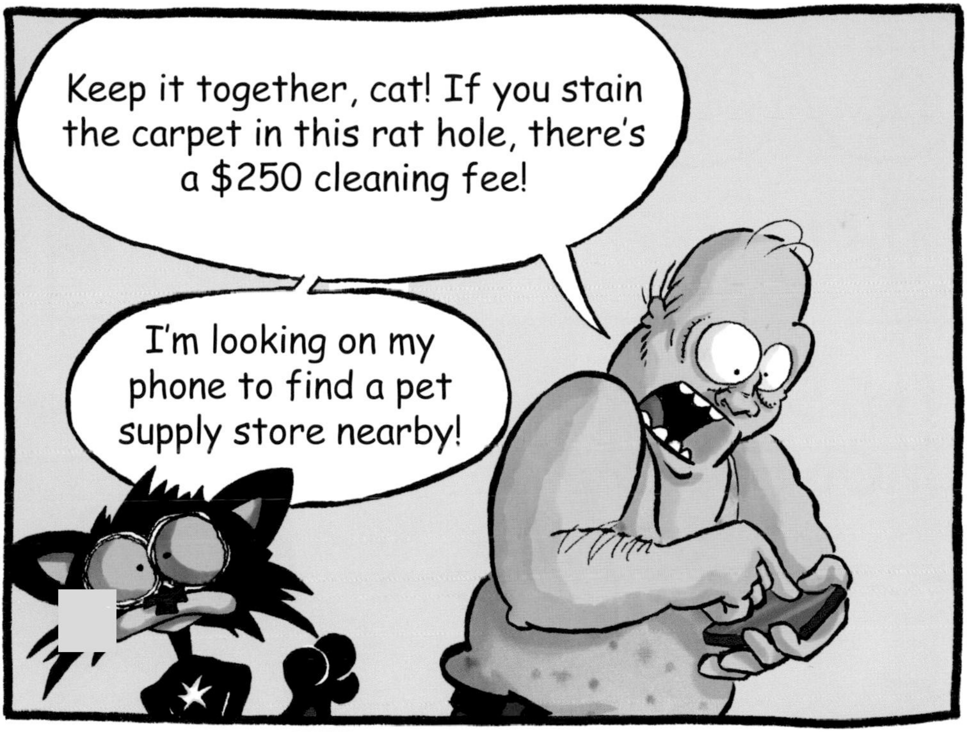
Keep it together, cat! If you stain the carpet in this rat hole, there's a $250 cleaning fee!
I'm looking on my phone to find a pet supply store nearby!

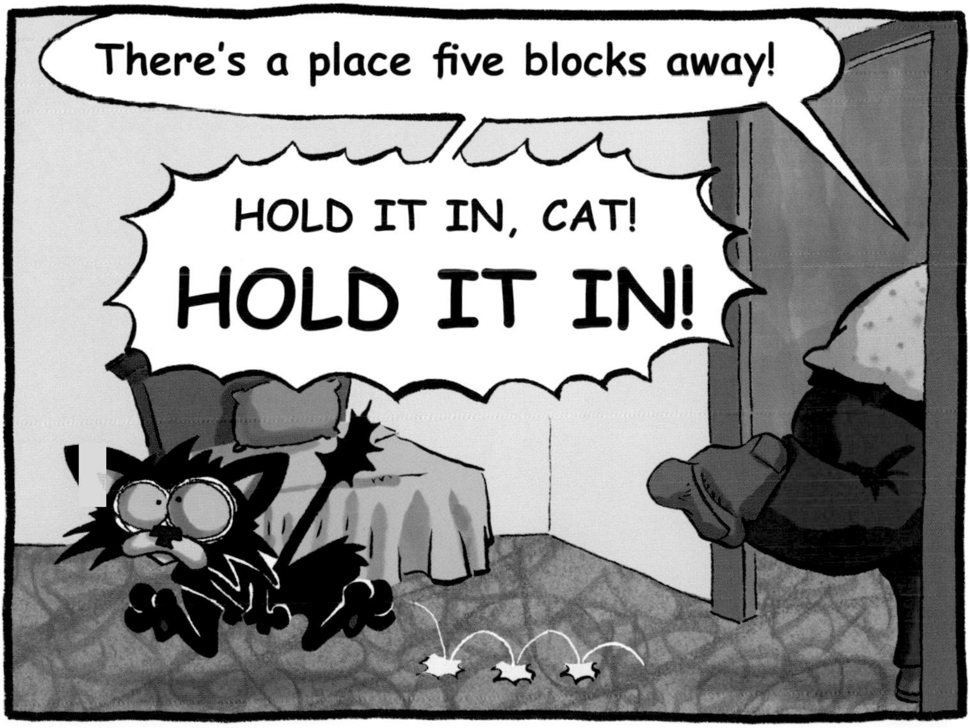
There's a place five blocks away!
HOLD IT IN, CAT!
HOLD IT IN!

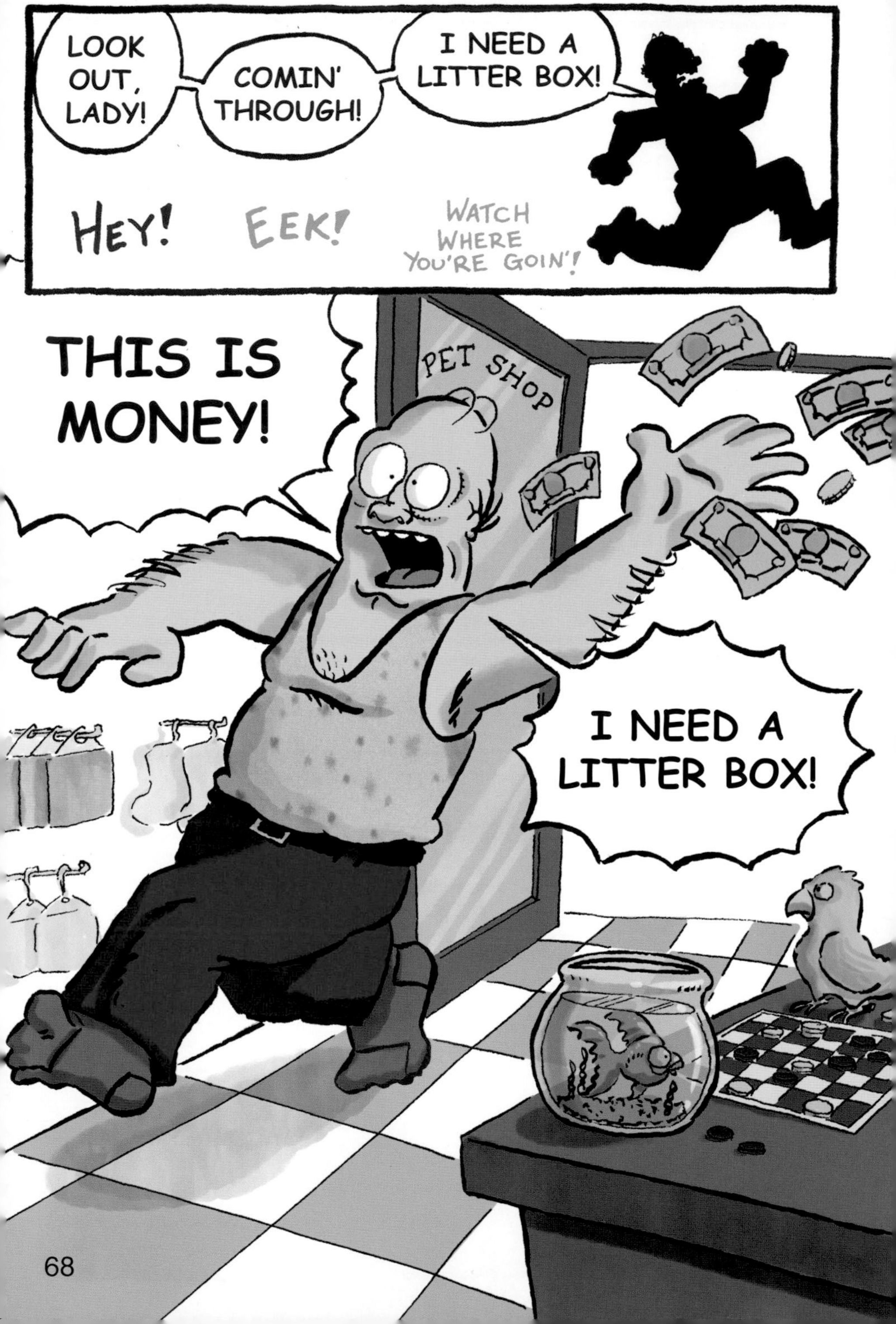
LOOK OUT, LADY!
COMIN' THROUGH!
I NEED A LITTER BOX!
HEY!
EEK!
WATCH WHERE YOU'RE GOIN'!
THIS IS MONEY!
PET SHOP
I NEED A LITTER BOX!

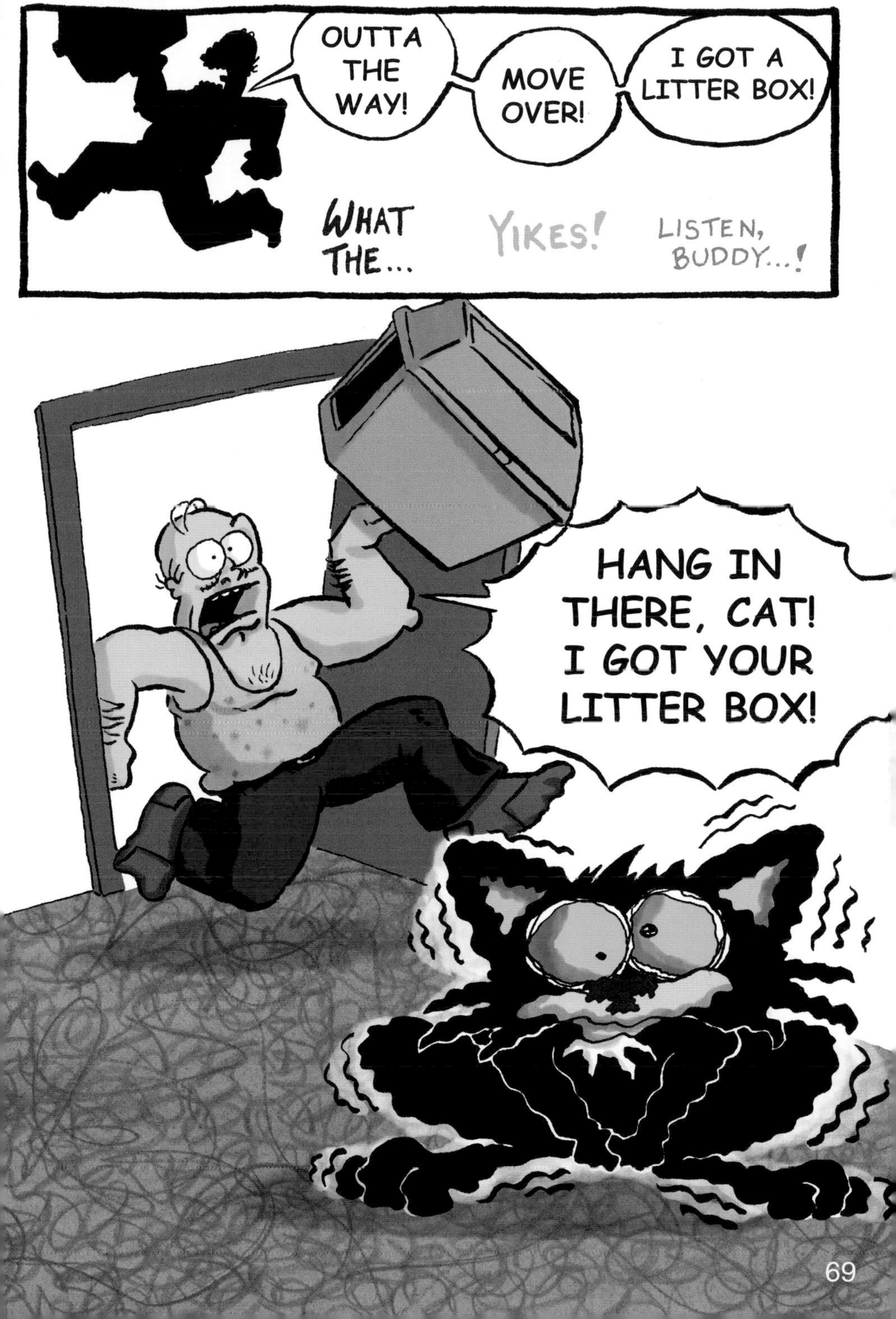
OUTTA THE WAY!
MOVE OVER!
I GOT A LITTER BOX!
WHAT THE...
YIKES!
LISTEN, BUDDY...!
HANG IN THERE, CAT! I GOT YOUR LITTER BOX!

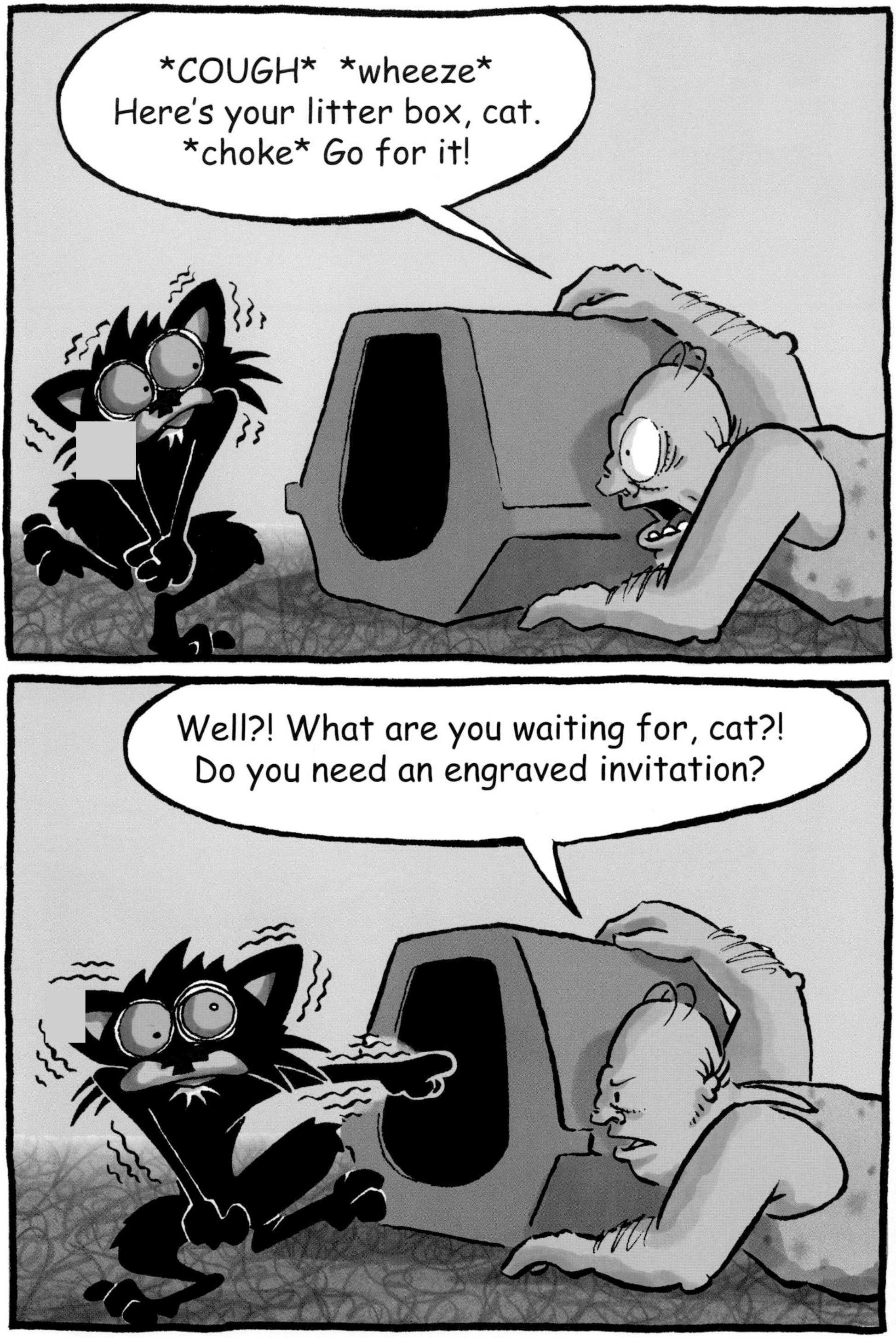
COUGH *wheeze* Here's your litter box, cat. *choke* Go for it!
Well?! What are you waiting for, cat?! Do you need an engraved invitation?

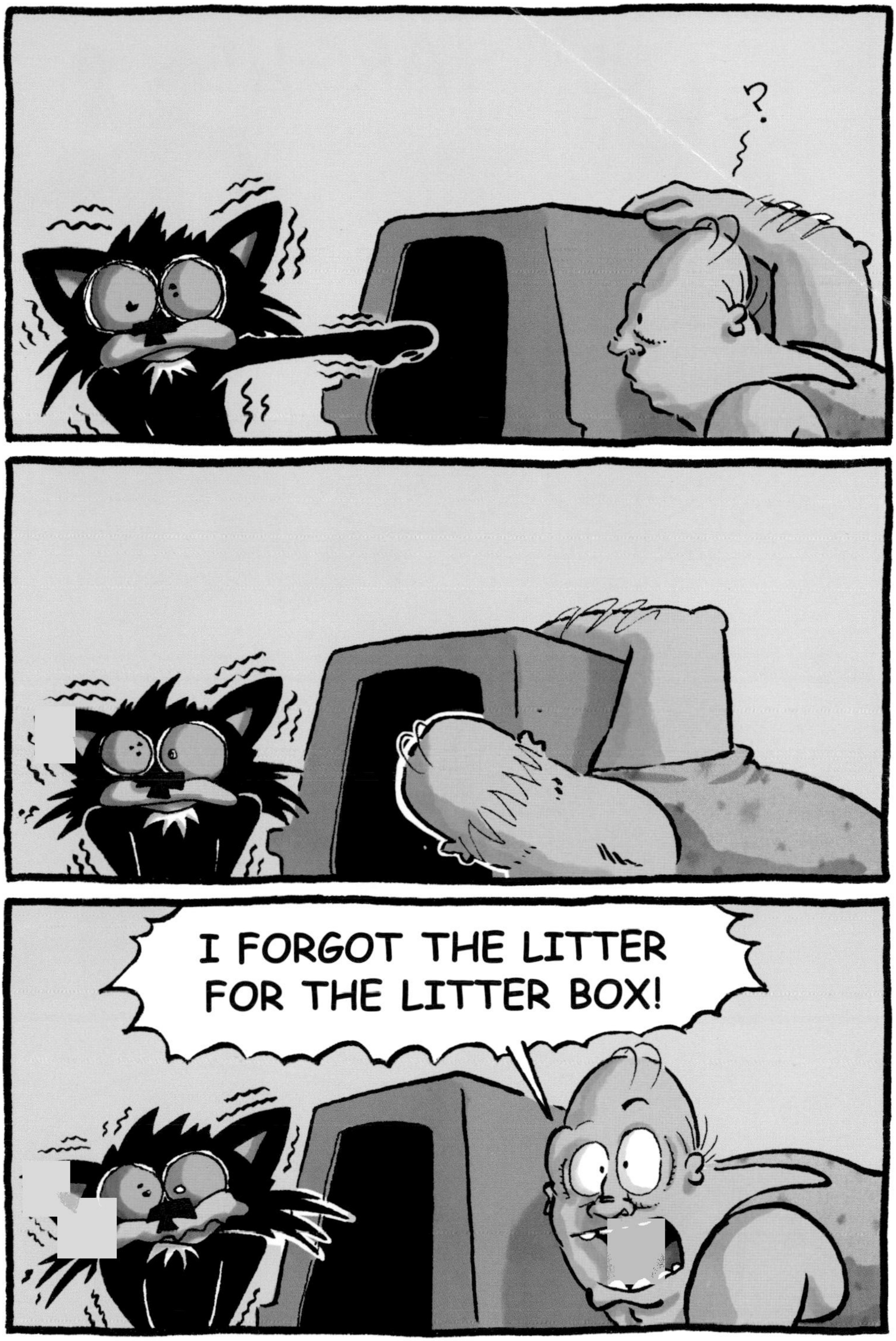
?
I FORGOT THE LITTER FOR THE LITTER BOX!

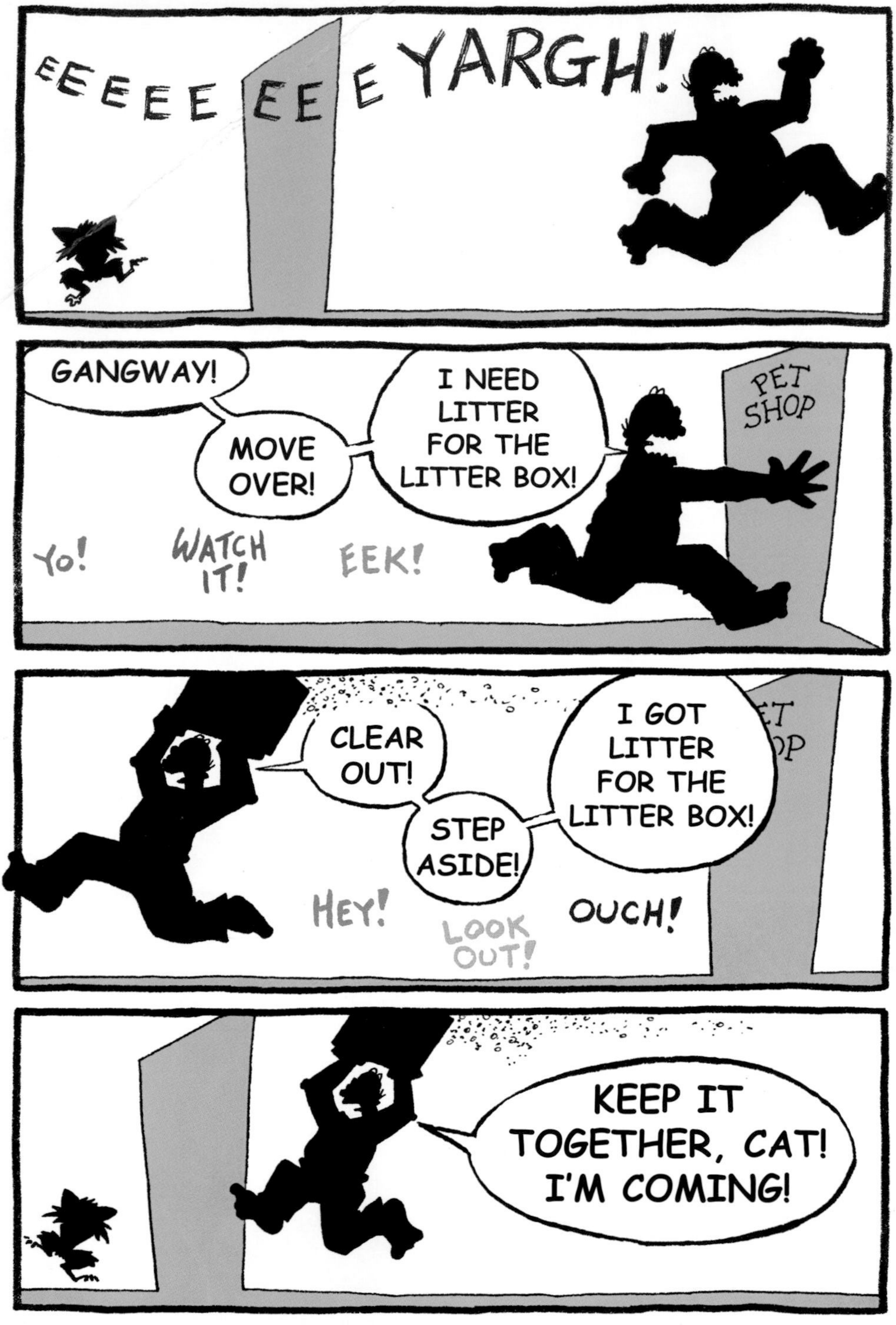
EEEEE EE EYARGH!
GANGWAY!
MOVE OVER!
I NEED LITTER FOR THE LITTER BOX!
PET SHOP
YO!
WATCH IT!
EEK!
CLEAR OUT!
STEP ASIDE!
I GOT LITTER FOR THE LITTER BOX!
HEY!
LOOK OUT!
OUCH!
KEEP IT TOGETHER, CAT! I'M COMING!

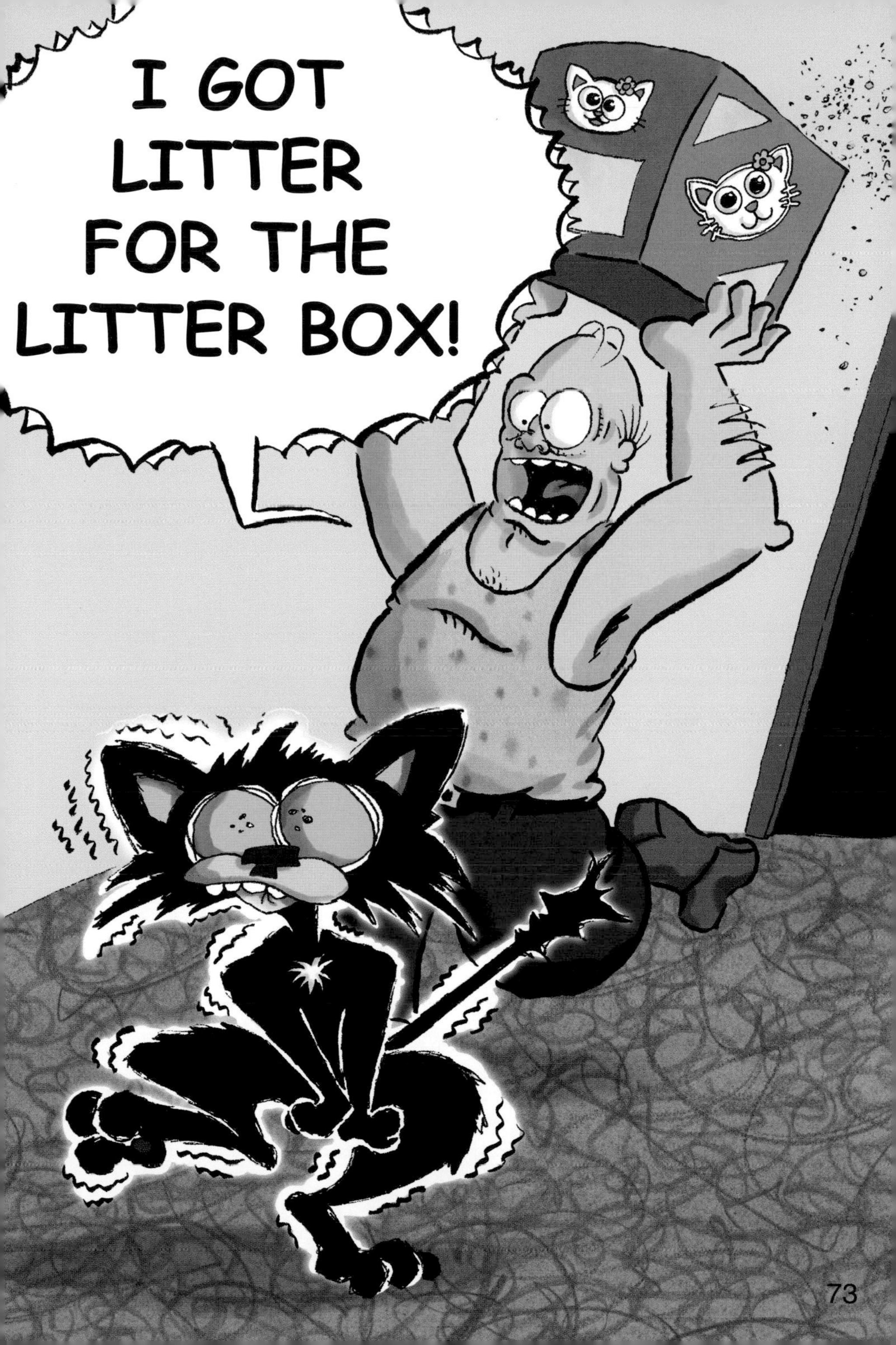
I GOT LITTER FOR THE LITTER BOX!

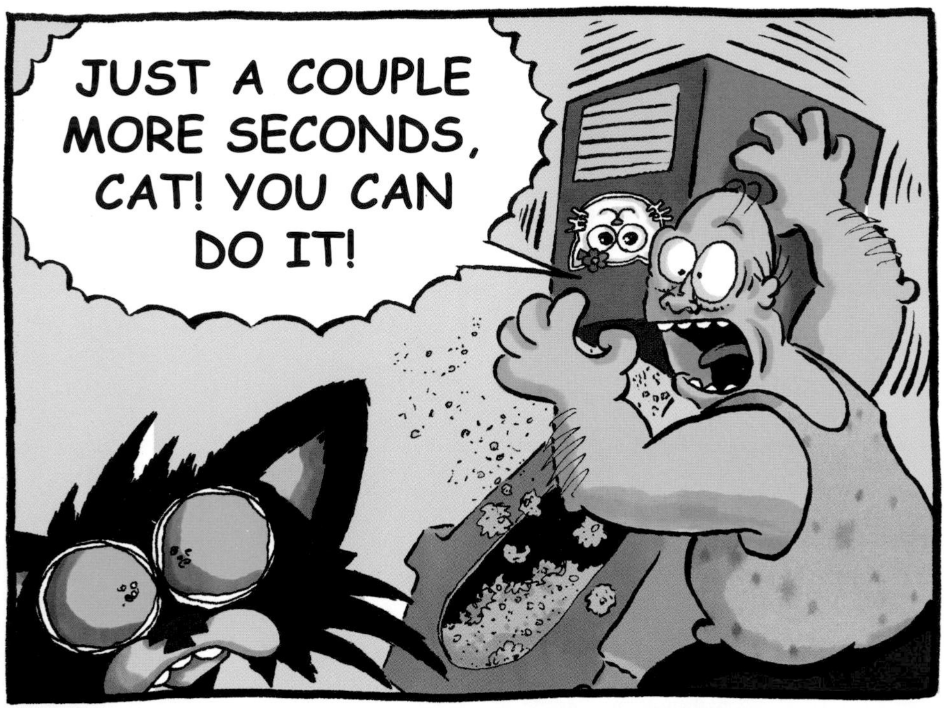
JUST A COUPLE MORE SECONDS, CAT! YOU CAN DO IT!

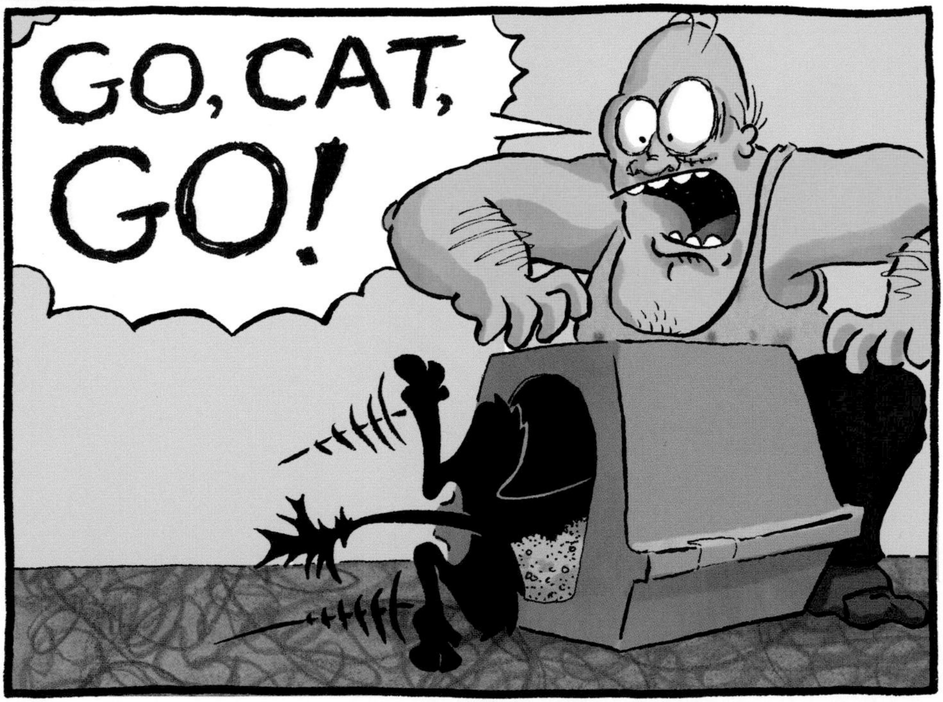
GO, CAT, GO!

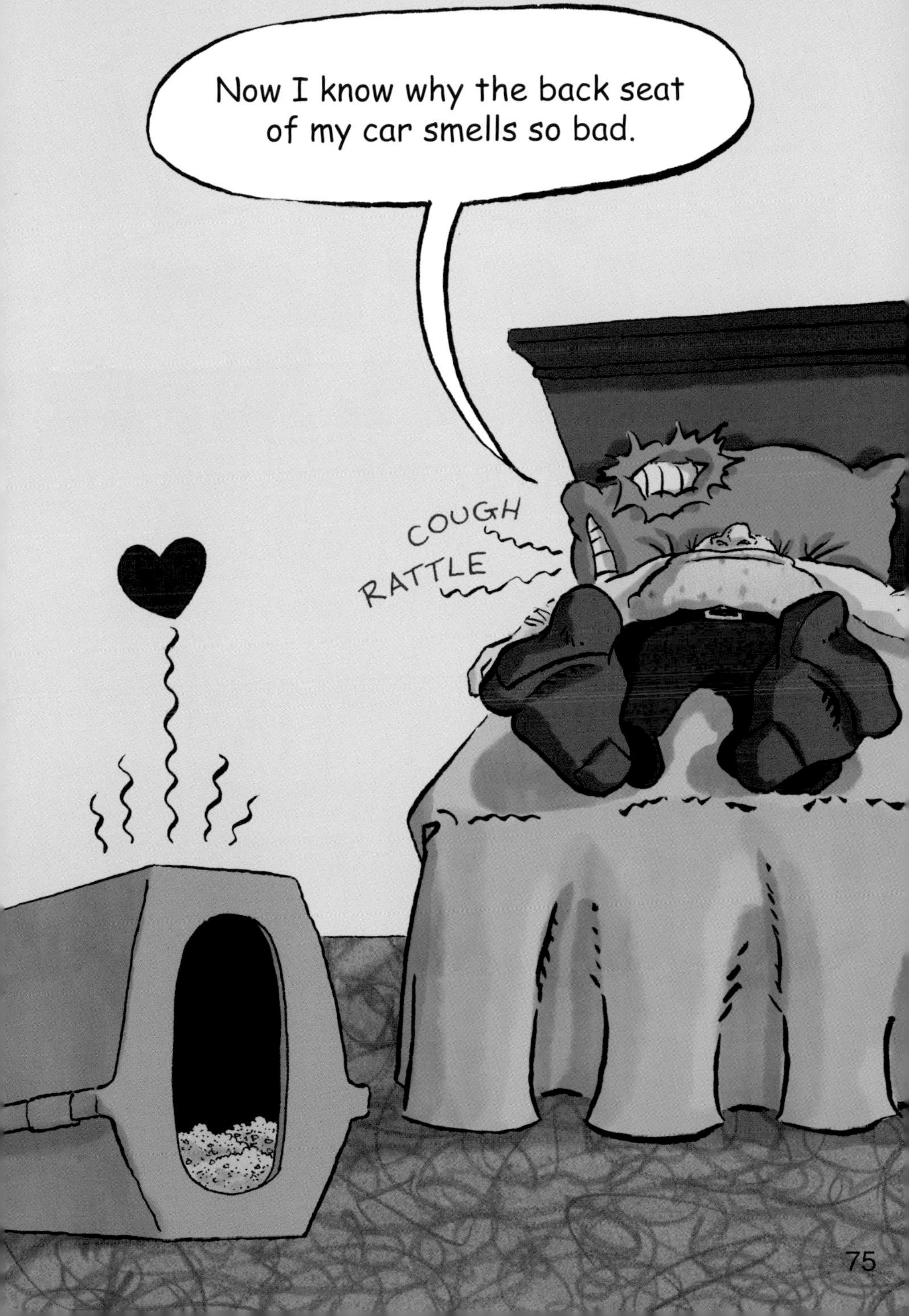
Now I know why the back seat of my car smells so bad.
COUGH
RATTLE

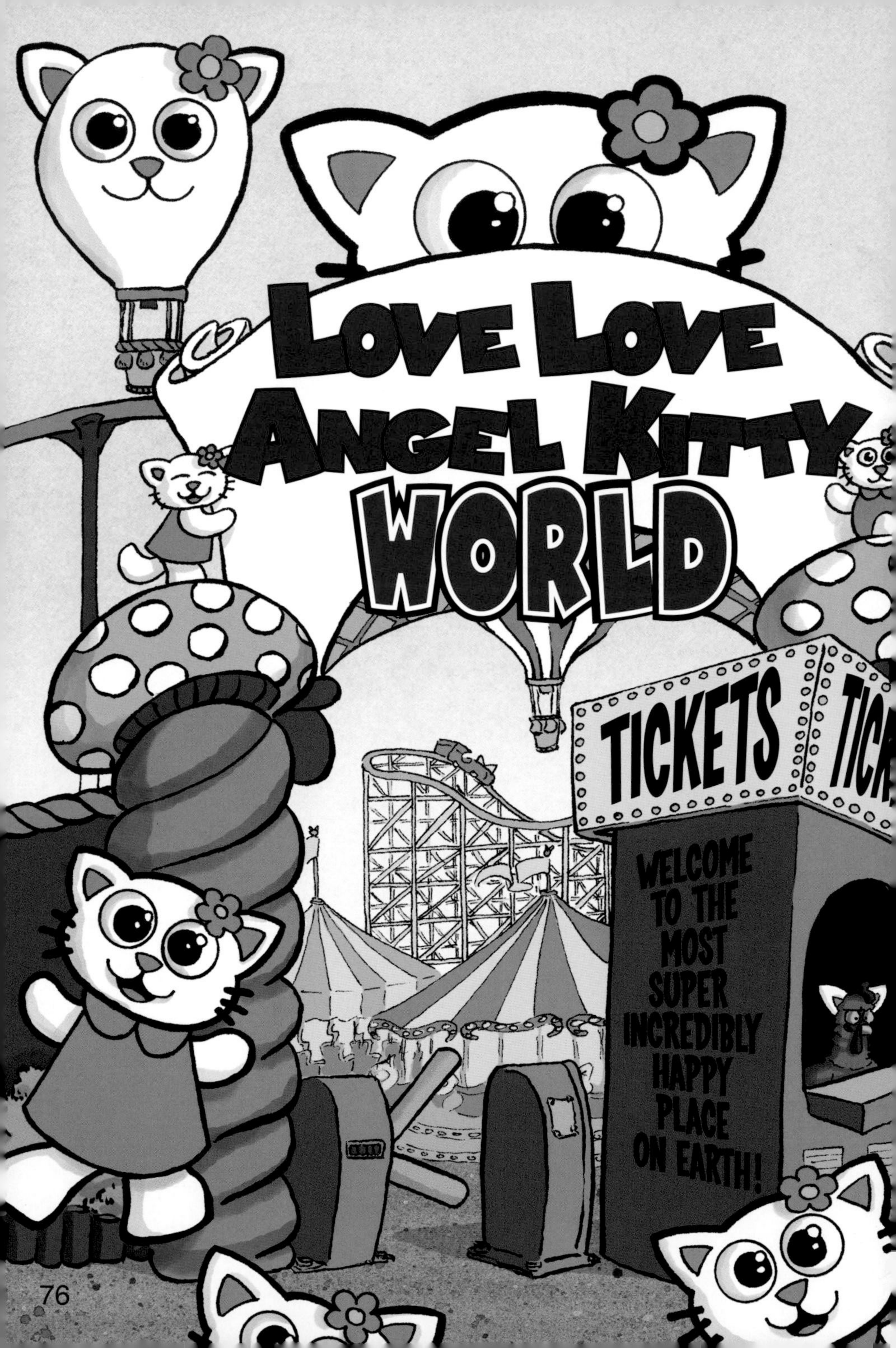
LOVE LOVE ANGEL KITTY WORLD
TICKETS
WELCOME TO THE MOST SUPER INCREDIBLY HAPPY PLACE ON EARTH!

• CHAPTER FIVE •

FINALLY

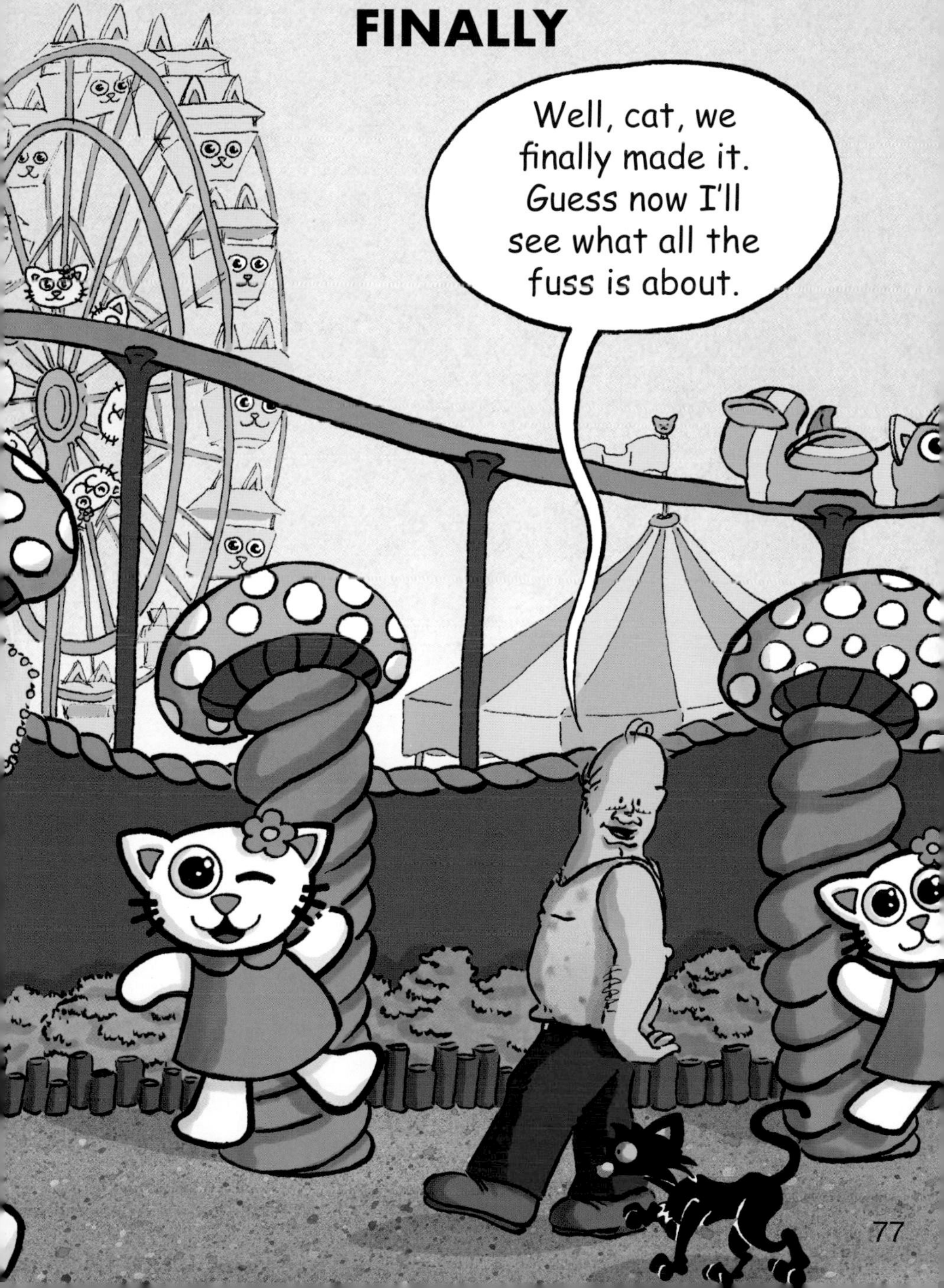
Well, cat, we finally made it. Guess now I'll see what all the fuss is about.

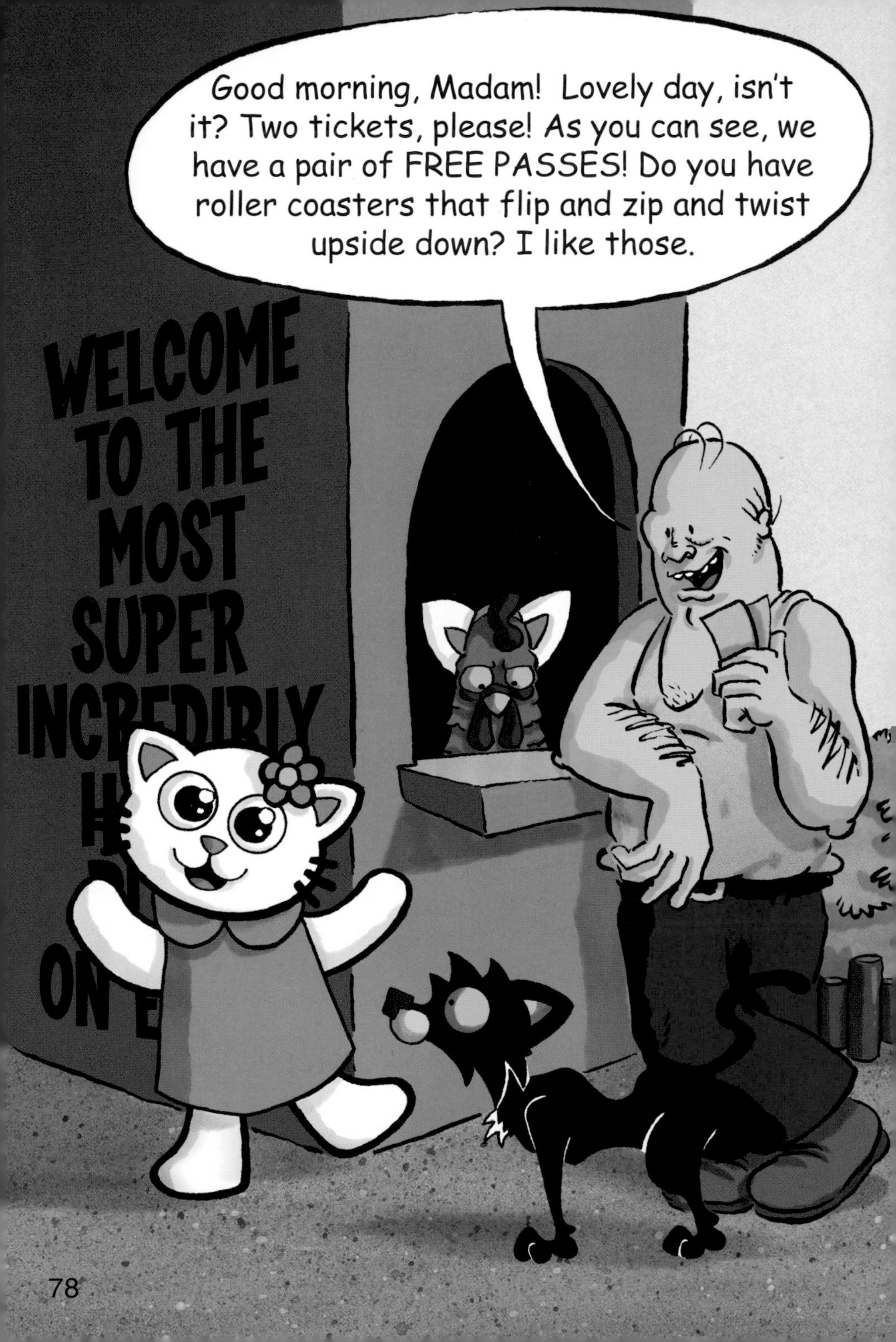
Good morning, Madam! Lovely day, isn't it? Two tickets, please! As you can see, we have a pair of FREE PASSES! Do you have roller coasters that flip and zip and twist upside down? I like those.
WELCOME TO THE MOST SUPER

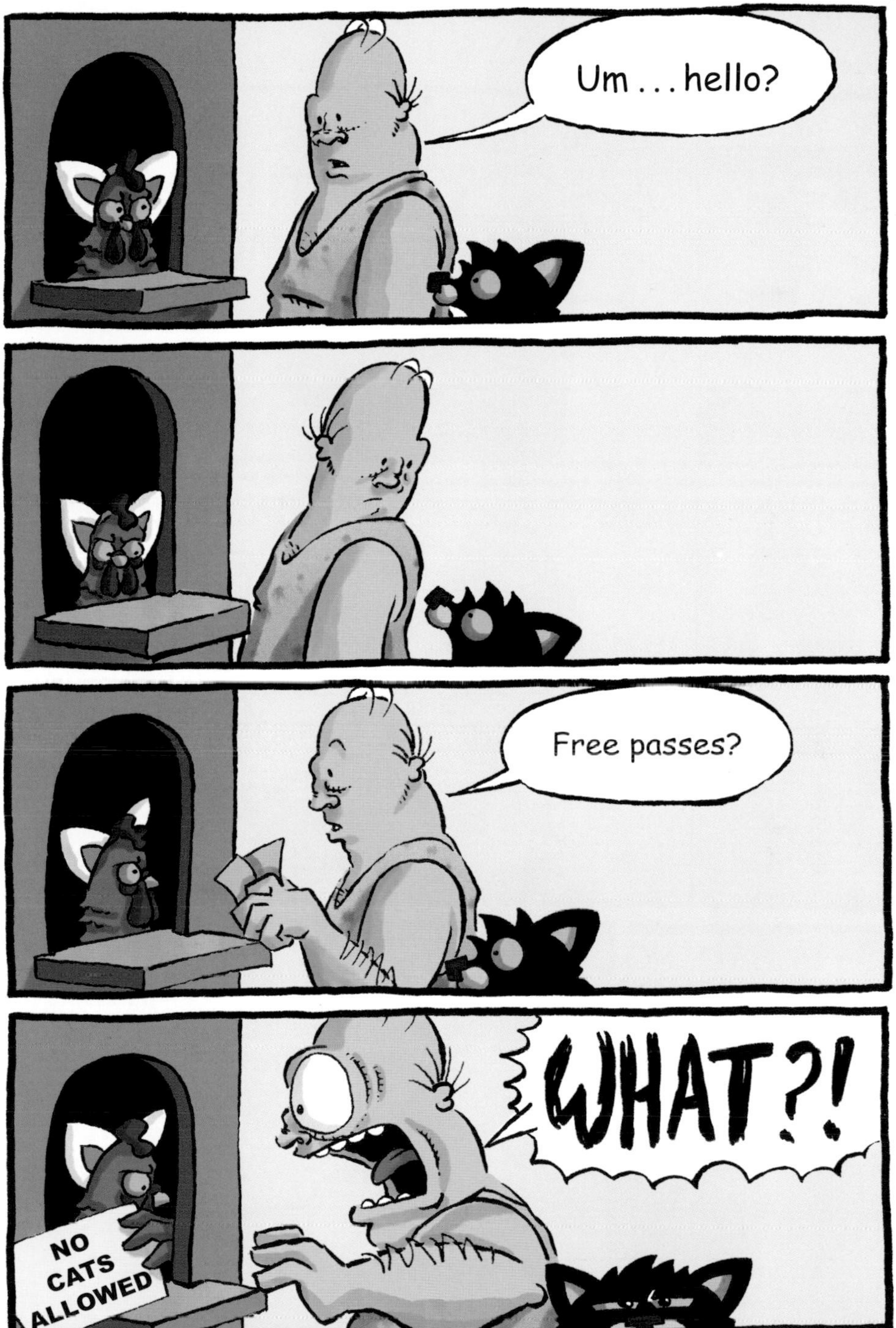
Um . . . hello?
Free passes?
WHAT?!
NO CATS ALLOWED

THE SEVEN STAGES OF UNCLE MURRAY'S PANIC • PART TWO

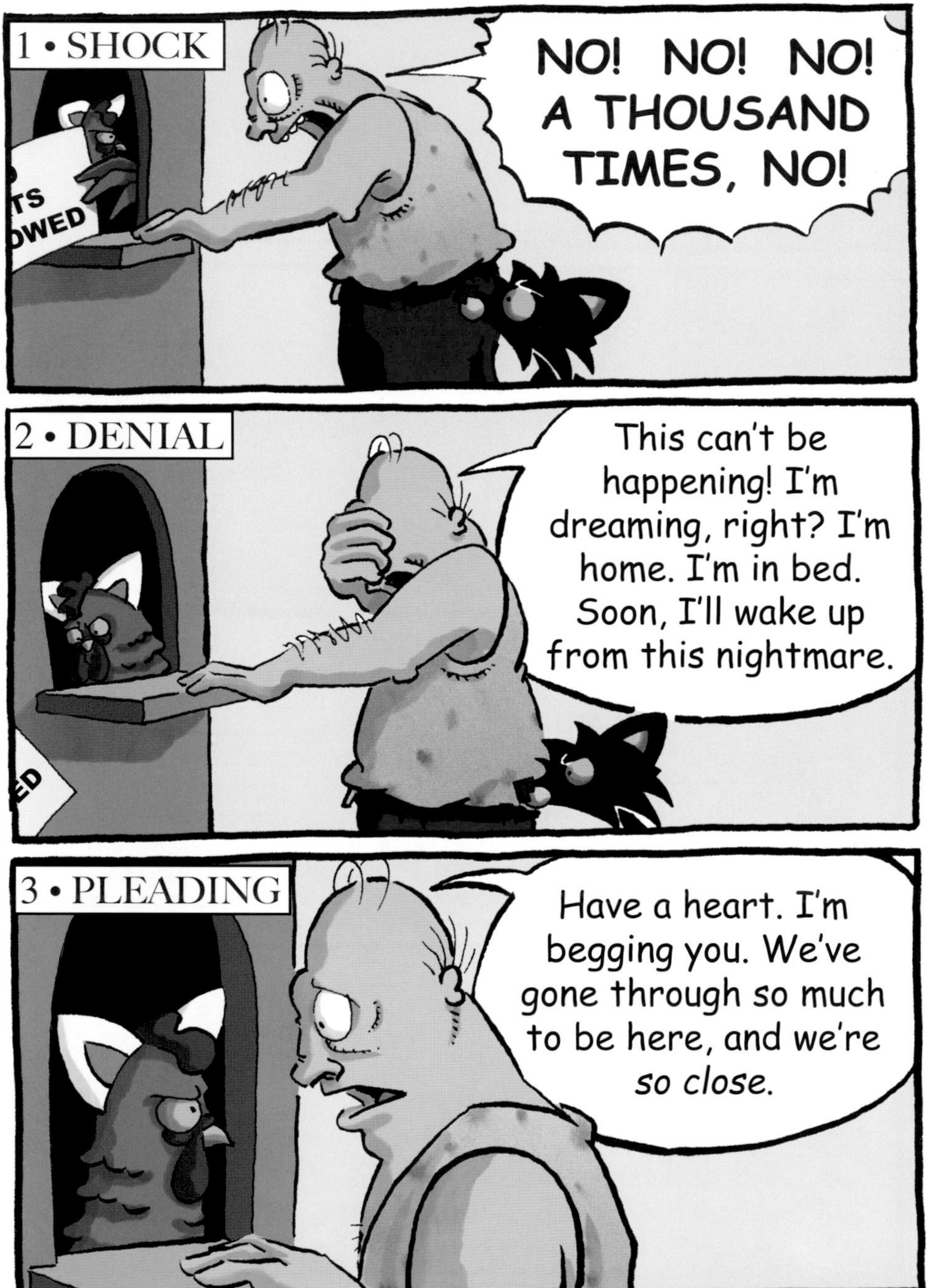
1 • SHOCK
NO! NO! NO! A THOUSAND TIMES, NO!
2 • DENIAL
This can't be happening! I'm dreaming, right? I'm home. I'm in bed. Soon, I'll wake up from this nightmare.
3 • PLEADING
Have a heart. I'm begging you. We've gone through so much to be here, and we're *so close.*

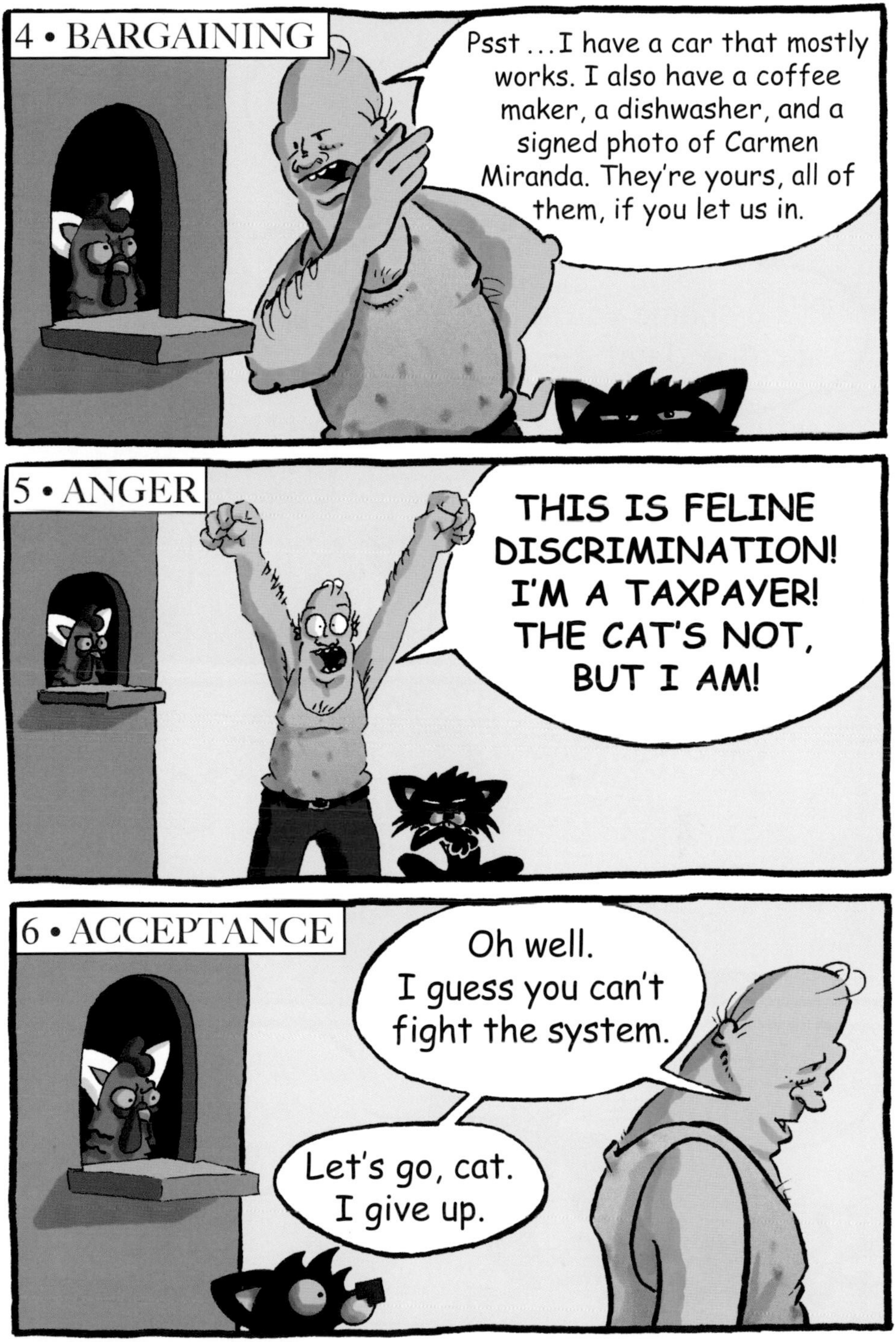
4 • BARGAINING
Psst . . . I have a car that mostly works. I also have a coffee maker, a dishwasher, and a signed photo of Carmen Miranda. They're yours, all of them, if you let us in.
5 • ANGER
THIS IS FELINE DISCRIMINATION! I'M A TAXPAYER! THE CAT'S NOT, BUT I AM!
6 • ACCEPTANCE
Oh well. I guess you can't fight the system.
Let's go, cat. I give up.

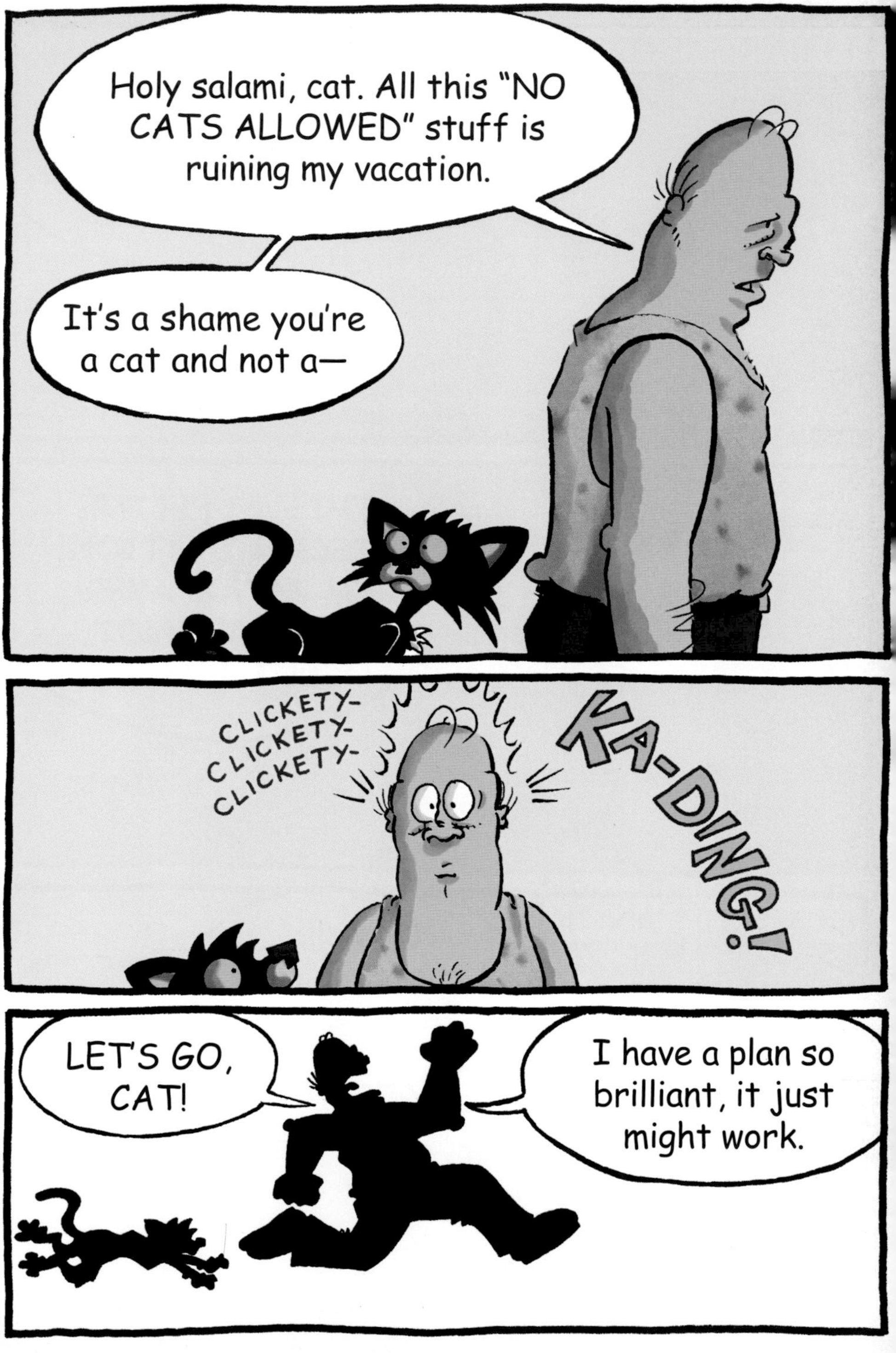
Holy salami, cat. All this "NO CATS ALLOWED" stuff is ruining my vacation.
It's a shame you're a cat and not a—
CLICKETY-CLICKETY-CLICKETY-
KA-DING!
LET'S GO, CAT!
I have a plan so brilliant, it just might work.

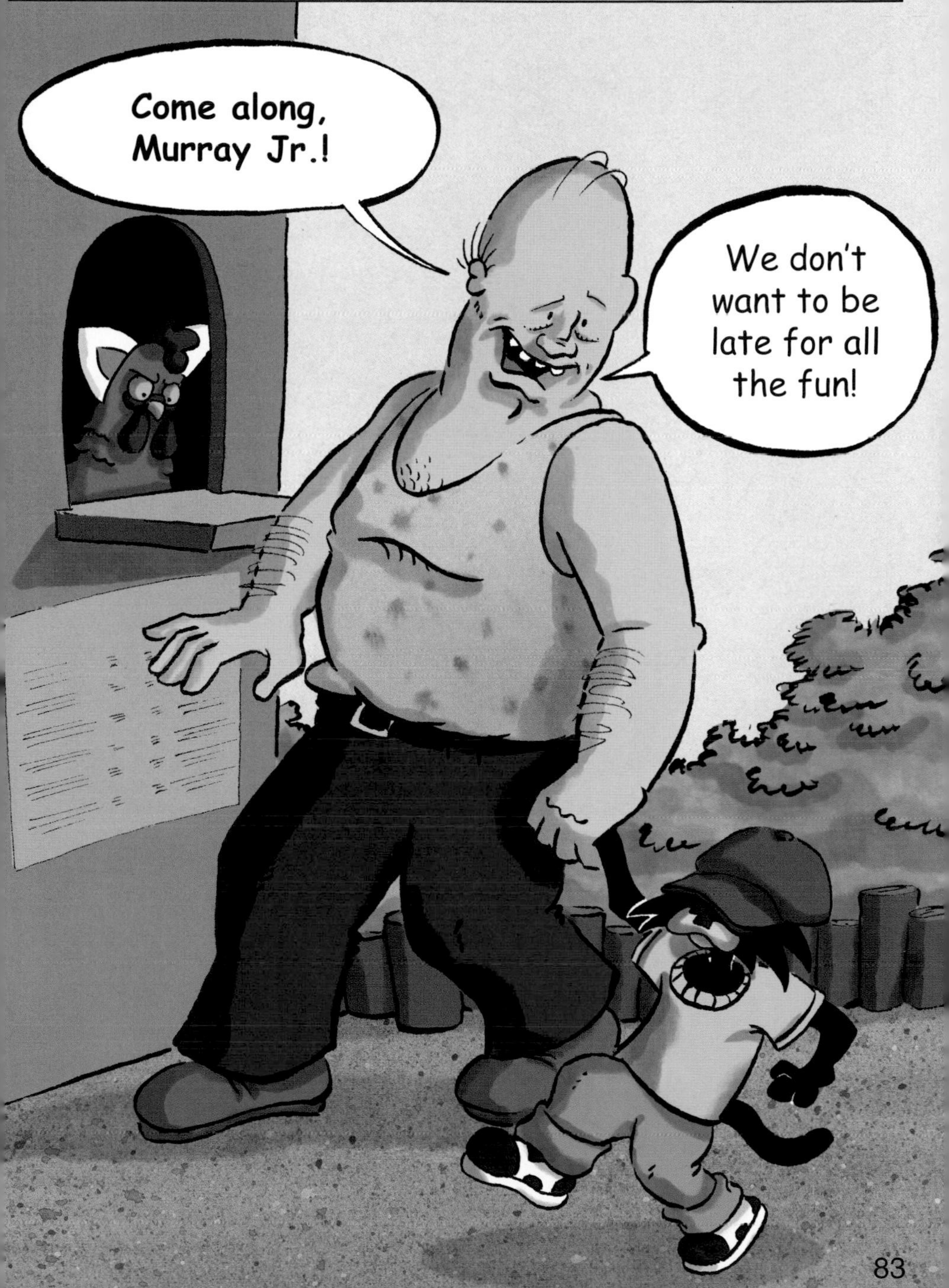
Come along, Murray Jr.!
We don't want to be late for all the fun!

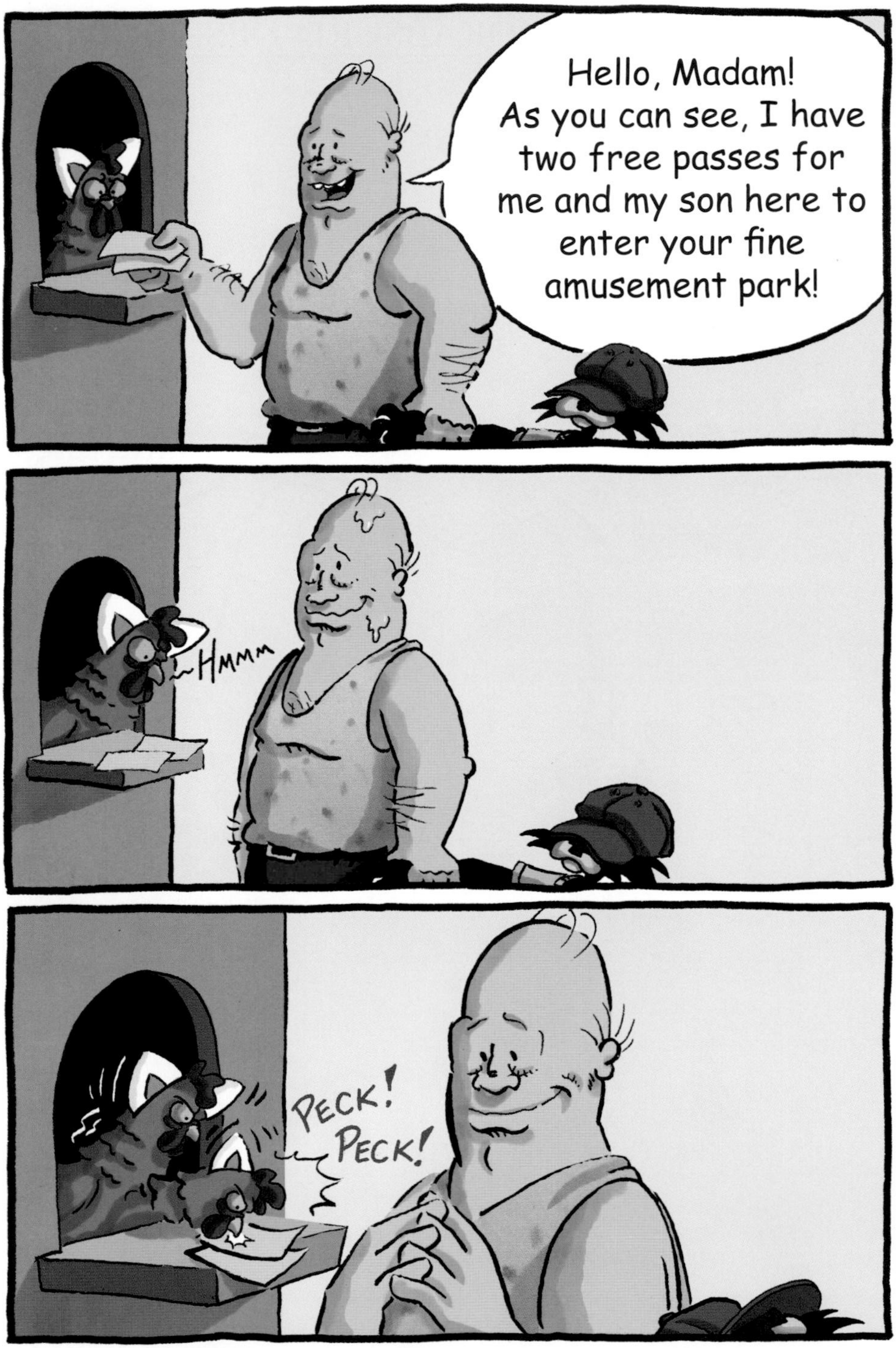
Hello, Madam! As you can see, I have two free passes for me and my son here to enter your fine amusement park!
HMMM
PECK! PECK!

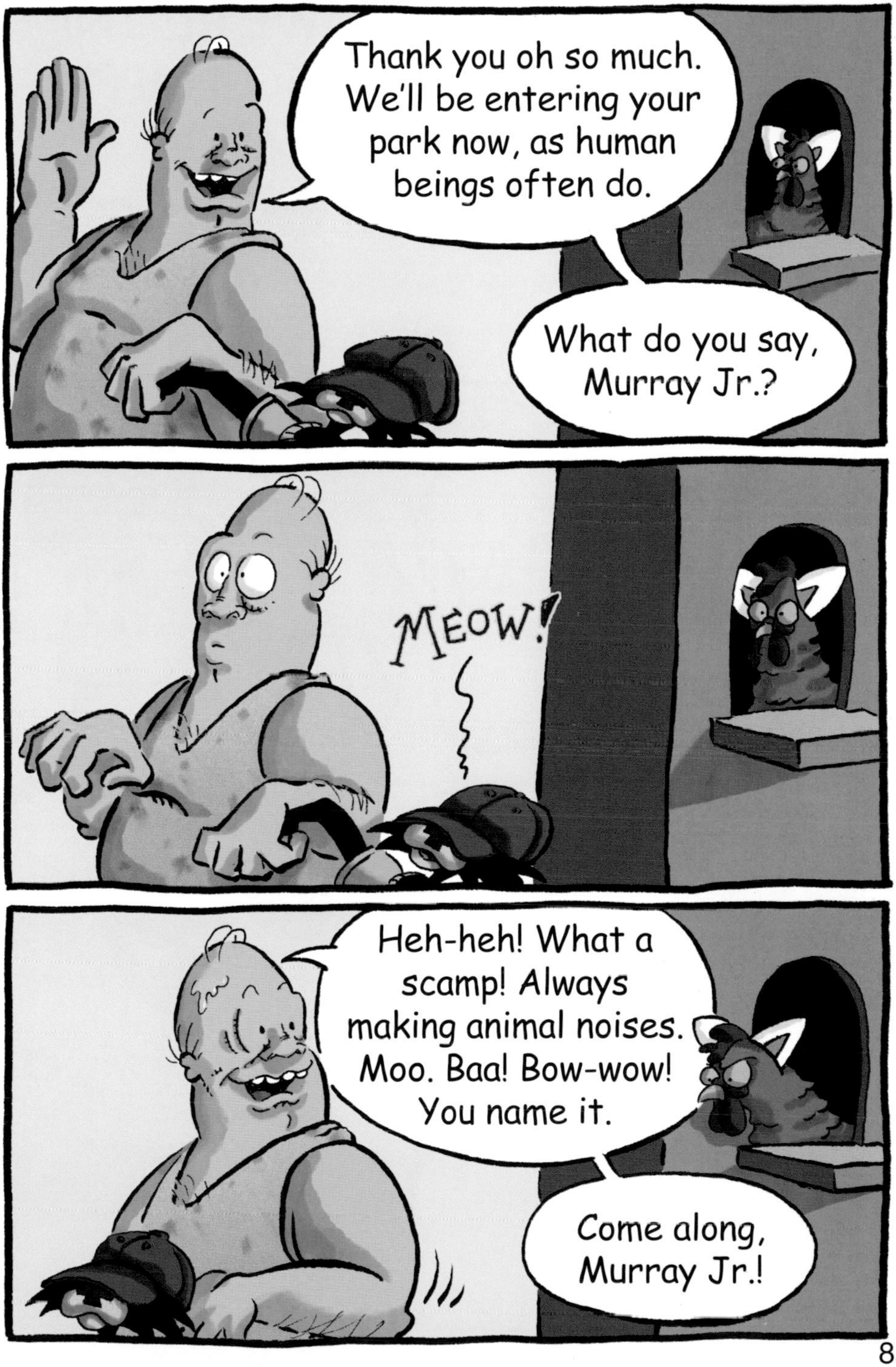

Thank you oh so much. We'll be entering your park now, as human beings often do.
What do you say, Murray Jr.?
MEOW!
Heh-heh! What a scamp! Always making animal noises. Moo. Baa! Bow-wow! You name it.
Come along, Murray Jr.!

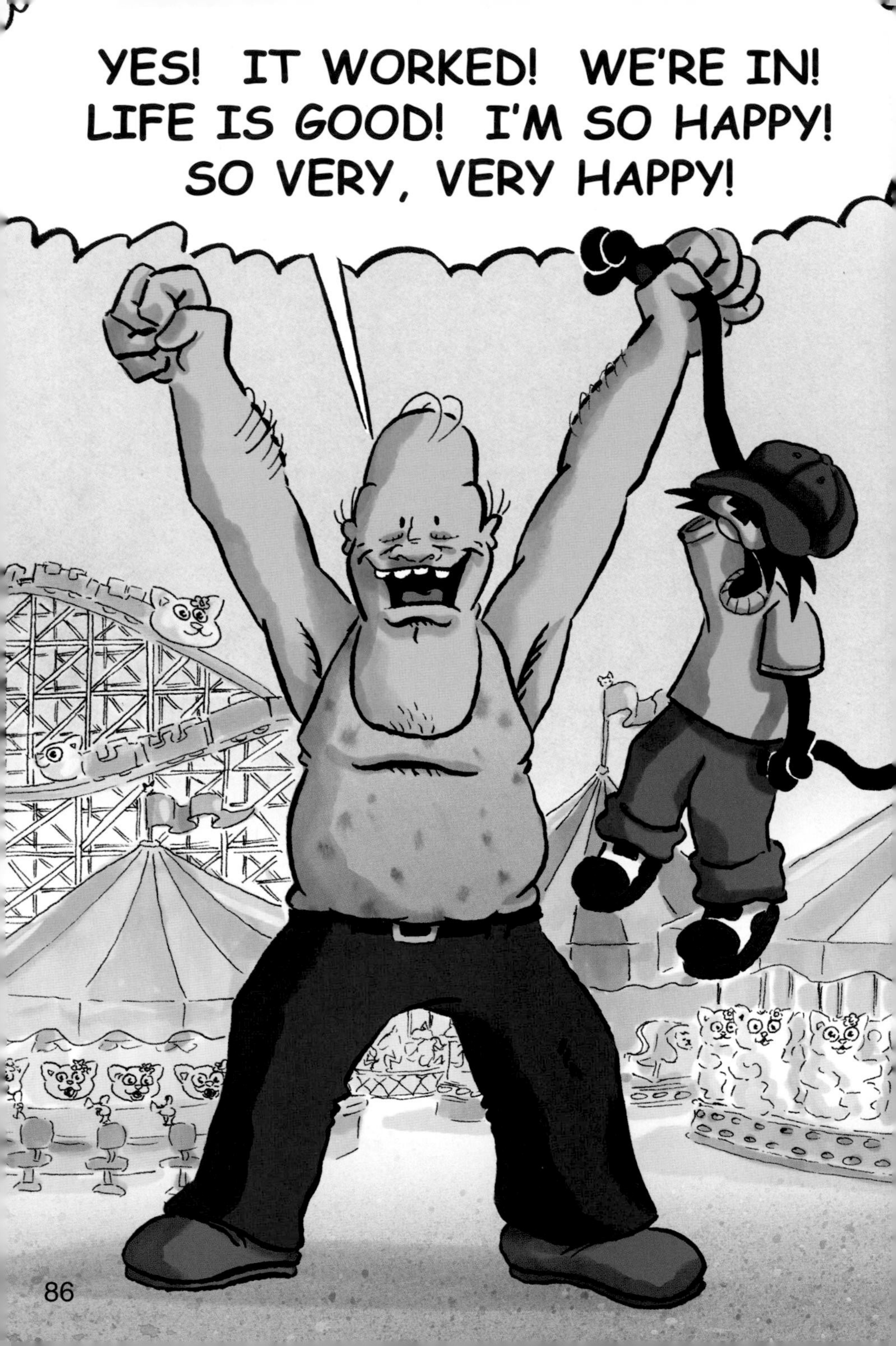
YES! IT WORKED! WE'RE IN! LIFE IS GOOD! I'M SO HAPPY! SO VERY, VERY HAPPY!

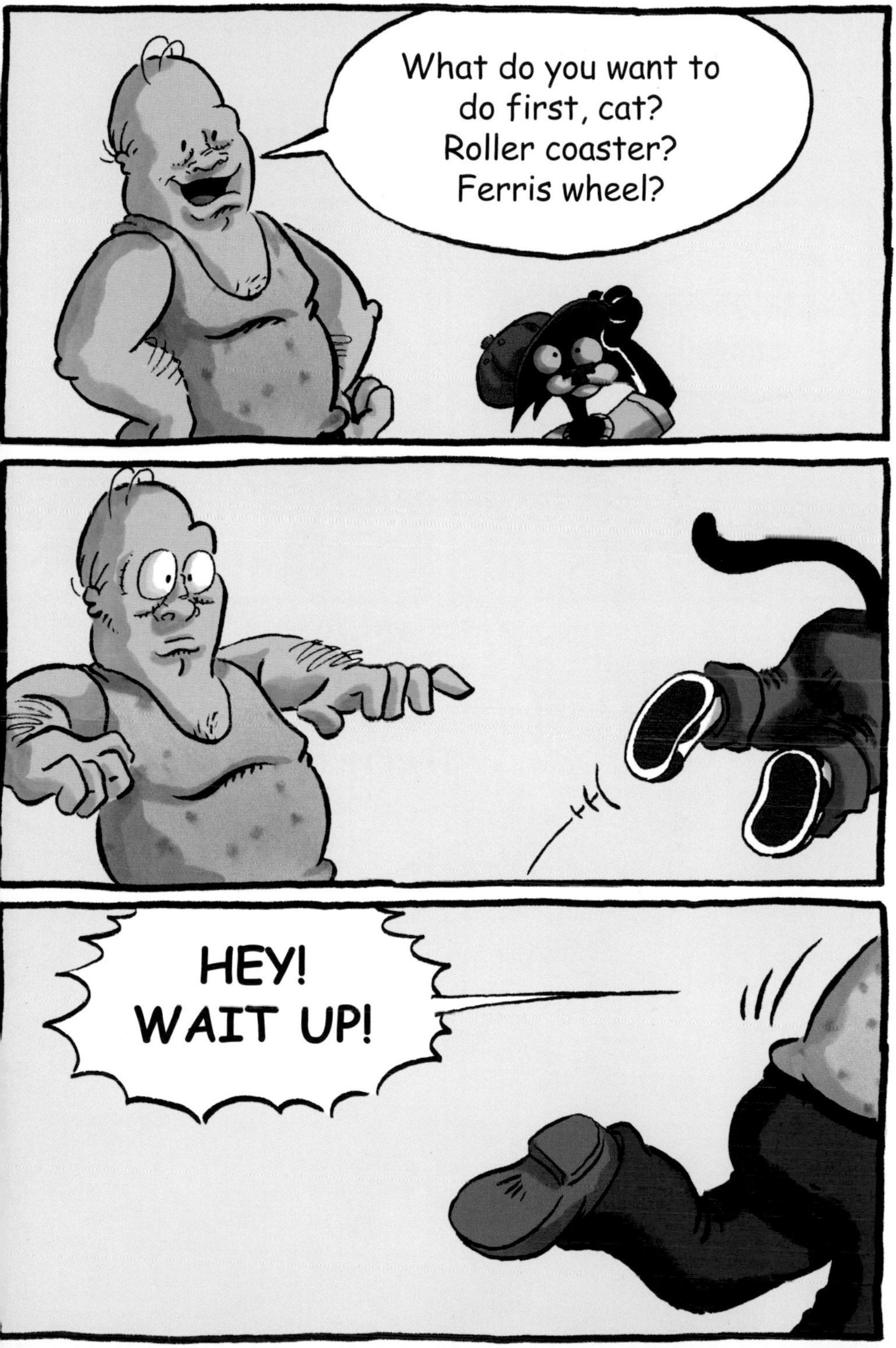
What do you want to do first, cat? Roller coaster? Ferris wheel?
HEY! WAIT UP!

•CHAPTER SIX•

INSIDE THE PARK

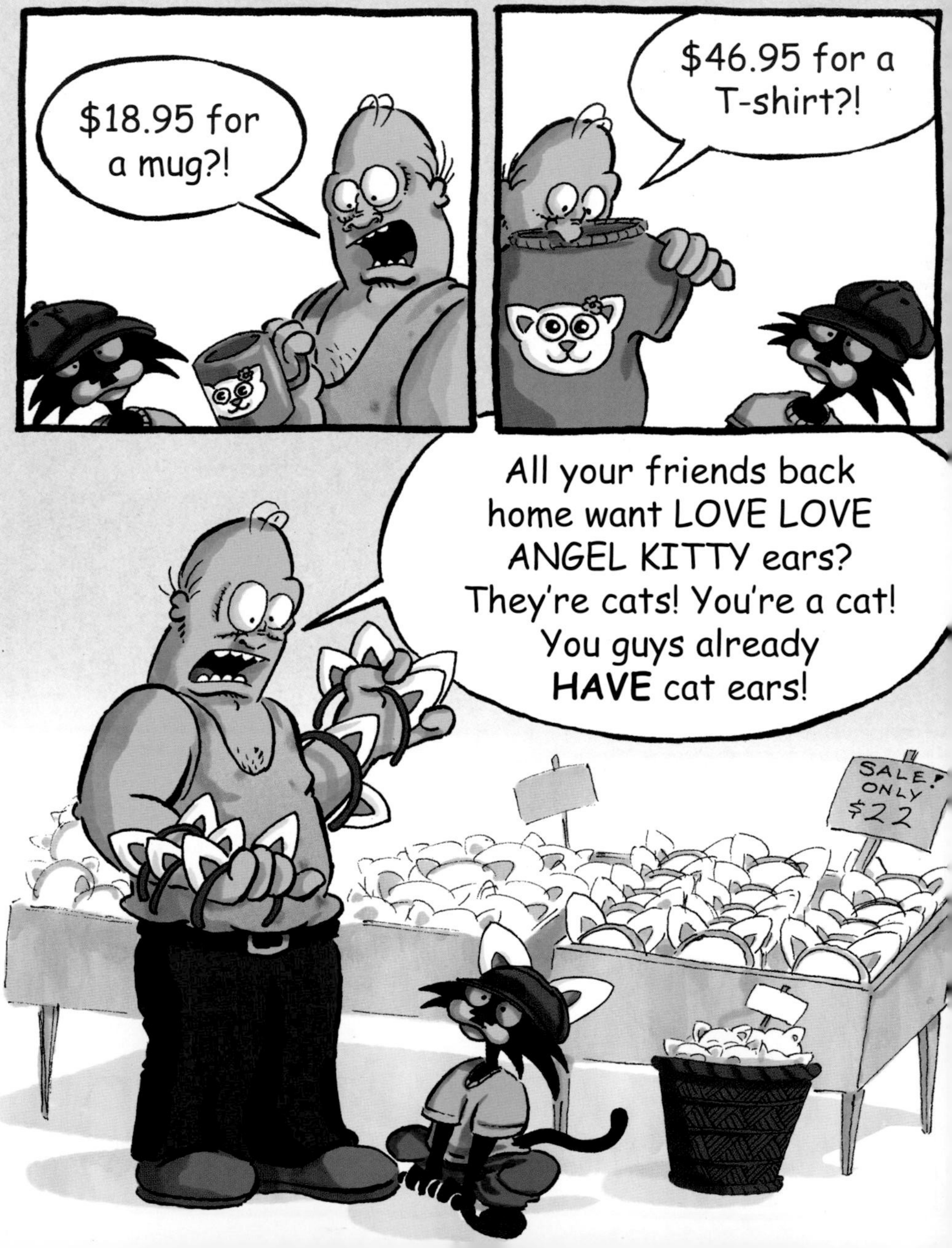
$18.95 for a mug?!
$46.95 for a T-shirt?!
All your friends back home want LOVE LOVE ANGEL KITTY ears? They're cats! You're a cat! You guys already **HAVE** cat ears!
SALE! ONLY $22

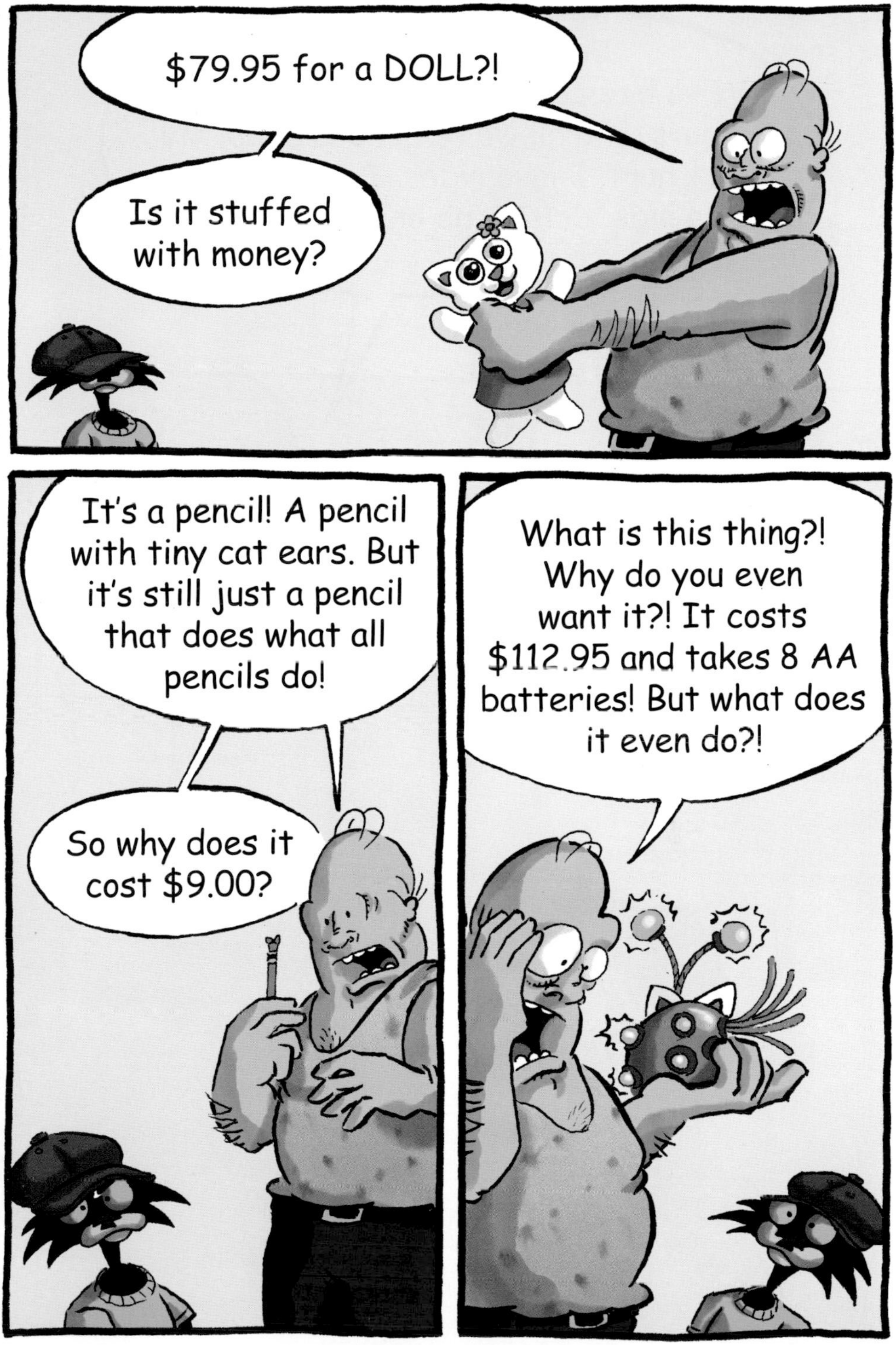
$79.95 for a DOLL?!
Is it stuffed with money?
It's a pencil! A pencil with tiny cat ears. But it's still just a pencil that does what all pencils do!
So why does it cost $9.00?
What is this thing?! Why do you even want it?! It costs $112.95 and takes 8 AA batteries! But what does it even do?!

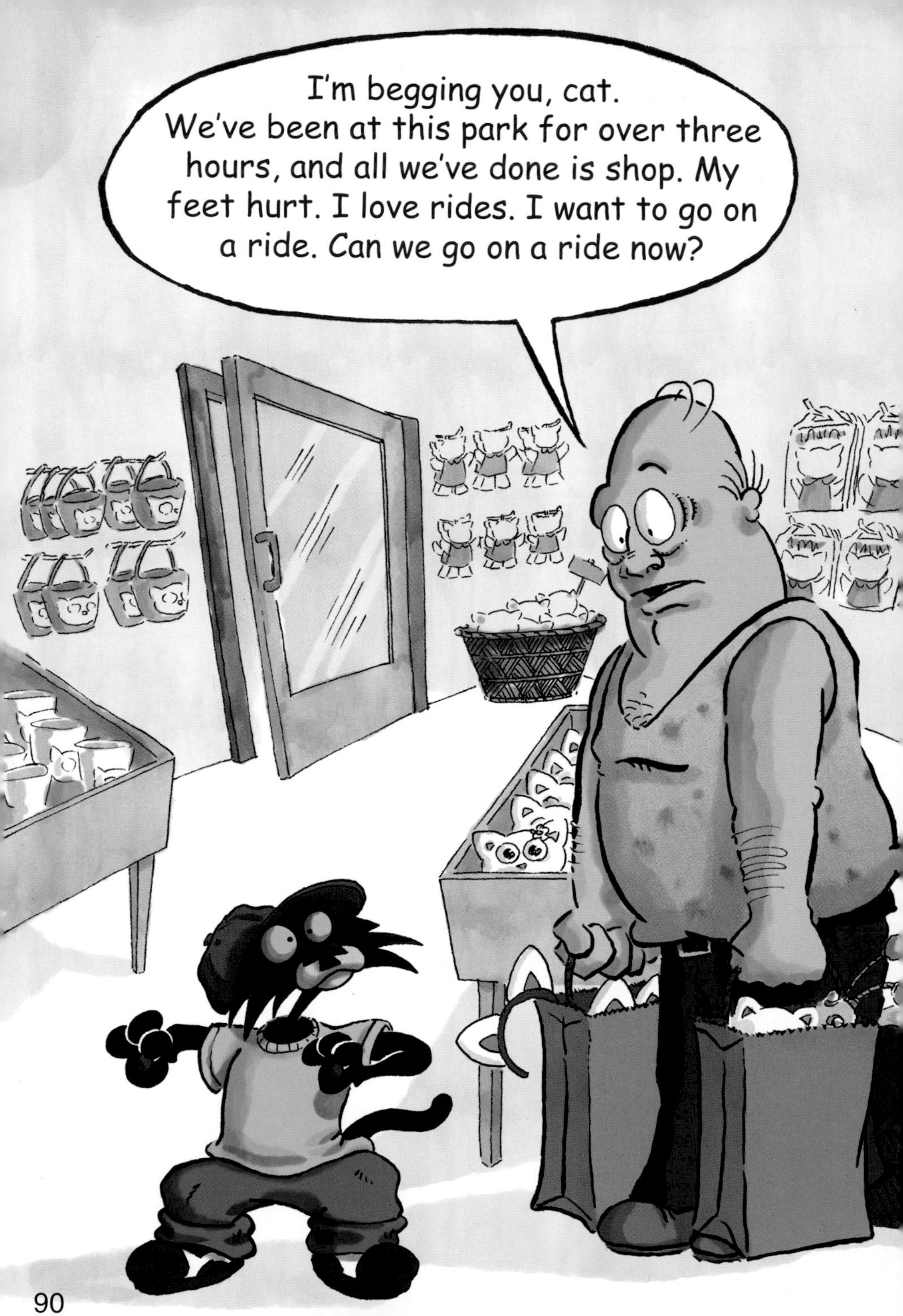
I'm begging you, cat. We've been at this park for over three hours, and all we've done is shop. My feet hurt. I love rides. I want to go on a ride. Can we go on a ride now?

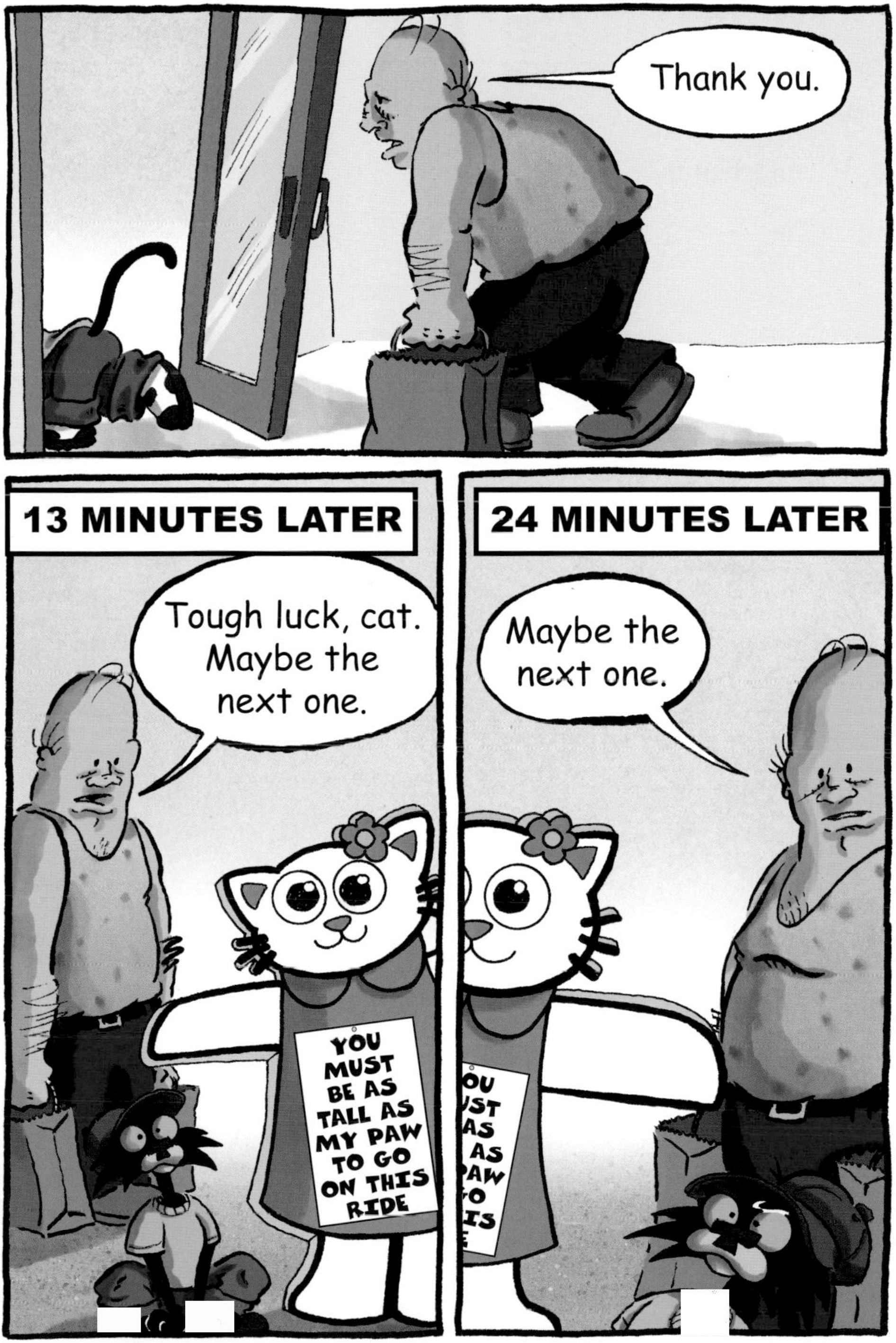
Thank you.
13 MINUTES LATER
Tough luck, cat. Maybe the next one.
YOU MUST BE AS TALL AS MY PAW TO GO ON THIS RIDE
24 MINUTES LATER
Maybe the next one.

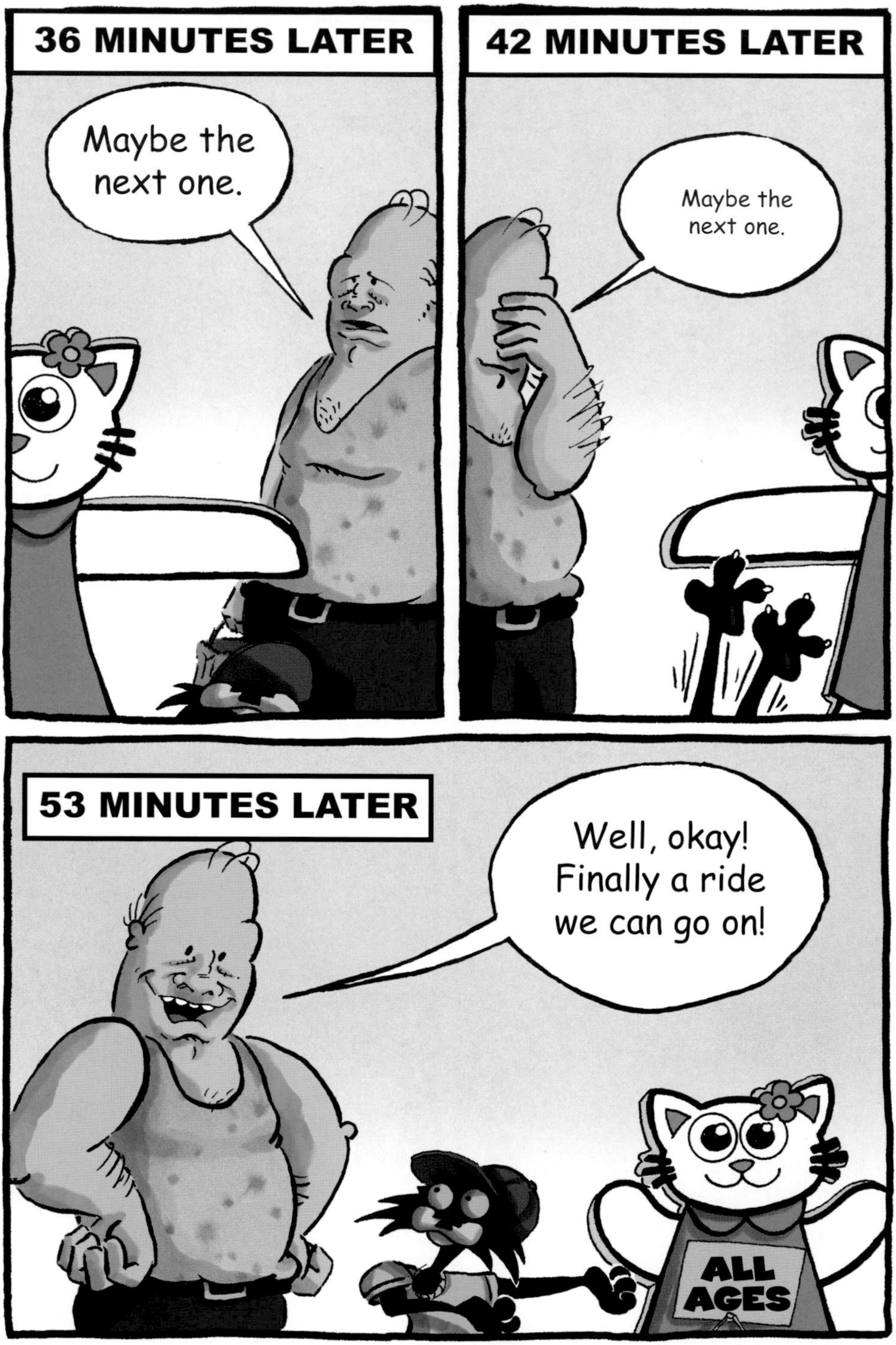
36 MINUTES LATER
Maybe the next one.
42 MINUTES LATER
Maybe the next one.
53 MINUTES LATER
Well, okay! Finally a ride we can go on!
ALL AGES

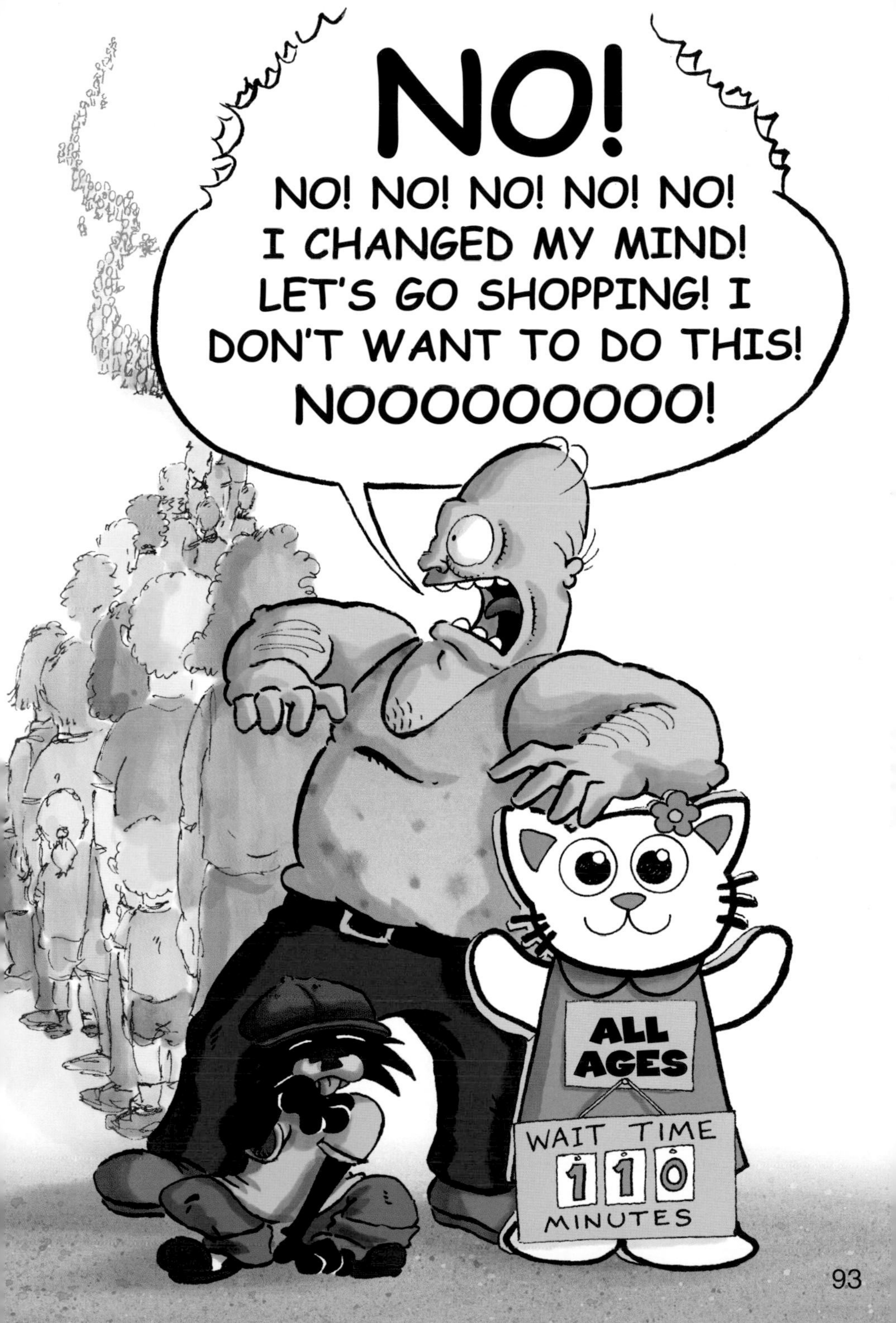
NO!
NO! NO! NO! NO! NO!
I CHANGED MY MIND!
LET'S GO SHOPPING! I
DON'T WANT TO DO THIS!
NOOOOOOOOO!
ALL AGES
WAIT TIME
110
MINUTES

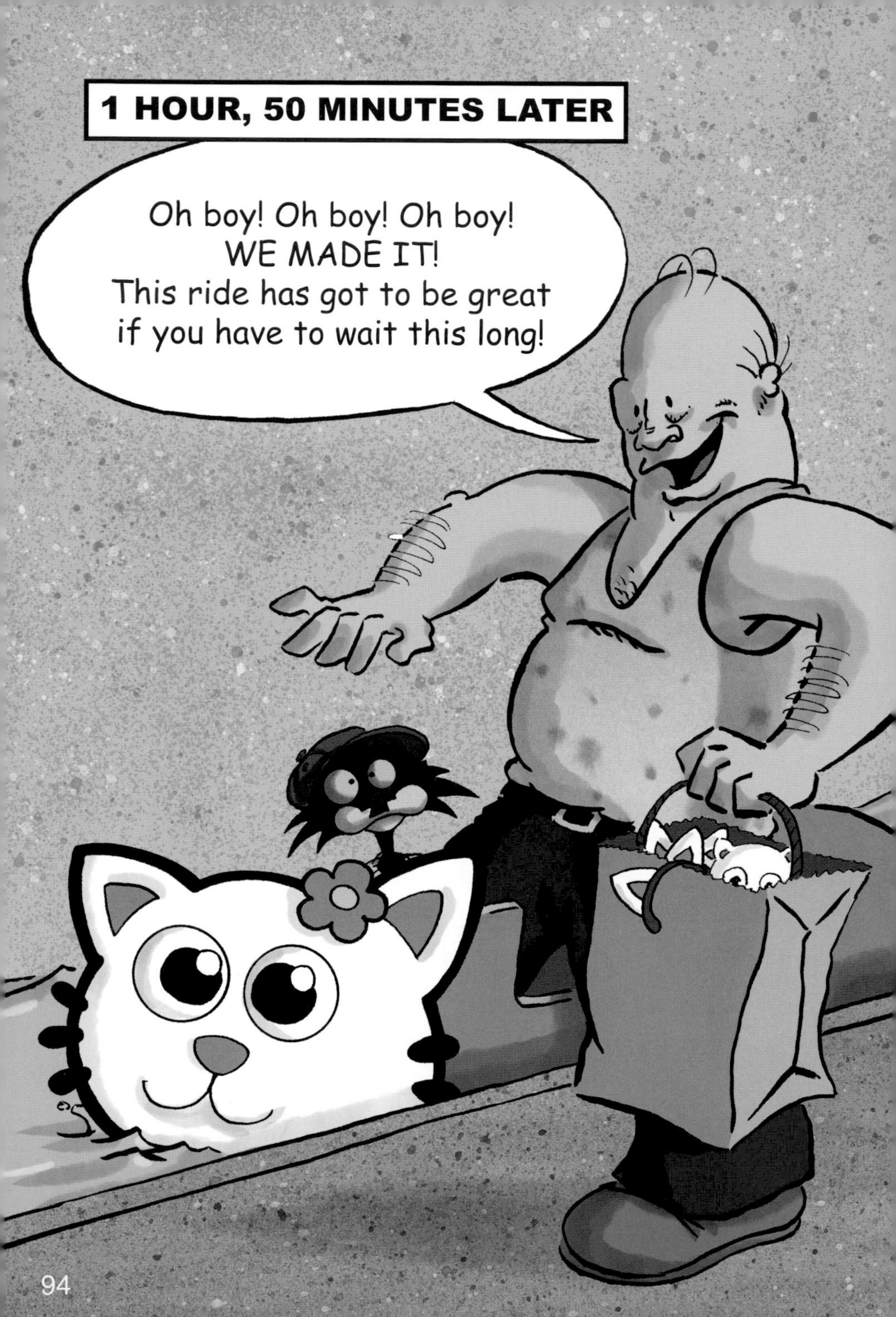
1 HOUR, 50 MINUTES LATER
Oh boy! Oh boy! Oh boy! WE MADE IT! This ride has got to be great if you have to wait this long!

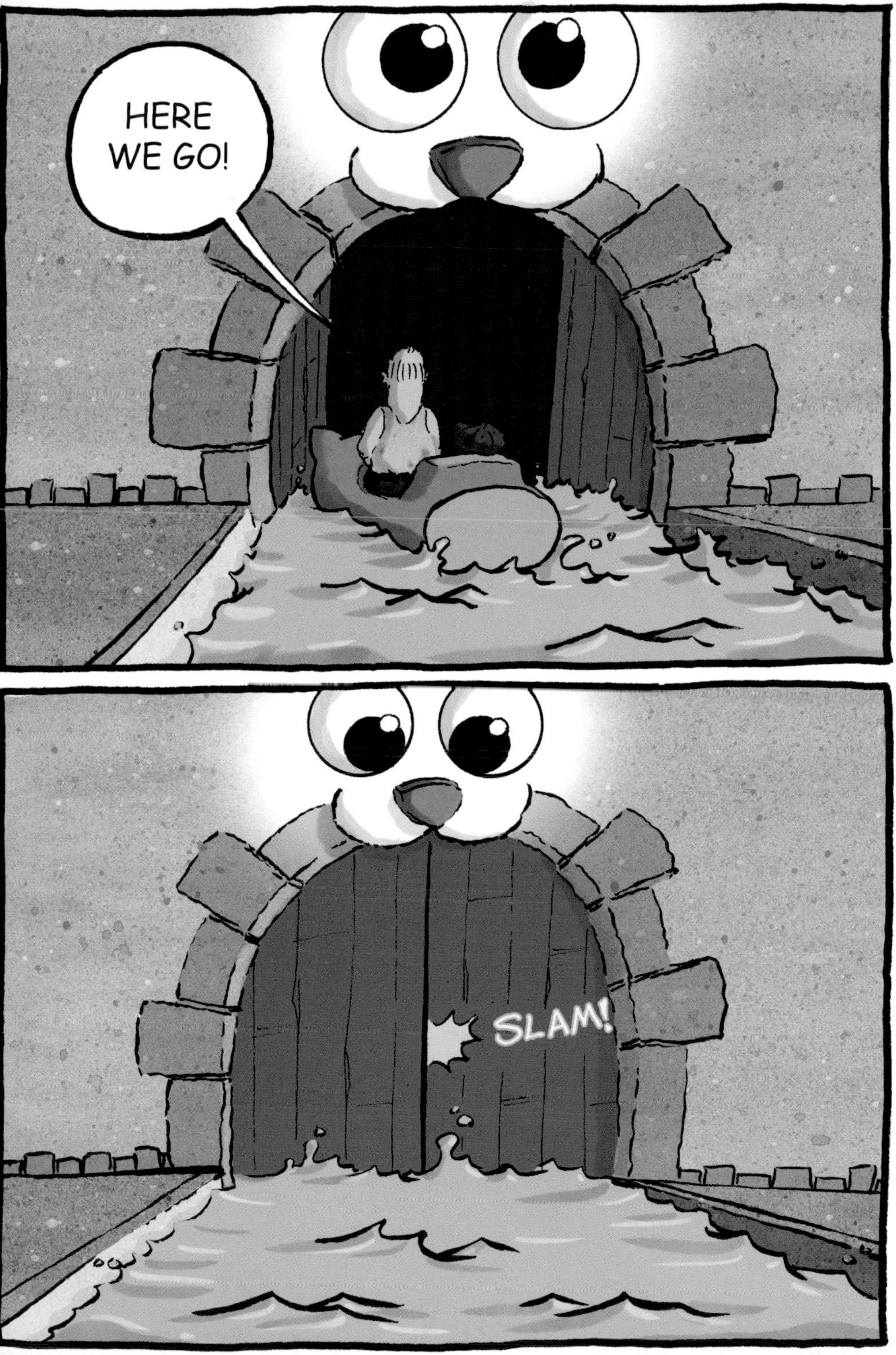
HERE WE GO!
SLAM!

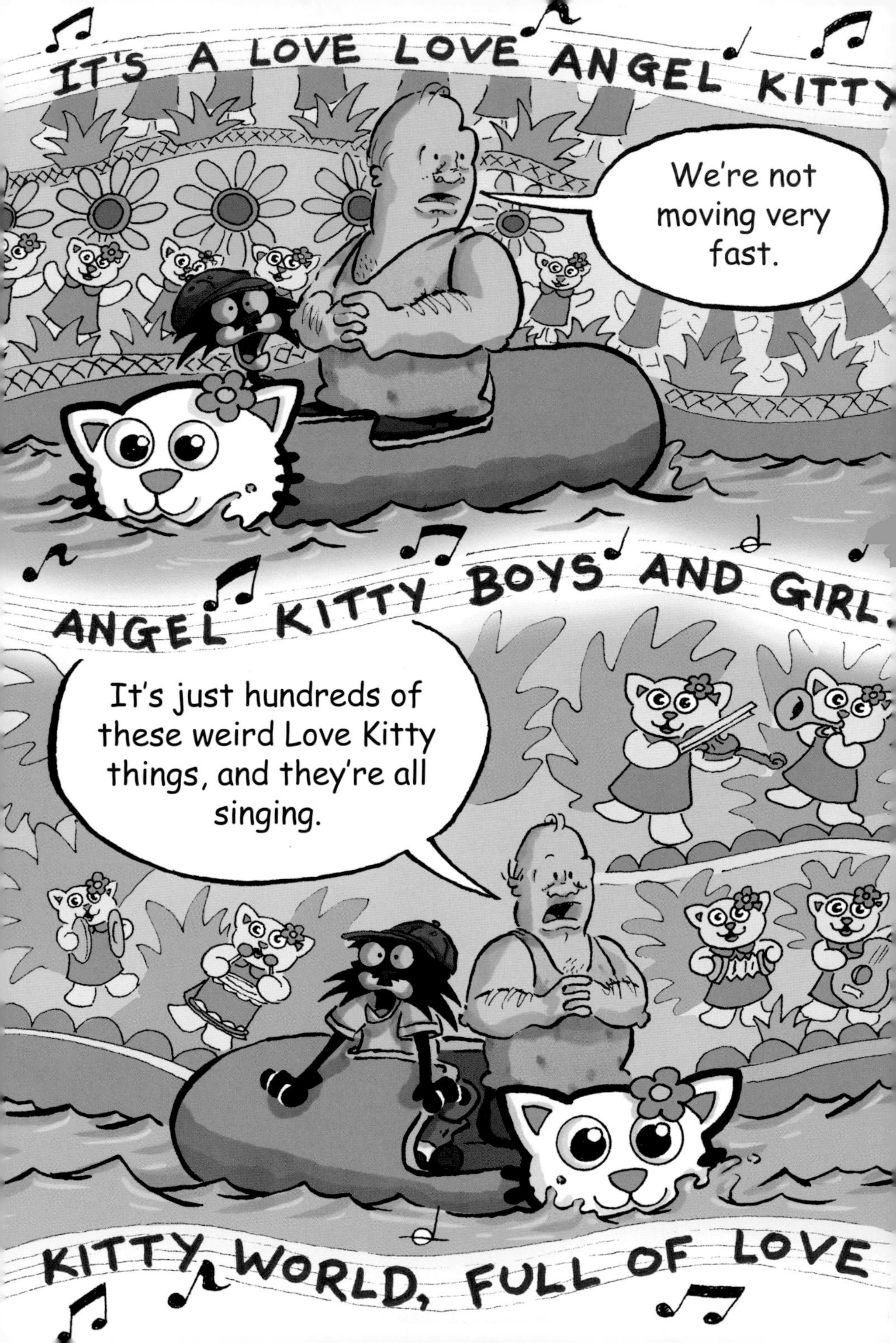
IT'S A LOVE LOVE ANGEL KITTY
We're not moving very fast.
ANGEL KITTY BOYS AND GIRL
It's just hundreds of these weird Love Kitty things, and they're all singing.
KITTY WORLD, FULL OF LOVE

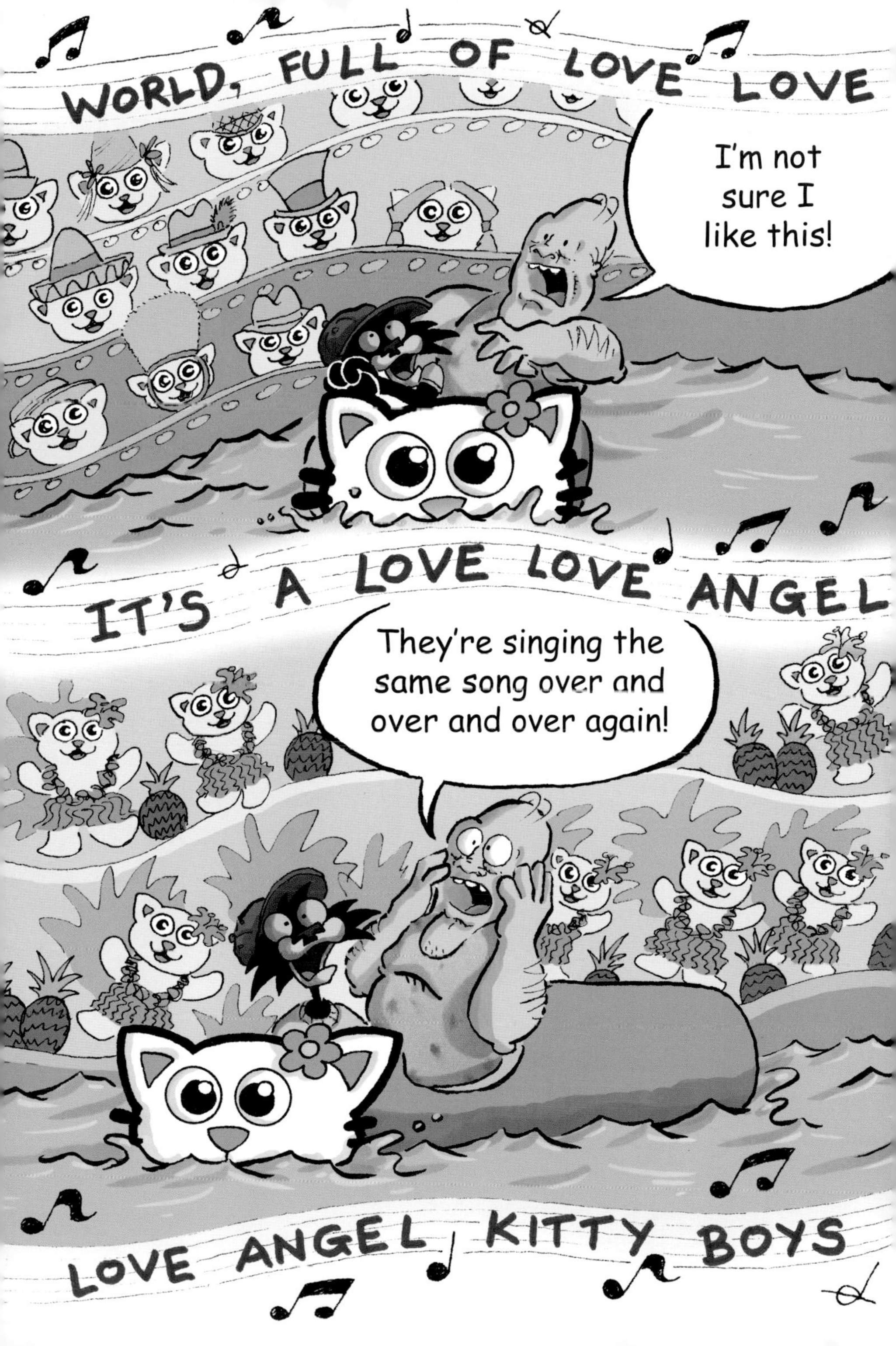
WORLD, FULL OF LOVE LOVE
I'm not sure I like this!
IT'S A LOVE LOVE ANGEL
They're singing the same song over and over and over again!
LOVE ANGEL KITTY BOYS

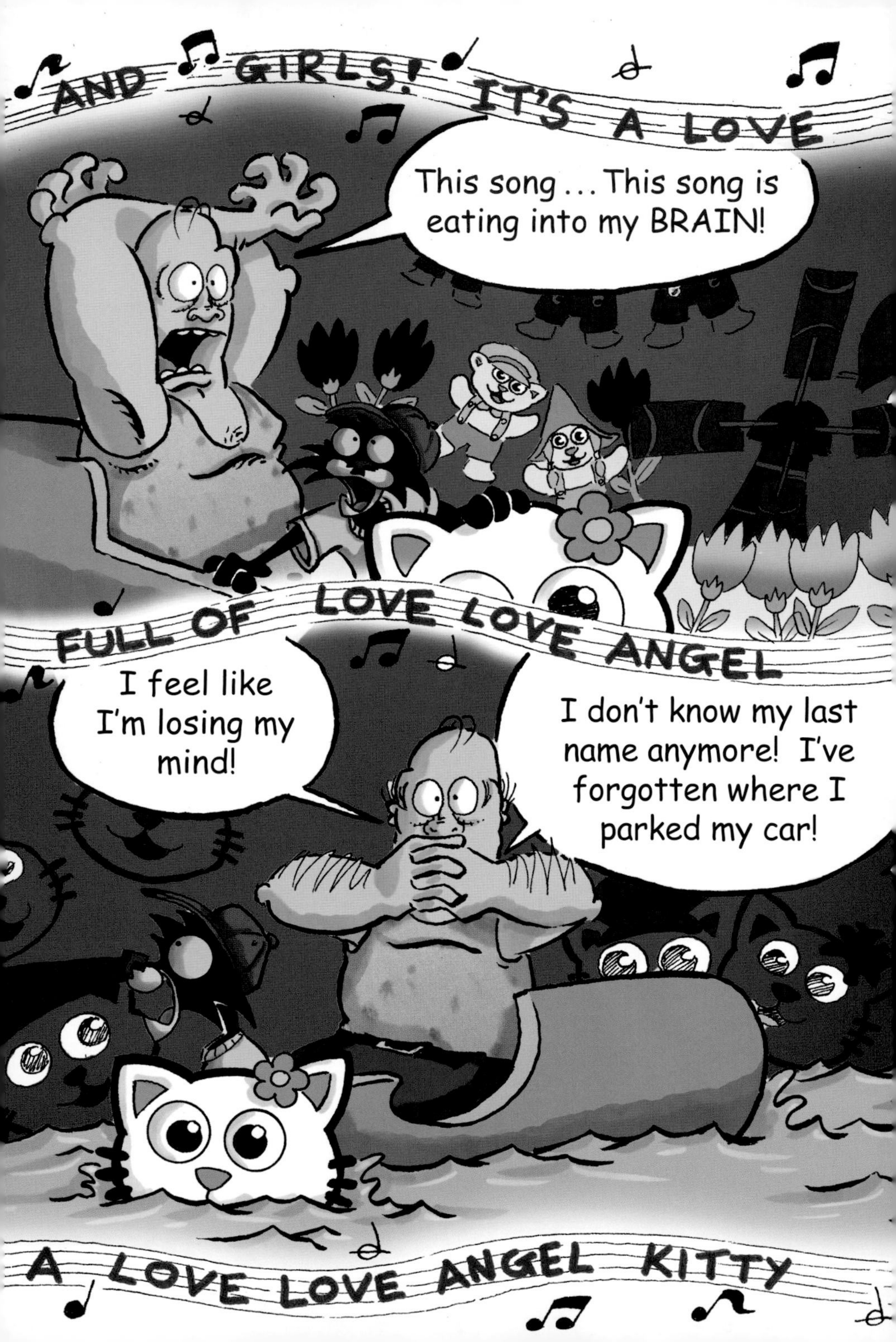
AND GIRLS! IT'S A LOVE
This song . . . This song is eating into my BRAIN!
FULL OF LOVE LOVE ANGEL
I feel like I'm losing my mind!
I don't know my last name anymore! I've forgotten where I parked my car!
A LOVE LOVE ANGEL KITTY

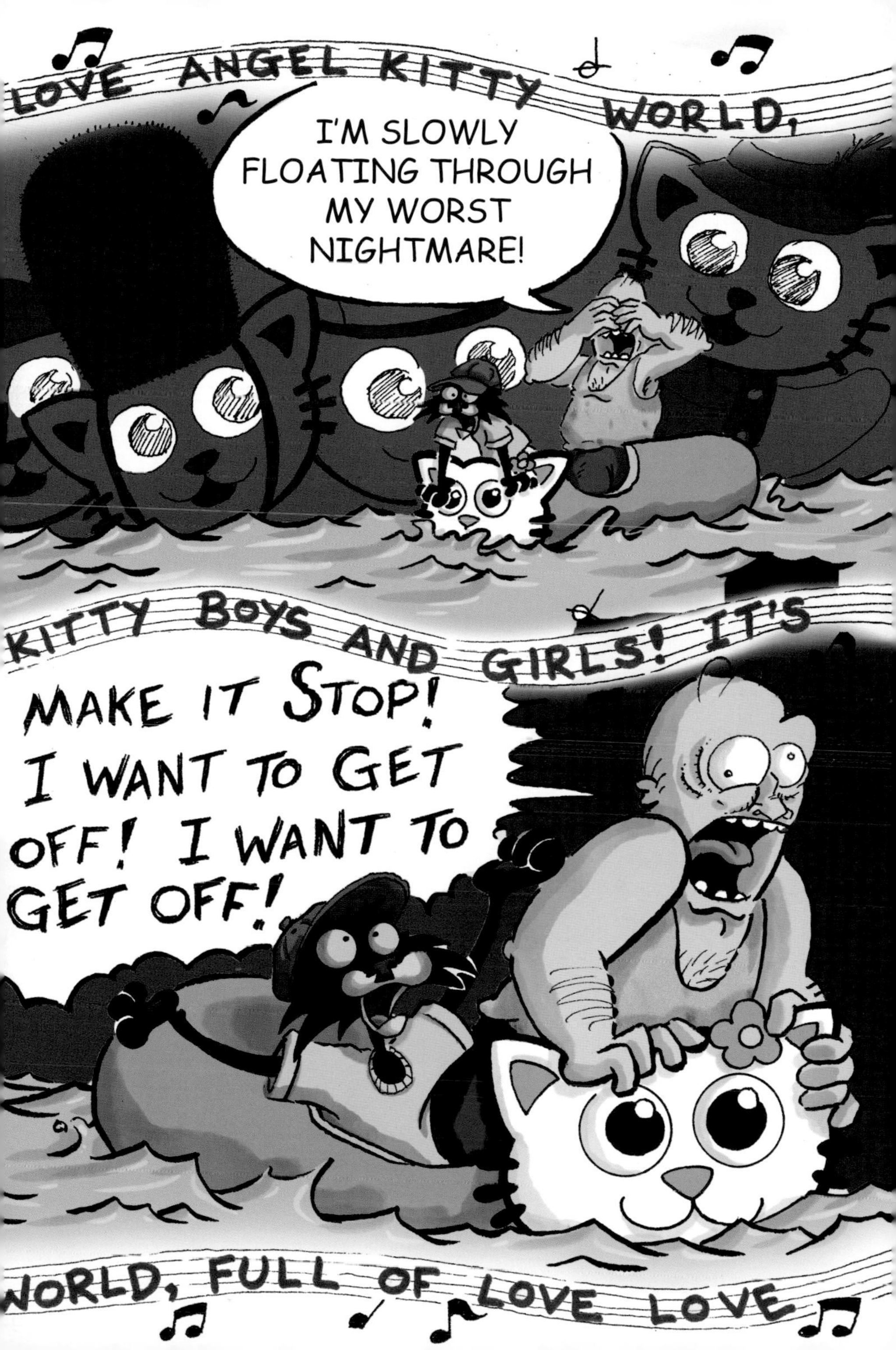

LOVE ANGEL KITTY WORLD,
I'M SLOWLY FLOATING THROUGH MY WORST NIGHTMARE!
KITTY BOYS AND GIRLS! IT'S
MAKE IT STOP! I WANT TO GET OFF! I WANT TO GET OFF!
WORLD, FULL OF LOVE LOVE

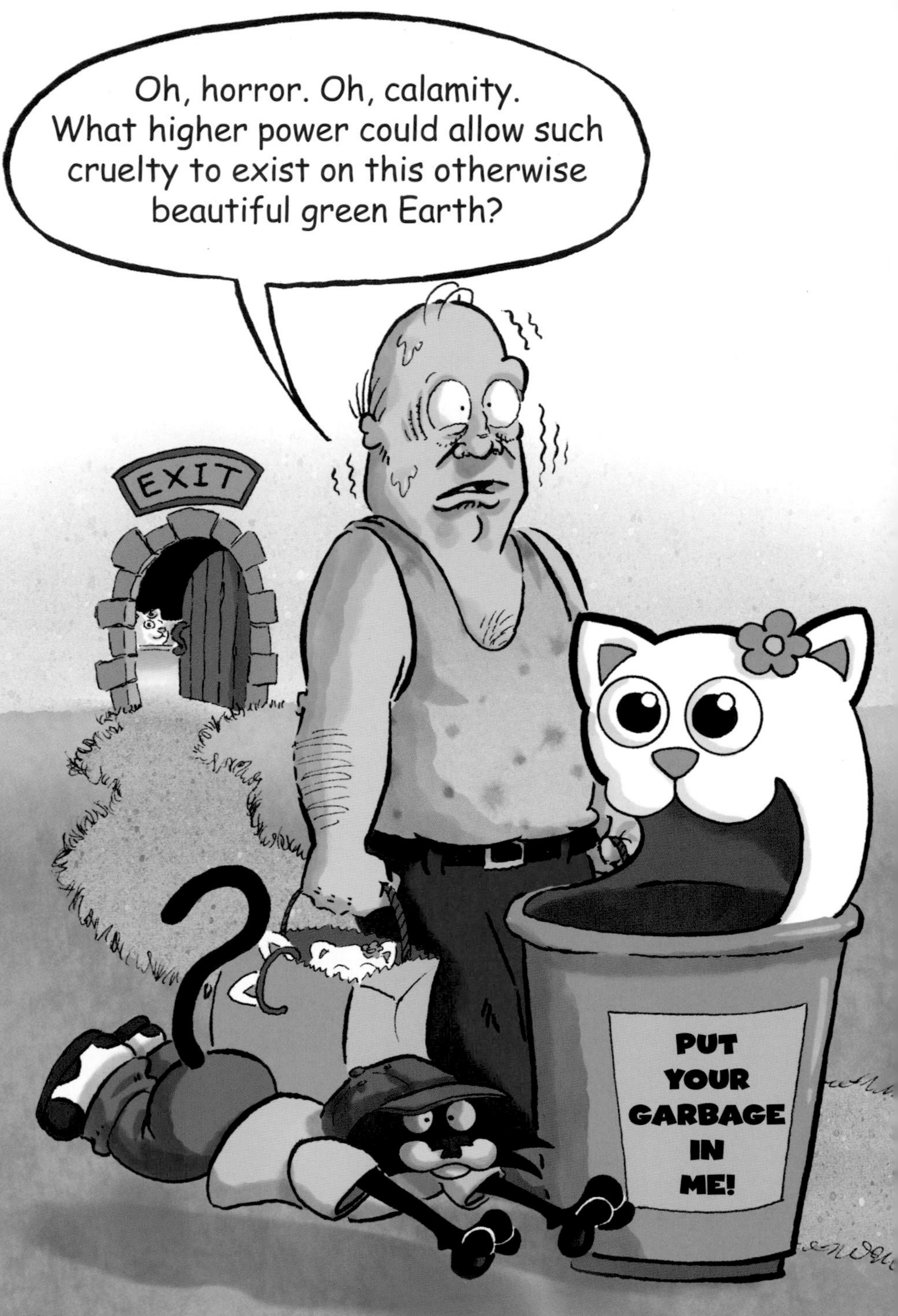
Oh, horror. Oh, calamity. What higher power could allow such cruelty to exist on this otherwise beautiful green Earth?
EXIT
PUT YOUR GARBAGE IN ME!

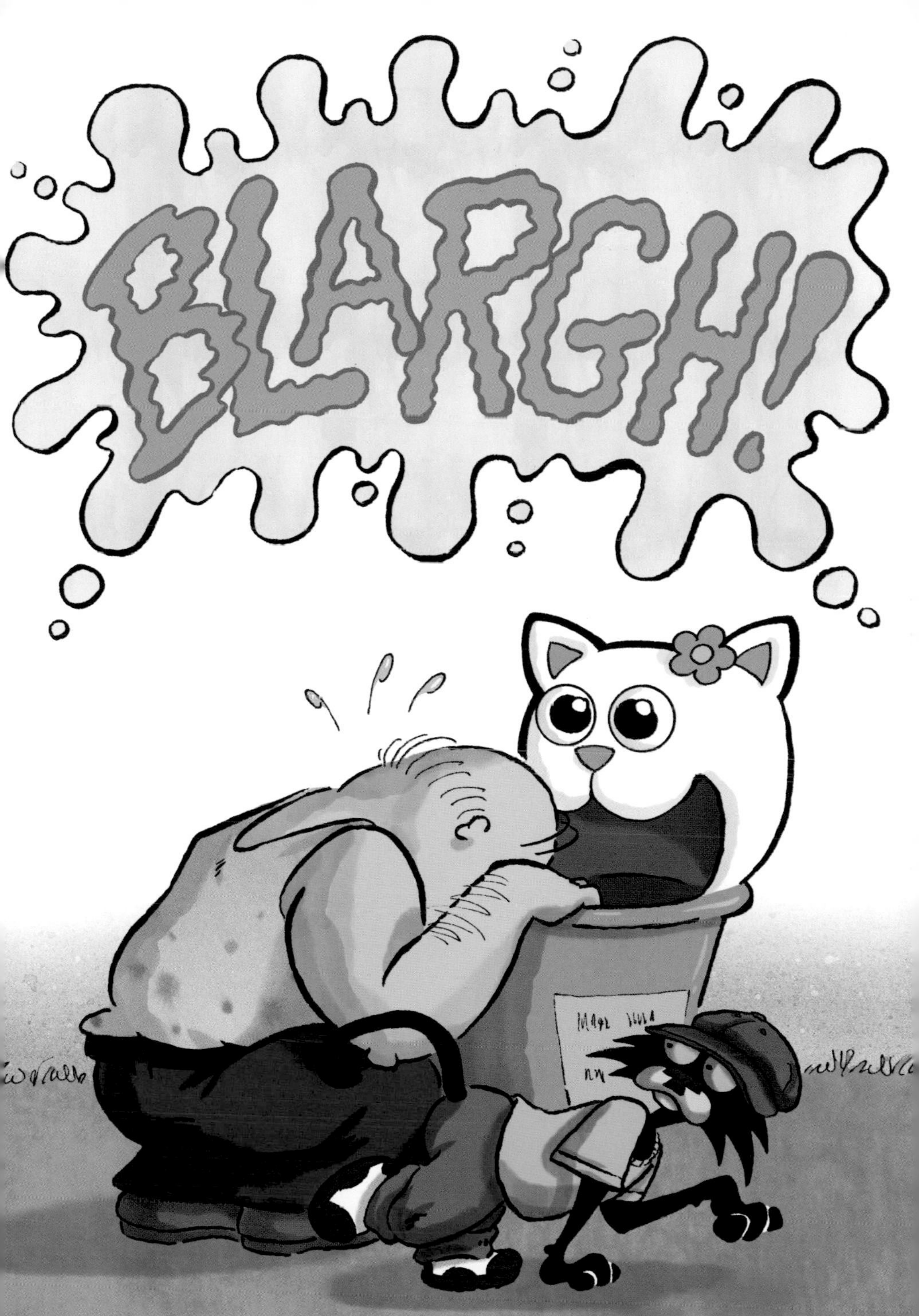
BLARGH!

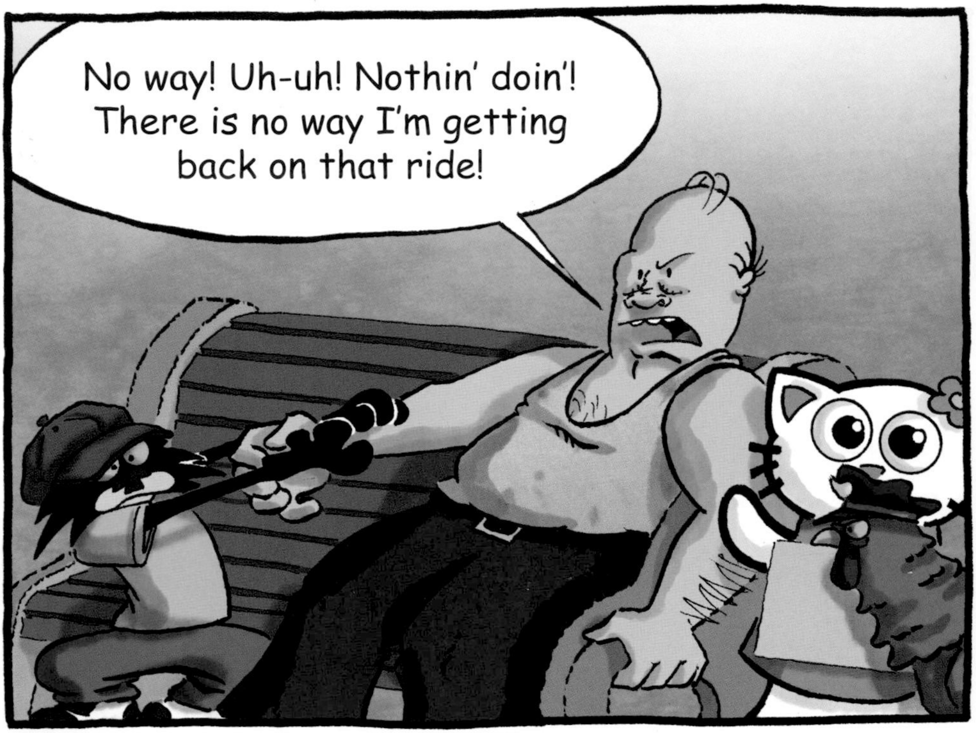
No way! Uh-uh! Nothin' doin'! There is no way I'm getting back on that ride!

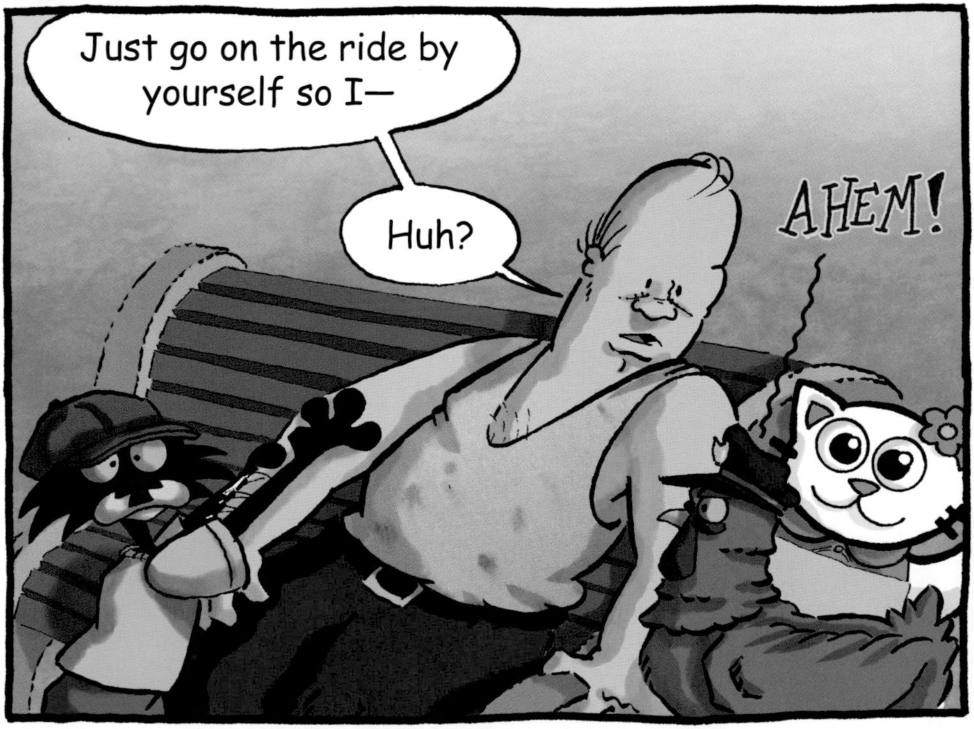
Just go on the ride by yourself so I—
Huh?
AHEM!

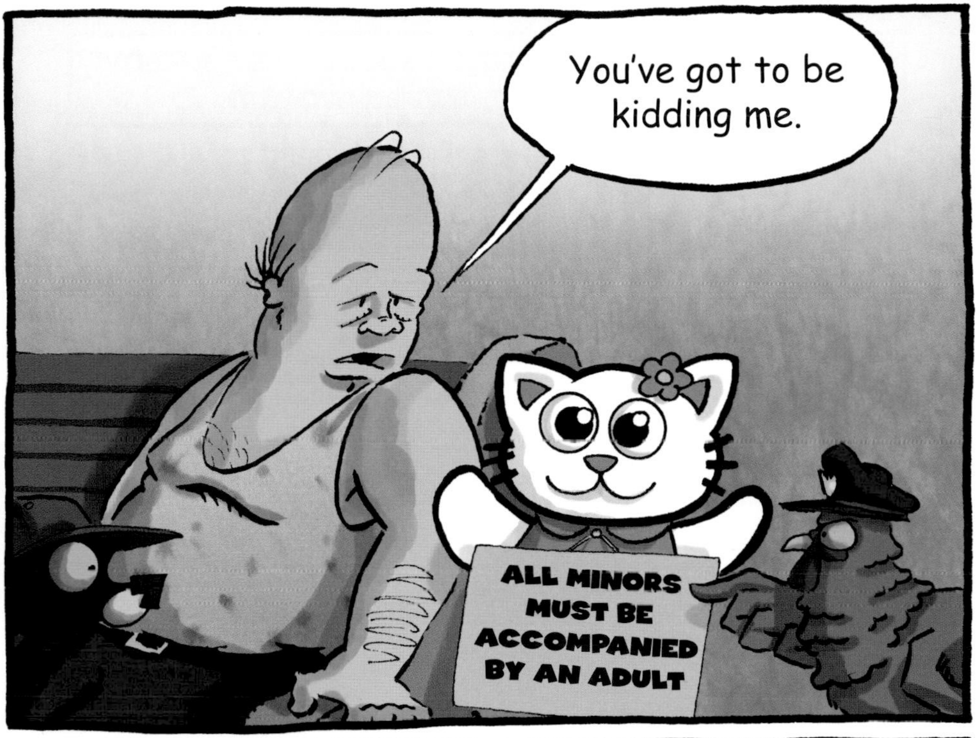
You've got to be kidding me.
ALL MINORS MUST BE ACCOMPANIED BY AN ADULT

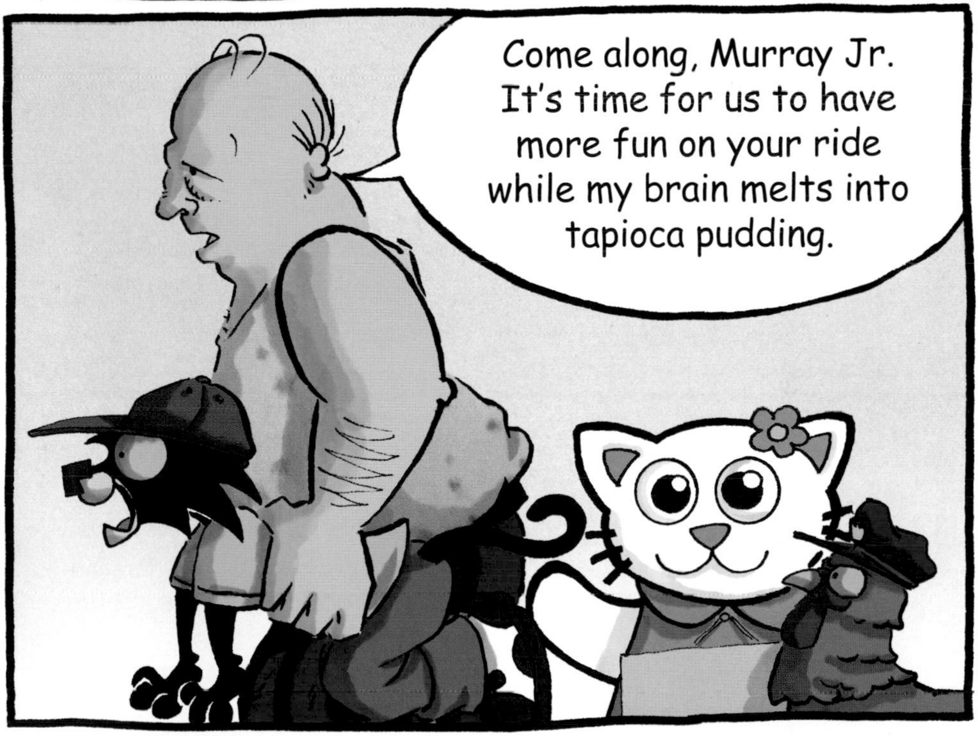
Come along, Murray Jr. It's time for us to have more fun on your ride while my brain melts into tapioca pudding.

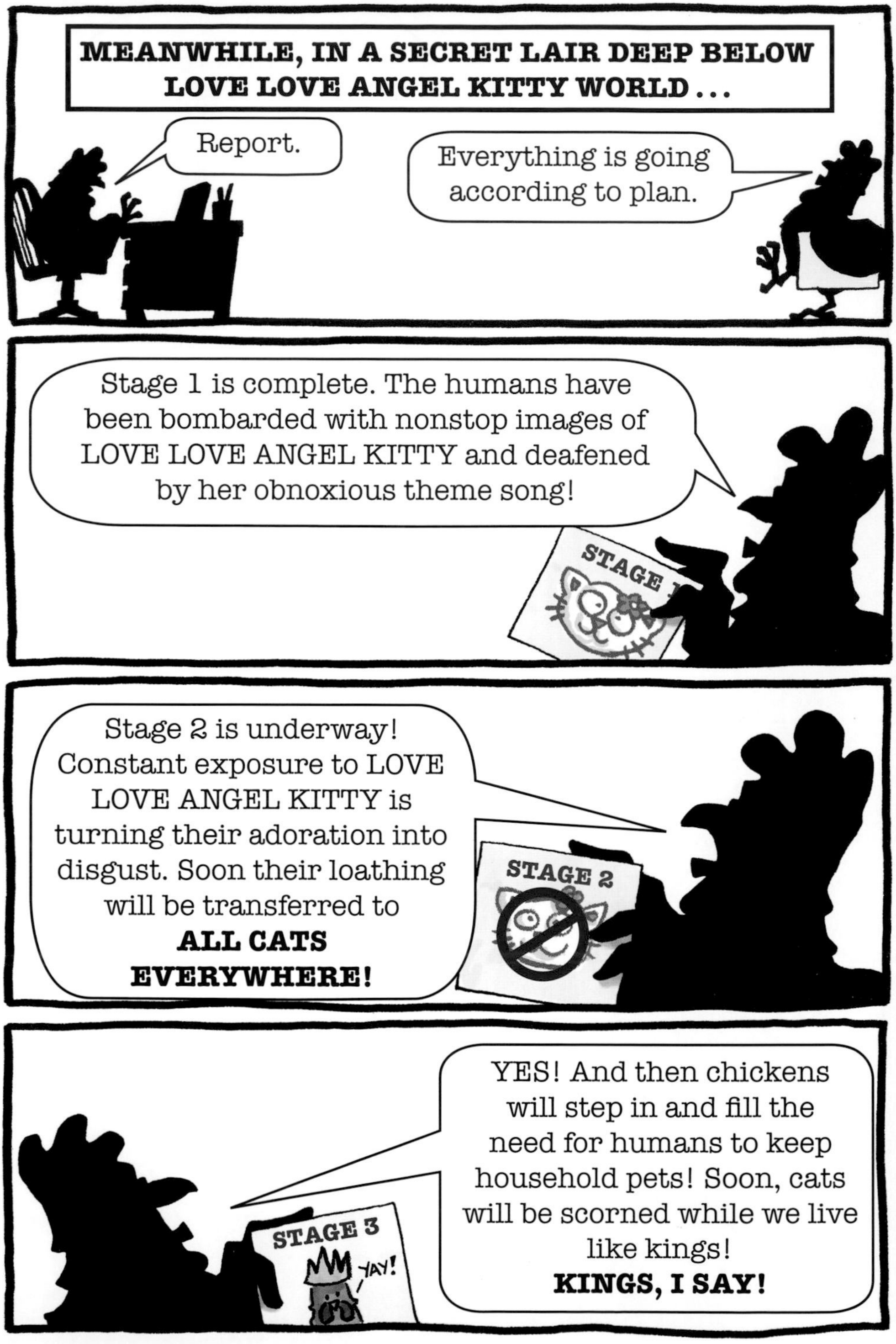

MEANWHILE, IN A SECRET LAIR DEEP BELOW LOVE LOVE ANGEL KITTY WORLD . . .
Report.
Everything is going according to plan.
Stage 1 is complete. The humans have been bombarded with nonstop images of LOVE LOVE ANGEL KITTY and deafened by her obnoxious theme song!
STAGE 1
Stage 2 is underway! Constant exposure to LOVE LOVE ANGEL KITTY is turning their adoration into disgust. Soon their loathing will be transferred to **ALL CATS EVERYWHERE!**
STAGE 2
YES! And then chickens will step in and fill the need for humans to keep household pets! Soon, cats will be scorned while we live like kings! **KINGS, I SAY!**
STAGE 3
YAY!

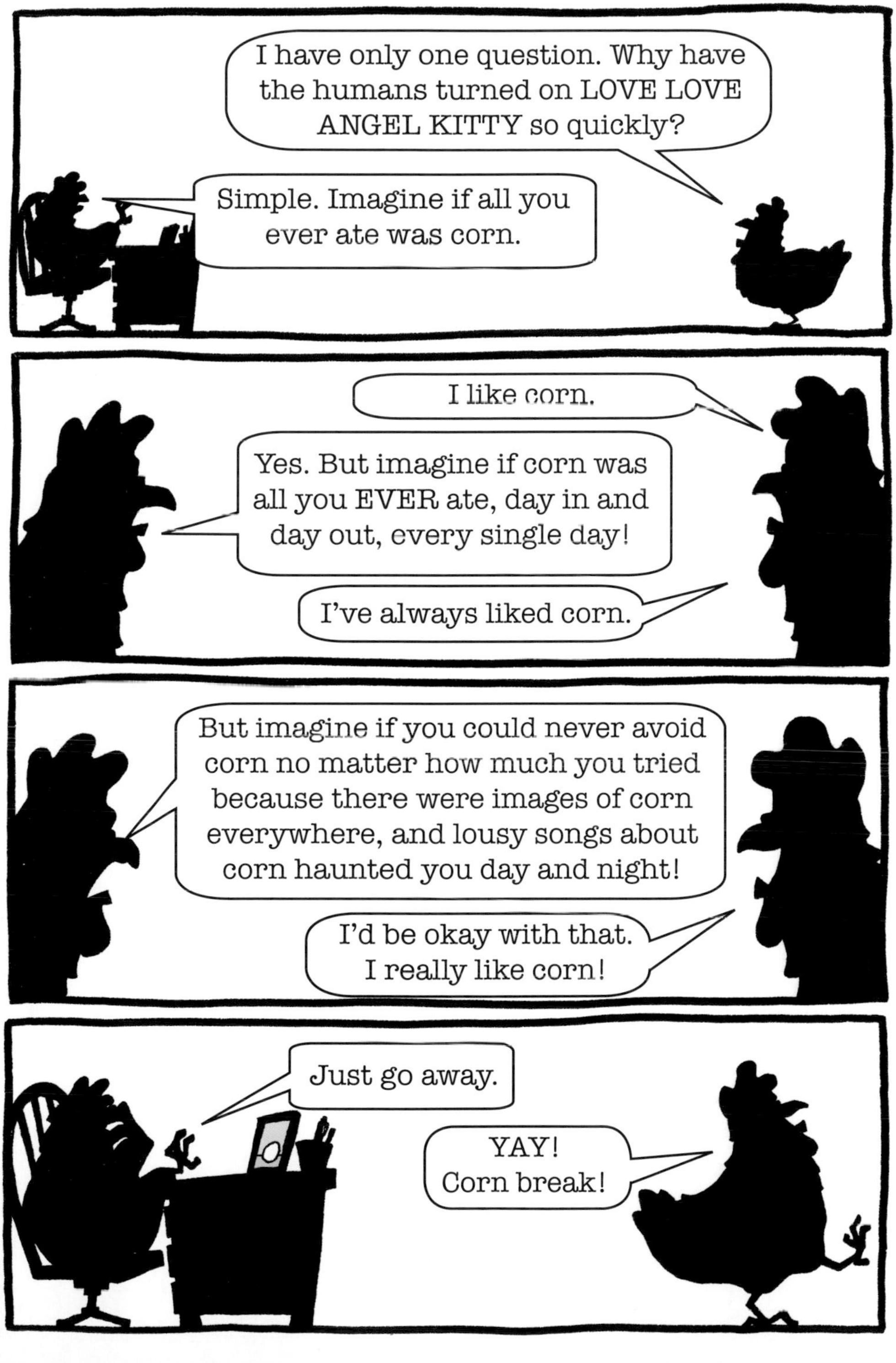
I have only one question. Why have the humans turned on LOVE LOVE ANGEL KITTY so quickly?
Simple. Imagine if all you ever ate was corn.
I like corn.
Yes. But imagine if corn was all you EVER ate, day in and day out, every single day!
I've always liked corn.
But imagine if you could never avoid corn no matter how much you tried because there were images of corn everywhere, and lousy songs about corn haunted you day and night!
I'd be okay with that. I really like corn!
Just go away.
YAY! Corn break!

• CHAPTER SEVEN •

14 RIDES LATER

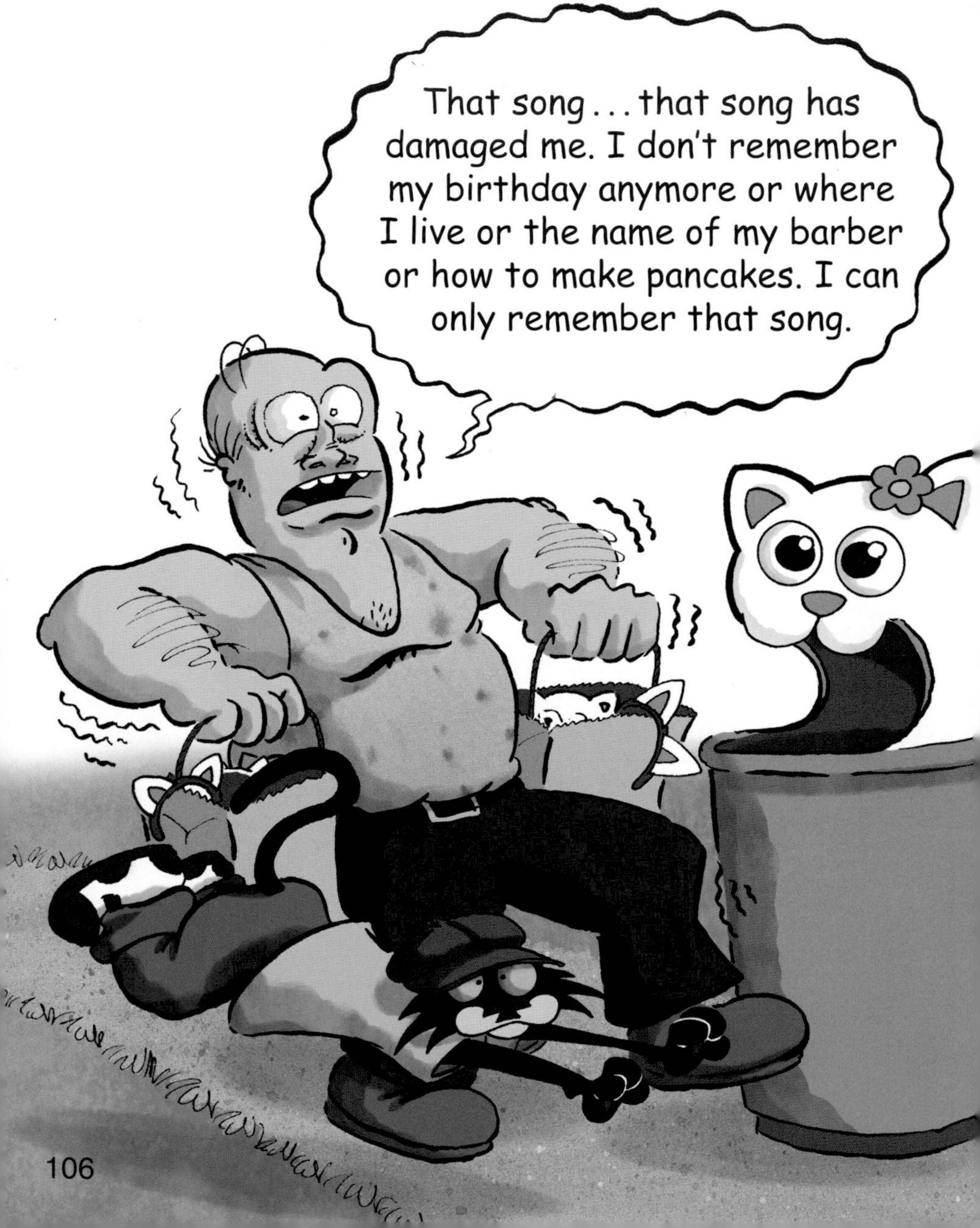
That song . . . that song has damaged me. I don't remember my birthday anymore or where I live or the name of my barber or how to make pancakes. I can only remember that song.

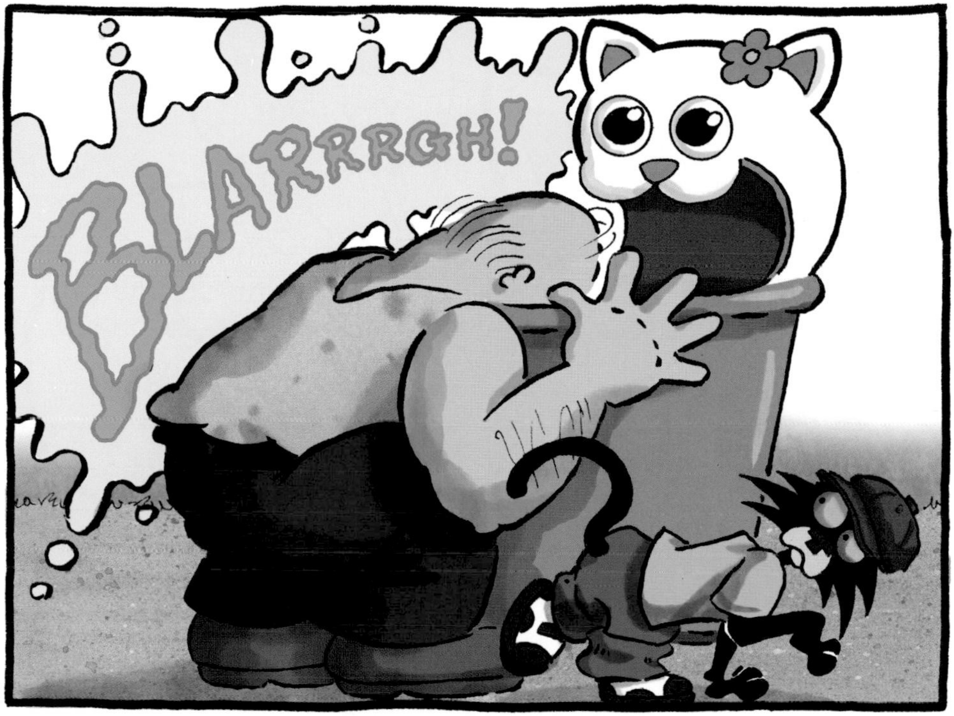
BLARRRGH!

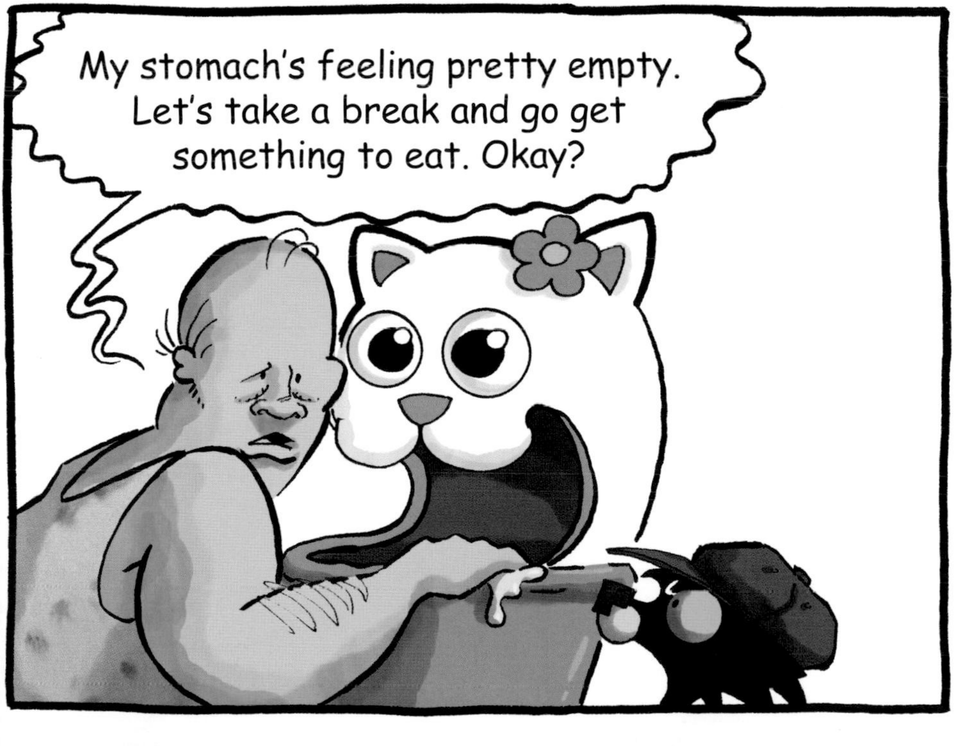
My stomach's feeling pretty empty. Let's take a break and go get something to eat. Okay?

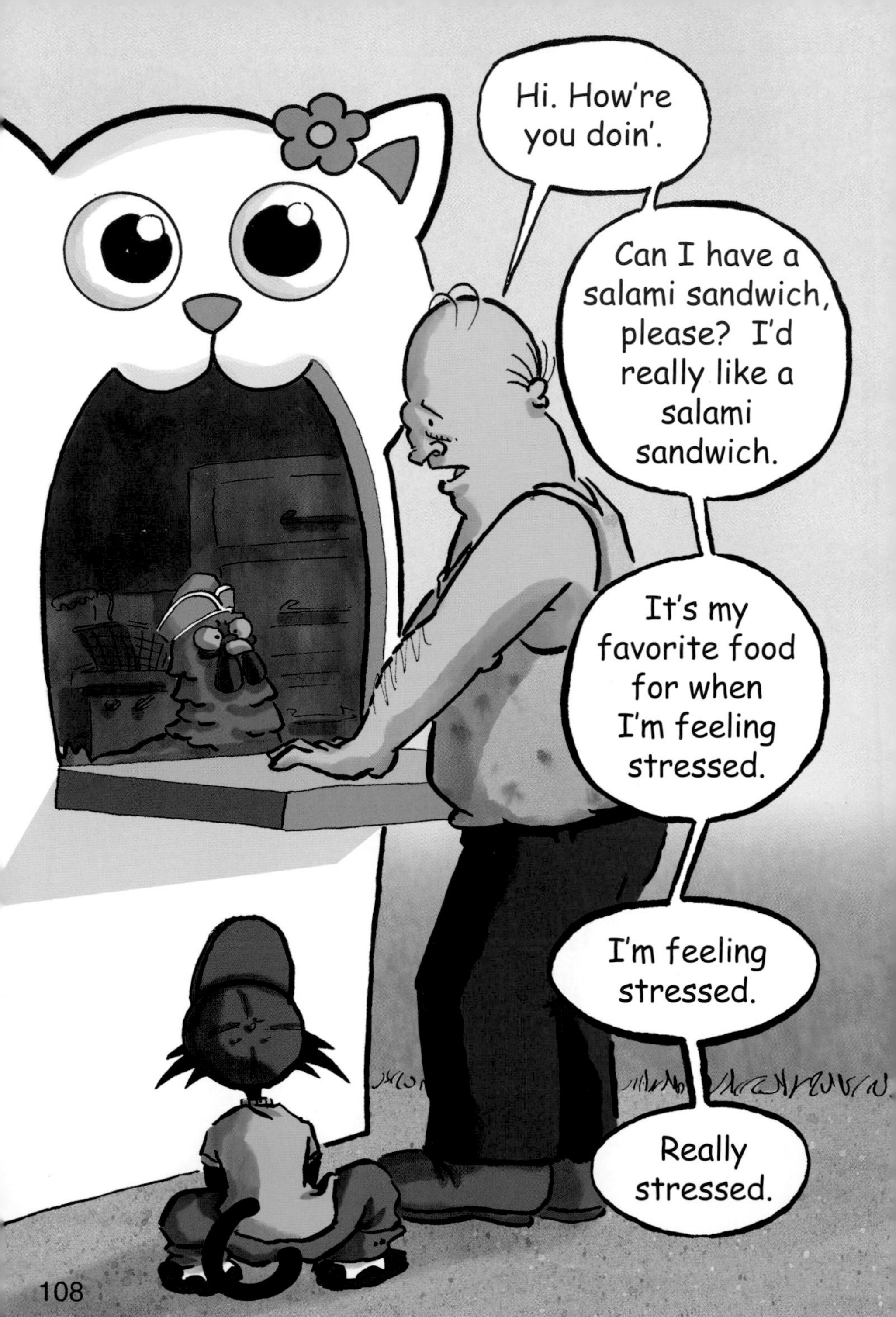
Hi. How're you doin'.
Can I have a salami sandwich, please? I'd really like a salami sandwich.
It's my favorite food for when I'm feeling stressed.
I'm feeling stressed.
Really stressed.

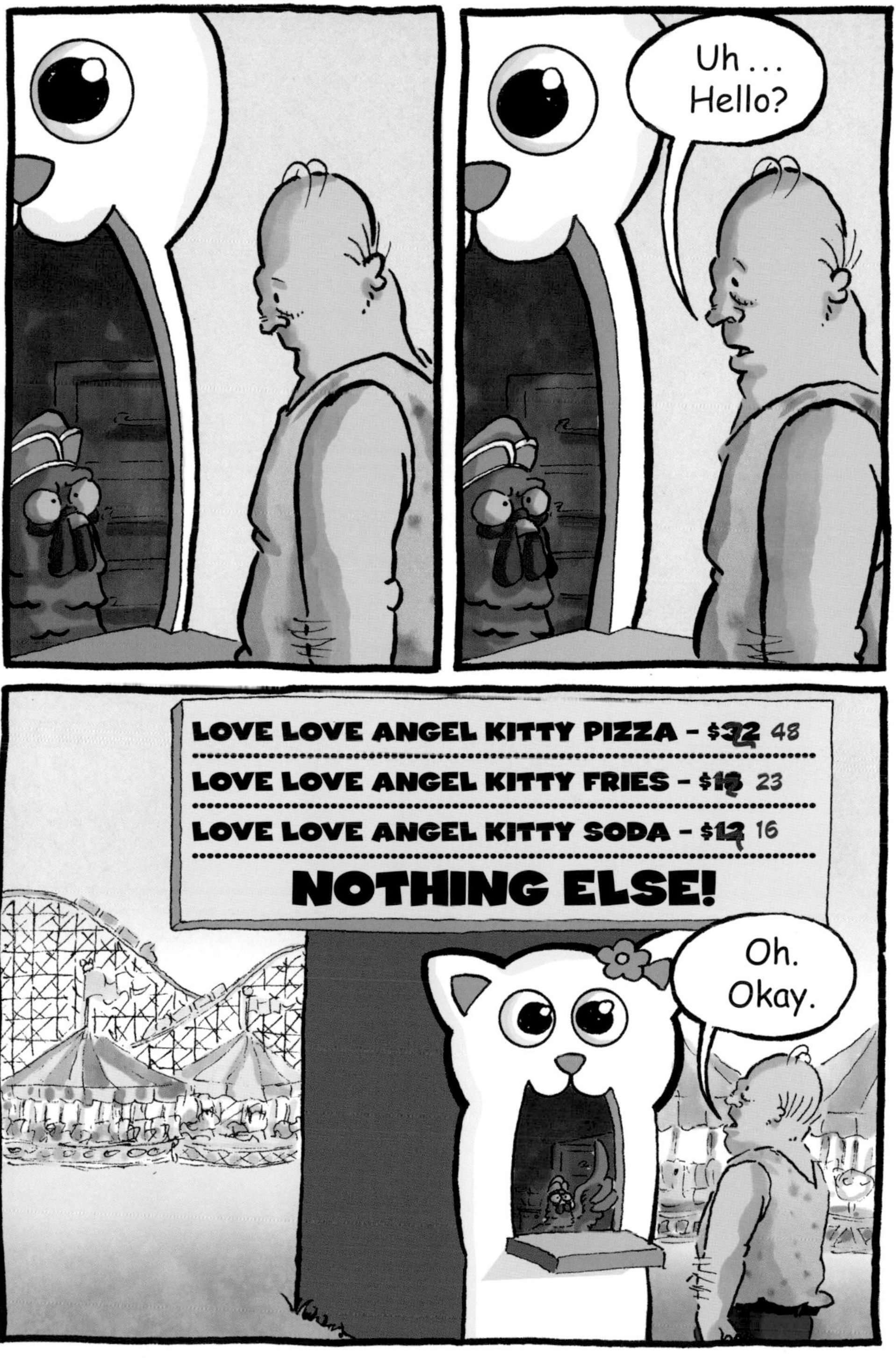
Uh . . .
Hello?
LOVE LOVE ANGEL KITTY PIZZA – $32 48
LOVE LOVE ANGEL KITTY FRIES – $18 23
LOVE LOVE ANGEL KITTY SODA – $12 16
NOTHING ELSE!
Oh.
Okay.

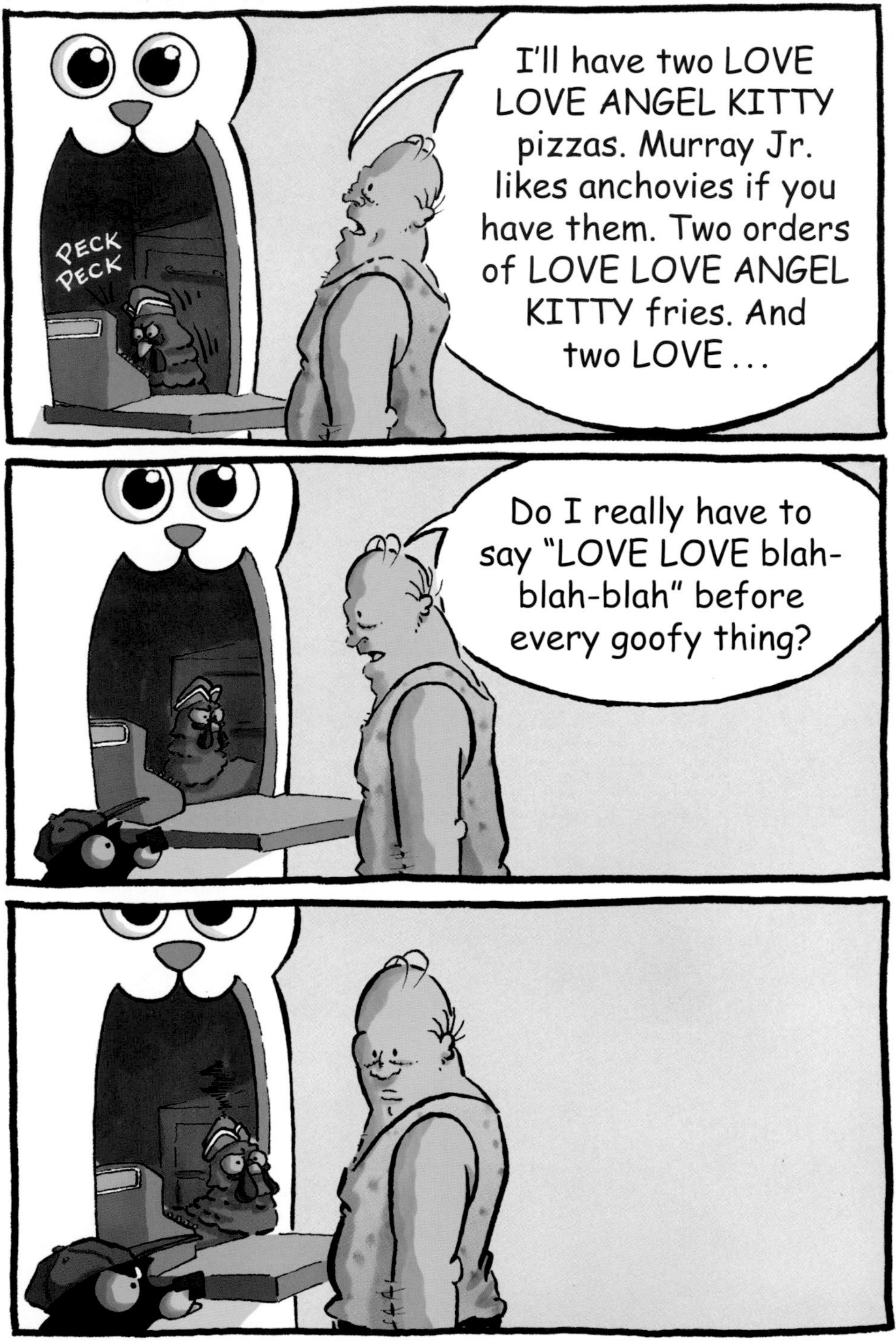
I'll have two LOVE LOVE ANGEL KITTY pizzas. Murray Jr. likes anchovies if you have them. Two orders of LOVE LOVE ANGEL KITTY fries. And two LOVE . . .
PECK PECK
Do I really have to say "LOVE LOVE blah-blah-blah" before every goofy thing?

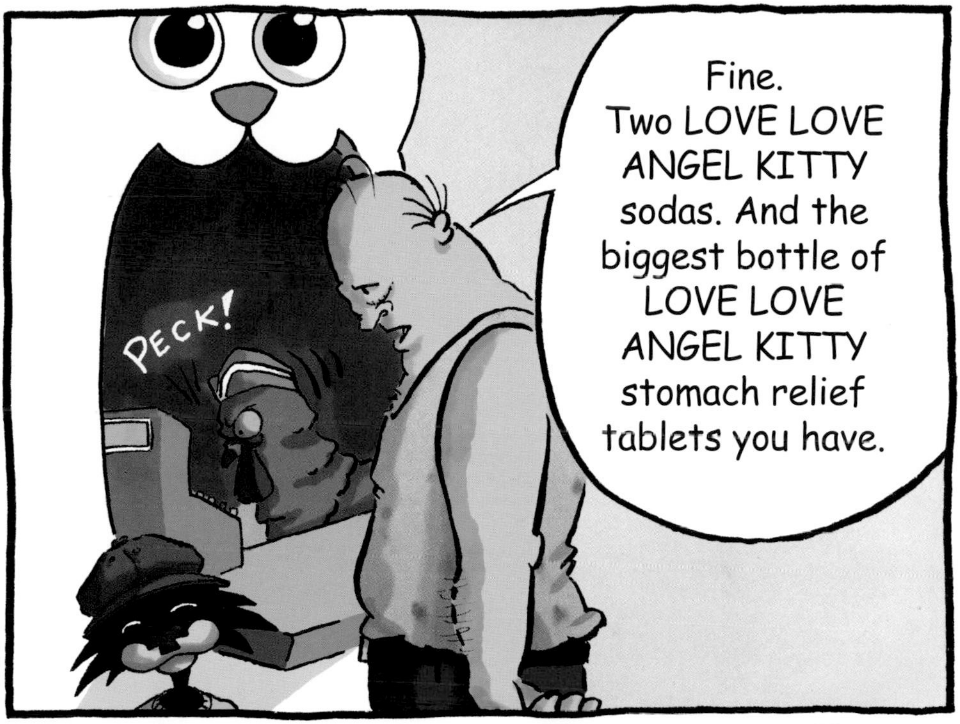
Fine.
Two LOVE LOVE ANGEL KITTY sodas. And the biggest bottle of LOVE LOVE ANGEL KITTY stomach relief tablets you have.
PECK!

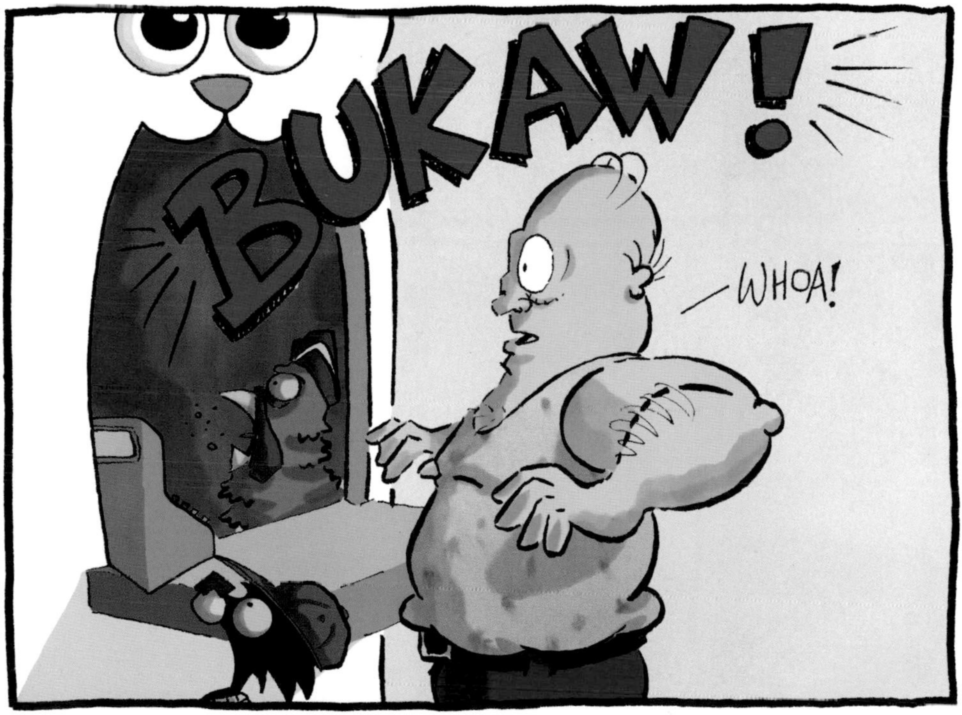
BUKAW!
WHOA!

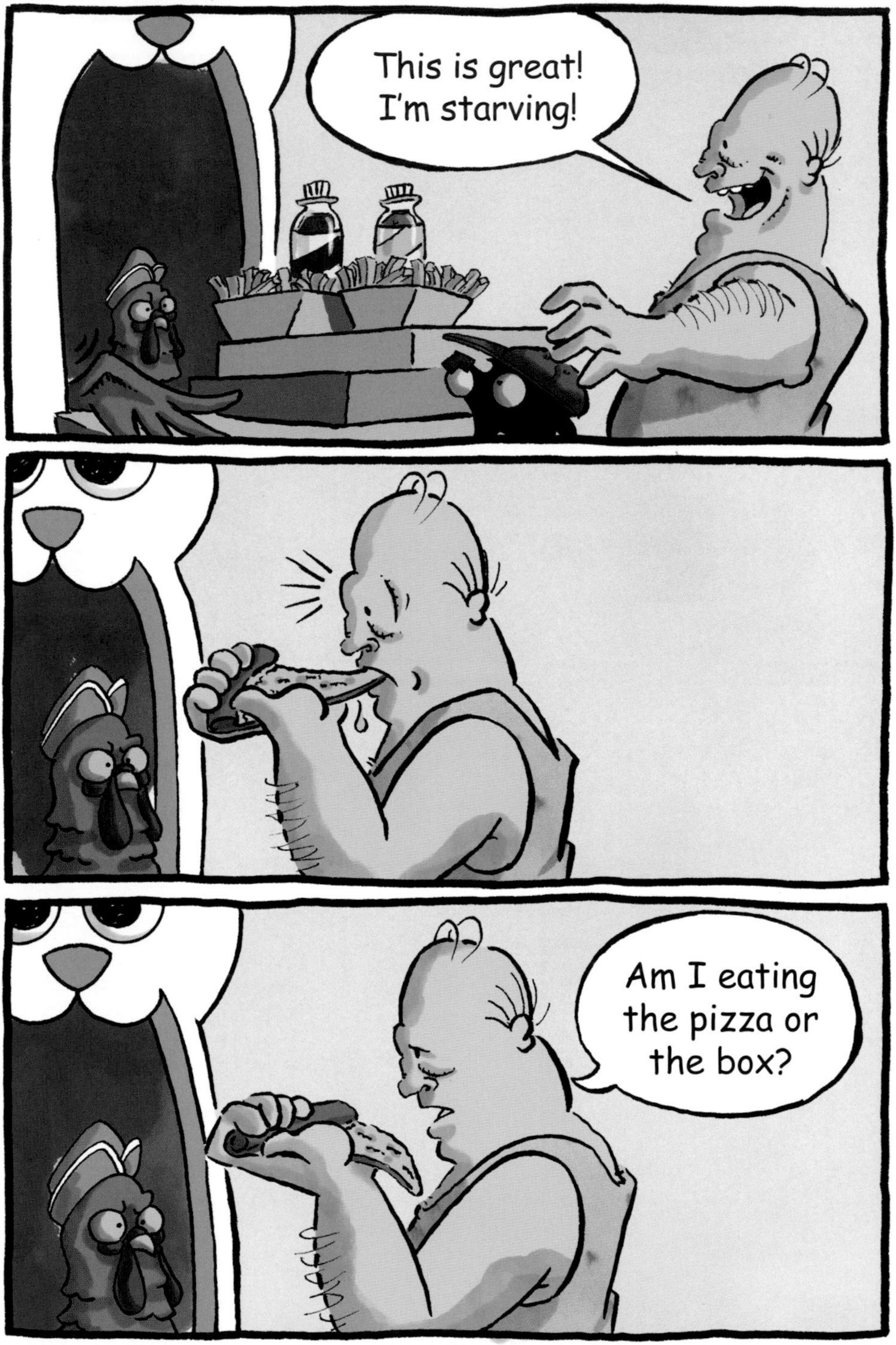
This is great! I'm starving!
Am I eating the pizza or the box?

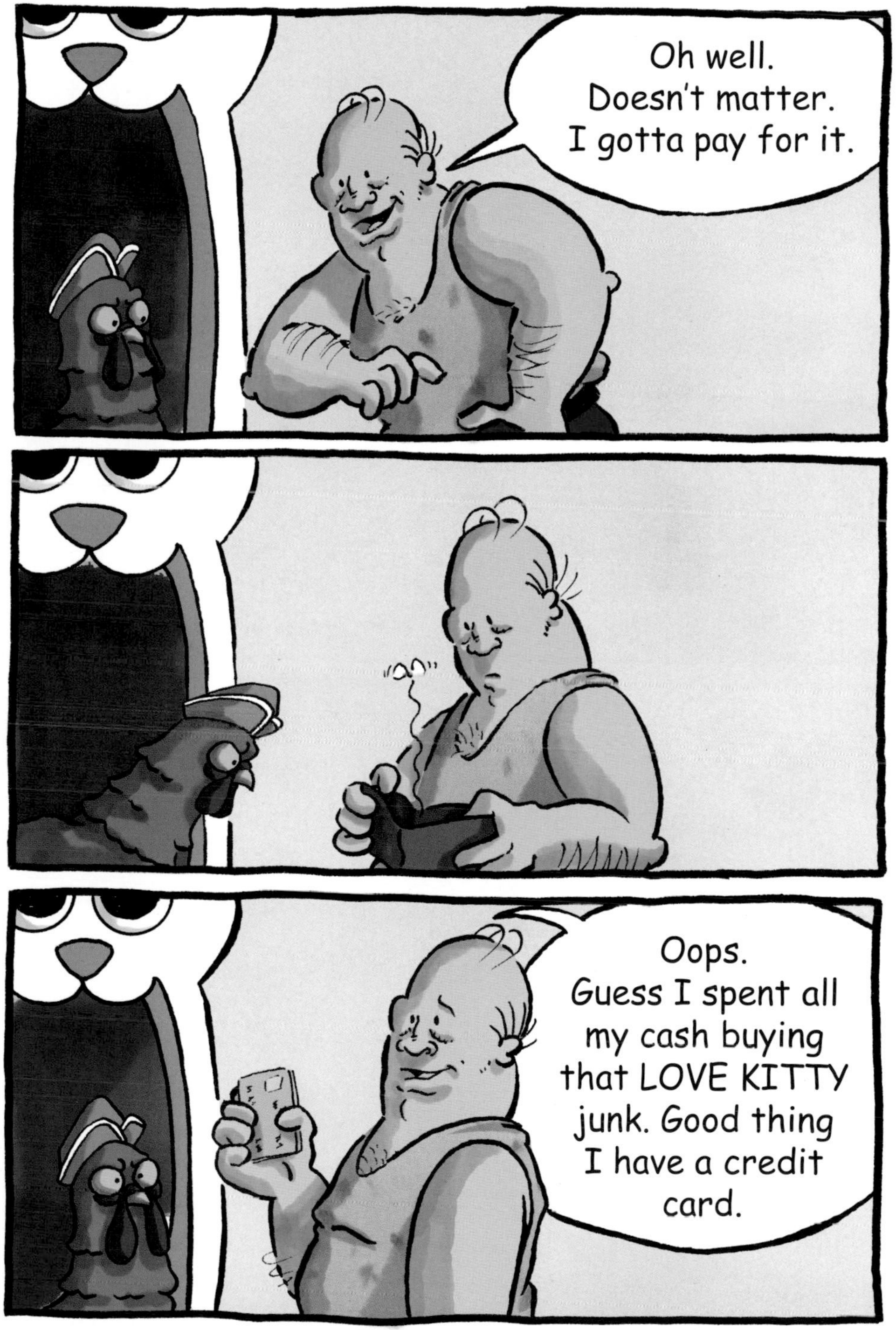
Oh well.
Doesn't matter.
I gotta pay for it.
Oops.
Guess I spent all
my cash buying
that LOVE KITTY
junk. Good thing
I have a credit
card.

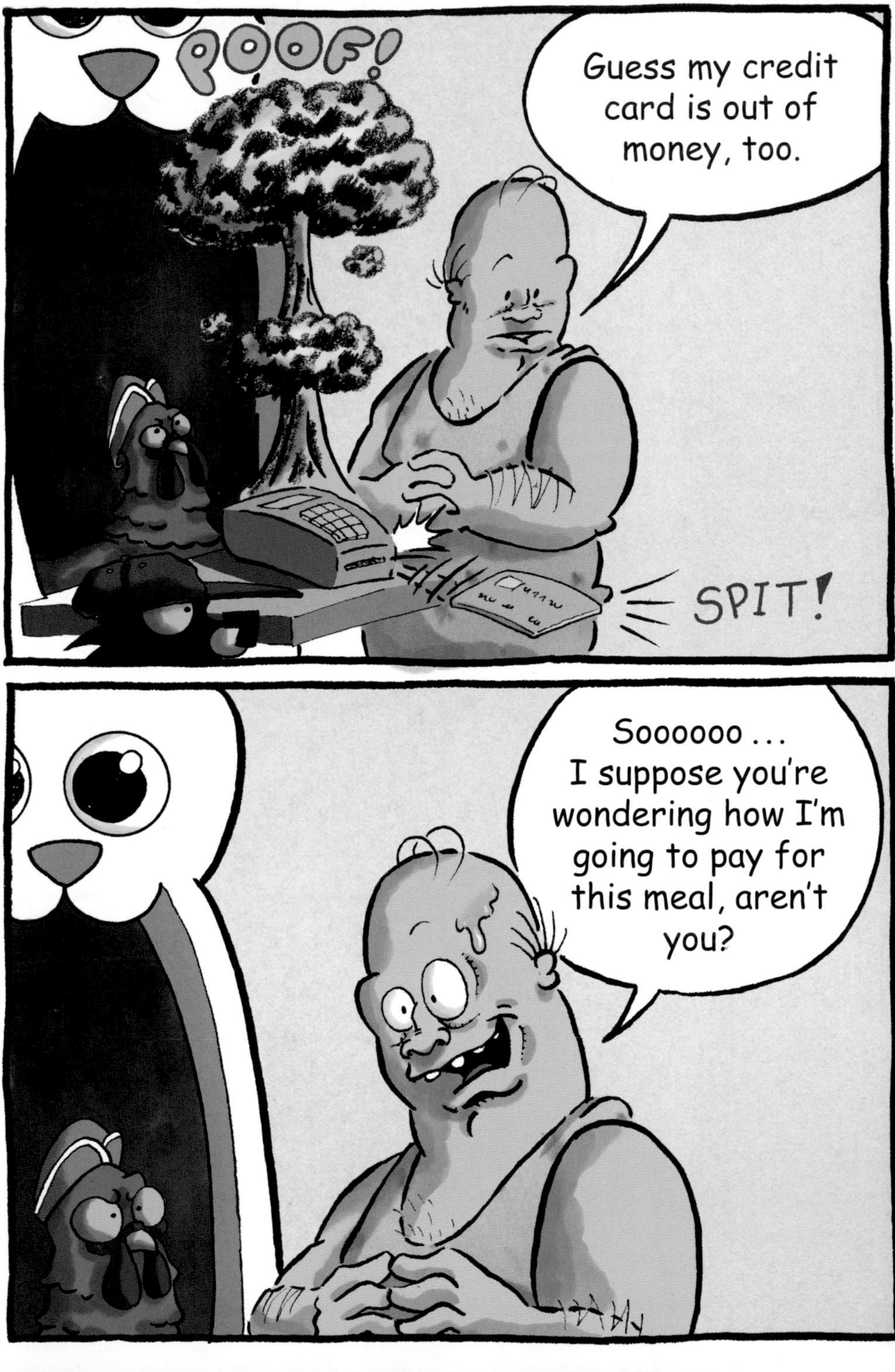
POOF!
Guess my credit card is out of money, too.
SPIT!
Soooooo . . . I suppose you're wondering how I'm going to pay for this meal, aren't you?

THE SEVEN STAGES OF UNCLE MURRAY'S PANIC • PART THREE

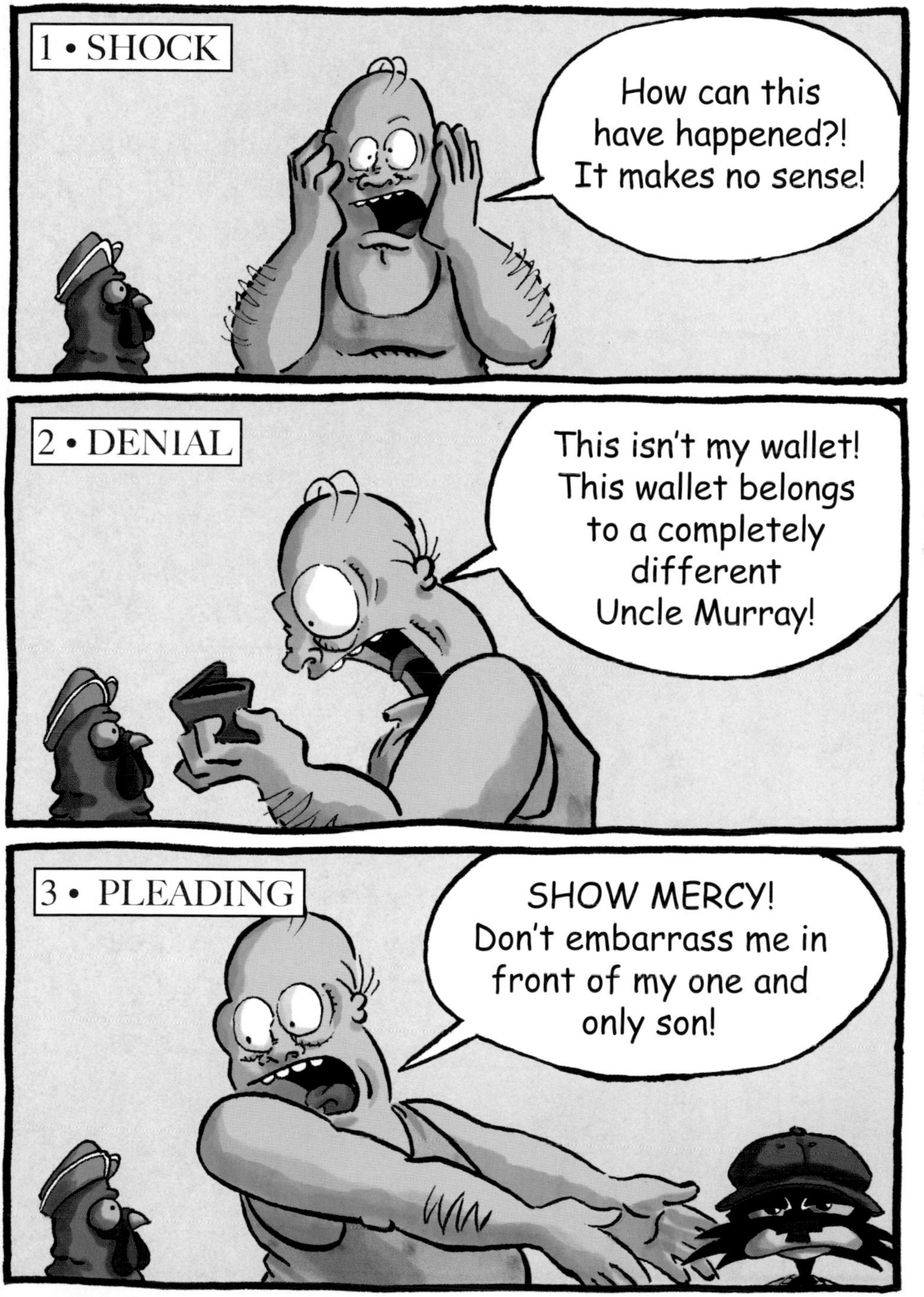
1 • SHOCK
How can this have happened?! It makes no sense!
2 • DENIAL
This isn't my wallet! This wallet belongs to a completely different Uncle Murray!
3 • PLEADING
SHOW MERCY! Don't embarrass me in front of my one and only son!

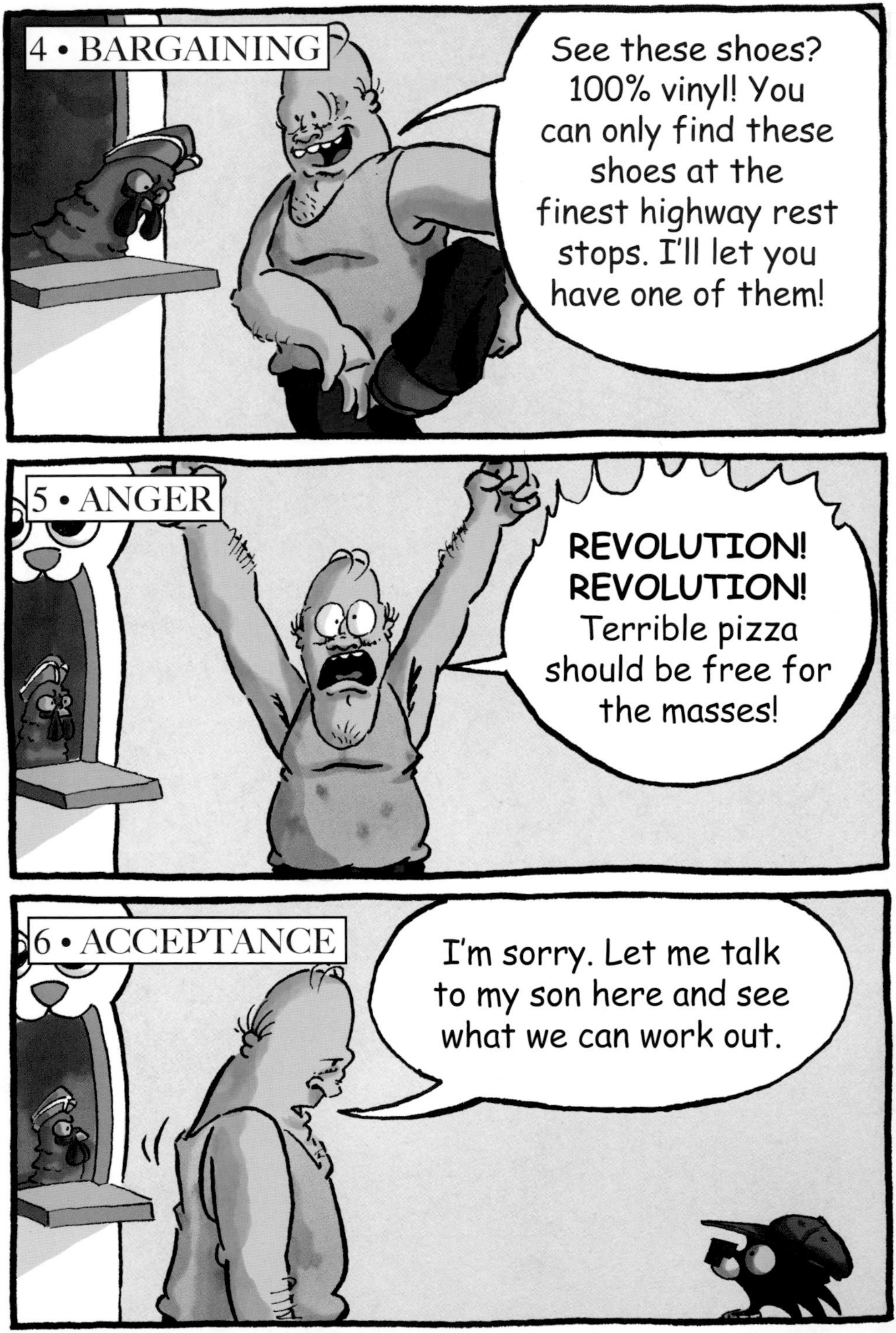
4 • BARGAINING
See these shoes? 100% vinyl! You can only find these shoes at the finest highway rest stops. I'll let you have one of them!
5 • ANGER
REVOLUTION! REVOLUTION! Terrible pizza should be free for the masses!
6 • ACCEPTANCE
I'm sorry. Let me talk to my son here and see what we can work out.

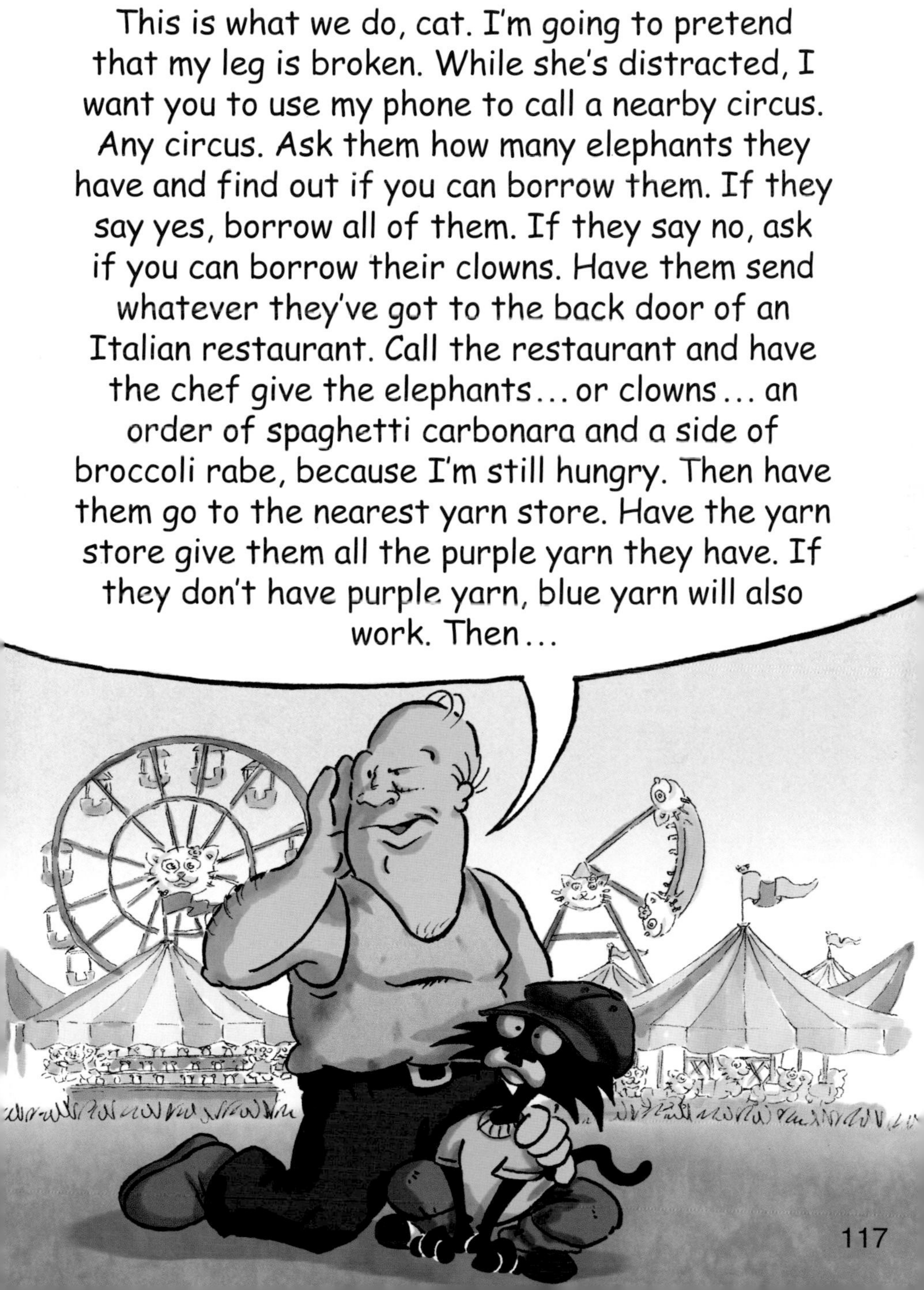
This is what we do, cat. I'm going to pretend that my leg is broken. While she's distracted, I want you to use my phone to call a nearby circus. Any circus. Ask them how many elephants they have and find out if you can borrow them. If they say yes, borrow all of them. If they say no, ask if you can borrow their clowns. Have them send whatever they've got to the back door of an Italian restaurant. Call the restaurant and have the chef give the elephants... or clowns... an order of spaghetti carbonara and a side of broccoli rabe, because I'm still hungry. Then have them go to the nearest yarn store. Have the yarn store give them all the purple yarn they have. If they don't have purple yarn, blue yarn will also work. Then...

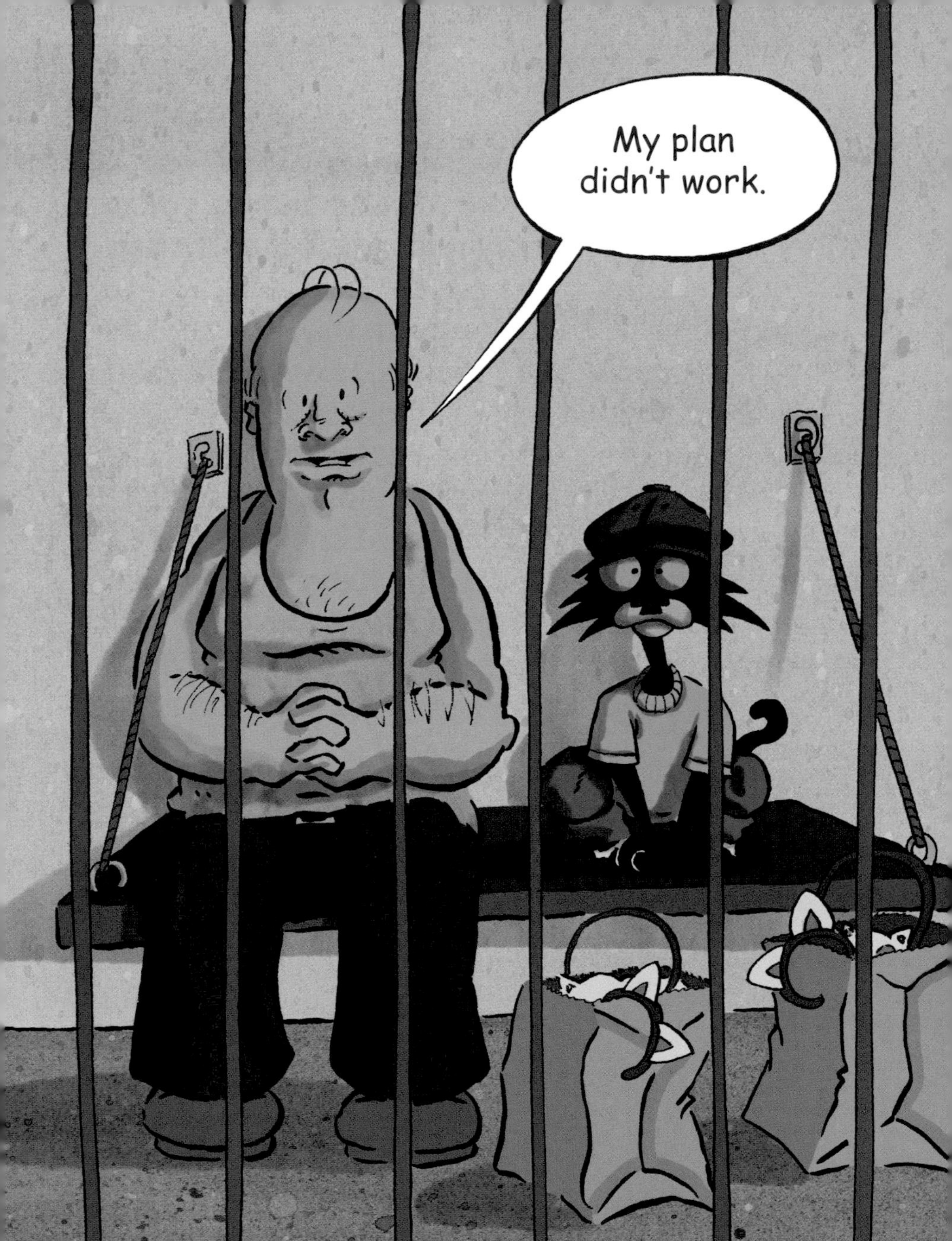
My plan didn't work.

•CHAPTER EIGHT•

LOVE LOVE ANGEL KITTY JAIL

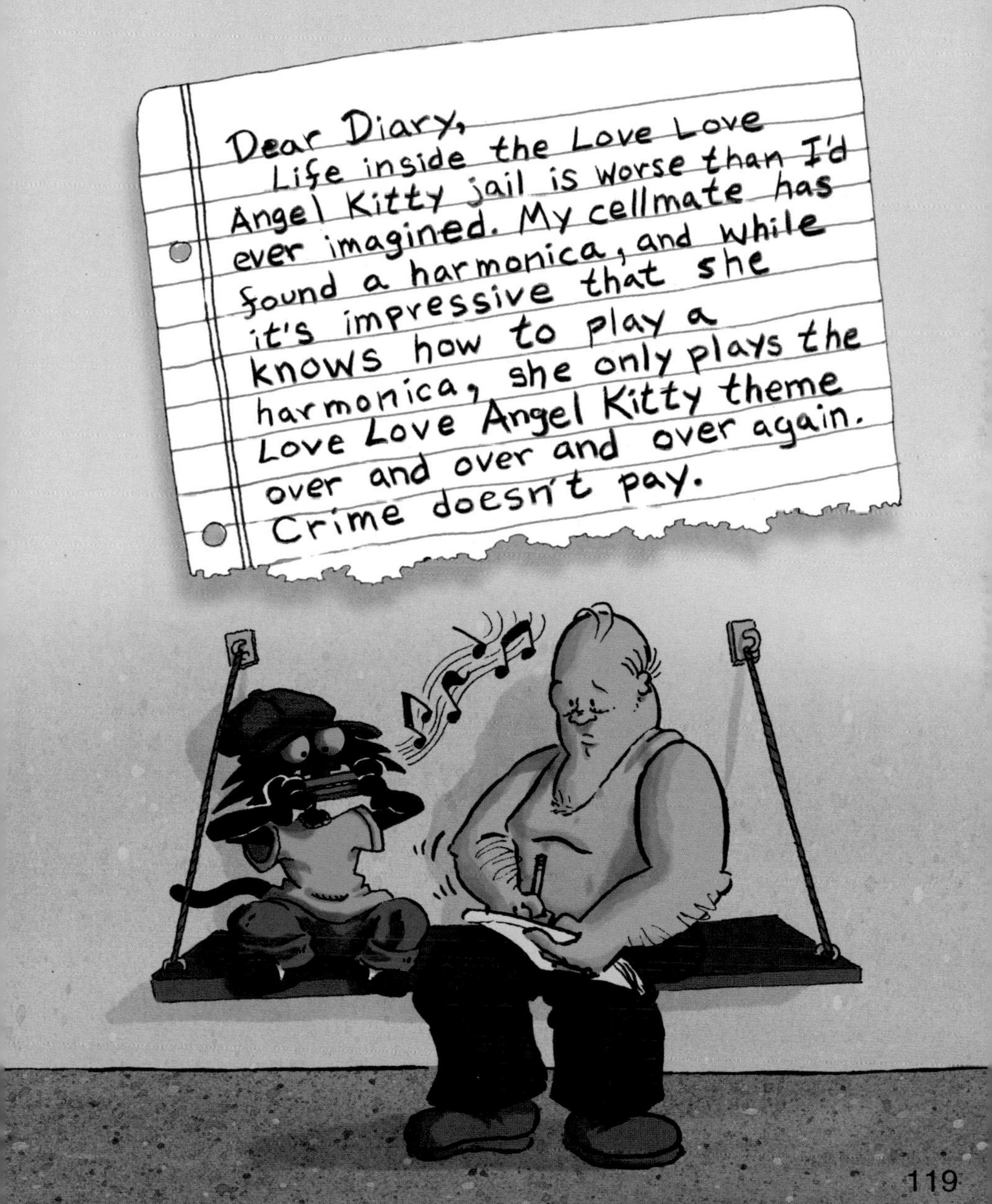
Dear Diary,
Life inside the Love Love Angel Kitty jail is worse than I'd ever imagined. My cellmate has found a harmonica, and while it's impressive that she knows how to play a harmonica, she only plays the Love Love Angel Kitty theme over and over and over again.
Crime doesn't pay.

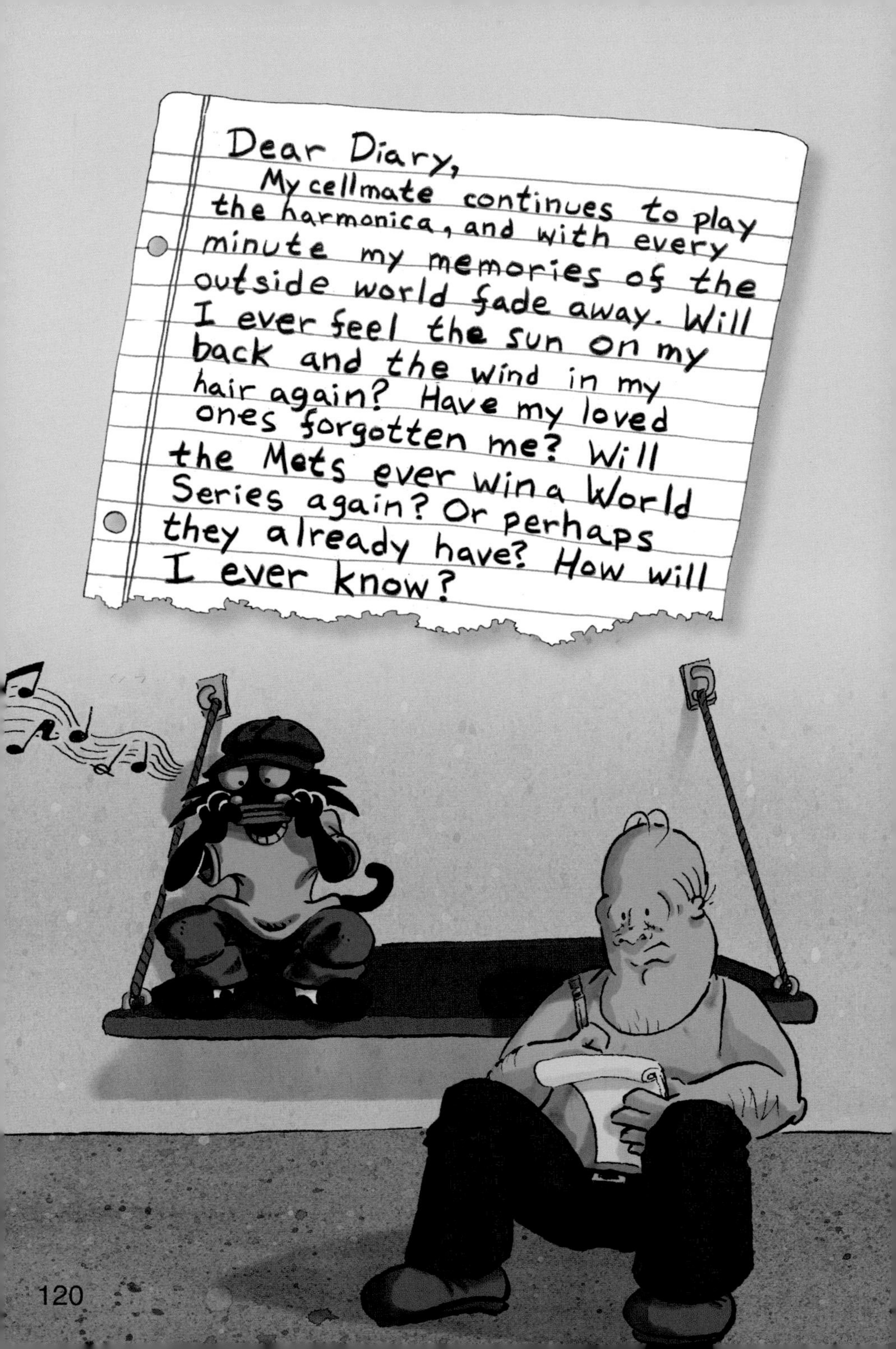
Dear Diary,
My cellmate continues to play the harmonica, and with every minute my memories of the outside world fade away. Will I ever feel the sun on my back and the wind in my hair again? Have my loved ones forgotten me? Will the Mets ever win a World Series again? Or perhaps they already have? How will I ever know?

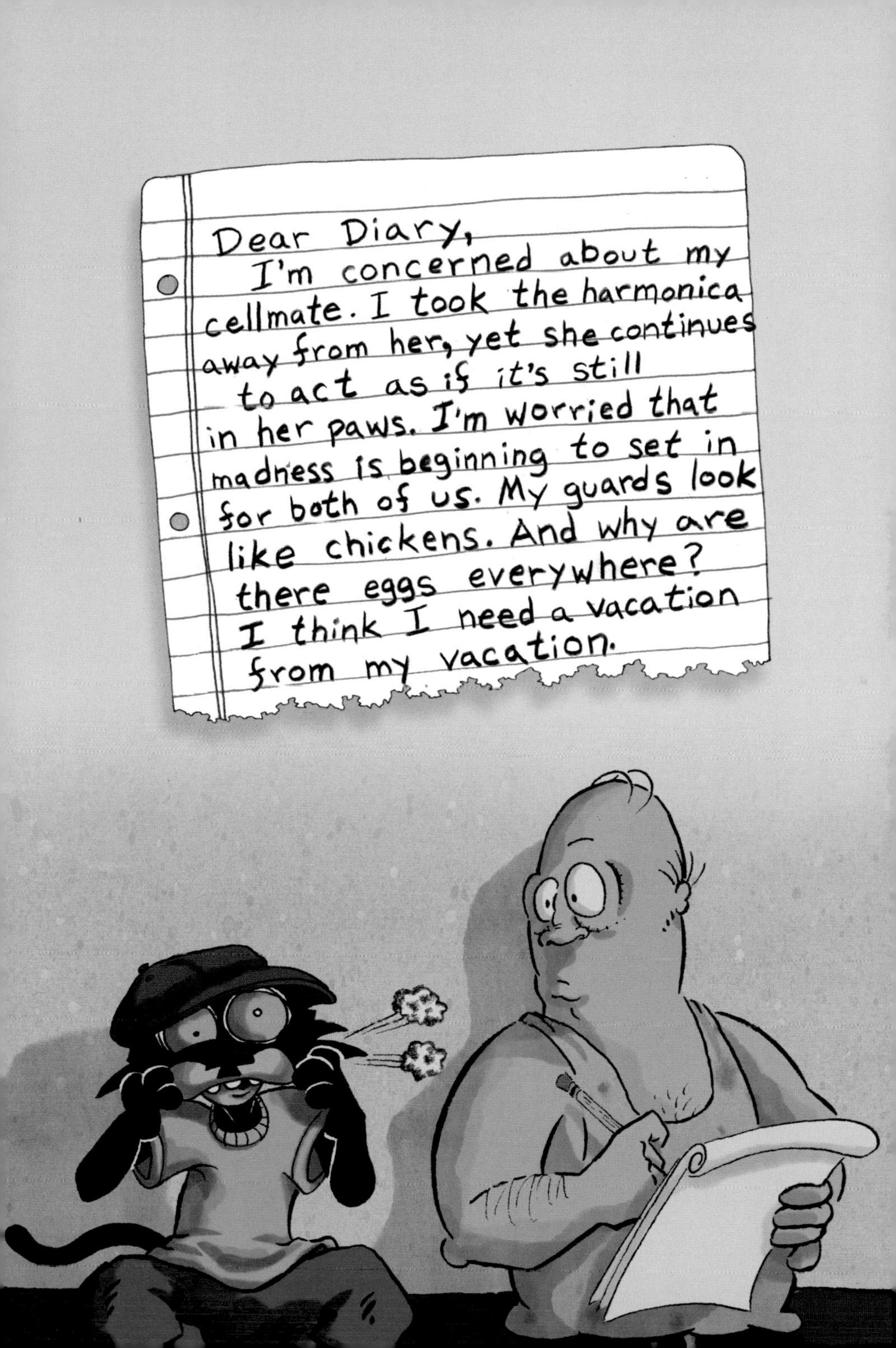
Dear Diary,
I'm concerned about my
cellmate. I took the harmonica
away from her, yet she continues
to act as if it's still
in her paws. I'm worried that
madness is beginning to set in
for both of us. My guards look
like chickens. And why are
there eggs everywhere?
I think I need a vacation
from my vacation.

Dear Diary,
I think even my cellmate has grown tired of this place—not just the jail but this entire park. She looks bored, sleepy, and unhappy. Neither of us is happy, which is ironic because

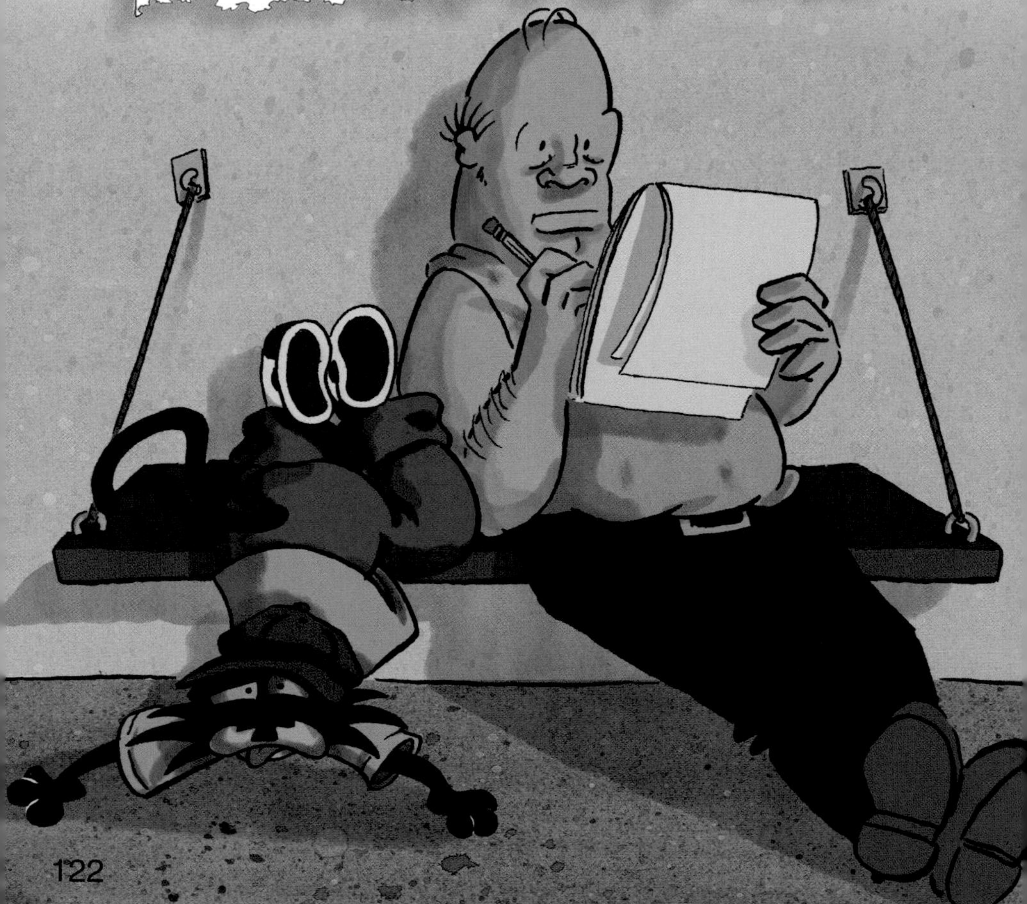

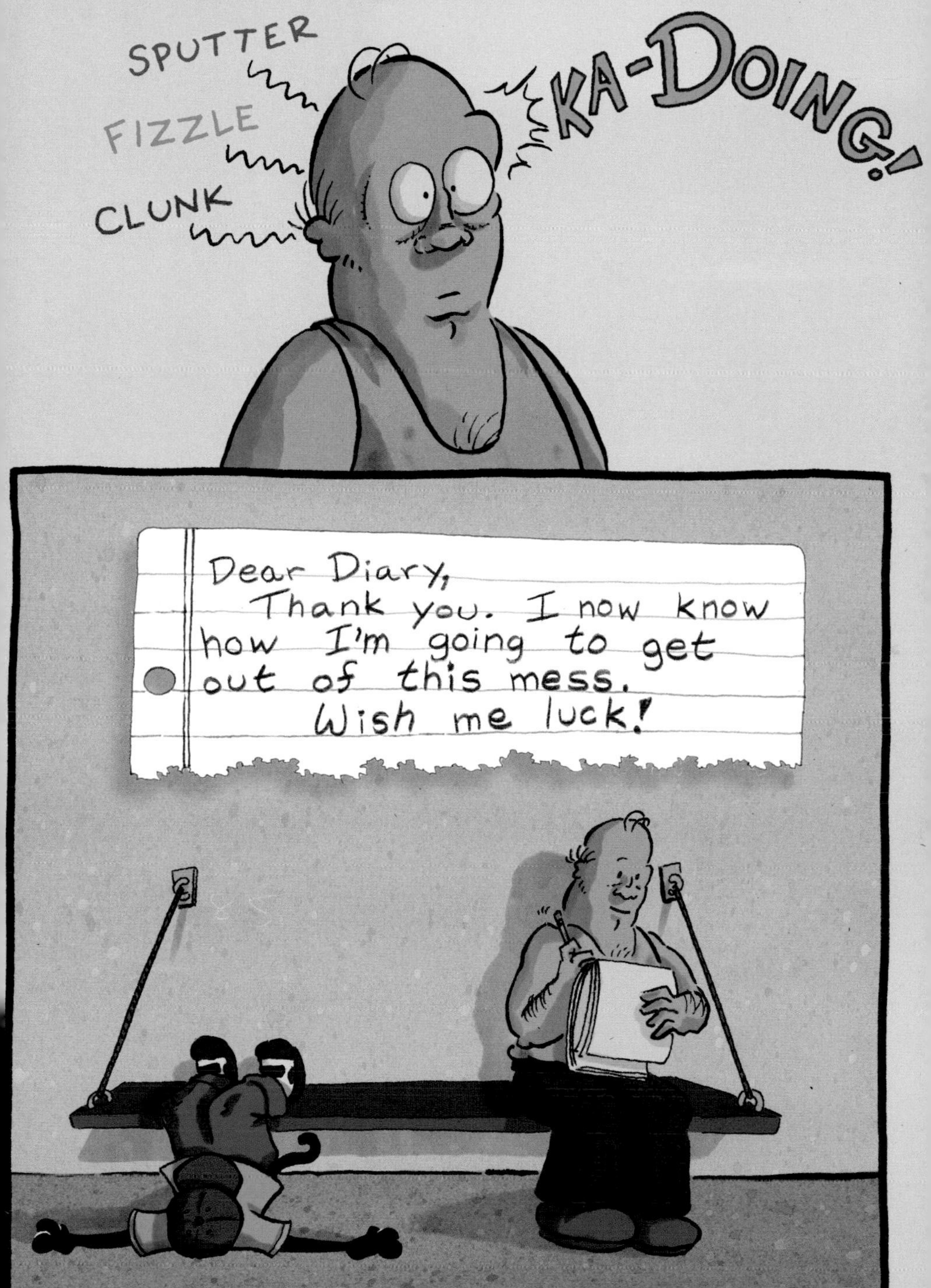
SPUTTER
FIZZLE
CLUNK
KA-DOING!
Dear Diary,
Thank you. I now know how I'm going to get out of this mess.
Wish me luck!

• CHAPTER NINE •

THE TRIAL OF UNCLE MURRAY (AND KITTY)

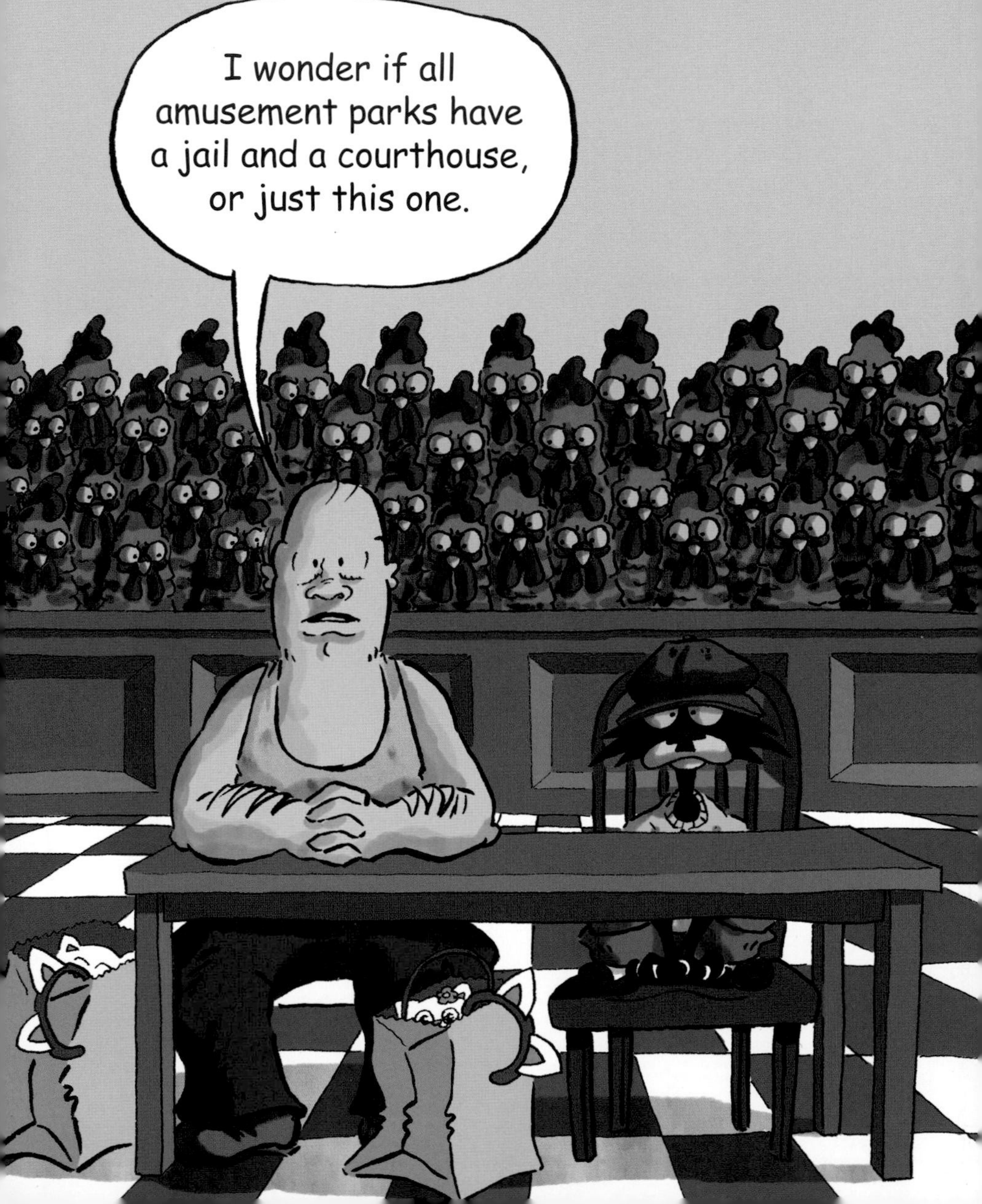

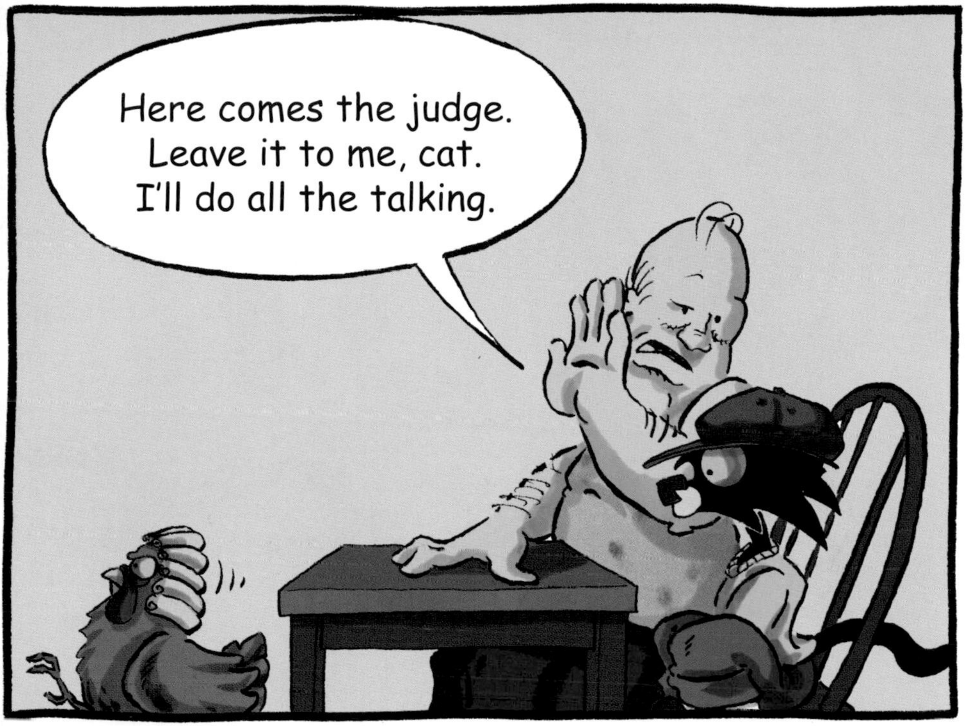
Here comes the judge. Leave it to me, cat. I'll do all the talking.

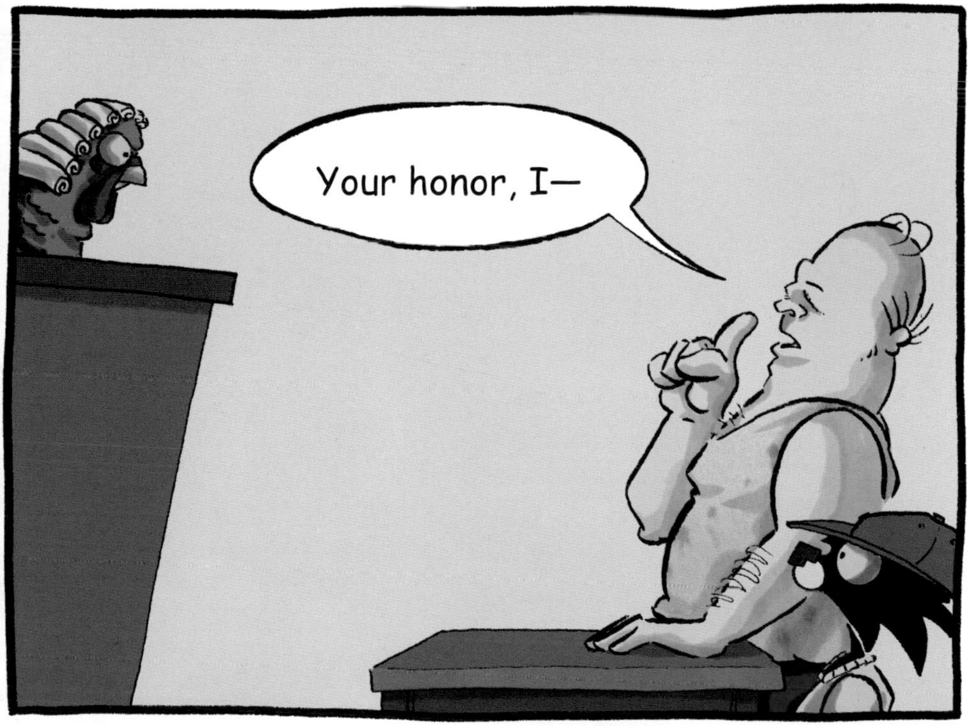
Your honor, I—

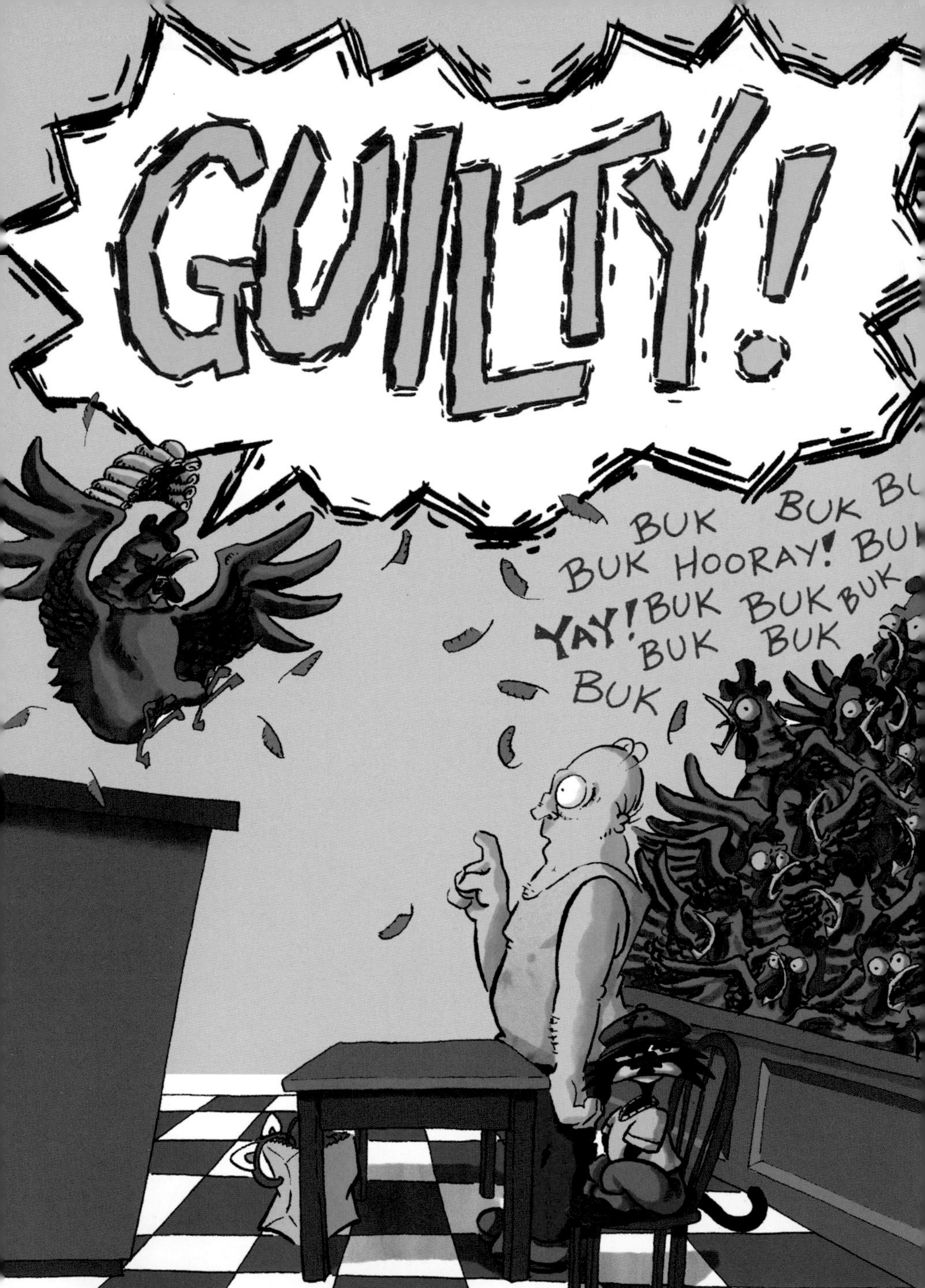
GUILTY!
BUK BUK BU
BUK HOORAY! BU
YAY! BUK BUK BUK
BUK BUK
BUK

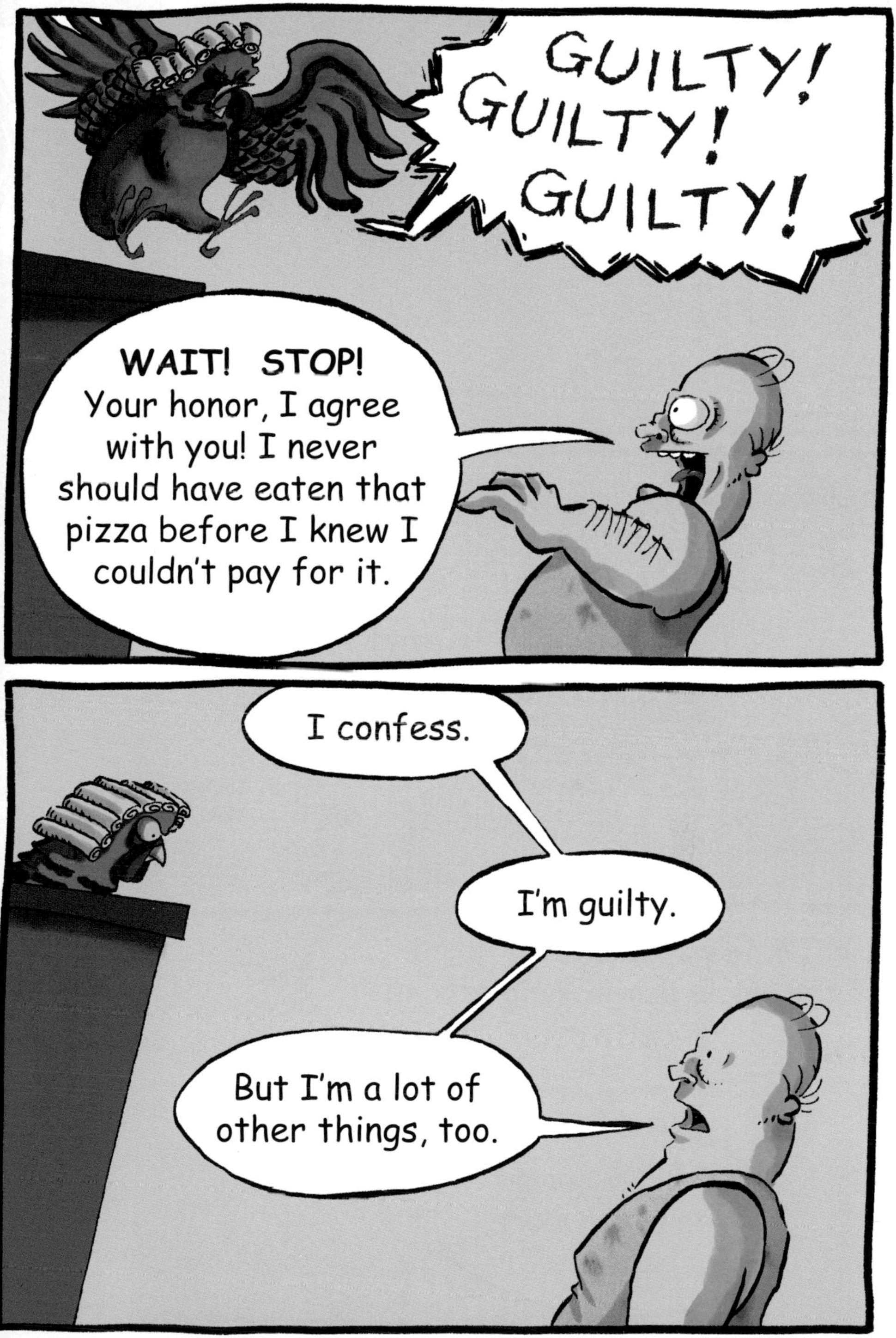
GUILTY! GUILTY! GUILTY!
WAIT! STOP! Your honor, I agree with you! I never should have eaten that pizza before I knew I couldn't pay for it.
I confess.
I'm guilty.
But I'm a lot of other things, too.

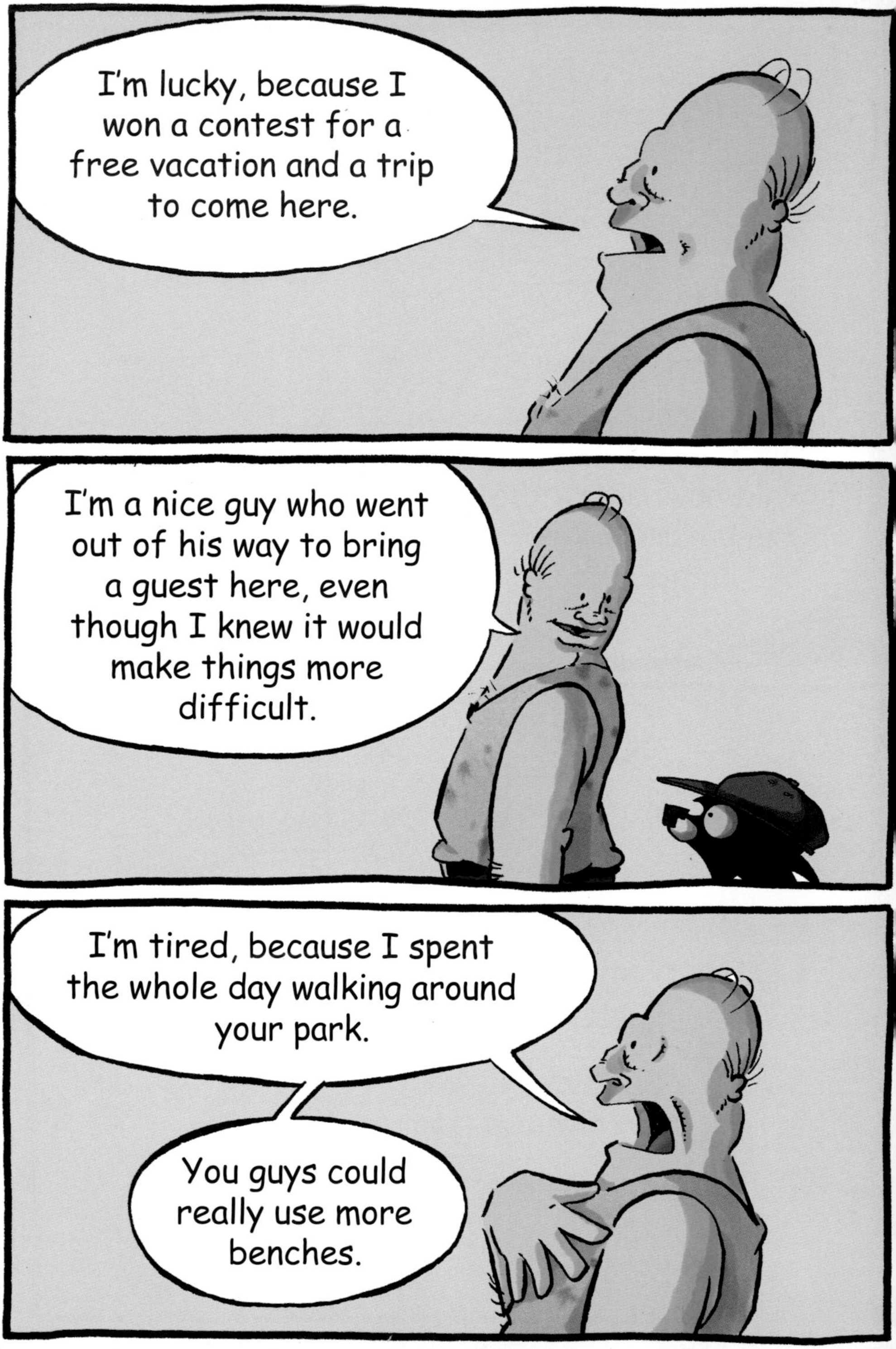
I'm lucky, because I won a contest for a free vacation and a trip to come here.
I'm a nice guy who went out of his way to bring a guest here, even though I knew it would make things more difficult.
I'm tired, because I spent the whole day walking around your park.
You guys could really use more benches.

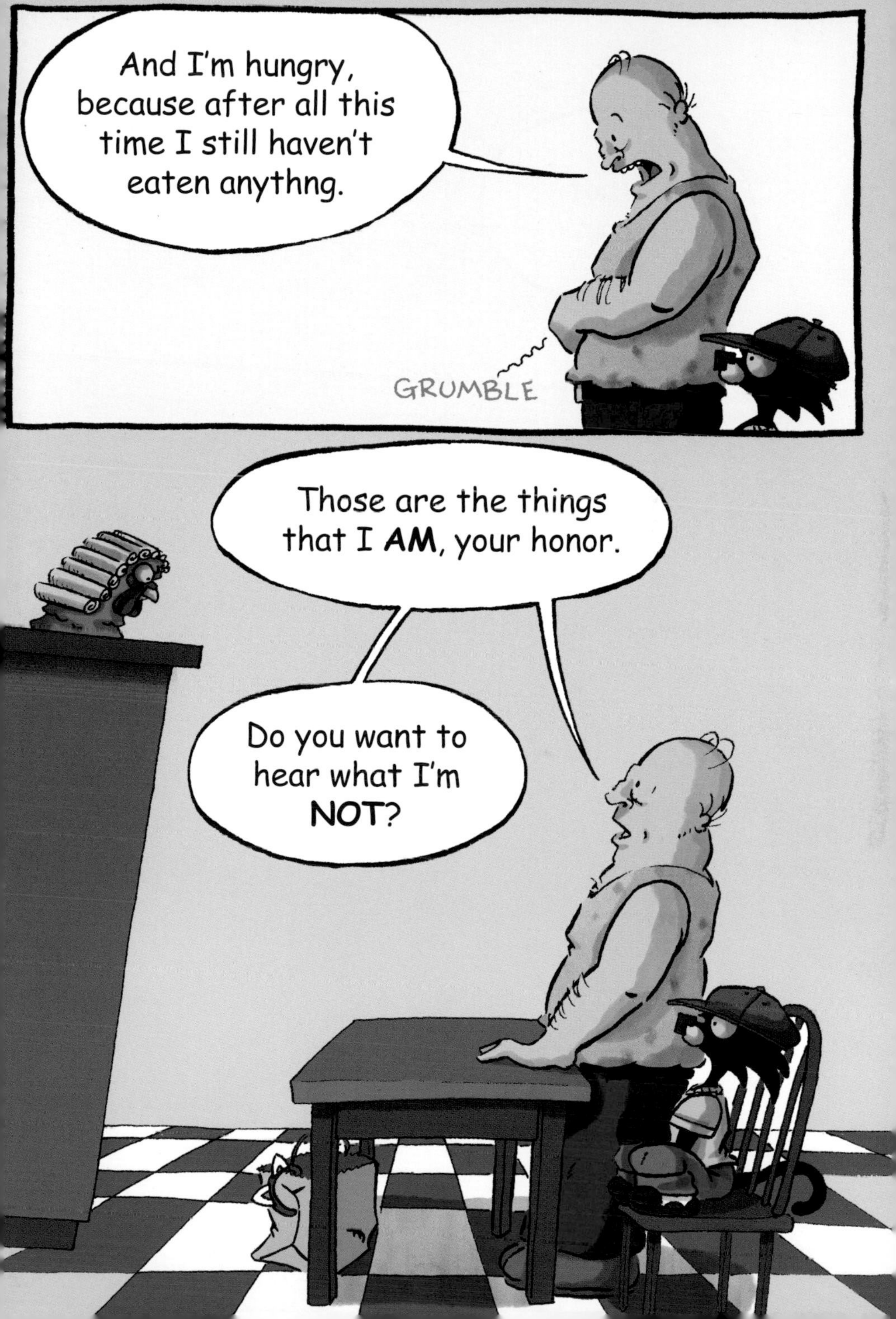
And I'm hungry, because after all this time I still haven't eaten anythng.
GRUMBLE
Those are the things that I **AM**, your honor.
Do you want to hear what I'm **NOT**?

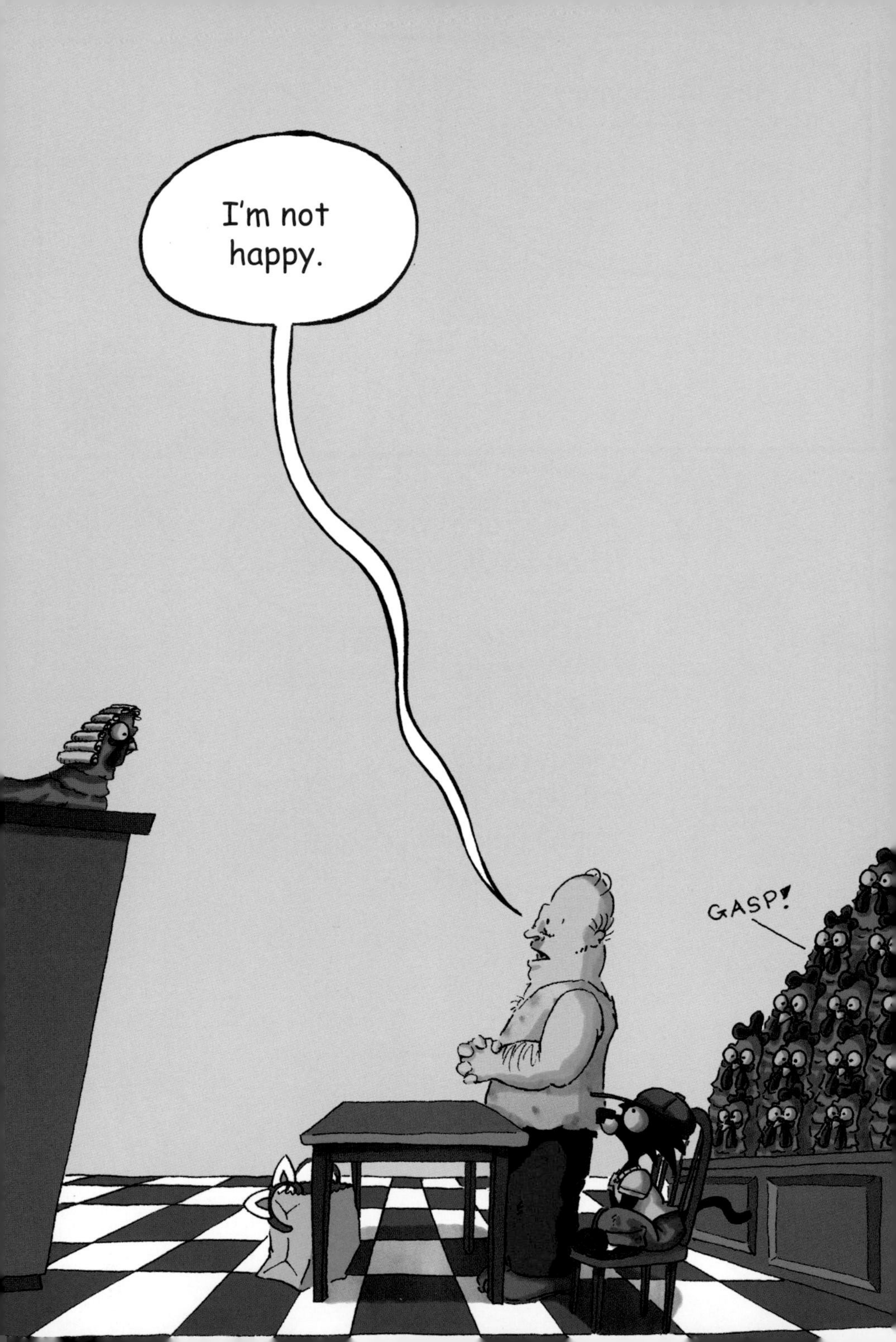
I'm not happy.
GASP!

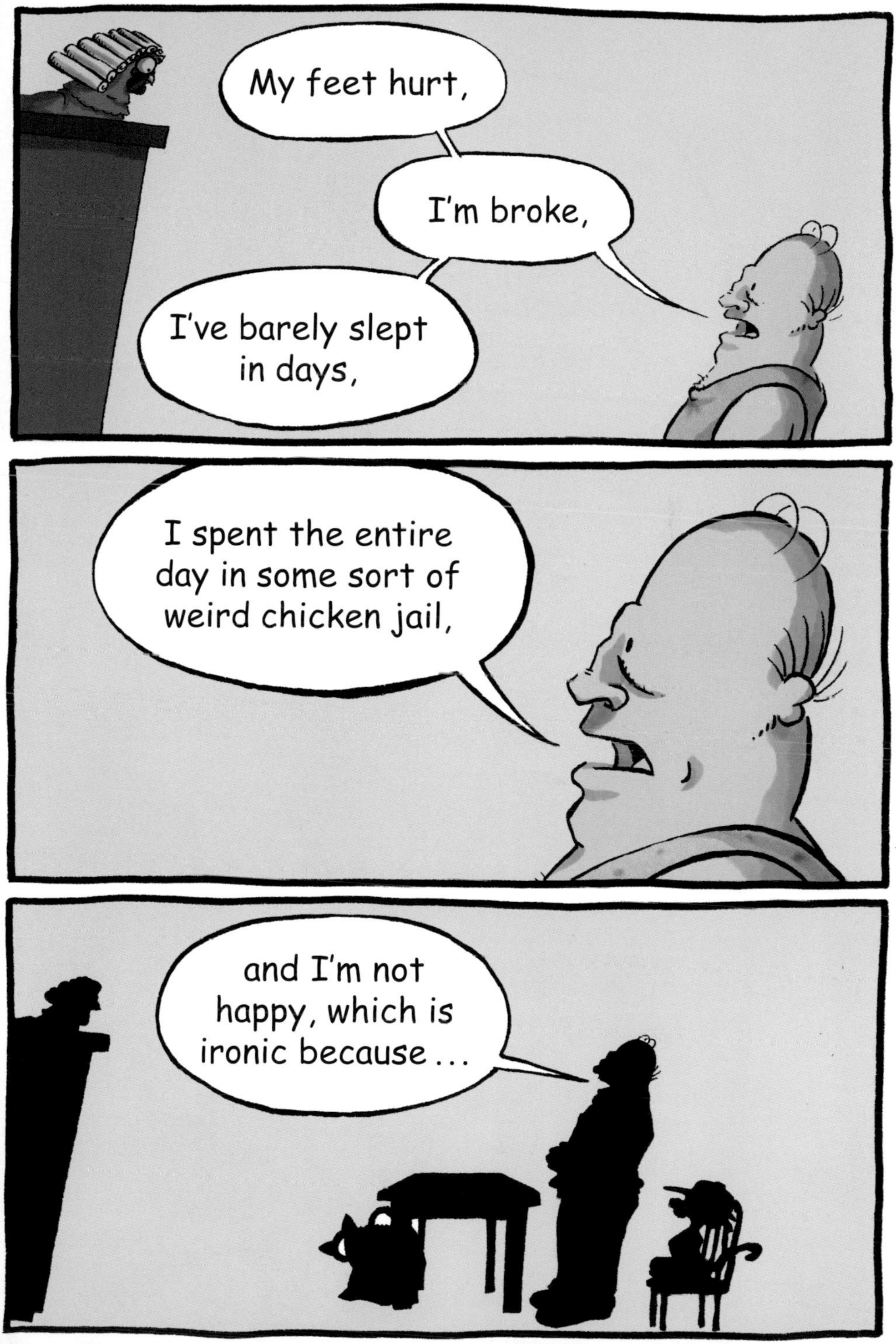
My feet hurt,
I'm broke,
I've barely slept in days,
I spent the entire day in some sort of weird chicken jail,
and I'm not happy, which is ironic because . . .

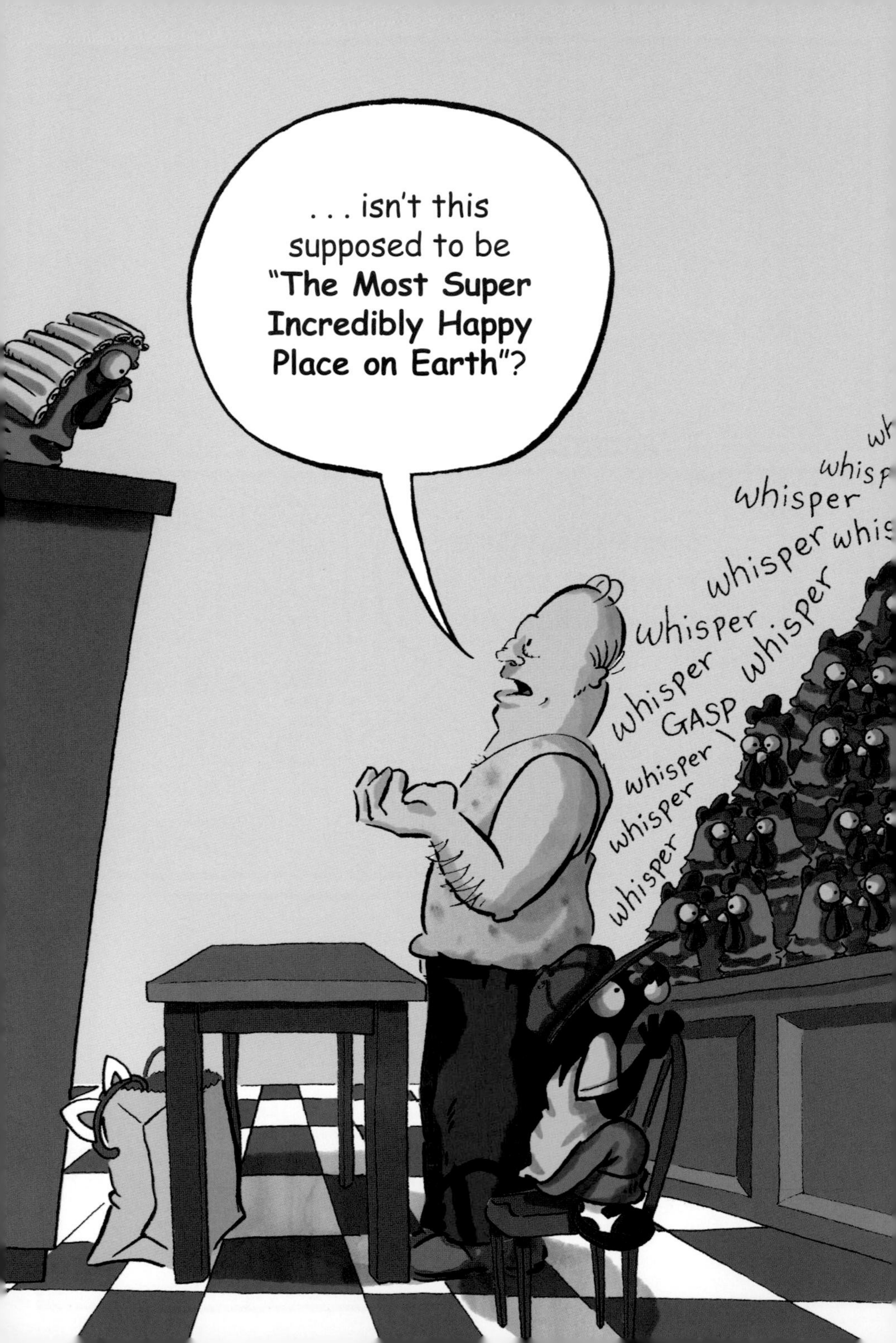
. . . isn't this supposed to be **"The Most Super Incredibly Happy Place on Earth"**?
whisper
whisper
whisper
whisper
whisper
whisper
GASP
whisper
whisper
whisper

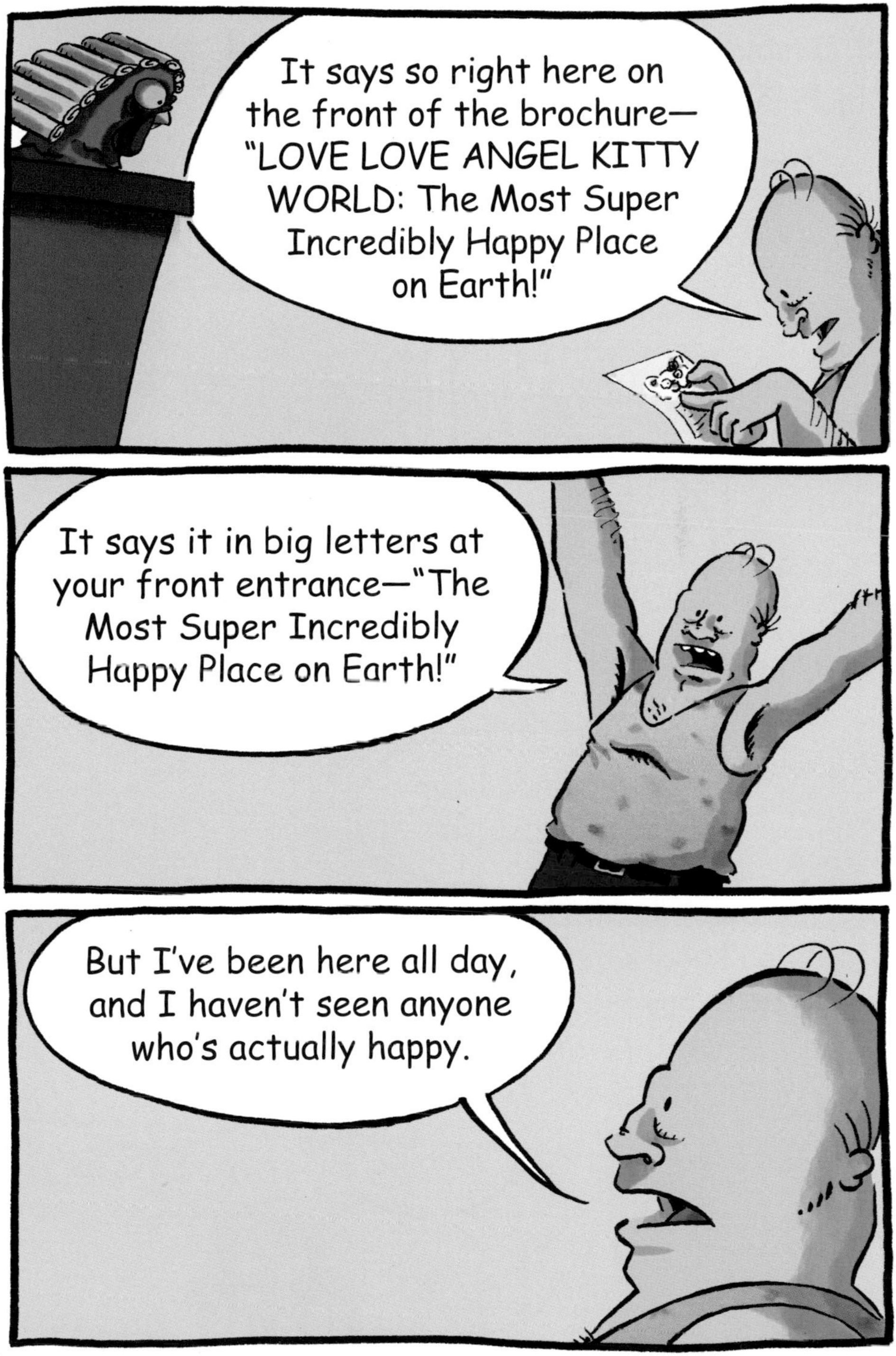
It says so right here on the front of the brochure—"LOVE LOVE ANGEL KITTY WORLD: The Most Super Incredibly Happy Place on Earth!"
It says it in big letters at your front entrance—"The Most Super Incredibly Happy Place on Earth!"
But I've been here all day, and I haven't seen anyone who's actually happy.

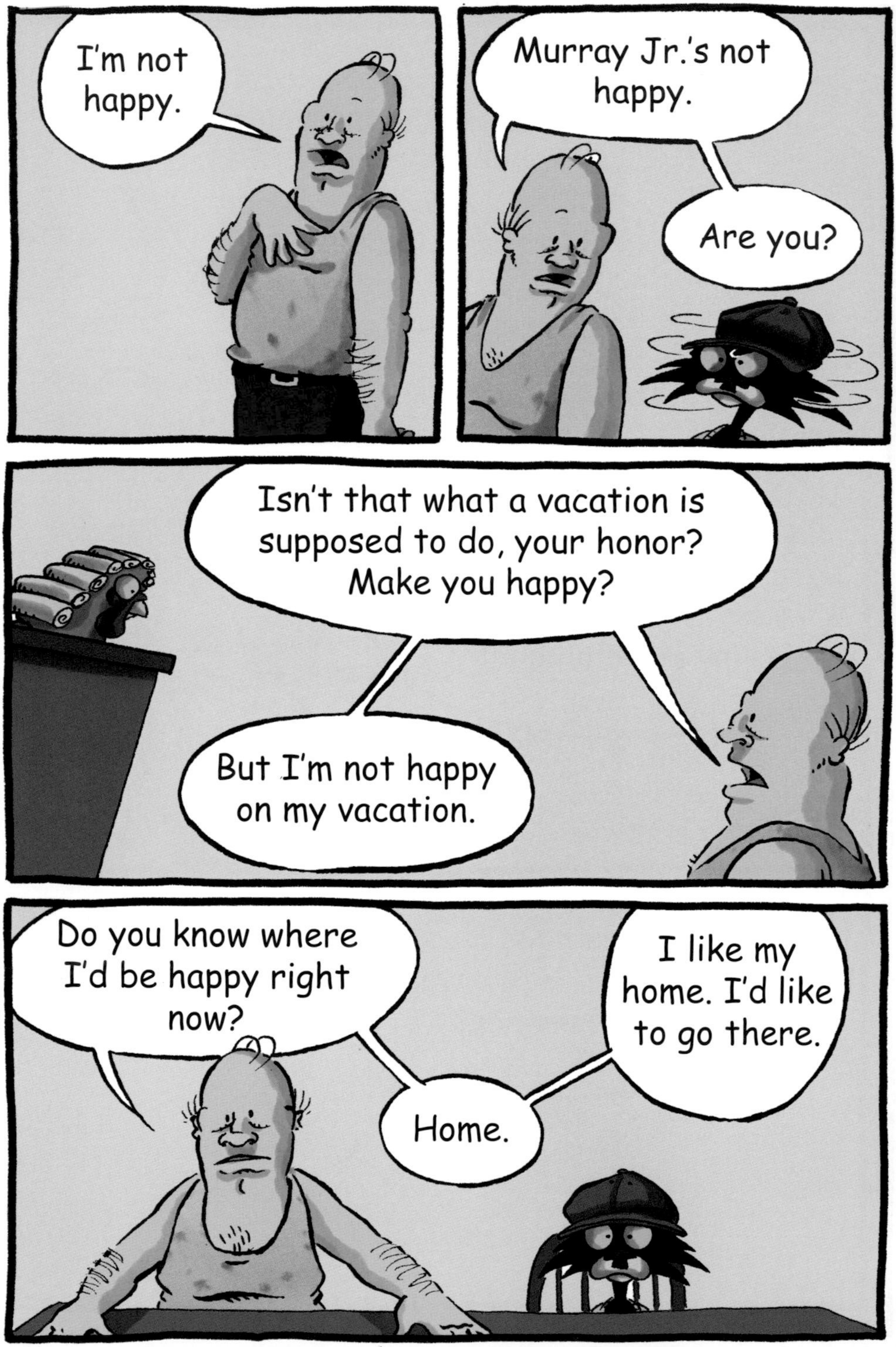
I'm not happy.
Murray Jr.'s not happy.
Are you?
Isn't that what a vacation is supposed to do, your honor? Make you happy?
But I'm not happy on my vacation.
Do you know where I'd be happy right now?
Home.
I like my home. I'd like to go there.

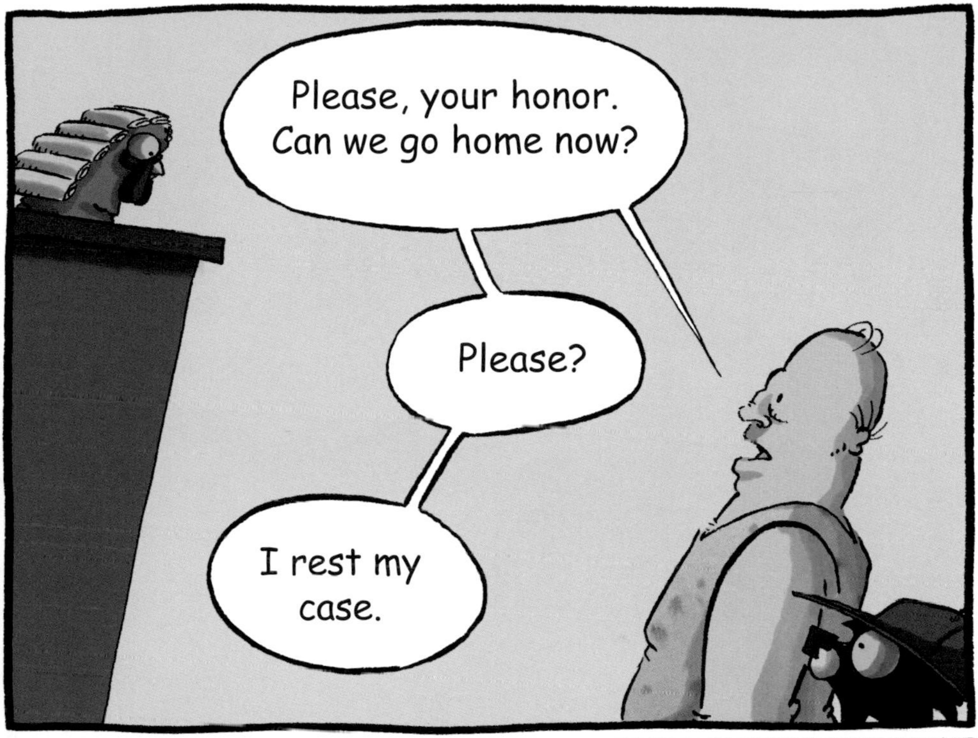
Please, your honor. Can we go home now?
Please?
I rest my case.

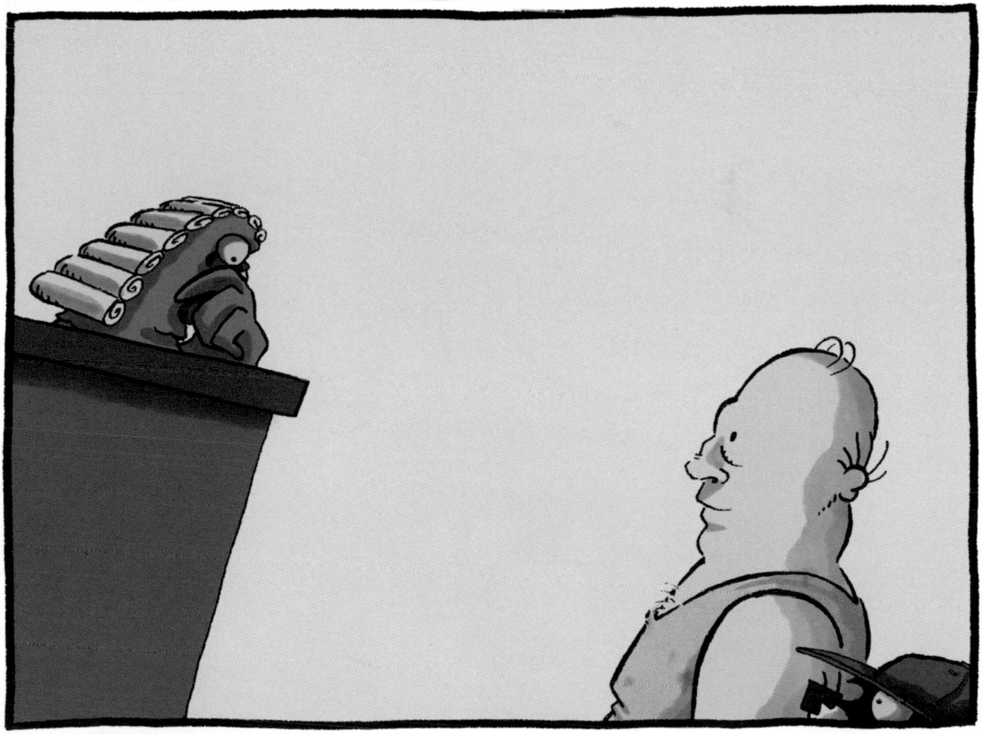

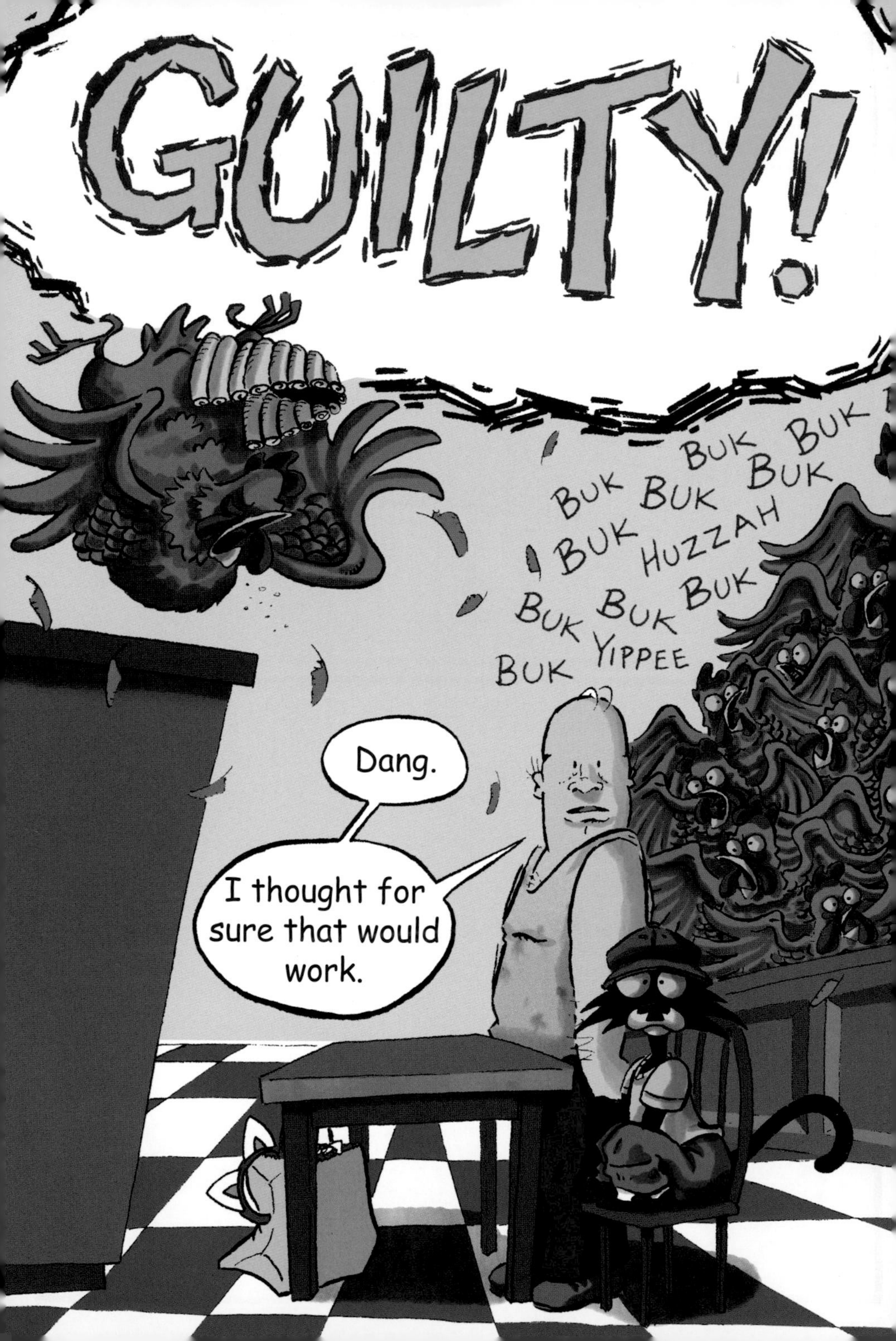
GUILTY!
BUK BUK BUK BUK BUK BUK BUK
HUZZAH
BUK BUK BUK BUK
YIPPEE
BUK
Dang.
I thought for sure that would work.

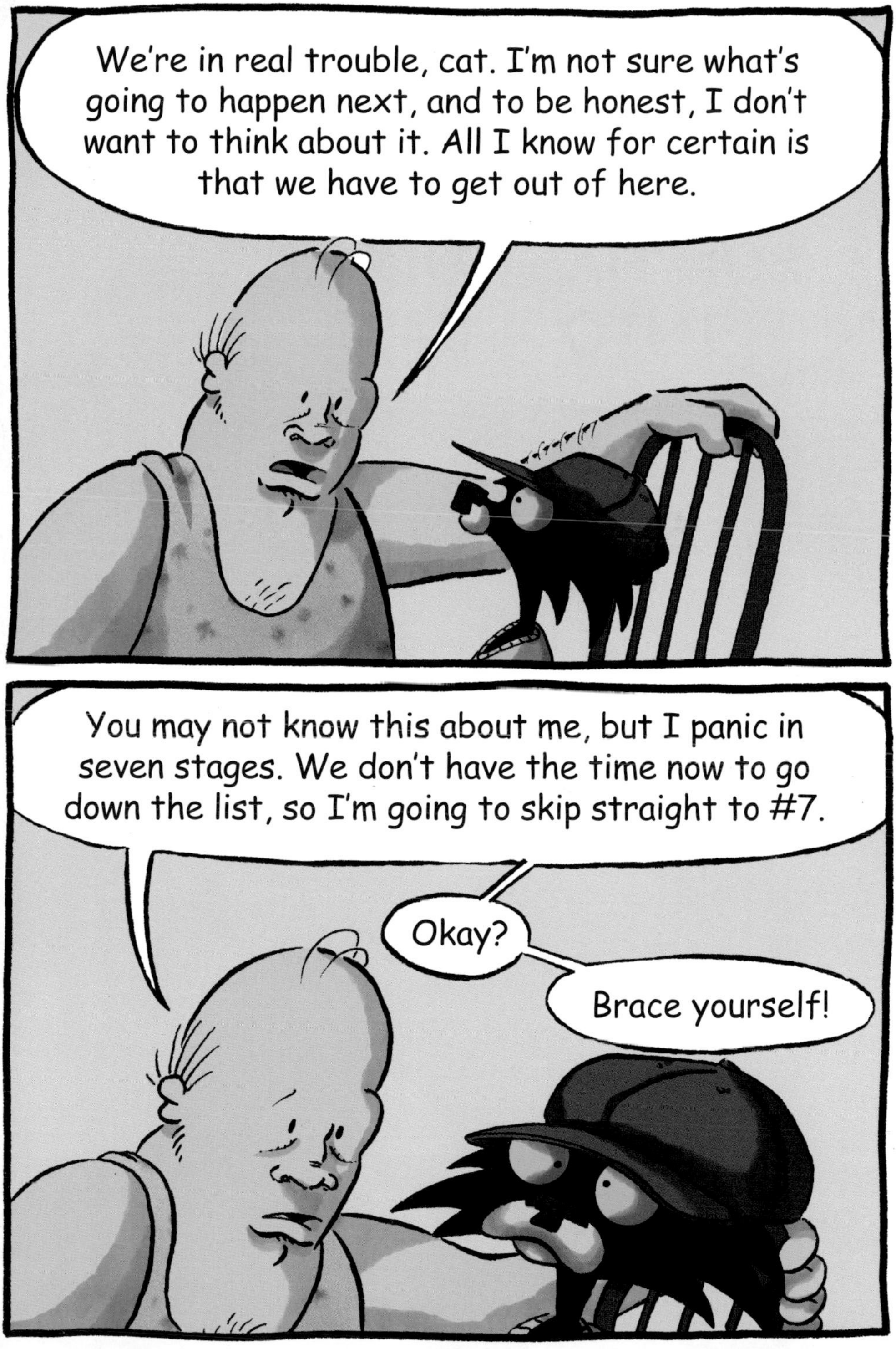
We're in real trouble, cat. I'm not sure what's going to happen next, and to be honest, I don't want to think about it. All I know for certain is that we have to get out of here.
You may not know this about me, but I panic in seven stages. We don't have the time now to go down the list, so I'm going to skip straight to #7.
Okay?
Brace yourself!

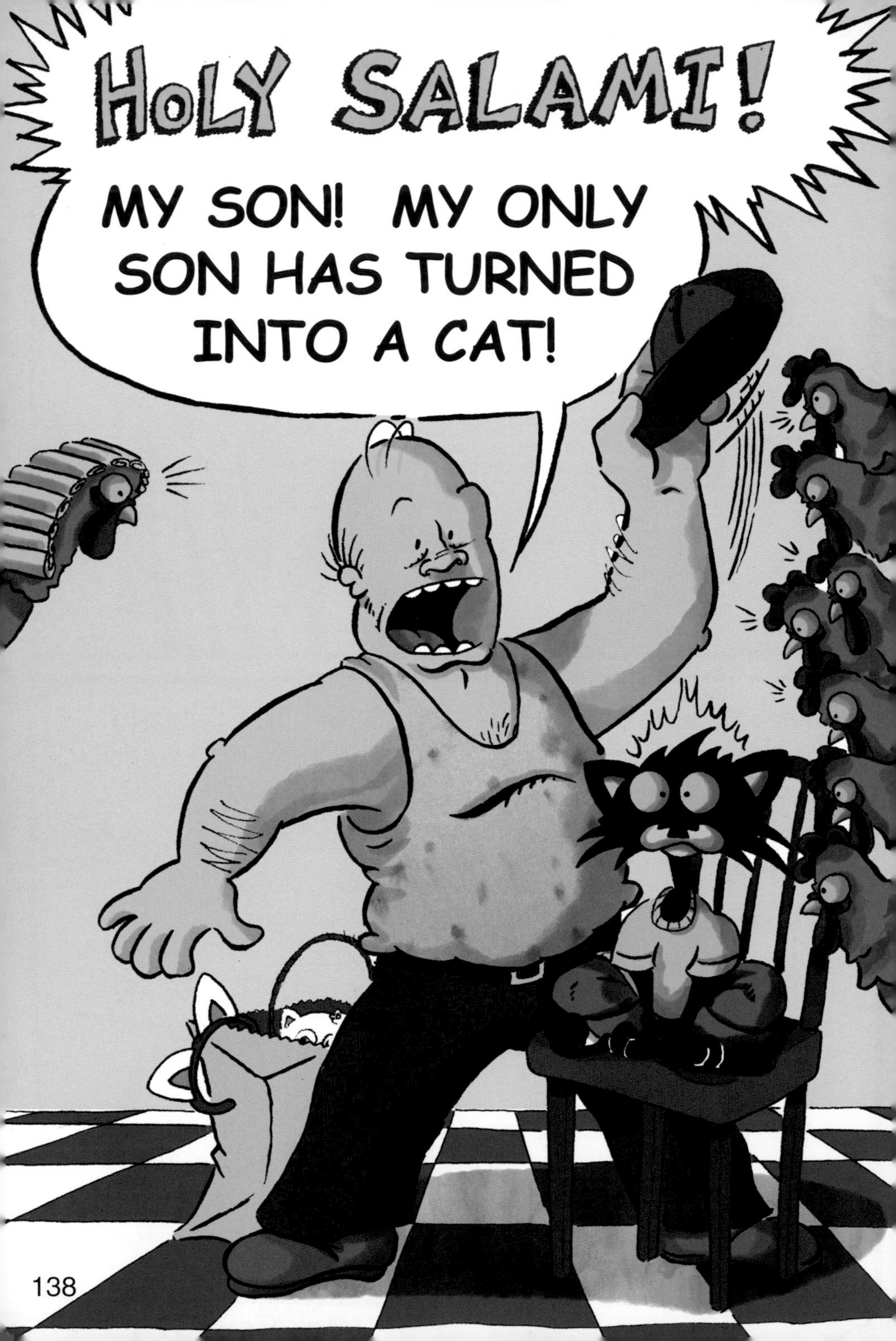
HOLY SALAMI!
MY SON! MY ONLY SON HAS TURNED INTO A CAT!

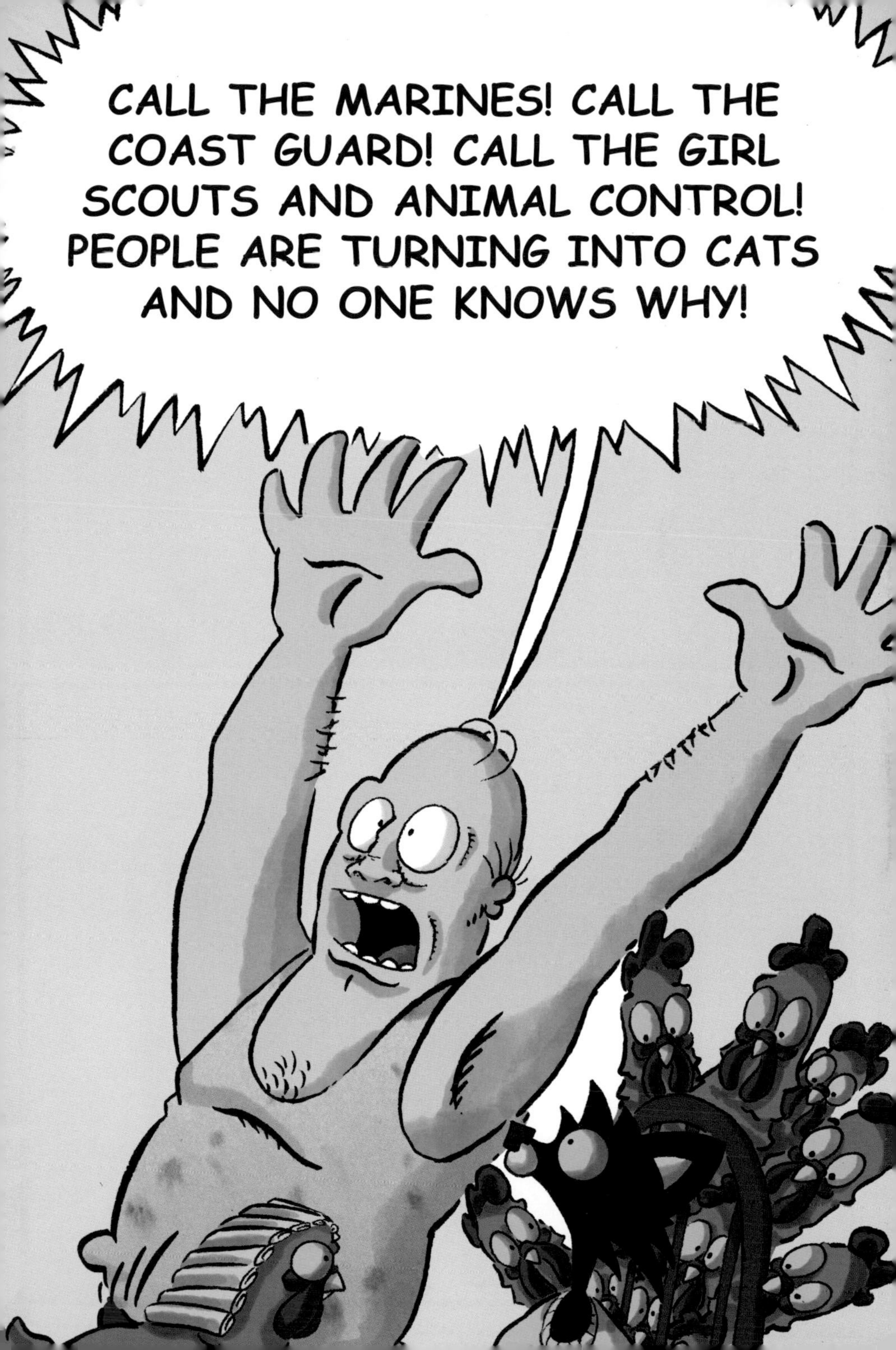
CALL THE MARINES! CALL THE COAST GUARD! CALL THE GIRL SCOUTS AND ANIMAL CONTROL! PEOPLE ARE TURNING INTO CATS AND NO ONE KNOWS WHY!

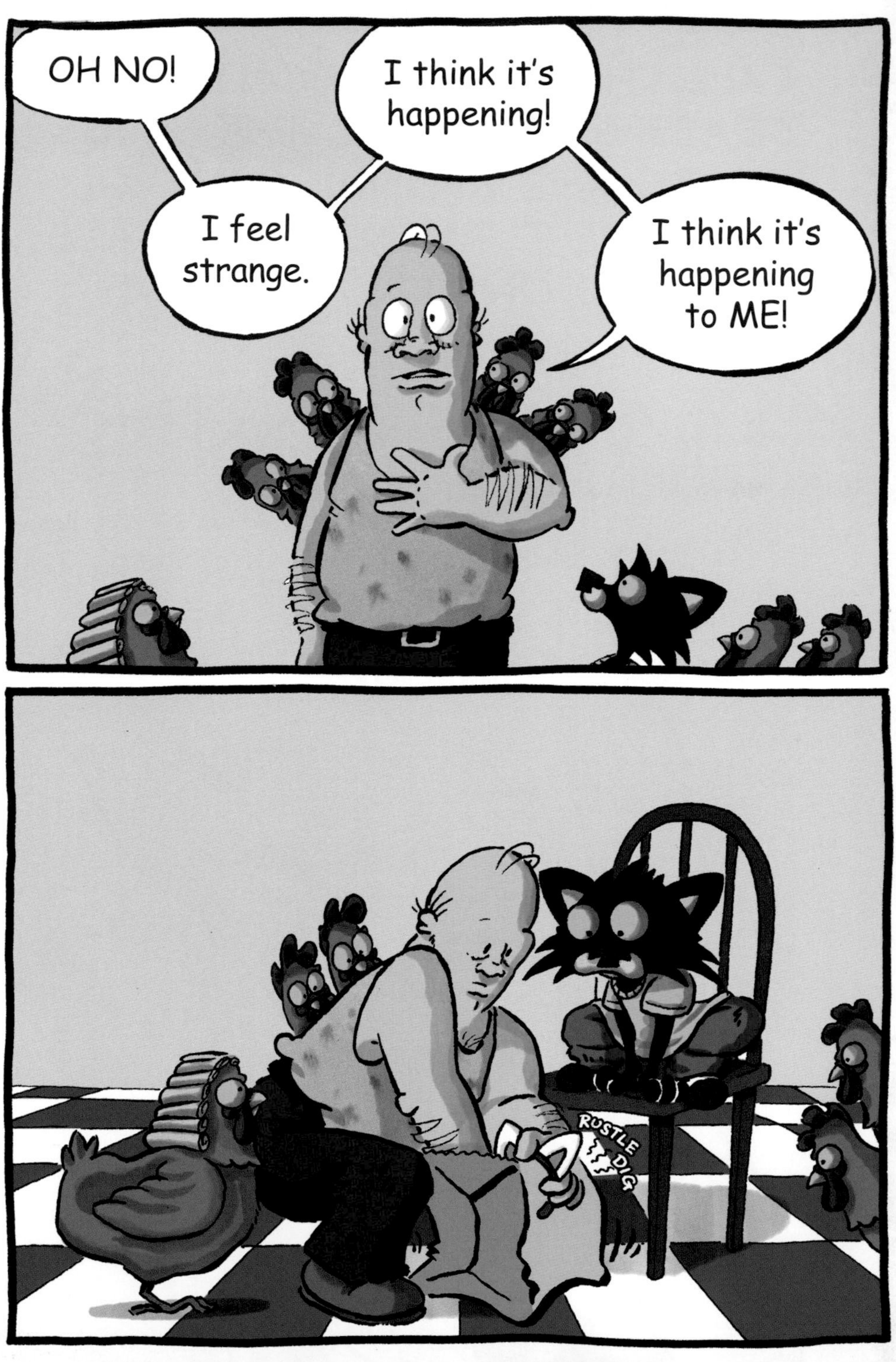
OH NO!
I think it's happening!
I feel strange.
I think it's happening to ME!
RUSTLE
DIG

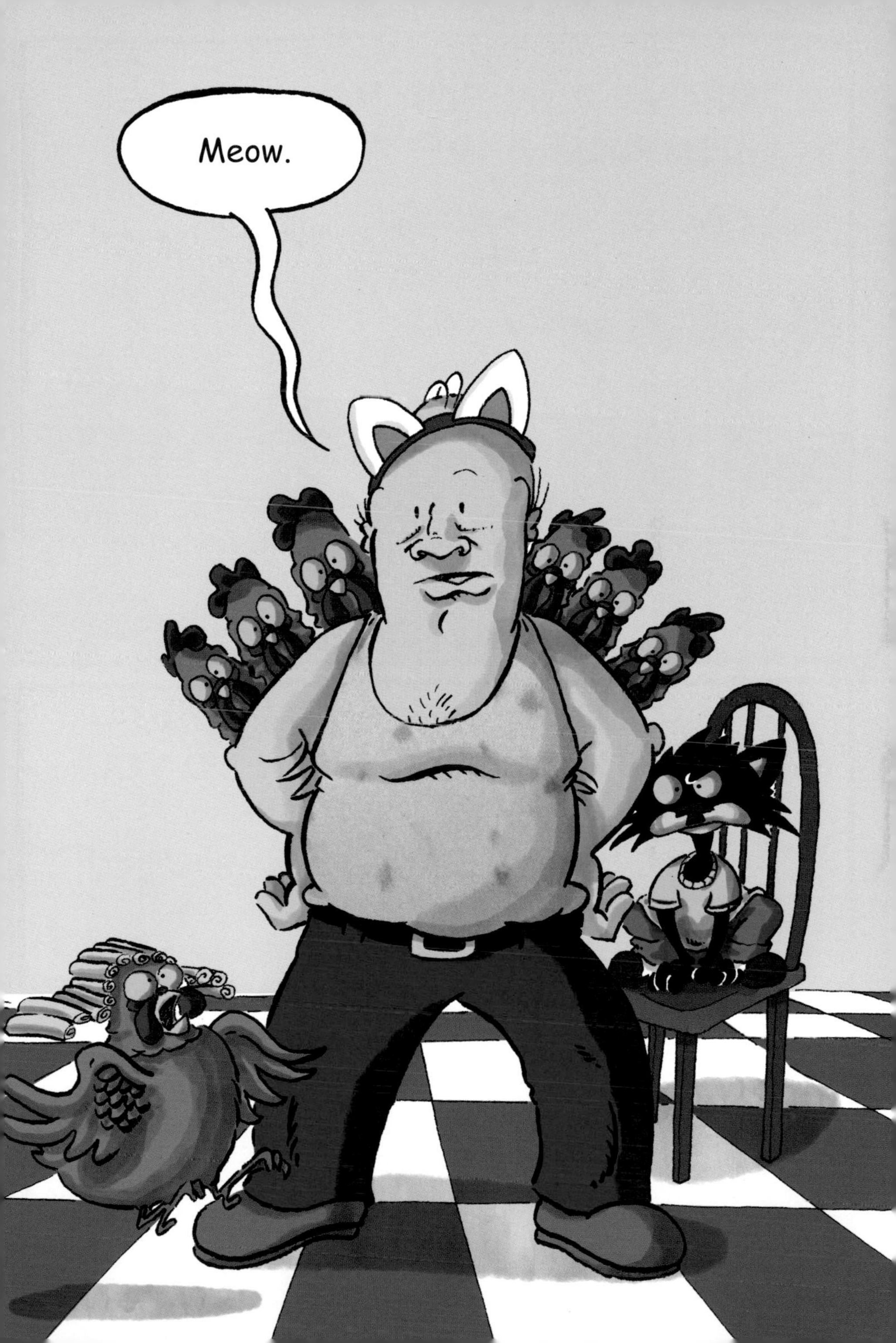
Meow.

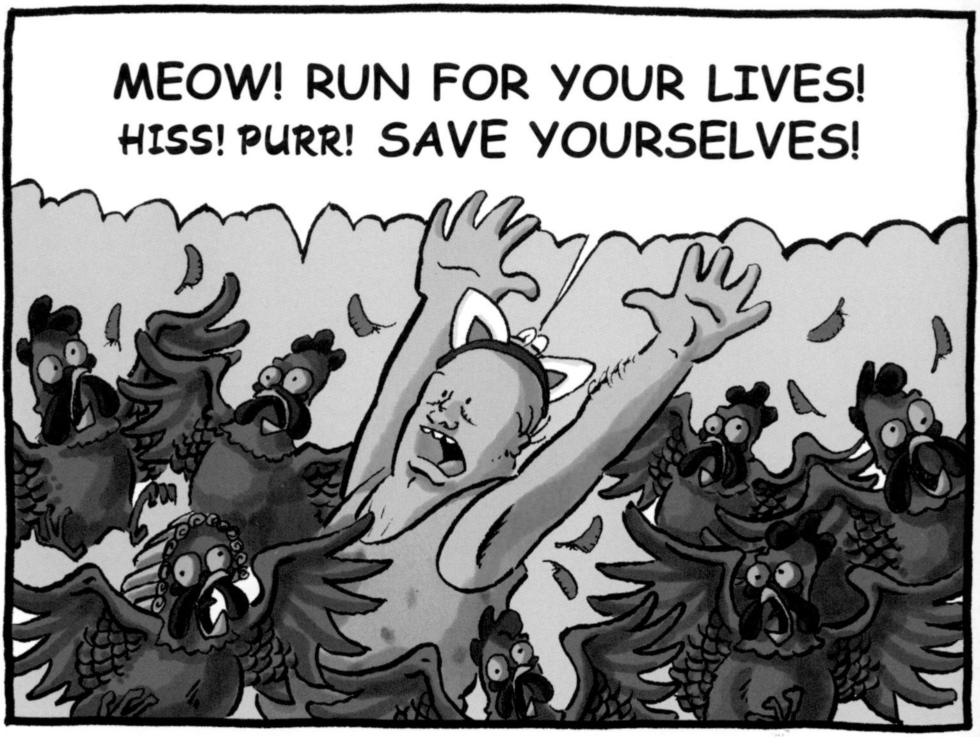
MEOW! RUN FOR YOUR LIVES!
HISS! PURR! SAVE YOURSELVES!

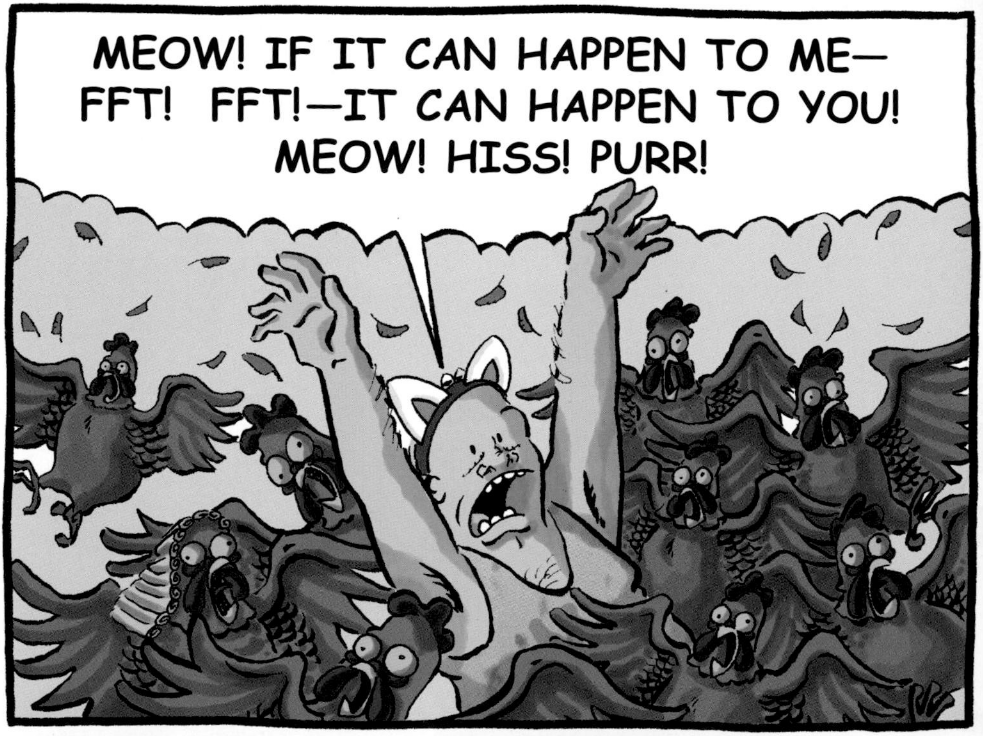
MEOW! IF IT CAN HAPPEN TO ME—
FFT! FFT!—IT CAN HAPPEN TO YOU!
MEOW! HISS! PURR!

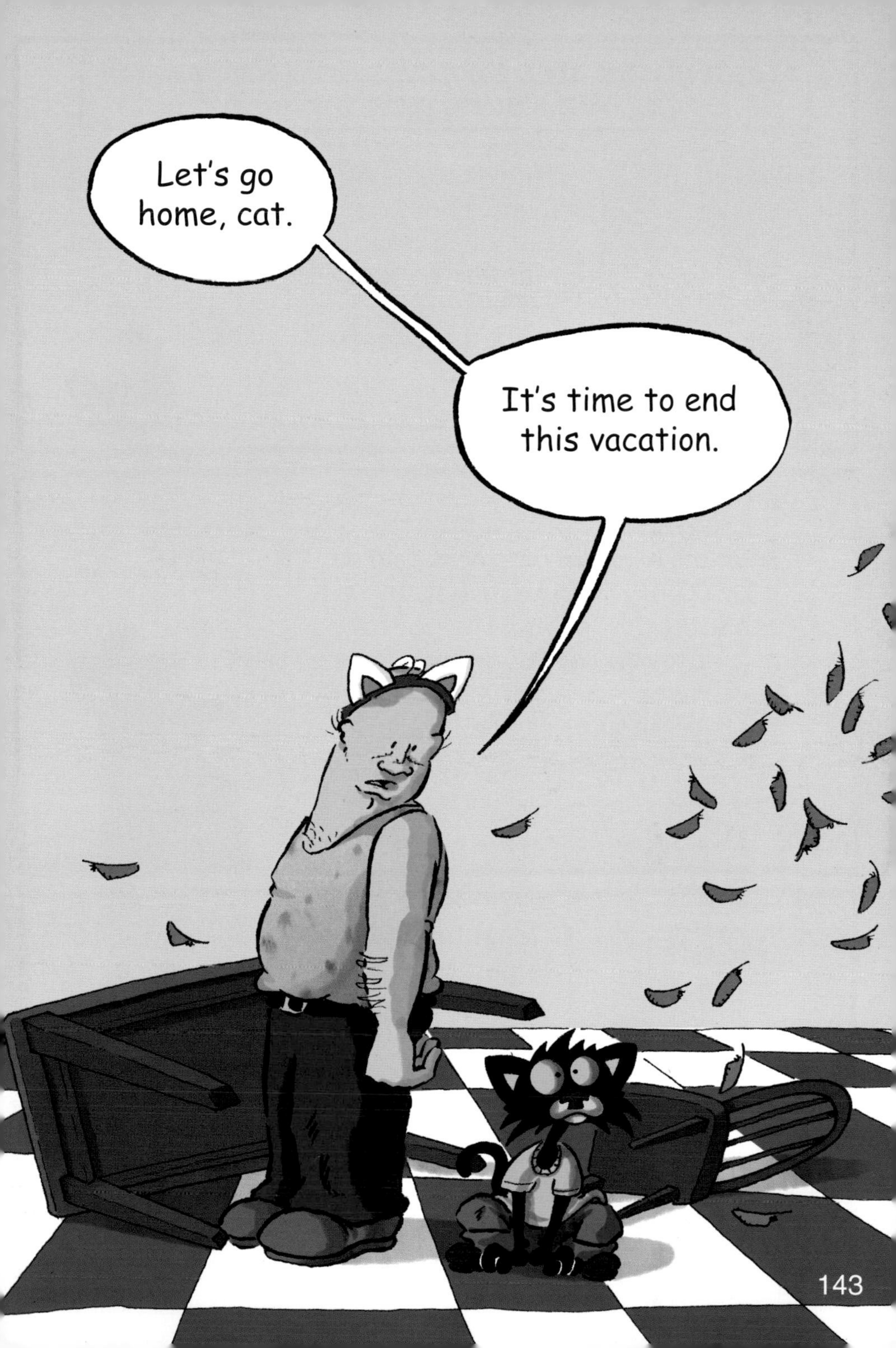
Let's go home, cat.
It's time to end this vacation.

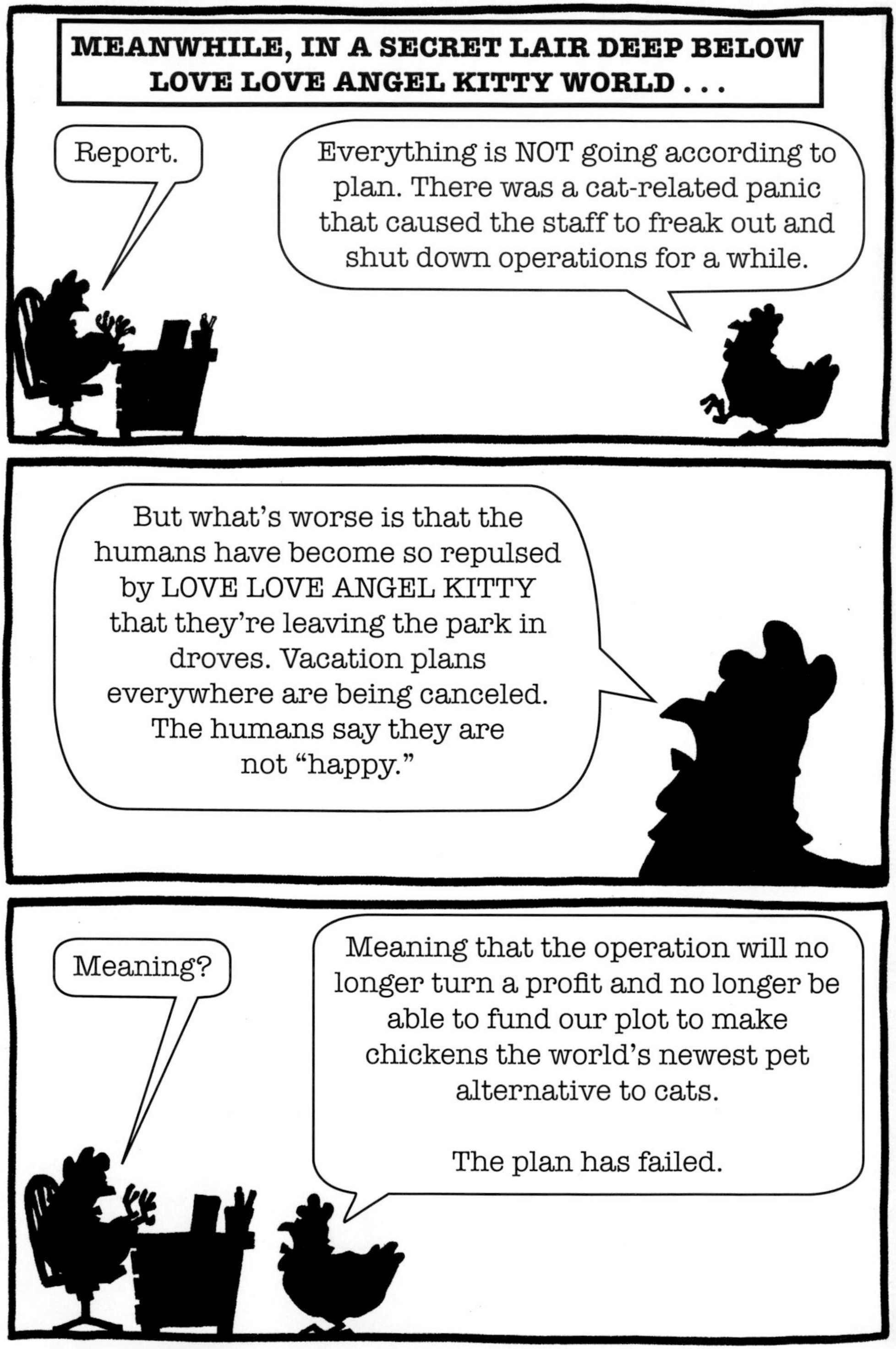
MEANWHILE, IN A SECRET LAIR DEEP BELOW LOVE LOVE ANGEL KITTY WORLD . . .
Report.
Everything is NOT going according to plan. There was a cat-related panic that caused the staff to freak out and shut down operations for a while.
But what's worse is that the humans have become so repulsed by LOVE LOVE ANGEL KITTY that they're leaving the park in droves. Vacation plans everywhere are being canceled. The humans say they are not "happy."
Meaning?
Meaning that the operation will no longer turn a profit and no longer be able to fund our plot to make chickens the world's newest pet alternative to cats.
The plan has failed.

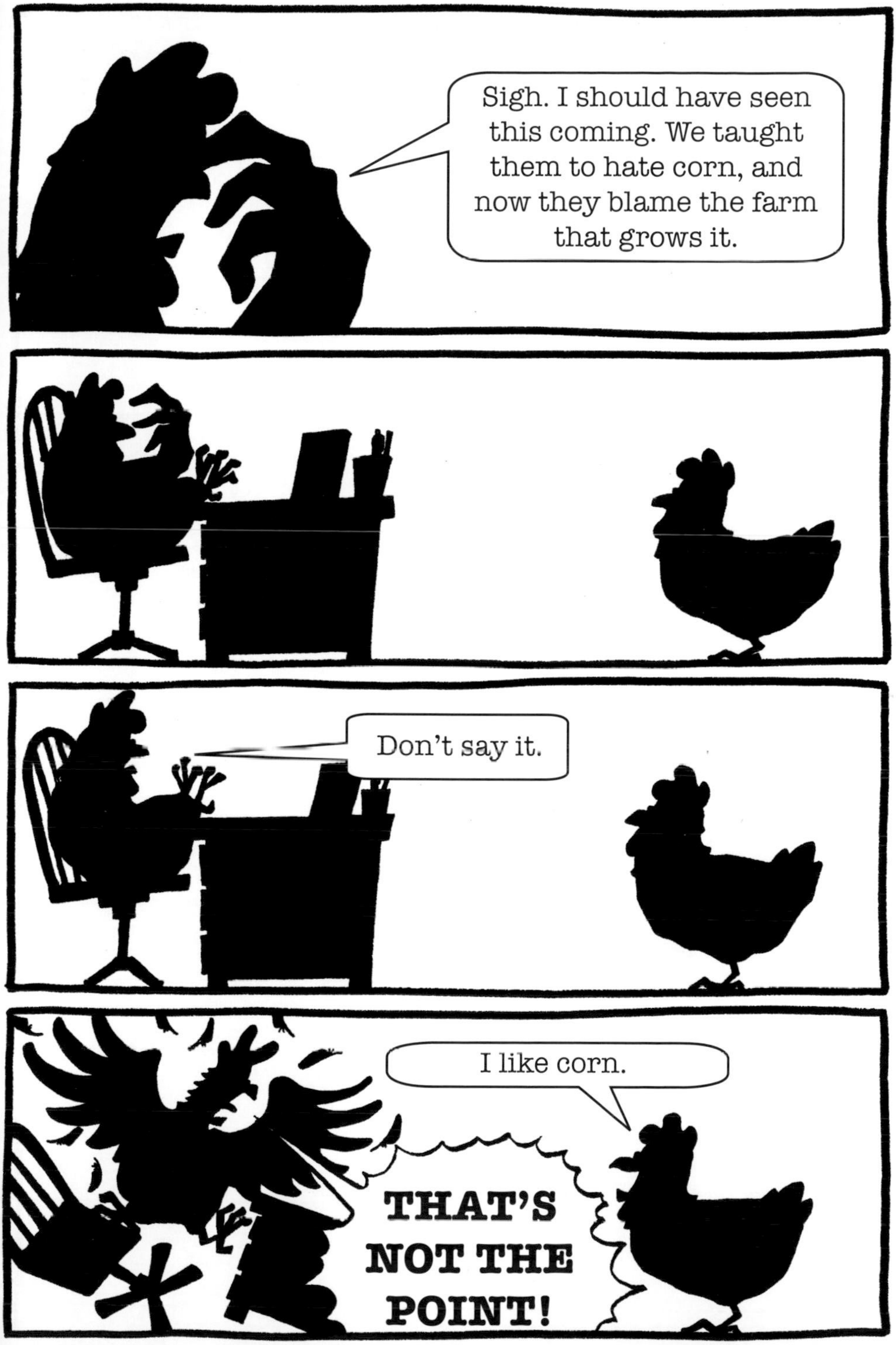
Sigh. I should have seen this coming. We taught them to hate corn, and now they blame the farm that grows it.
Don't say it.
I like corn.
THAT'S NOT THE POINT!

• CHAPTER TEN •

HOME AGAIN

Welcome home, Kitty!
Welcome home, Uncle Murray!

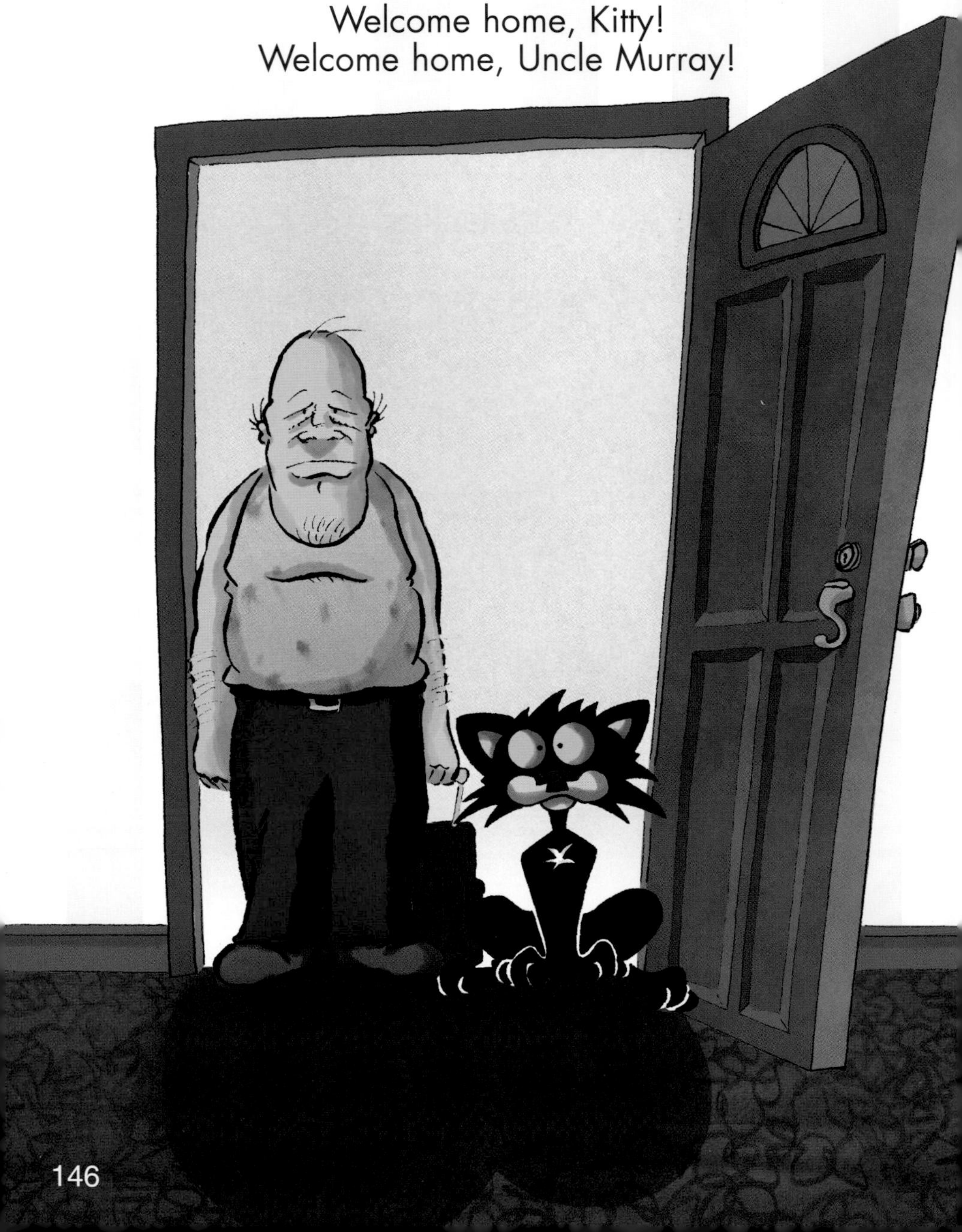

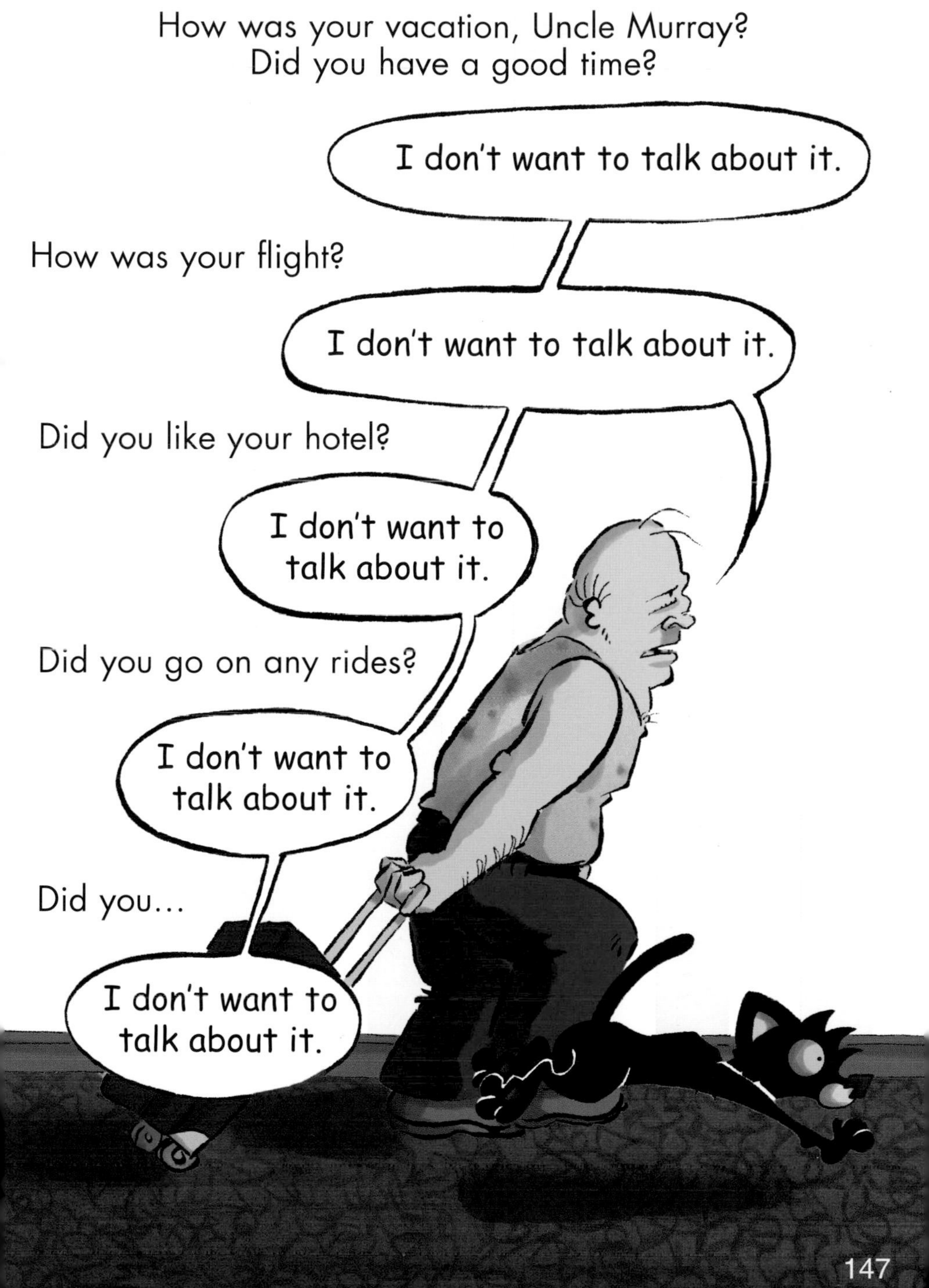
How was your vacation, Uncle Murray?
Did you have a good time?
I don't want to talk about it.
How was your flight?
I don't want to talk about it.
Did you like your hotel?
I don't want to talk about it.
Did you go on any rides?
I don't want to talk about it.
Did you...
I don't want to talk about it.

All of Kitty's friends dropped by to see if you brought them LOVE LOVE ANGEL KITTY ears like they hoped you would.

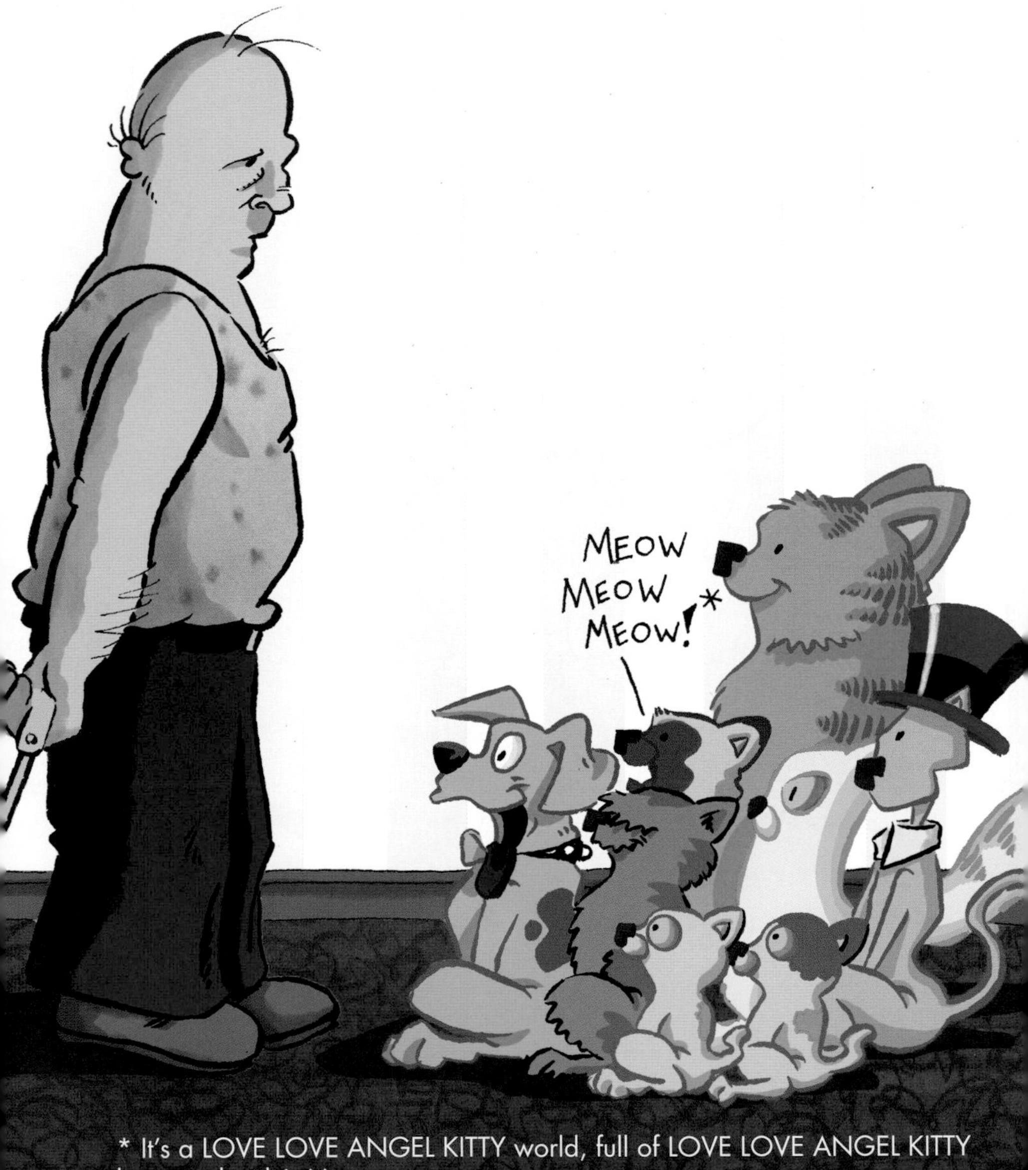
MEOW
MEOW
MEOW!*

* It's a LOVE LOVE ANGEL KITTY world, full of LOVE LOVE ANGEL KITTY boys and girls! It's a . . .

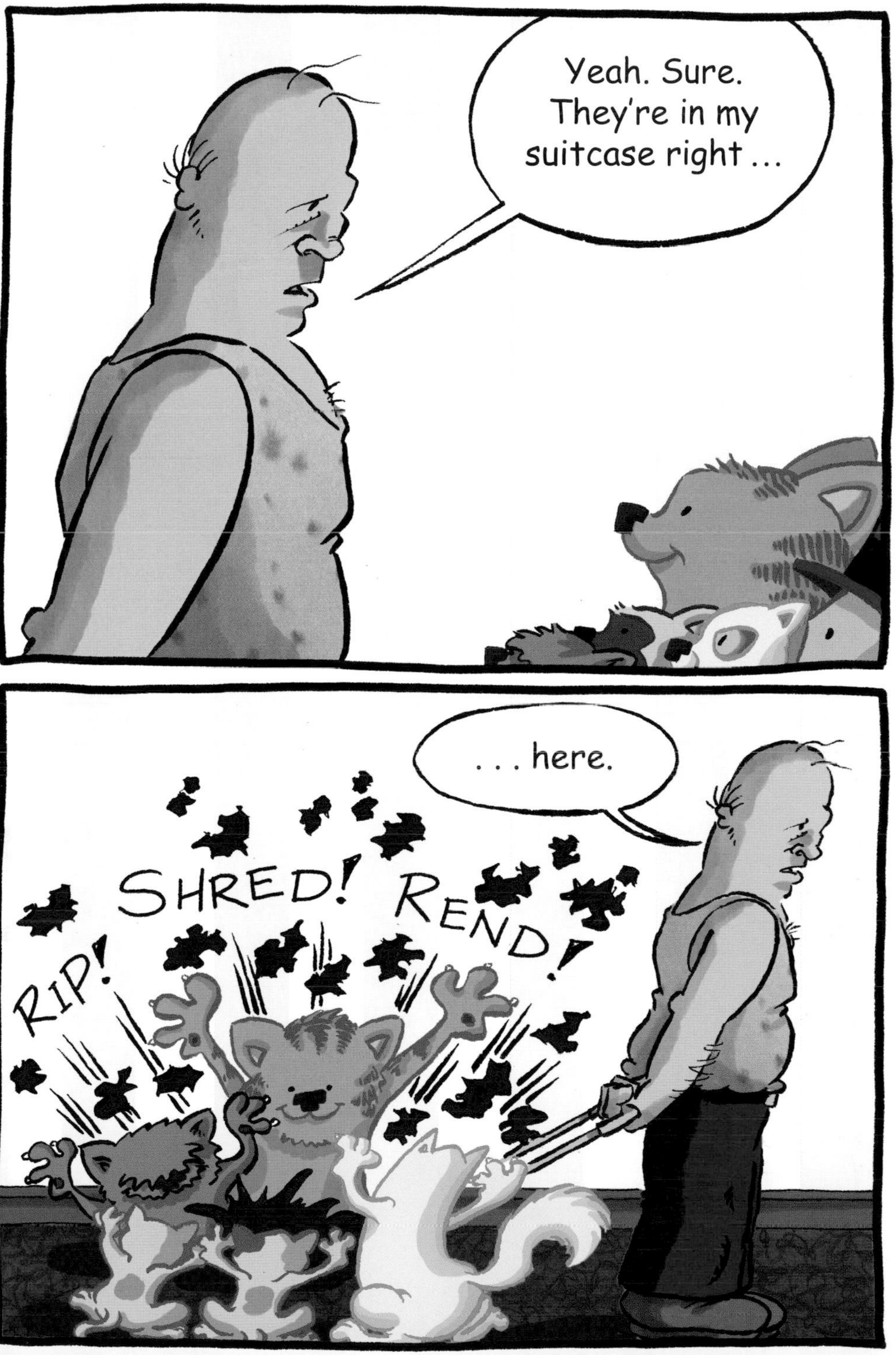
Yeah. Sure. They're in my suitcase right ...
. . . here.
SHRED!
REND!
RIP!

The kitties KNEW you'd come through, Uncle Murray. You always do. So they have some surprises for you.

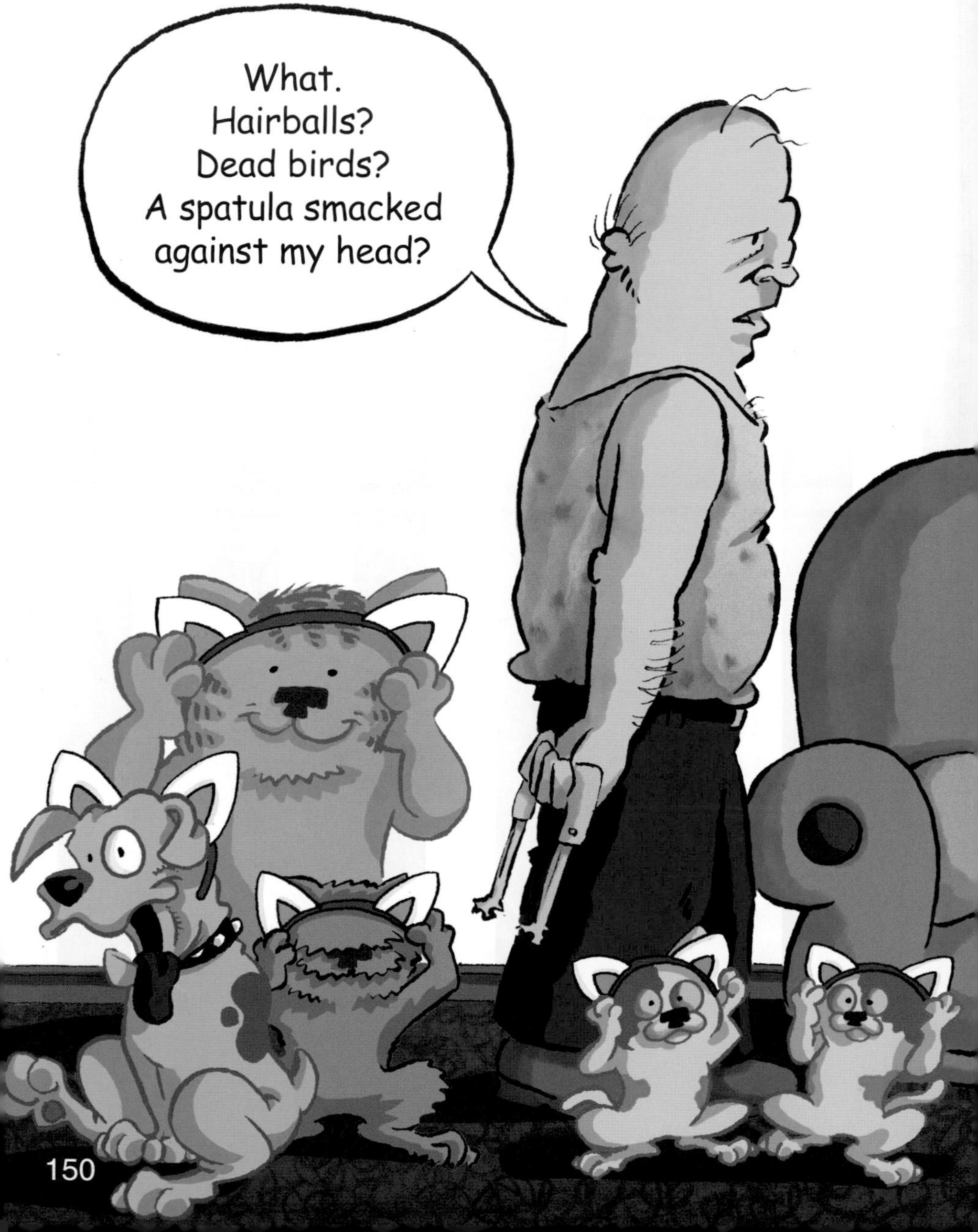
What.
Hairballs?
Dead birds?
A spatula smacked against my head?

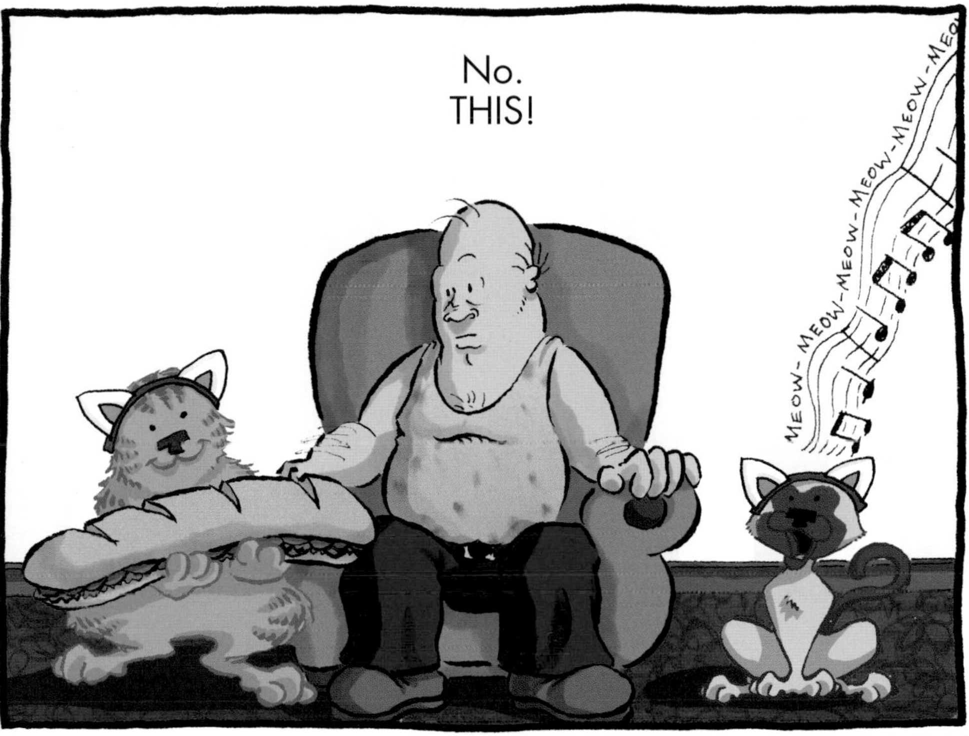
No.
THIS!
MEOW-MEOW-MEOW-MEOW-MEOW-MEOW-MEO

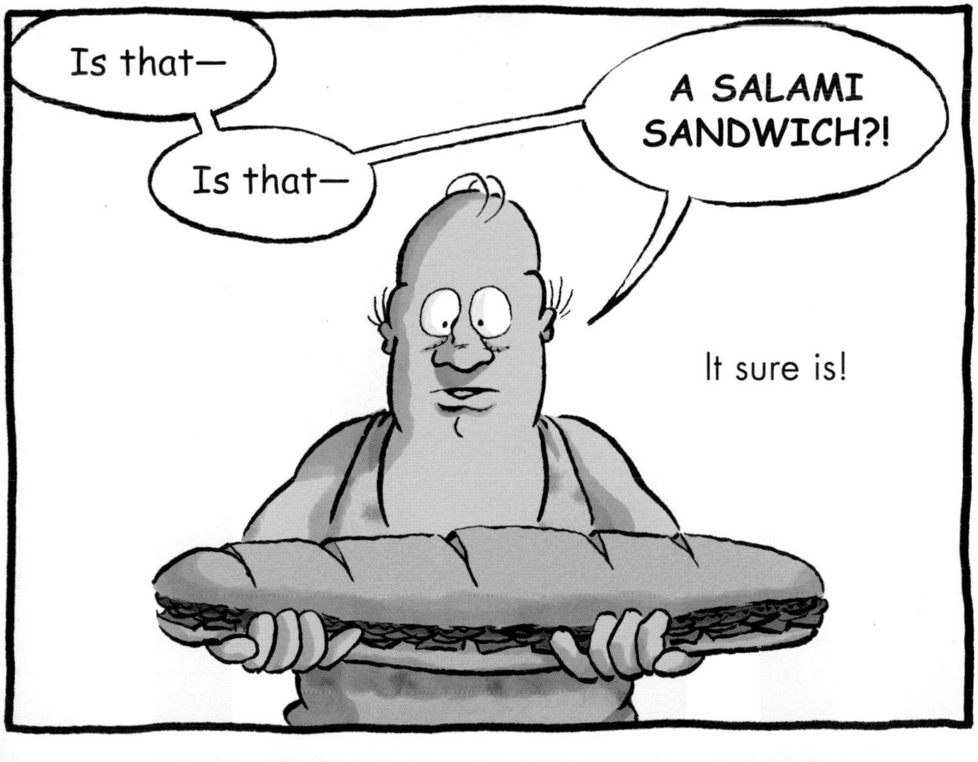
Is that—
Is that—
A SALAMI SANDWICH?!
It sure is!

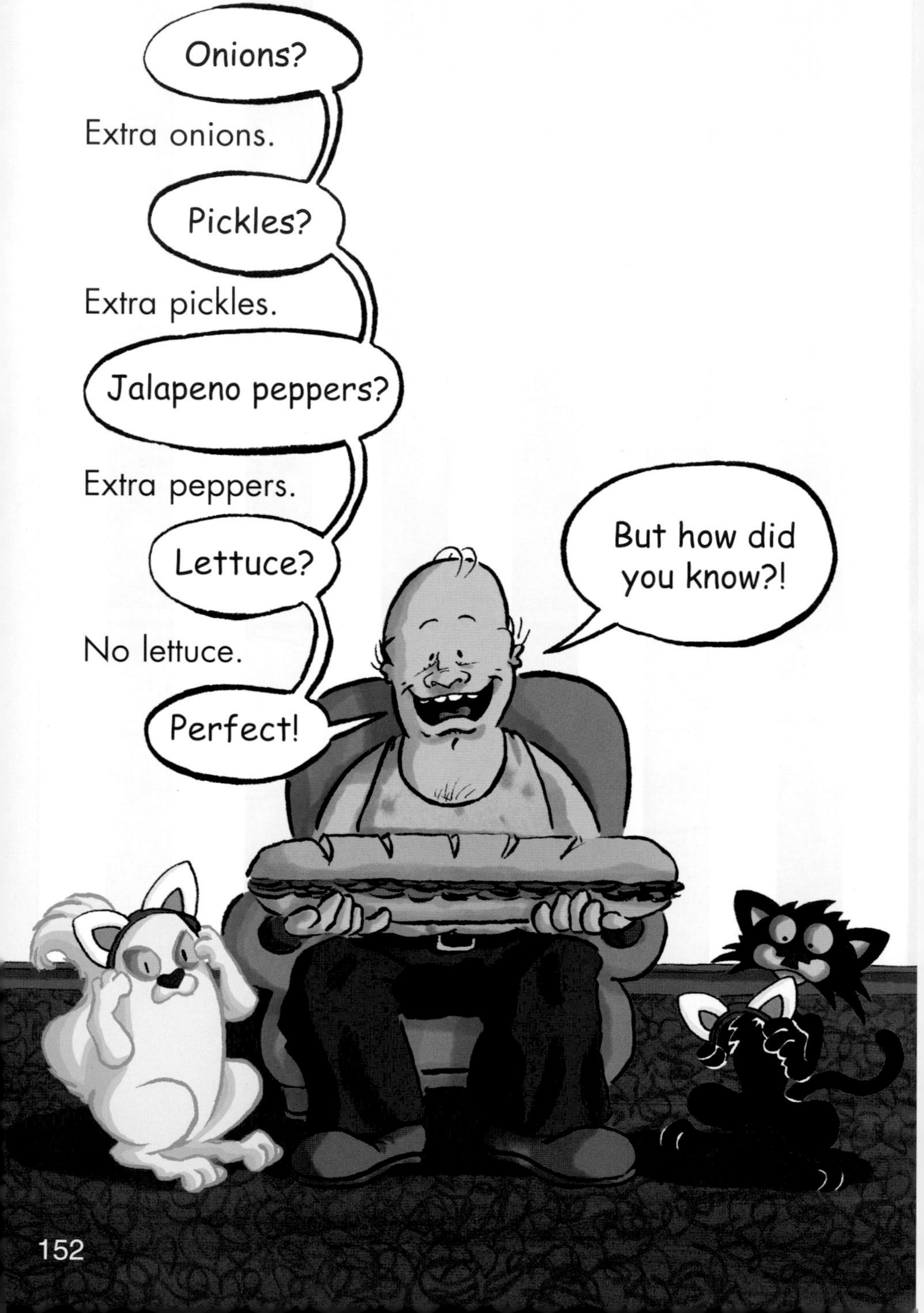

Onions?
Extra onions.
Pickles?
Extra pickles.
Jalapeno peppers?
Extra peppers.
Lettuce?
No lettuce.
Perfect!
But how did you know?!

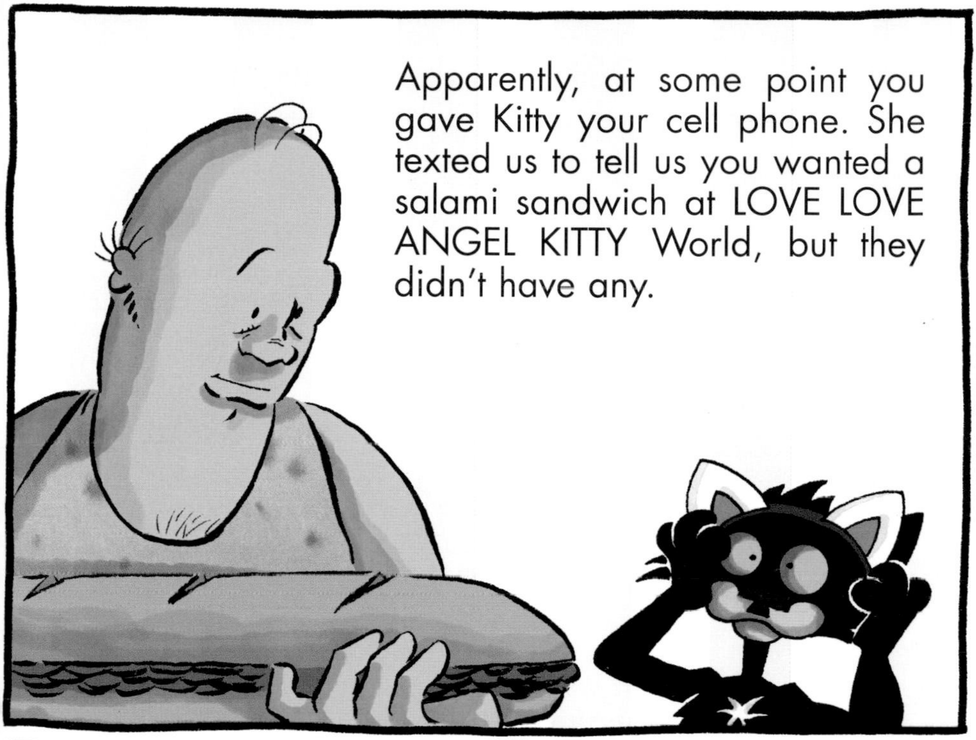
Apparently, at some point you gave Kitty your cell phone. She texted us to tell us you wanted a salami sandwich at LOVE LOVE ANGEL KITTY World, but they didn't have any.

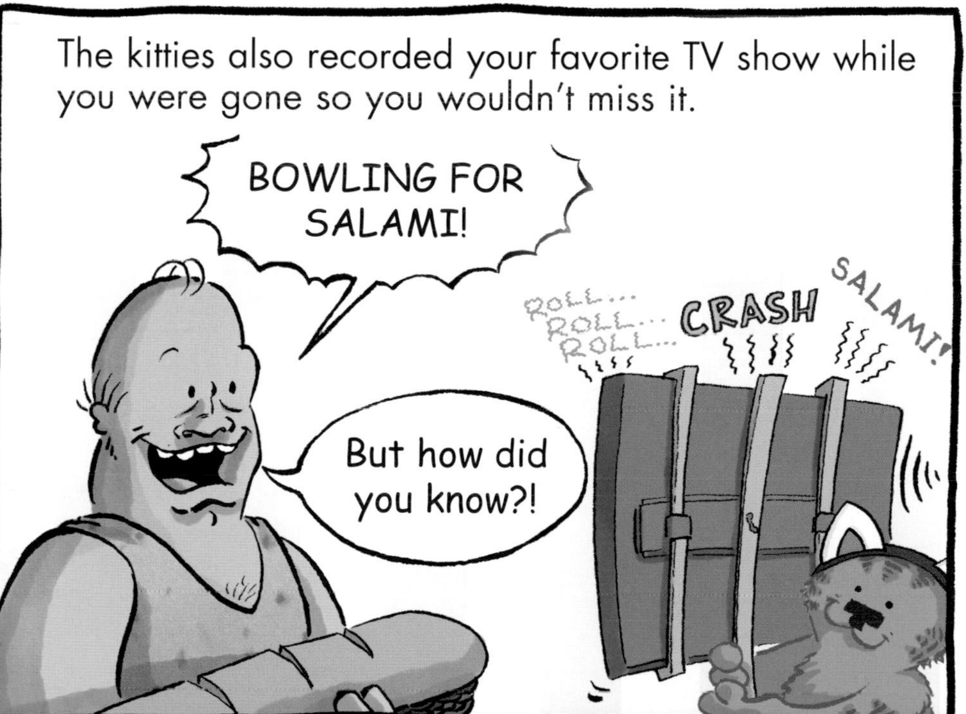
The kitties also recorded your favorite TV show while you were gone so you wouldn't miss it.
BOWLING FOR SALAMI!
But how did you know?!
ROLL... ROLL... ROLL...
CRASH
SALAMI!

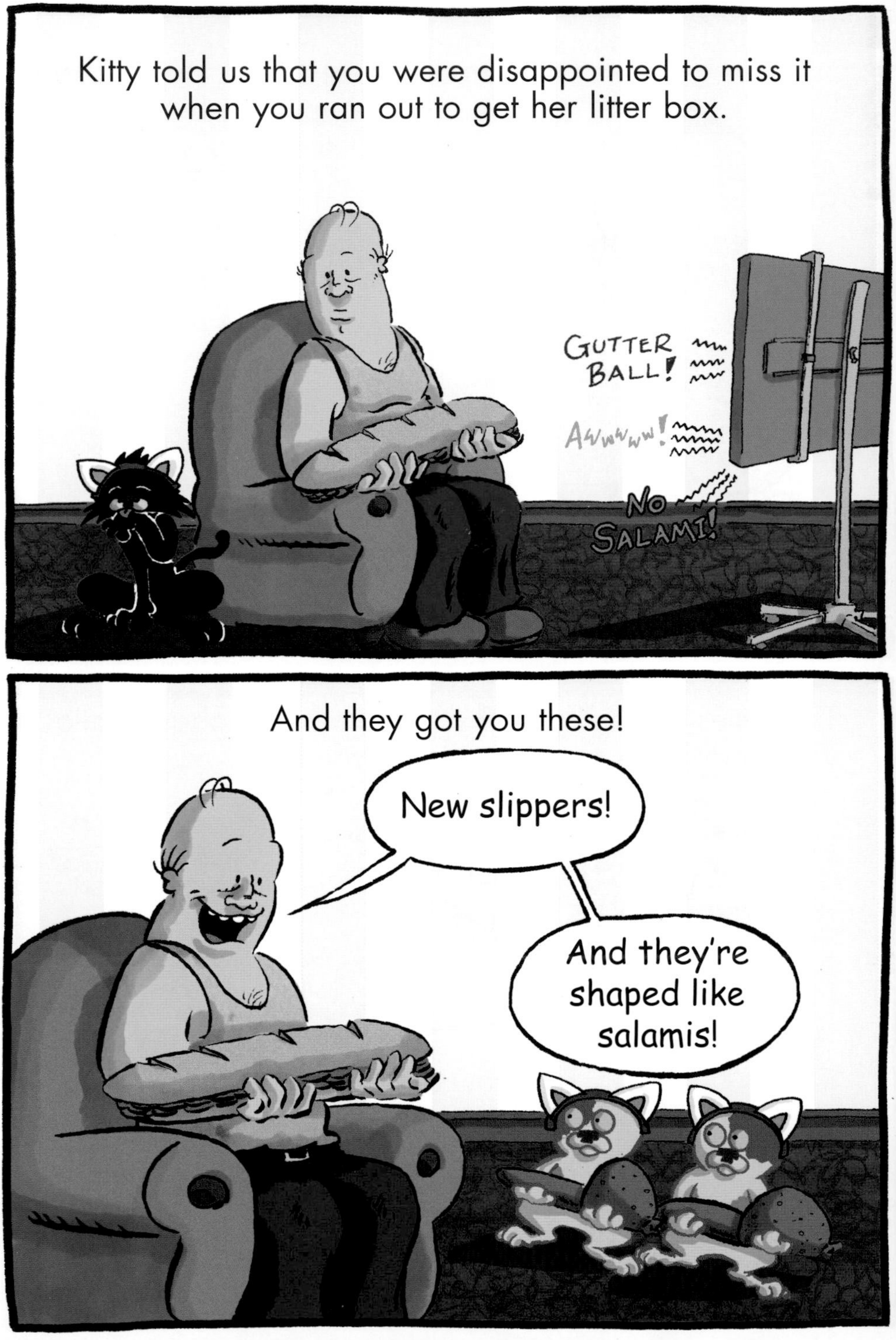
Kitty told us that you were disappointed to miss it when you ran out to get her litter box.
GUTTER BALL!
Awwwww!
NO SALAMI!
And they got you these!
New slippers!
And they're shaped like salamis!

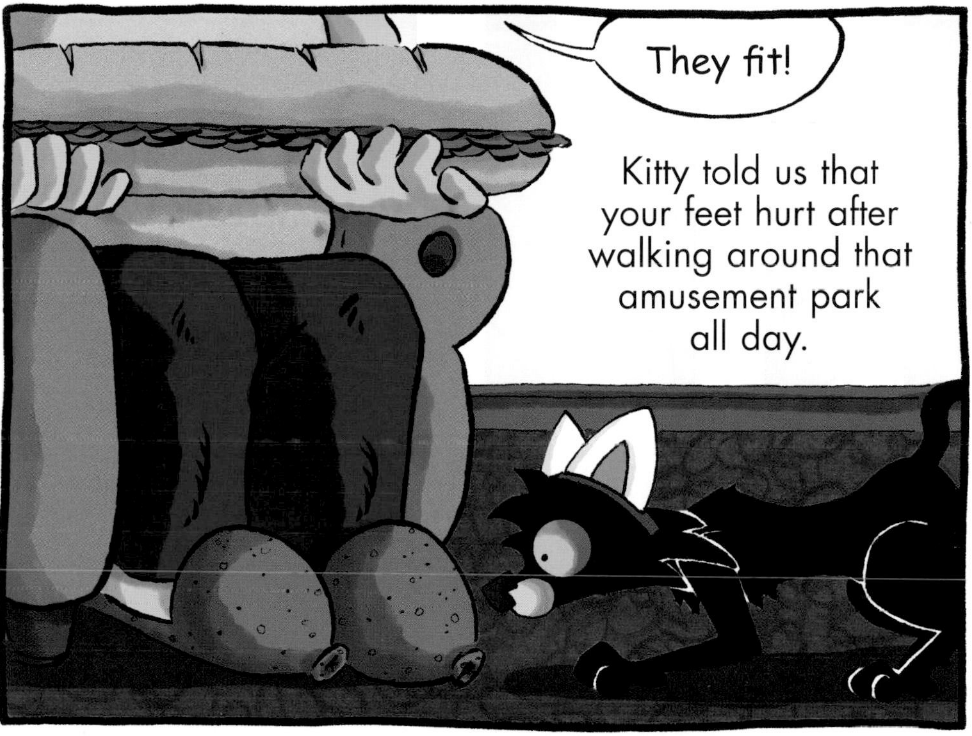
They fit!
Kitty told us that your feet hurt after walking around that amusement park all day.

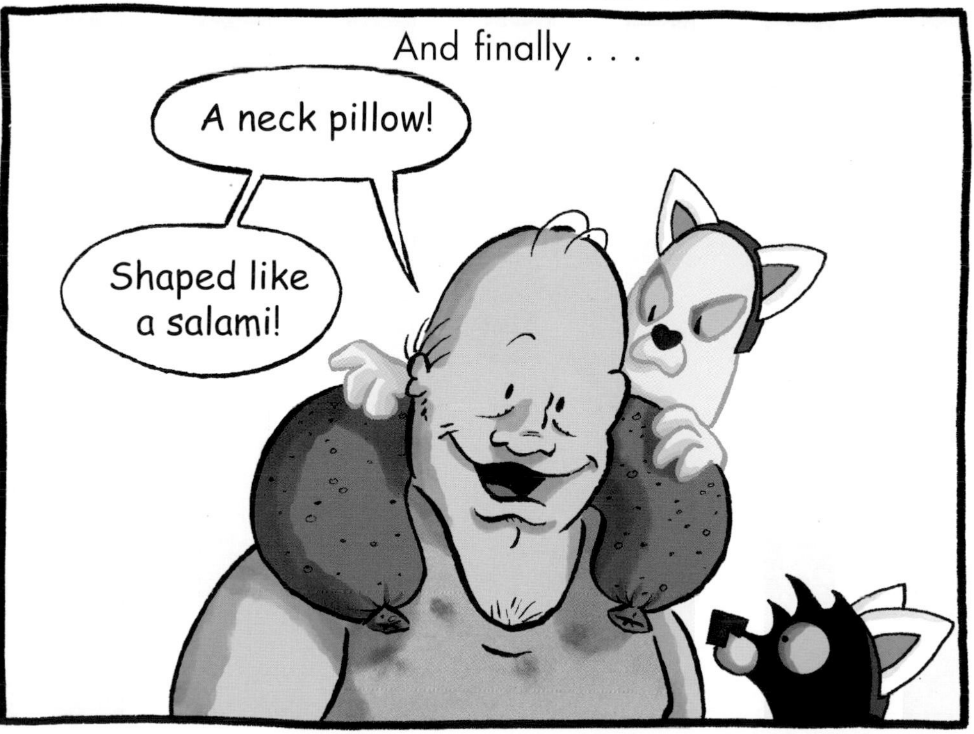
And finally . . .
A neck pillow!
Shaped like a salami!

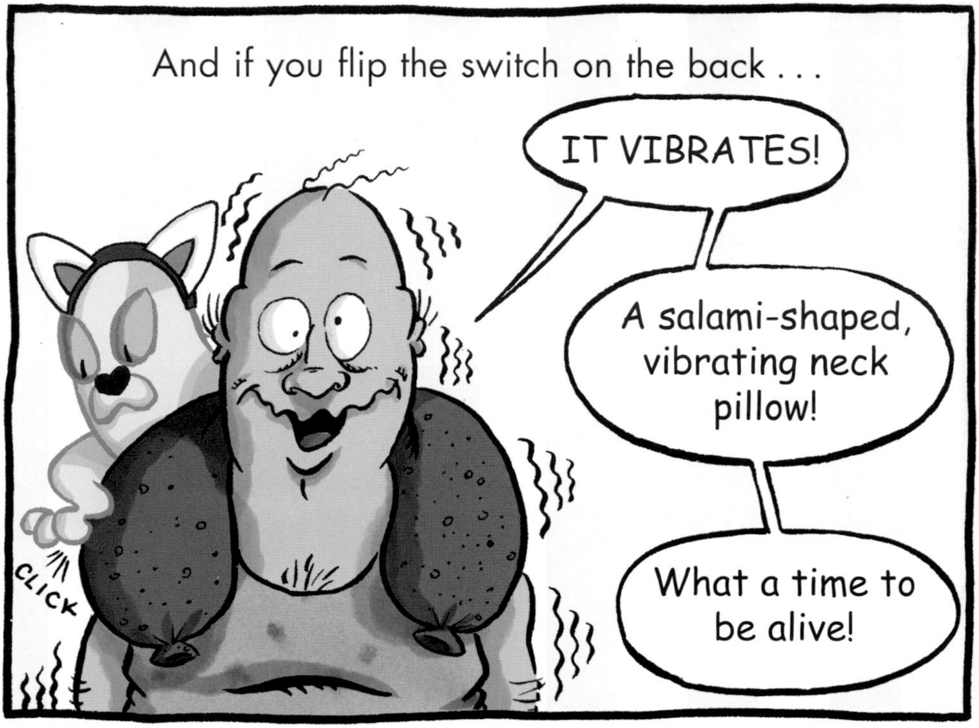
And if you flip the switch on the back . . .
IT VIBRATES!
A salami-shaped, vibrating neck pillow!
What a time to be alive!
CLICK

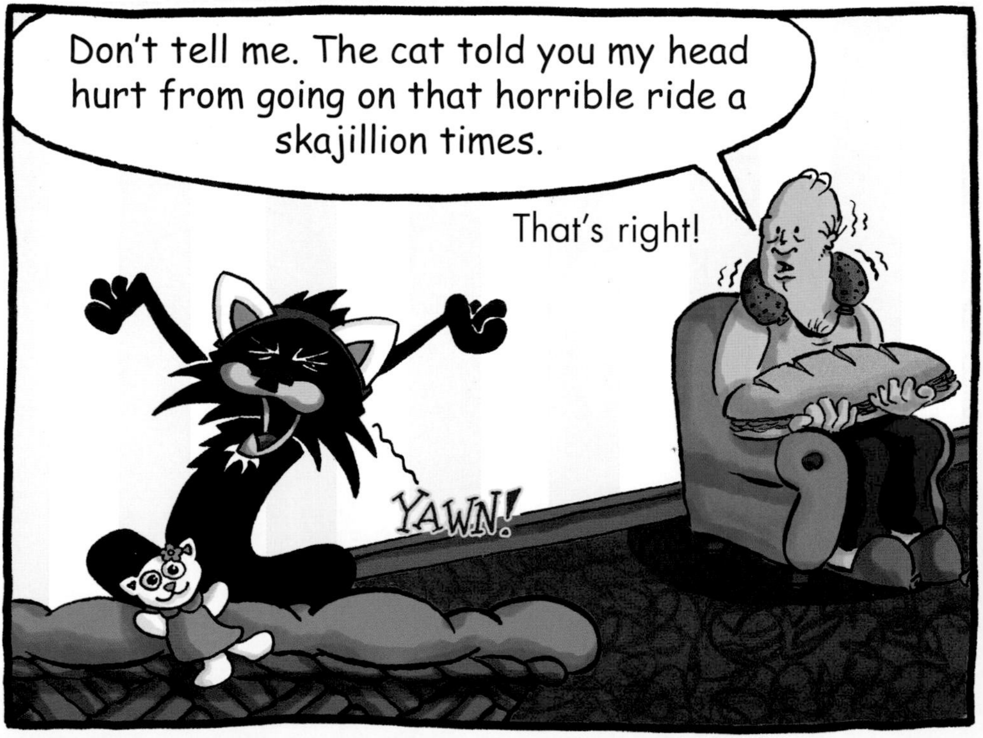
Don't tell me. The cat told you my head hurt from going on that horrible ride a skajillion times.
That's right!
YAWN!

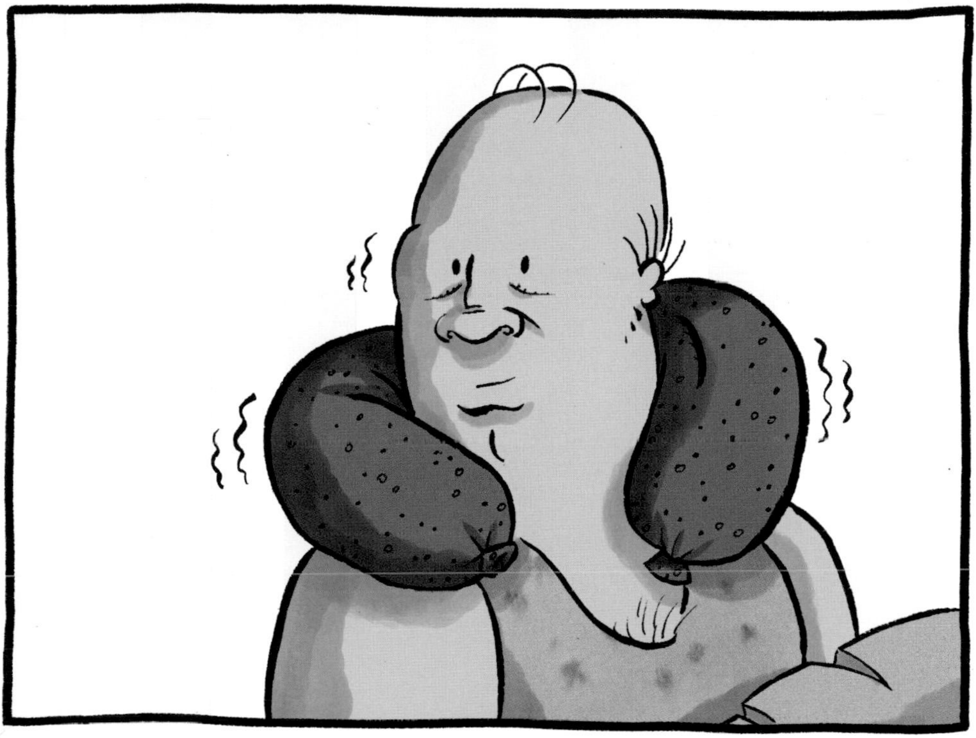

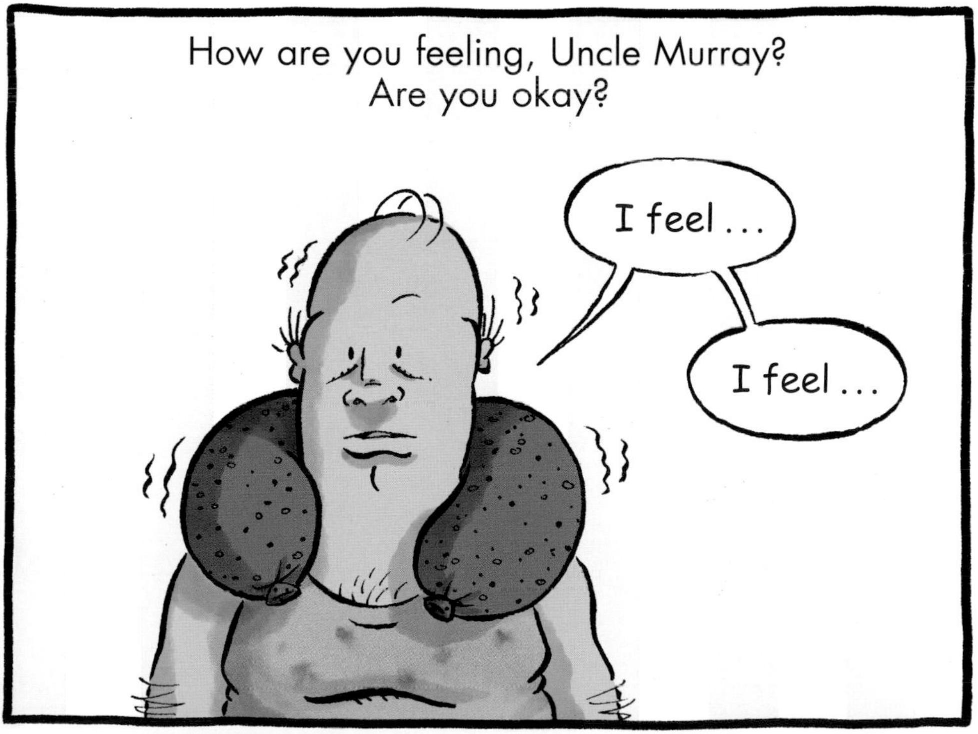
How are you feeling, Uncle Murray?
Are you okay?
I feel . . .
I feel . . .

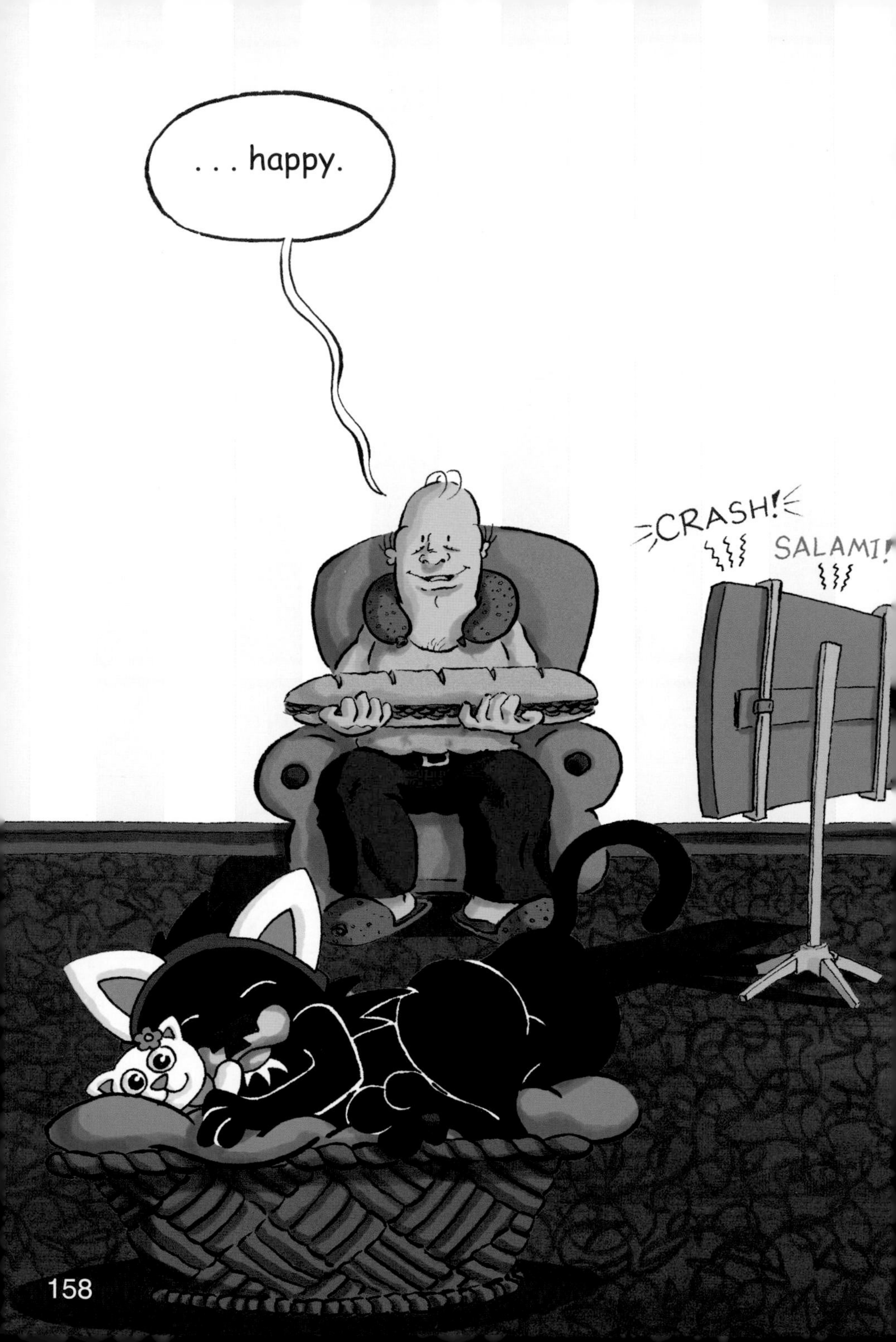
. . . happy.
CRASH!
SALAMI!

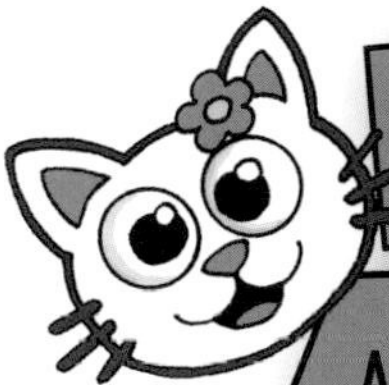

THE LOVE LOVE ANGEL KITTY THEME SONG

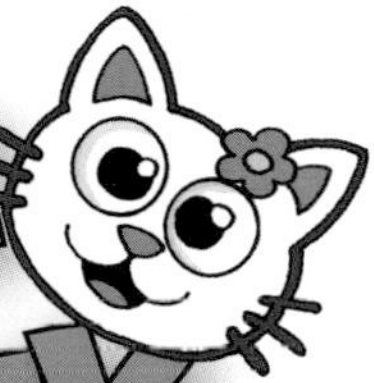

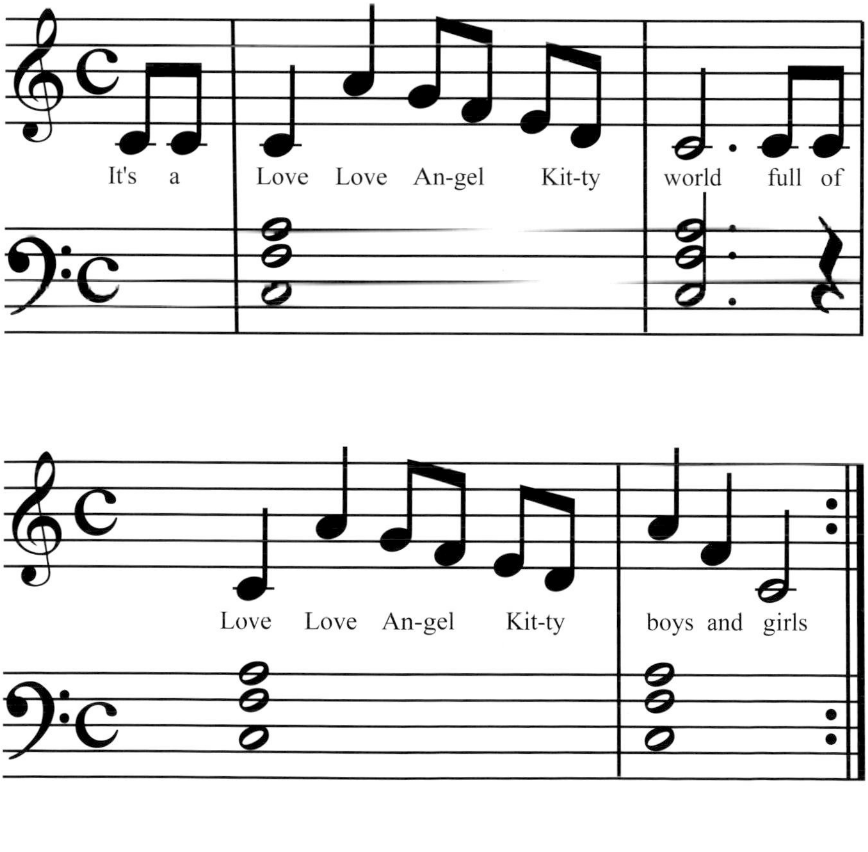
It's a Love Love An-gel Kit-ty world full of
Love Love An-gel Kit-ty boys and girls

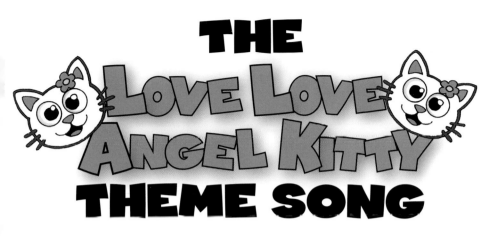

• ABOUT THE AUTHOR •

NICK BRUEL is the author and illustrator of the phenomenally successful Bad Kitty series, including *Bad Kitty Meets the Baby* and *Bad Kitty for President*. Nick has also written and illustrated popular picture books, including *A Wonderful Year* and his most recent, *Bad Kitty: Searching for Santa*. Nick lives with his wife and daughter in Westchester, New York. Visit him at **nickbruelbooks.com**.